THE HAUNTINGS OF FATE

THE CHRONICLES OF EDGAR HAROLD

SIMON SAYERS-FRANKLIN

Twitter: @EdgarHaroldUK
Facebook: The Chronicles of Edgar Harold

ISBN: 9781522087670

For Betty -

Without you, none of this would have been possible.

"Every second has a meaning,
Day after day, the world still spins.
Great barriers act as invisible pins;
All holding the fabric of time and space
Relatively in the very same place.

How would you cope,
Armed with nothing but hope to
Ready you for the dark times to come?
Over the barriers you will go,
Living your life, to help other's lives flow.
Deaf you will be to the Raven's crow."

PROLOGUE

March. 1993.

The red haired boy bombed into the bathroom wearing his stripy pyjamas. He carried a teddy bear dressed in a monk's robe with a hood covering its cute, fuzzy face. He lifted it up, looked into its glassy blue eyes and smiled as he placed it upon the shelves at the foot of the bath. The steaming water ran fast and the bathtub filled quickly while a thick, steamy mist swirled from the hot water and engulfed the bathroom in its haze.

'Edgar, you'd better not put Teddy in the bath again,' his mother, Priscilla, shouted from his bedroom across the upstairs landing as she prepared his bed for bedtime. 'He might need a wash but only boys and girls go in the bath. Teddy goes in the washing machine.'

Edgar wasn't listening and in her heart, Priscilla knew her words would be unheard. Her son was a force of his own. He was good and he was gentle but he was a very distracted child and often seemed to be in an entirely different world of his own.

WHOOSH

A strong gust of wind suddenly blew through the house without any explanation.

'Shut the window, Edgar!' Priscilla, shouted from his bedroom and Edgar looked glum, annoyed that he faced the blame for something he hadn't done again.

'I didn't do it!' Edgar shouted in reply as he zoomed around, spinning in circles with his arms stretched out until he fell over, laughing. 'Biggy did!'

He lay there, looking up at the high ceiling, beaming to himself as a figure dressed in a white monk's habit appeared from the clouds of steam that filled the bathroom. His hood covered the top of his face in shadow so only the end of his long nose and his thin mouth could be seen. The man lifted a finger to his lips and Edgar nodded, giggling to himself.

'Are you ready for your bath, Edgar?' his mother asked from his bedroom across the hall.

'No. I'm playing with Biggy.'

Edgar's mother flung his pillow back onto his bed and sighed. She hid her face in her hands and exhaled as they slid down to cover her mouth. She took a moment to collect herself and tried to hide her despair. She had grown frustrated with Edgar's constant talk of his imaginary friend whom he blamed for everything and this was the final straw.

'Biggy doesn't exist, love. If he did mummy would be able to see him,' she retorted, coming to stand on the threshold of Edgar's bedroom. She looked across the hallway but was oblivious to the man hiding behind the bathroom door, still holding his finger up to his lips to try and keep little Edgar quiet.

'He does. I'm watching him,' Edgar replied, laughing as he

looked towards the mirror, his gaze fixed upon the monk in the corner and they smiled kindly at one another like old friends acknowledging the other's arrival.

Edgar waved at his mother cheekily as she turned around with a hefty sigh and redirected her attention to making his bed.

'Hello Biggy,' Edgar whispered, shuffling shyly from one foot to the other. The tall man always had this effect on young Edgar. His giant stature that had earned him the nickname Biggy and his hidden face were intimidating but his friendly nature instantly erased that fear.

'Hello Edgar,' Biggy replied, 'can I ask you a favour?'

'What?' Edgar sighed.

'I need to borrow something from you,' Biggy said with an air of superiority. He lifted his hood down and Edgar saw his face properly for the first time.

Biggy was a middle-aged man with short, dark hair that sat neatly trimmed upon his head. His eyes were bright blue and gleamed as he beamed down at the child. He didn't just smile with his mouth – it was with his eyes too and the kindly wrinkles in the corners; the slight crows feet that crinkled with the onset of ageing. Biggy pointed at the teddy bear that stood on the shelves at the other side of the room and Edgar shook his head.

'No. You can't have my toys,' Edgar squealed irritably, as any child would. He stomped his feet and Biggy glanced from side to side, worried that Edgar's mother would come running to him.

'One day, you'll understand, Edgar. It may take a long time, you might even be as old as me, but one day you will understand...I

promise,' Biggy whispered, a trace of desperation in his tone.

'But mummy gave me that Teddy on the day I –'

'Came out of her tummy, I know,' Biggy replied.

Edgar looked confused and didn't speak. He turned silent and tilted his head, eyes narrowed in puzzlement.

'Edgar! Come here love, mummy needs to talk to you,' Priscilla shouted.

'How did you know that?' Edgar asked the ghost.

'I've been following you and I always will,' he replied. 'Don't worry. I'm a friend, Edgar and one day, you will understand. I promise.'

The ghost grinned at the child and nodded, pointing at the teddy bear, as if asking once more for Edgar to give him it.

'Edgar! Come here darling,' his mother shouted again from across the hall and Edgar shook his head furiously at the ghost.

'I have to go,' Edgar whispered as he turned to leave the bathroom.

'I know.'

Edgar's mother sat on his bed and watched him approach with her arms outstretched welcomingly. He trundled across the hall and into her embrace.

With the child gone, Biggy took this moment as an opportunity to stride across the bathroom and take the teddy bear dressed as a monk from the shelves but as his fingers clasped around its soft fur, he heard raised voices down the hall.

'Come on, Edgar. If Biggy existed, mummy would really see him,' Priscilla tried but Edgar frowned and shook his head. He was *having none of it.*

WHOOSH

A gust of wind blasted through the bathroom, so forcefully that it made the windows rattle and a painting of a boat sailing across an ocean bathed in a red sunset fall down with a CRASH.

'Edgar! I thought I told you to close the window.'

'No. Biggy must have done it...'

'He doesn't exist!'

'He does. He likes me so I can see him but mummy can't, silly mummy,' Edgar jested in a sing-song voice, laughing as he pulled his mother into the bathroom and looked behind the door. Biggy was long gone.

'The window's shut...what caused that draft?' Priscilla asked worriedly – a trace of confusion etched across her face as she stared at the closed window and picked up the painting that lay face first on the floor. The glass in the frame had shattered and a web of cracks covered the picture beneath.

'Told you so!' Edgar exclaimed, his eyes widening as they fell upon the empty shelf where his teddy bear had sat only moments before. 'Where's Teddy?' Edgar squealed, bursting into tears. 'I want my Teddy. Biggy took him. Where did Biggy take him?'

'Edgar! Please, stop...this is getting weird now,' Priscilla shrieked, clinging to her son's hand tightly as she realized that maybe he was right – perhaps there had been a ghost in the house.

After all, that was the only way to explain the mysterious draft and the disappearance of Teddy who never ever came back.

TWELVE YEARS LATER...

– CHAPTER ONE –

GHOSTS OF THE PAST

It was a sweltering summer day near the end of July and a teenage boy trudged slowly up the cobble-stoned hill towards his home as the burning sun beat down on his back. He paused for a few seconds to remove his leather trench coat and tried to cram it into his already bursting school bag to no avail. This boy was Edgar Harold and there was nothing special about him at all.

Edgar was a tall, skinny boy with pale skin that occasionally broke out in spots like all normal teenagers and his eyes were bright blue. His long, wavy hair was tied up in a ponytail as usual and he scrunched up his eyes against the glare of the sun. Edgar was a quiet, shy person; the kind of kid who shrank away into the background at school, the last one to be picked for sports teams and the one nobody ever invited to parties. At school they called him names: *"Werewolf"* was their favourite because of his long hair, thick, unruly eyebrows and the wispy whiskers that had started to grow upon his top lip. They also mocked his slightly bulbous nose and his red hair which he had taken to dying black, hoping to hide one of the more obvious reasons to bully him, still, it didn't make much difference. Everyone already knew the truth. It didn't matter now. For the next six weeks, he was free and then he would only have one more year to endure.

He stumbled on in the intense heat – this must have been the hottest summer he'd ever known and he tried to speed up, eager to finally be home but his heavy, black boots slowed him down.

Edgar loved the old, worn boots that had been given to him on his fifteenth birthday, a matter of months ago. They were old but he didn't care. He had seen many new pairs just like them but none had the strange insignia under the soles – a metal circle indented in the boot, containing a pentagram with two crossed swords in the middle. He had no idea what it meant but he suspected it must be the logo of a company that no longer existed.

He was nearly half way up the hill now, coming closer to a quaint street of terraced houses that turned off to the right and linked the steep hill to a churchyard which was home to the ancient church of St. Mary and was cluttered with an assortment of ancient graves and mausoleums.

Finally, Edgar reached the street halfway up the hill and he turned onto it. As he slumped along, he could see his house at the far end through the heat haze that rose all around him, making his surroundings shimmer and wobble faintly.

In the distance, past the churchyard and upon a steep tree-covered hill, Edgar could see the long, skeletal battlements of a ruined castle which dominated the costal headland. This castle had stood at the very top of this hill like a guardian watching over the old town of Scarborough; a vast labyrinth of old, terraced houses that lined the cobbled streets, narrow alleyways and flights of crooked, uneven steps that ran down to the seafront.

Edgar reached his front door and sighed a breath of relief. It was good to be home. He had lived in the same house all his life – there had been plenty of opportunities to move but his mum had always refused, claiming she didn't want to move too far away from Edgar's grandparents. It was a simple house, just one in a long line of an average brick terrace but it was home; it had been for fifteen years now and Edgar simply could not imagine living anywhere else.

The door was a deep royal red but the old paint had flaked off over the years and a rusted hanging basket dangled down above it. It had hung there for at least two years while the dead flowers still drooped over the edge like shriveled up, dry roots, trying to dig deeper for water. The dead plants had been left there as a contribution to the "Scarborough in Bloom" competition to find the best decorated house or garden in the town. Sadly, Edgar didn't have a garden so he and his mum settled to try to make the house look nice at the front. Unfortunately the flowers had withered within a week so Priscilla had just laughed and said they'd win if it was "Scarborough in *Gloom,*" since that day, the hanging basket had stayed as a long lasting memorial to their morbid sense of humour.

Edgar fumbled around in his pocket to find his keys as he reached his home but a shrieking voice from the other side of the street made him jump out of his skin.

'ASTI! OI! ASTI!'

Edgar glanced back, rolling his eyes. He recognized the hoarse, croaking shrieks as those of old Mrs. Franks who lived over the road.

The withered old lady dressed in a dirty brown pinafore and teal cardigan stood upon her doorstep with her flyaway hair sticking out at all angles. Her eyes were magnified by her thick, brown-framed glasses that might have been fashionable in the nineteen-seventies perched halfway down her hooked nose so that she had to tilt her head back to see out of them properly. She leaned, hunched on her walking stick and continued to shout.

Edgar sighed and made his way over the road to calm her down. Mrs. Franks had shown signs of dementia for as long as Edgar could remember but with no family to care for her she had dealt with it alone with only the odd visit from nurses to check up on her.

'Are you okay Mrs. Franks?' he asked kindly, showing concern for his elderly neighbour who was almost half his height and looked so frail that a sudden gust of wind might blow her away.

'My Astyanax hasn't come home. The little blighter could have gone anywhere – they do, cats you know, and I'm scared incase them air raid sirens go off and he's lost out here while them Germans bomb us some more. They already ruined the castle last time, they did...*and* killed a poor child.'

'The Germans are all gone, Mrs. Franks. The war ended sixty years ago and I'm afraid Astyanax died when he fell from your roof a during that storm last summer,' Edgar said, trying to sound as sympathetic as possible but Mrs. Franks just stared blankly at him.

'Oh...yes...I remember now. Yes, yes...well, I'd better go get the kettle on, Madge'll be here soon. It was nice to see you, Edwin, you're a good lad, you are.'

Mrs. Franks chuckled to herself as she turned and shuffled back towards her open front door beyond which a narrow corridor piled high with wonky towers of old books and boxes could be seen in the gloom.

'Oh, I'm nothing special, Mrs. Franks and by the way, it's Edgar.'

'I doubt I'll remember my dear boy, I doubt I'll remember,' Mrs. Franks chuckled madly, more to herself than to Edgar, as she closed the door behind her.

Edgar shook his head, confused by the oddities of the eccentric old woman and headed back over the road to his door. He let himself into the house and went through the narrow hallway into the living room with a sigh of relief to be home at last.

The living room was massive considering the compact size of his small terraced house. A scarlet sofa was pushed up against the open-plan staircase and in the opposite corner was a matching armchair next to an alcove, filled with pine shelves that were stuffed with books. These books contained subjects of history, medicine, castles and survival in extreme circumstances as well as an assortment of fiction and there were so many that there was no space in between for any new additions to the collection.

The sofa and chair matched the colouring of the carpet and in front of the window were several big, squashy cushions where Edgar loved to sit with a book while sunlight streamed in through the window behind him, giving him sufficient light to read.

Edgar rushed upstairs and headed to his own little bedroom, which looked even smaller because of all the junk he had collected in there over the years. Piles of books and computer games cluttered his floor; a vast assortment of posters clung to his walls promoting films and his favourite bands so that many pairs of beady eyes watched him as he took off his school uniform and threw the clothes in a messy heap on the floor.

It was then, the framed photo on the desk caught his eye and made him smile. It was a taken last summer and showed a group of people, all beaming widely. Edgar was in the middle; his toothy grin just a flash of metal (thank God the braces were gone now) and he was surrounded by several others: Claudia - a short girl with olive skin, big brown eyes and ash blonde ringlets. There was Alvin – a tall, skinny boy with sharp, pointy features. Next to him stood Charity who, despite being nearly half his height, was clearly Alvin's sister and there was Vicky too. Again, like her siblings Alvin and Charity, her pretty face was pointed and elfish; her long dark hair was tied up in a braid and she beamed, her arms around her siblings shoulders, then finally on the end were Kieran and Hector – two of the more recent friends to have joined the group.

These people were Edgar's best friends, but none more than Alvin. He sat down on the edge of the bed, still wearing nothing but his underwear and a smile crossed his lips as he touched the photo longingly. Today had been terrible – probably one of the worst days at school in a long time...but soon that would change! It was time for the re-enactment season and Edgar could go away to live a medieval life with these wonderful people and immerse himself in history. It was a life so far removed from his own miserable existence of being bullied and suffering; it was a life of exploration and adventure and he couldn't wait to go and spend time with these people once more. The long wait was almost over.

'Just a couple of weeks, guys,' he whispered to the people in the photo as he placed it back on the desk, his thoughts on the adventures they would soon be having together.

After what felt like an age, just laying on the bed, day-dreaming about the adventures to come, Edgar managed to pull himself back to reality, get dressed and go back down stairs. As he came around the corner and looked down into the living room, he stopped in his tracks. Frozen. There was something in the corner of the room near the kitchen doorway – a tall shape of a man. It flickered in and out of focus; stretching, shrinking and breaking like a TV channel that wasn't tuned properly. Edgar stared and blinked several times, hoping he was seeing things; praying the ghost was just in his mind. The shape stayed and Edgar laughed to himself.

A cold shiver shot down his spine. He hadn't seen anything like this for years – not since he was three. Not since the day the ghost had stolen his teddy bear. The mysterious monk had promised back then, that one day Edgar would understand why. He said it might take a long time but it had been twelve years and Edgar was still no wiser as to why the ghost had taken his teddy bear and the haunting memory of that moment had remained vivid and chilling on the surface of his mind, his entire life defined by that moment.

'Biggy?' Edgar asked curiously, inching down the stairs, refusing to take his eyes off the ghost. He froze, leaning over the banister, transfixed by the flickering form. 'Biggy, is that you?'

The figure of the man turned slowly to face him. It was undoubtedly the ghost he remembered from his childhood. A tall, thin man dressed in a white monks robe.

'Why now?' Edgar demanded, his heart slowing to an almost dead beat. He stared, unable to believe his stinging eyes, not wanting to blink in case the ghost vanished. 'It's been twelve years!'

'Edgar...' the ghost said solemnly, his voice crackling as he spoke, looking at Edgar. 'You can see me?'

He pulled down the hood and revealed his handsome face, something he had never done when Edgar was a child. He had always been so enigmatic until their final meeting...but there was something wrong. The vivid image of the face under the hood that had stayed with him for so long did not match what he saw now. The man he remembered had a strong-featured face; a heavy brow and a large nose between twinkling blue eyes. This man's face was pale and pointed, his nose was thin and his eyes were brown. There were no similarities at all other than the short dark hair and that created one enormous question in Edgar's mind: *If it hadn't been Biggy in the bathroom that night, so long ago, then who had it been?*

'Yeah...I can see you...but you're not...' Edgar replied in a quiet, strangled tone. This was a surprise that he hadn't been expecting. He thought the ghost was gone forever.

'Not what?' Biggy asked, his voice echoing eerily.

'You're not the same man who stole my Teddy bear,' Edgar said in disbelief. He shook his head. Maybe he was mistaken – perhaps, like anyone trying to recall a detail from long ago, time had eroded his memory. Surely that was the only explanation.

'I never stole your teddy bear,' Biggy insisted, furrowing his brow in confusion.

'Where have you been, Biggy?'

'Firstly, I believe you are now mature enough to call me by my real name – Brother Bradley,' he said, coming to the centre of the room. He looked up at Edgar who leaned over the banister of the staircase above him. 'And secondly, I never left.'

'But I haven't seen you in twelve years!' Edgar replied bitterly. 'All those times I needed a friend...a *real* friend and you were gone! My own mother tried to convince me that you were in my head! She took me to doctors and they made me believe I was wrong. I thought I imagined you.'

'Things are changing,' the ghost interrupted, a sharp edge to his voice. '*You* are changing and I have a feeling we'll be getting better acquainted again rather soon.'

'What do you mean?' Edgar probed nervously. It had been so long since he had seen Brother Bradley that he had forgotten how intimidating and frightening his flickering, distorting form was to behold. The ghost looked at Edgar, a gleam in his eye and muttered:

'Every second has a meaning,
Day after day, the world still spins.
Great barriers act as invisible pins;
All holding the fabric of time and space
Relatively in the very same place.

How would you cope,

Armed with nothing but hope
Over the barriers you will go to
Ready you for the dark times to come?
Living your life, to help other's lives flow.
Deaf you will be to the Raven's crow.'

'I almost forgot about that,' Edgar said. 'You used to say it every time before you vanished...but you never told me...what does it mean?'

Edgar stared at the ghost, his mouth hanging wide open, unable to believe that he had returned after all these years. The ghost didn't reply with anything other than a simple wave of his hand and he faded from sight – gone.

'Wait! Biggy...I mean Brother Bradley! Come back!' Edgar pleaded as he jumped down the last of the stairs and ran to the place where the ghost had stood. There was no sign of him other than a faint, cold tingle in the air.

Edgar's white cat, Star, stirred on the sofa. She stretched, yawned and meowed at Edgar then jumped to the ground and weaved around his legs lovingly.

'I love you too, Star,' Edgar laughed as he sat down on the sofa and let the cat climb on his lap. He stroked her head and she purred contentedly. 'You slept through that didn't you?'

The cat meowed again and headbutted Edgar's chin affectionately.

BANG, BANG, BANG. The knock at the door startled Edgar. He pushed Star aside gently but she dug her claws into his leg, determined to stay.

He swore at the cat as he jumped to his feet and dashed to answer the door. He peeked through the peephole to see who it was. A plump, severe looking woman stood outside wearing a garish red t-shirt that she attempted to hide under a smart, black velvet jacket. It was his mother - Priscilla.

Edgar opened the door for her, standing aside to let her in. She was a little shorter than him and her shoulder-length brownish-blond hair seemed windswept. She swiped it out of her blue eyes that were framed by rectangular glasses. Priscilla had a kind, friendly appearance but Edgar knew too well that she was the kind of woman who took no prisoners and was not ashamed to speak her mind.

'Biggy...I saw him,' Edgar blurted before Priscilla's foot had even made it over the threshold.

'What?' she sneered, rolling her eyes. 'I thought you gave up on that when you were three.'

'I did but I just came downstairs after I got changed and he was there.'

The urgency in his tone made Priscilla wonder if he was telling the truth but she just shook her head as she flopped into her chair in the corner of the living room beside the bookcase.

'Did you just nod off and have a funny dream?'

Edgar shook his head feverishly and Priscilla merely shrugged her shoulders.

'I'm sorry love, but one strange occurrence twelve years ago isn't enough to make me believe in him, especially since you've not spoken about it since that night.'

'But I have talked about him! You just never pay attention!'

'This house isn't haunted, Edgar,' Priscilla retorted with a heavy sigh.

'Fine. Don't believe me but I know what I saw,' Edgar spat defensively. His heart still hadn't recovered from the shock and his gut twisted with frustration because his mother wouldn't listen to him. 'I walked over the spot where he stood and it was all cold and tingly,' Edgar protested and Priscilla closed her eyes as if to pretend she couldn't hear. 'He was here!'

'Anyway, did you have a good last day at school?' She asked, changing the subject quickly.

'It was alright.'

'You're a terrible liar,' Priscilla said, raising an inquisitive eyebrow.

Edgar froze. He didn't want to talk about it. He never wanted to talk about it because that meant reliving the moments, it meant admitting certain things had happened and he had been weak enough to let them. He had tried to fight back in the past but it only made things worse; now he had learned to just take it and deal but he prefered to suffer in silence. It was hard enough to live it once.

'Spencer started on me again,' Edgar sighed after a moment and he sank down on the sofa.

'What happened?'

'Nothing bad... At least I don't have to put up with him for six weeks,' Edgar replied, forcing a smile and refusing to speak of what had happened with the bully.

'Come on, Edgar,' Priscilla said, giving Edgar that knowing look; a look that proved she knew it was worse than he would let on. Something only a mother's intuition would pick up on.

'I'm fine, really,' Edgar lied, staring at the ground and twiddling his thumbs. He wished he could tell her the truth but it was too much. It would only hurt her.

'You're not fine.'

'Okay,' he knew from her reaction that she wouldn't let it rest until he told her what had happened. 'Spencer and Julian beat me up and shoved me in a locker just before the last bell.'

'You what?'

Priscilla's eyes almost popped out of their sockets.

'I don't want talk about it. Mr. Wise caught them, thankfully. If it weren't for him, I'd be stuck in a locker and shut up in the school for the summer.'

Priscilla stared at Edgar open-mouthed in horror. She sighed and shook her head.

'What are we going to do with you, eh?'

'I dunno. Kill me?' Edgar joked without thinking. He stared down at the Star who had jumped back onto his lap and settled on him. She dug her claws into his leg as if to scold him.

'Stop being so dramatic, Edgar,' Priscilla replied austerely. 'If Spencer starts bullying you again just let me know and I'll tell his mum.'

'What? You know his mum?' Edgar exclaimed. If only he had known this before then maybe he wouldn't have had to suffer at the hands of the merciless bully.

'We used to be friends back at school. She was there for me when your father left but you were so little...' Priscilla said sadly. Her icy blue eyes, so much like Edgar's, swam with tears but she held them back and her voice trembled but she managed to keep it under control.

Edgar was taken aback and words failed him. He had never heard Priscilla speak about his father in years. The most she had ever revealed about him was that he left before Edgar had even been born – it was just a simple fact that he had grown up with. He didn't know how to feel but having never known the man made it easier. It had meant that he didn't miss him because he couldn't miss what he had never known and that was a small comfort but sometimes, like now, he knew that Priscilla missed him; that the man she had married had truly broken her heart.

Edgar was lost for words, he hated seeing his mother in this state. It was rare but in these moments he could see through her teary eyes and into her mind – into her very soul. He could sense how much she hurt and yet he never dared to pry or ask questions. It was just an unspoken thing between them – an understanding and no words were ever needed for Priscilla to know that Edgar was there for her, to support her. Her son meant everything and it was for him that she stayed strong.

'It's time, Edgar. You're old enough to understand the truth,' Priscilla began hesitantly and Edgar looked confused. He frowned, not quite knowing what to expect and his mother continued. 'Your father left to look for his brother who went missing. I always thought he'd come back...thought we could have been a family.'

The words were so unexpected that they flew right over Edgar's head and it took a moment for him to comprehend what he had just been told. As the words slowly formed into a cohesive sentence in his brain his eyes widened and his jaw dropped.

'Dad left to look for his brother – *my uncle*?' Edgar thought out loud. He didn't know how to feel. A fire of anger burned in his gut that twisted tight like a serpent inside him. His head swam dizzyingly and a wave of nausea swept over him. 'And he just left you alone with me? What a selfish bast-'

'Your father was a good man, Edgar!' Priscilla interjected defensively, her gaze severe and her voice as sharp and cutting as a knife. 'He and his brother were inseparable.'

'You never mentioned my uncle! Ever!' Edgar raged, furious about the secret that had been kept from him. 'It's like I don't even known my own family!'

'For all I knew he could have been dead. I thought it best to-'

'I don't care what you thought! You kept secrets from me! We promised each other...ever since I was a kid, right back as far as I remember...No secrets. Only honesty.'

'I'm sorry, Edgar,' Priscilla said, lifting her glasses to wipe a tear from her eye. 'He really meant the world to your father. And when he vanished, I learned the harshest lesson of love. Sometimes, if you love someone completely, you have to let them go.'

Edgar's ignorance infuriated her – he had never known his father and would certainly never know him like she had. 'He always promised he'd come back...he never did. Maybe he lied to me, maybe he died out there. Maybe he didn't find his brother and is still looking. I don't know...but I have you and so I deal with it.'

'Sorry,' Edgar muttered quietly, knowing that he had pushed things too far.

'No, I'm sorry, Edgar. I shouldn't have snapped like that,' Priscilla apologized sincerely, her eyes still swimming with tears. 'It's just that you look so much like him when we were your age and it's so hard not knowing where he is, if he's alive or dead or if he'll ever come back even if he is alive.'

'It's alright, mum. You've brought me up alone for fifteen years. We don't need him,' Edgar said sympathetically and his mother feigned a weak smile. Edgar looked at her, forcing a smile of support but she didn't return the eye contact. Instead, she stared at the old boots on his feet. 'They were his you know. He left them for you when he went - said you'd be old enough to appreciate them when you turned fifteen.'

'These boots are my dad's?' Edgar gasped as he stared down at the worn leather boots on his feet. He had always assumed they were just a simple present – an old, second hand pair of the boots he had always wanted. He had been so happy when he unwrapped them on the morning of his fifteenth birthday, knowing Priscilla would have struggled to afford even a second hand pair. They had been everything to him but now it turned out they were so much more – they were all that might be left of his father: The man he never knew and for the last six months he had worn them religiously and never even known.

'Yeah,' Priscilla replied. 'You really are his double, Edgar. Sometimes I just look at you and all I see is him.'

'But what's so special about a pair of old boots?' Edgar scoffed incredulously.

'Nothing...but they were his.'

'I have to ask you something serious, mum,' Edgar asked cautiously, unsure of how his question might be received. 'Do you honestly think he might still be out there, somewhere? Do you think he might come back one day?'

Priscilla froze. She opened her mouth to speak and her voice caught in her throat. Edgar looked puzzled and eventually she spat the words out.

'I honestly don't know. I hope so.'

Silence fell over them and Priscilla got up to turn on the TV. She flicked through the channels and stopped on the news. Edgar remained deathly quiet, his mind on his father and the fact that the boots had been his. Deep down he wished that he'd had the opportunity to meet the man who had once walked in them and he felt a cold tingle shoot down his spine. For all he knew, he could be wearing the boots of a dead man – that the simple item of clothing that he loved and wore daily meant so much more.

He looked up to the television, his eyes brimming with tears but he held them back. He glanced at his mum who sat in her chair in the corner of the room but she didn't notice. She was too wrapped up in her own thoughts, concentrating on the news in which a solemn woman in a garish dress announced the deaths of two men, a woman and several police officers in a vicious stand off in New Jersey.

Edgar blinked back the tears that blurred his vision and wiped his eyes with his sleeve. His vision cleared instantly and he spotted something that made the hairs on the back of his neck stand on end; the ghost of Brother Bradley re-appeared.

It stood beside the television, his expression solemn and his eyes sad.

'Mum…he's there,' Edgar said, pointing a shaking hand towards to the ghost.

'What?' Priscilla asked, staring in the direction that Edgar pointed. The ghost shook its head and Edgar looked confused.

'Brother Bradley – Biggy – the ghost. Can't you see him?'

Edgar's eyes remained fixed upon the flickering, distorting shape of the man, wondering why Priscilla couldn't see. He was there; shimmering, stretching and shrinking like a reflection on water.

'I can't see a thing, Edgar. You must be tired, honey.'

'No, mum! I swear! He's right there. How can you not see the seven foot tall ghost when it's right in front of you?' Edgar turned to her, his face twisted with frustration but when he looked back, the ghost was gone once more.

Edgar's heart sank.

Maybe he was imagining things but surely that would make him crazy.

'Look, I want to believe you, Edgar but there's no proof that ghosts exist. I think you're imagining things, darling.'

'I swear, I'm not,' Edgar protested, anger and frustration taking control.

'Has the sun got to you today?' Priscilla laughed, trying to pin the blame for Edgar's hallucinations on something she could class as logical. 'It *has* been really hot, maybe you've just got sunstroke or something.'

'No, mother!' he protested furiously 'I know what I saw.'

'I think you need some fresh air, we'll go for a walk after tea,' Priscilla said and Edgar nodded irritably. He didn't want to go for a walk – he just wanted his mother to believe him.

*

The sky had almost completely darkened now and amidst the blanket of deep blues and purples that faded into blackness, the moon shone brightly above them and stars had appeared, twinkling pinprick gems in the sky.

Edgar and Priscilla trooped along the street together and past the ancient, ruined, sandstone wall that was the only reminder of a settlement left by the Cistercian monks that had once lived there centuries ago. They climbed up the flight of uneven steps and along the path that led to the door of the impressive church with its giant, blue clock face which told the time: eleven-fifteen with its golden Roman numerals and glittering metallic hands upon its squared spire.

They wound their way along the paths, past the garden of remembrance that was bordered by a rose bush and around the side of the church to a quiet, darkened area beside two broken towers of stone which marked the original far-end of the building before that whole wing was destroyed by Oliver Cromwell in the English Civil War a few centuries before.

It was dark here. There were no streetlights which made it spooky but in addition to the haunting atmosphere was Anne Bronte's grave, gleaming and covered in flowers as a mark of permanent respect to the long lost writer. Just beyond her grave and over the wall stood the Towers – an ancient house that sat upon the hillside just below the ancient castle gates. It looked like a small castle, itself – with two turrets at either side of the house.

The only sound was the rustle of tree branches as the gentle wind swept through them and the quiet hooting of the owls. Edgar and Priscilla sprawled on the grass, staring up at the vast expanse of space above them. Edgar's hand shot into the air and pointed as he spotted a meteor split the blackness with a trail of silver.

'Did you see that?' Edgar exclaimed excitedly.

His mum nodded, not taking her eyes off the sky. Another three zoomed past, so fast they would have been easy to miss but Edgar spotted them and squealed with joy.

'There's so many!' Priscilla gasped, turning to look at Edgar who just lay flat on his back, staring straight up above him.

'Yeah. It's amazing,' Edgar replied in a breathless tone, a smile on his lips. 'I'd better make a wish.'

'Go on then.'

Edgar screwed his eyes up tightly and thought hard. He thought of all the things he wanted in his life. He wondered if he could make a wish for each individual shooting star, or if one single

THE HAUNTINGS OF FATE

wish might strengthen it with the combined force of several stars. Still, there was only one real wish that came to his mind.

'I wish everything would change – that things will get better,' he thought and the idea consumed him until it hurt. He kept the wish in his head, his eyes shut so tight that his whole face scrunched and wrinkled, making him look like he was in pain while he wished with all his might.

'Did you make a good one?' Priscilla asked as Edgar opened his eyes and looked around once more.

'I did, did you?' Edgar asked, looking at his mother curiously and when she nodded sadly but elaborated no further. Deep down, Edgar knew exactly what she had hoped for – the same thing she always did - his father's return.

36

– Chapter Two –
The Old Woman and Her Coin

'COME ON! WAKE UP!' shouted Priscilla as she stormed into Edgar's bedroom and flung his curtains open so that the room was filled with bright, blinding light. 'I'm at work in an hour and I'm stuck in that bloody museum all on my own so you're coming to keep me company!'

'Oh, no. You're not getting me in that shit hole!' Edgar retorted venomously as he pulled the duvet over his head and tried to go back to sleep.

'Oh, yes I *am* getting you into that *shit hole*,' Priscilla replied seriously and glared at Edgar in the way that warned him not to push his luck. Edgar groaned again; Priscilla tutted under her breath and stormed out of the room.

Edgar opened his eyes to a squint, peeked out from under the duvet at the clock on his desk and groaned. It was only half past eight – far too early to be awake on the first day of the school holidays, in his opinion.

Edgar dragged himself from his bed, staggered across the room, yawning and caught a glimpse of himself in the mirror. He had to look twice to believe how exhausted he looked – his face was gaunt and drawn, his bloodshot eyes drooped and his hair was a tangled mess. The room behind him looked blurry so he wiped his eyes again and blinked wearily; somebody stood behind him.

'Brother Bradley?' Edgar gasped. 'Again? What do you want with me?'

Edgar turned to face the ghost behind him but in that split second, the ghost had faded and was gone. Edgar shivered, a feeling of unease creeping over his entire body. Why had the ghost appeared now? What did it want with him? Still, he forced the thoughts to the back of his mind as he got dressed and ready to go and spend the day with Priscilla at the museum.

*

It was a beautiful day and the sun burned bright in the sky with no clouds to block out the heat that already rose to searing temperatures despite being so early in the day.

'You alright?' Priscilla asked, noticing Edgar's glum expression as he slumped along beside her, staring down at the ground.

'Yeah. Just still surprised after what you told me last night,' Edgar replied quietly and his mother nodded.

'We can talk more about it if you want,' she said softly. 'I know it's come as a shock but like I said, you're old enough to know now.'

'I know.'

'Sorry I never told you sooner but you know you've got me and I haven't done such a bad job of bringing you up with Scarlet and Robert, have I?' Priscilla laughed and her bright, cheerful smile was infectious for a moment. Even Edgar, in his sombre mood, couldn't resist returning the cheeky grin.

It wasn't long until they arrived at the Rotundra museum where Priscilla worked. The tall and cylindrical building was very old and had been the first purpose built museum of geology. It was made of sandstone and topped with a domed roof like an upside down bowl. Over the years, as the collections had grown, a long wing had been added to each side.

In front of the museum there was a bank of flowers and shrubs with a long metal fence running along the front and a flight of steps at each side that led up to a gravel path to the entrance.

'Do I have to come here today? It's so boring,' Edgar complained as his mother unlocked the doors and let them in. 'It's a nice day. I don't want to be stuck inside,' he muttered, scowling as he followed his mother inside.

'It gets me money, so we can have nice things, keep a roof over our heads and go re-enacting,' Priscilla replied shooting him an icy cold look that told Edgar to shut up and get on with it.

The thought of re-enactments made him smile. He loved nothing more than escaping from the world to live as a medieval person and he knew that soon enough the re-enactment season would begin and so would his adventures with the friends he could only meet at the events during the summer months each year.

Feeling slightly uplifted with this thought fresh in his mind, Edgar ran around frantically after Priscilla, helping her to unlock all of the doors, turn the lights on, set up the activities for children and put the signs up outside on the front gate. Then at ten o' clock the doors of the museum opened to the public.

The warm sun streamed through the open door and windows, spreading a cheerful glow around the yellow painted walls. Edgar sat in the office on a broken computer chair, spinning in circles to try and alleviate his boredom but instead only made himself feel sick. He wished he could be anywhere but there. He hated it.

Outside, the warm sun shone in the cloudless sky and the cool sea was just down the road, visible from the doorstep. It was cruel temptation to see the tourists enjoying their day out, splashing and swimming in the cool, refreshing water.

Priscilla sat behind the desk reading a book about medieval archers while Edgar, flicked through a pile of papers Patrick had left on his desk with a note:

Priscilla,
A little history about your house.
Hope you find it as interesting as I did.
Patrick xx

Kisses?

Was it normal for a boss to add kisses to a note for an employee?

Curiously, Edgar flicked through the file. It contained pictures, maps and drawings of the old town and he read the pages detailing how the site where his house was now built used to be a Cistercian monastery, then later, over the ruins a manor house had been built. There was an old photo of the manor – it was grandiose and must have filled half of the street. It was surrounded by a high gate and a big wall.

The notes about the manor detailed how it burned down in the late 1800's and how the family who lived there had barely survived. The children escaped with minor burns but the father had died – there had been rumours of a curse placed upon them by a gang of pirates that he had run into at sea.

Edgar thought it was a load of rubbish. What proof was there of curses and supernatural powers but the idea of his house being built over the remains of a monastery fascinated him. He knew the old, crumbling wall at the end of the street that ran along the hill to the steps into the churchyard was an ancient remainder of the old monastery so it only made sense that the site would have stretched the extra few metres to where his house now stood.

It always intrigued him, thinking about the past and how places used to be; like right now in the Rotundra museum, his imagination would wander. The place had been the first purpose built museum of Geology in the country. It was set up and run by a man called William Smith who had a large collection and an interest in local geology, and since it had opened it had attracted thousands of visitors. When he wandered its halls and climbed its staircases, Edgar found himself imagining that he were following in the footsteps of so many others – how many other people had walked in his footsteps long before he tread them himself? He could feel the past around him, almost physically see the ghosts bleeding through time and space to keep him company.

He got up and wandered from the office and around to the west wing. He spent his time there peeking in the dusty glass display cases lit by flickering fluorescent lights. They were filled with curiosities from the Roman era: coins, pieces of pottery, examples of Roman clothing. It was exceedingly dull except for the hollowed out pillar in the middle of the room in which stood a long, black coffin hewn from a tree trunk and a blackened skeleton – The Gristhorpe Man.

Edgar pressed his face against the glass to see more clearly without the reflection of so many other lights getting in the way. Fascinated, his eyes tracked every inch of the skeleton. He was tall and his teeth were perfectly intact. Edgar couldn't help but feel unsettled when he examined the body through the glass. It was eerie how the ancient skull stared right back at him, eyeless and dead.

Tearing himself away from the Gristhorpe Man, Edgar moved back into the central cylinder, ignoring his mother who was too engrossed in her book to speak to him and he began to climb the spiral staircase into the upstairs.

The upper floor of the museum was absolutely stunning and even though he saw it most days, Edgar still felt a rush of surprise as the room came into view. Far above a skylight let the sun stream in through the top of the domed roof and all around the circular room were original Victorian wooden cases with thin, flimsy glass. Each case home to artifacts from Greeks, Egyptians, Mayans and a whole array of historical cultures. A smaller, wooden spiral staircase led up to an upper gallery which was inaccessible to the public. Around the edge of the balcony for the upper gallery was a long painted map showing the strata of the Yorkshire coast.

Edgar looked around briefly but found himself quickly bored. It was all too familiar. He knew every single thing in the museum off by heart and so he went back down to the office and attempted to keep occupied.

A tiny bell tinkled as the door opened and Edgar found himself unable to believe someone had actually bothered to visit while the weather was so glorious.

'Hello,' someone said. He recognized the voice – the Scottish accent was familiar. He'd heard it many times and he couldn't help but smile.

'Hiya Betty,' Priscilla said waving in a friendly manner from behind the desk. 'Have you come to cheer us up and brighten our boring day?' she asked jovially.

Edgar jumped up off the chair and rushed out of the office to greet the old lady.

'BETTY!' Edgar exclaimed delightedly. Betty spotted him and grinned. She had one of those infectious smiles and every time she grinned, her bright green eyes lit up and narrowed, not in a spiteful way but in a way which reflected her warm personality. Her long brown coat trailed along the floor when she walked and as usual she wore her black slippers which she always joked had steel toecaps.

Betty was a very old, very close, family friend who had known Edgar since he was a baby and often came around to his house to see him and Priscilla. He remembered back to when he was young and Betty had visited almost every day. He would be so excited to see her but after a while he would always be told to go and play in his room while the grown-ups talked. He never gave much thought to it, but now he was old enough to realise that Betty had been there to offer his mother help and support when she was feeling lost and lonely after his father had left. Betty had been the rock who kept Priscilla strong while she tried to deal with the problems of raising Edgar single-handedly.

Though of course, this had never mattered to Edgar. He had been blissfully unaware of his father's existence, much like some of the other children at school who had never known their fathers' either.

In their time together, Betty had taught Edgar all kinds of strange codes and little secrets which led to them playing games for hours on end and solving puzzles that they would set for each other. His favourite, which he remembered and still used to this day, was the Alphabet Code which involved turning letters into numbers to create secret messages.

'Hello love,' Betty said. They wrapped their arms around each other in a warm embrace and squeezed tightly. Edgar gasped in shock. Betty was exceptionally strong for her age.

'How's school?' she asked.

'Not bad,' Edgar replied, sighing as he broke away from Betty's crushing embrace. 'Thank God it's over for the summer.'

'Oh, my. I hope it's nothing too serious,' Betty said, looking concerned. Her round, wrinkled face scrunched up in pity.

'It'll be alright,' Edgar lied.

'Where is Doreen today?' Priscilla butted in. It was odd to see Betty out and about without her friend. They were practically inseparable.

'I went for an early morning walk and she was still in bed. I've been out since six o' clock,' Betty replied sadly.

'But that was six hours ago! Aren't you tired?' Edgar asked, looking at Betty, puzzled.

'I haven't found my coin today and you know that means I can't go home so it looks like I'm going to be here for a while,' Betty replied, looking disheartened. There was a tired sadness in her emerald eyes as she glanced all around and sighed.

This was nothing new – as odd as it sounded, Edgar was used to Betty and her need to find a coin before she could go home. It was her OCD– a strange quirk that she had been cursed with. It always upset Edgar to see the old woman so forlorn when she hadn't found a lonely penny on the street, so he put his hand into his pocket and felt around.

'Would you like a coffee?' Priscilla asked kindly, standing up behind the counter.

'Oh, yes please. It's unlikely I'll be going home for a while... I might have to borrow a metal detector from someone and look on the beach,' Betty joked with a grin and followed Priscilla into the staff room to make tea with her.

While her attention was diverted, Edgar pulled a penny from his pocket. He looked around; Betty perched on an old, creaky chair in the staff room, with her feet up on a cardboard box. What was that on the soles of her slippers? Edgar thought. It looked as though somebody had chiseled an intricate pattern into the bottom of them - a pattern that was exactly the same as the one on the bottom of his boots – a pattern he'd never given much thought. It was a symbol of a pentagram with a wobbly circle in the centre around two crossed swords. He assumed it was because the boots were old – maybe a vintage limited edition or something to that effect.

Staring at the soles of her slippers, from a distance he discretely dropped the coin on the floor so Betty would find it and be able to go home. No matter how odd this OCD was, Edgar felt sorry for Betty even if she was slightly mad in her old age. She was old and needed a home with heat and comfort where she could rest but how could she get this if she didn't find her coin?

'So, anything interesting going on with you lately?' Betty asked, giving Edgar a curious look over the rim of her mug as she took a sip.

'Not really, just school and all the usual stuff,' Edgar sighed. He'd rather avoid the subject if he could.

'Oh, you'll be finished soon,' she replied, sensing that Edgar didn't really want to talk about it. 'One more year and you're out.' Betty's encouraging tone wasn't enough to make him feel any better. They sat in silence for a moment.

'Betty...' Edgar began, 'You believe in ghosts and stuff don't you?'

'Of course. Seen a fair few in my life-time,' Betty replied. 'Why do you ask?'

'It's just...I'm going to sound mad but I used to see them when I was a kid-'

'Ah yes, I remember Priscilla telling me at the time,' Betty chuckled. 'You grew out of it though, didn't you?'

'The thing is, I don't think I did. It's been twelve years but he's back.'

'Really?' Betty replied darkly. She surveyed Edgar curiously. 'And what do you think that means?'

There was something about the way she looked him up and down that made him feel uneasy.

'I honestly don't know...but do you really think I'm seeing him or am I going crazy?' Edgar asked 'I don't even know if I believe what I've been seeing myself.'

Betty eyed Edgar beadily and took another sip of her coffee.

'I've seen enough ghosts in my life to know that you're *not* mad. It's those who see things and deny the truth who are.'

Edgar beamed at her.

'Thanks. I needed that,' he replied quietly.

Betty finished her coffee in the cramped staff room. She washed her mug, left it on the draining board and walked back into the shop area of the museum where she spotted the penny on the floor.

'Oh. A coin! I can go home now after all!' Betty exclaimed and Edgar smiled back innocently, trying to conceal the fact that he'd dropped the coin so that Betty could go. She turned to Edgar and flashed a quick wink at him. He blushed, knowing that Betty knew he had dropped it for her.

'You're too good to me,' she said, her gratitude showing in her wide grin.

'We can't have you searching all day, can we?' Edgar replied, unable to think of anything else to say.

'You've a kind heart, dear. You have had ever since you were a wee bairn, Edgar. It'll get you a long way in life.'

Edgar pondered on what Betty had said. Maybe he did have a kind heart but he'd never really thought about it. It was just the right thing to do and that was Edgar's nature – to do the right thing, especially when it came to Betty – the old woman who had been friends with his mother since before he could even remember.

She had been there his whole life – she had practically been family. He couldn't leave her in a vulnerable situation.

'Well, I'd best be off now,' Betty said quickly, clutching the coin tight in her withered, old hand. She smiled and turned to walk out of the museum, waving goodbye and shouting 'Thank you both, see you again soon.'

'Betty, before you go, I need to ask you something,' Edgar said quickly, before she left.

'What's that dear?' she asked.

'What does the symbol under your slipper mean?' Edgar said curiously. 'It's under my boot too…I don't even know what it stands for.'

He lifted his foot and showed Betty the underside of his boot but she shook off his question with a flick of her hand.

'Well, I'll have to tell you another day, I'm tired and I really have to go home,' she said quickly as if she was relieved to have an excuse to leave so abruptly and Edgar couldn't bring himself to argue. Again, it was his soft nature taking charge. He could have easily demanded an answer there and then, but all he could think about was how long Betty had been out wandering around and how exhausted she must be. For that reason, he just let her go.

'Bye Betty!' he said, grabbing the old lady for a huge hug. Betty chuckled to herself, hugged him tightly back and planted a big kiss on his cheek.

'See you soon, Edgar,' she said, gripping his shoulders before pulling him in for one last squeeze. Her arms were shockingly strong for her age and Edgar almost thought she might break his ribs.

'Don't I get one?' Priscilla chimed sadly.

'Of course you do, dear. Of course you do.'

Betty let go of Edgar and crossed over to Priscilla to give her a hug but the bell tinkled as a lost looking tourist stumbled in wearing a hefty backpack – a typical rambler who looked out of place in the museum and would have been more at home a few miles out of town on the moors.

Betty stopped in her tracks as the man strode past her and strolled up to Priscilla at the desk.

'Is it free then?' he said

'I'm afraid not, sir. There is a small charge-'

'Small charge? Museums are meant to be free!'

'I'm afraid this one isn't but-'

'I want to come in for free.'

'What I'm trying to say, sir is that we have a small charge but that gives you access to our other museums in the town and also the art gallery too.'

The man began to rifle around his wallet for change, moaning out loud about how the museums in London are all free – a common reaction from far too many customers. Priscilla, however, had learned to just smile and get on with it even though her sparkling eyes, bright smile and pleasant tone indicated to Edgar that she would happily commit murder if it weren't illegal.

'I'll just see you next time,' Betty said quietly and waved as she let herself out. She stopped by the door, turned to Edgar and said:

'See you soon, darling.'

She waved, blew a kiss and then she was gone.

– CHAPTER THREE –

THE FALL OF KRINKA

Brother Dominic was good man and a Brother of the Cistercian Order, the white monks who had originated in France before spreading over Europe. He lived his simple life by the Bible with his fellow brothers in the Abbey of Rievaulx in Yorkshire, England.

The majestic Abbey that he called home stood proud in the vast wilderness of the rugged countryside. It was there that he had been welcomed as a young man after his father passed away, when he had nobody left to turn to. He had lived there for over a decade now and had adjusted to life well.

The routine became second nature to him and had it not been for the obvious signs of aging – the faint wrinkles, the gradual graying and balding of his auburn hair and the feelings of weariness and fatigue that only came with age, he would have expected his life to have been frozen in time. The same monotonous, simplistic routine day in, day out had almost killed him with its tedious nature.

Dominic wasn't meant for this kind of life but it was the only way to be safe – the only way to avoid becoming a vagrant on the streets where he would have to live a life of crime and risk hanging just to survive, however, that was all about to change.

Dominic had been careless. As time wore on, he would often venture away from the Abbey to go on pilgrimages which raised the suspicion of the other monks and it was only when Dominic returned from one of his mysterious journeys that he was overheard speaking to his closest friend, Brother Clement. The two of them had been locked away in the chapel, speaking in hushed tones about dimension travel and time travel – of demons and creatures of the dark and a warrior prophecised to slay them.

Those who overheard searched Dominic's room and found old notes scrawled in parchment about his ability to travel through different worlds with the aid of an artifact he called a travellers' token; a relic which they uncovered in a drawer with his diaries detailing his adventures. Fearing that Dominic had been touched by the Devil and consumed by his evil they took the travellers' token and destroyed it before confronting Dominic with an ultimatum. Terrified that the Devil they believed had taken their fellow brother would soon begin to taint those around him, they gave him one hour to leave the Abbey that served as sanctuary for so long or to face the consequence of his heresy.

During this final hour Brother Dominic packed a knapsack of his few vital belongings and paid a goodbye visit to his best friend, Brother Clement who had always been there for him to confide in; been there as a Brother and a friend despite his outrageous claims.

'So what will you do? Where will you go?' Clement asked nervously when Dominic told him that he was fleeing from the abbey for his own safety.

'On my travels I have heard tales of a place far away, over oceans, land and mountains where the Orders of our foreign Brothers are welcoming,' Dominic replied solemnly, bowing his head as he contemplated the dangers of the long, dangerous journey that lay ahead of him. 'And since they destroyed my means of travelling, I shall have to brave the journey the hard way.'

Clement looked concerned but Dominic smiled. That was just his nature – optimistic, even in the face of devastation.

'But how can you be certain that you will make it?' Clement demanded. He was worried for his friend now and it was beginning to show in his wavering voice and his wide, watery eyes as a tear rolled down his cheek.

'I will be fine, my dear Brother. I have my faith in the Lord and I know you shall pray for me when I am gone,' Dominic said serenely, placing a comforting hand on his fellow Brother's shoulder. It was obvious that he was hiding just how scared he really was from the way his fingers dug slightly into Clement's shoulder.

'What is the name of this paradise that you are headed to?' Clement asked, wondering where in the world could be safe for a monk who had been accused of witchcraft.

'It is the city of Krinka,' whispered Dominic with an air of mystery to his tone. 'To reach it I must travel across earth and oceans. I follow a dangerous path to a city on the edge of stone between sea and sand – a haven for those like me who have learned the secrets of travelling.'

'I wish you well Brother Dominic, but I cannot see why there was no other, easier option. Can you not re-think and find a more...

accessible place to flee to?' Clement asked anxiously, 'How long will it take you to reach this Krinka place that you speak of?'

'I do not know. I will have to walk far and build boats to get me across the oceans inbetween but I must go…and soon. If they catch me here after my expulsion time you do not want to know what they will do to me,' Dominic explained hurriedly as he turned his attention away from Clement and paced the room, trying to collect his thoughts. The fear returned. He knew what they would do if they caught him and it wasn't pleasant.

'What will they do?' Clement asked fearfully, biting his lip to hold back the tears as his friend paced solemnly.

'You know what they do to *witches,* do you not?' Dominic spat gravely. He stopped pacing briefly to look Clement in the eye. Clement trembled and nodded. His eyes widened.

'They burn them and that is why I shall bid you goodbye and good luck,' Brother Clement said as he crossed the room and took a thick, gnarled, walking stick from the corner which he passed to Brother Dominic. He took it without question and thanked Clement for his kindness.

'If you don't find a way to use it immediately, don't worry. There are many other uses for a stick aren't there?' laughed Clement as Dominic nodded and turned to the door.

'They aid with walking. They make good weapons and if the worst comes, it can serve as an oar when I make my way across the seas,' Dominic grinned and Clement chuckled, glad to see that his friend was remaining so upbeat despite the heavy circumstances of his departure.

'I shall miss you, Brother. Please, write to me and maybe one day I shall be able to follow you to this city of Krinka.'

'I doubt that will be so. When I leave here, all traces of me vanish. I am but a ghost. I am beyond shadow and time. I may not even make it to my destination,' explained Dominic grimly but his face was set, there was a sparkle in his steely eyes and he seemed determined.

'But how do you know where to go? How will you find this city?'

'The man I spoke of – the man I was condemned for speaking of, Father Danko, gave me a map when we met in the Black Belltower in the monastery of Grindlotha.'

'Danko?' Clement gasped, the name ringing in his ears with a strange familiarity.

'You know him?'

'Of course…it was he who came by me and told me to give you the stick. He trusted me because *you* trusted me,' Clement said suspiciously. 'But how did he-?'

Dominic beamed. He could see the confusion in Brother Clement's eyes – the thoughts almost visibly whizzing around his head. *"How did Danko get here if he's meant to be in a city half way across the world?"*

'He must have travelled,' Dominic replied with a sigh. 'Must be nice being so free.'

'If he can, why can't you? Why didn't he leave a spare token for you to use?'

Dominic looked anxious. His stomach twisted violently in a tight knot as he thought to his long, dangerous journey ahead.

'This is my test. If I am worthy of calling Krinka home, I shall make it. If not, I shall perish.'

Clement's expression was pained and he shook his head in despair – his fear for his brother's journey was overwhelming. He took Dominic's hand and squeezed it tightly around the gnarled stick.

'If you ask me, this is very important. There's a reason you should have it and though I know not what it is, I think you'd do well to keep it safe, Brother.'

'And so I shall. Danko works in mysterious ways as does our Lord,' Dominic said, glancing out of the window of the abbey into the cloisters below. A bell tolled the hour, echoing to signal Dominic's doom. 'The time has come for me to leave. I shall never forget your kindness, Clement but I must go before I am caught. If they see me now, I am as good as dead.'

'Goodbye…and take care, my Brother,' Clement said as he hurriedly pushed Dominic towards the door.

'Goodbye,' Dominic replied in a low, sad tone as he pulled up his hood and hugged Clement tightly. He didn't want to let go but after a moment, the sobering sound of the bells rang in his ears, he pulled away. 'I'll miss you.'

'I'll miss you too,' Clement said, his hand still on Dominic's arm.

'I'll always be with you,' Dominic said as he placed his hand on Clement's heart and leaned towards him and kissed him softly on the forehead.

'Go. Quickly before they see you.'

Dominic grimaced. He took a deep breath and sighed, then slung his knapsack over his shoulder and glanced over his back to see his best friend one last time as he crossed the threshold from the room to the cold, draughty corridor. He smiled at Clement who returned it weakly, knowing this would be the final time that they would see each other.

Dominic turned away and the door closed behind him slowly. It creaked and then banged as it shut, leaving Dominic alone in the corridor with the dreadful echo surrounding him; engulfing him in its dull thud. Dominic sped down the corridor as quickly and as light on his feet as he could possibly be. The abbey bells continued ringing loudly to signal that the time of exile had come. He rushed down the spiraling stone staircase at the end of the corridor; jumping two at a time and emerged into the cloisters.

Other monks stared at him with discontent through their little windows, which shone like miniature stars from the sides of the building. He sprinted across the sweeping lawns, through the herb gardens and past the chapel at the far side of the grounds and came towards the gates. The dirt path was lined with several of the elderly monks who had admitted him a decade before. They eyed him warily, their faces swallowed by their hoods and they chanted Latin prayers under their breath as Dominic slowed his pace to stride past them.

'You got what you wanted. I am leaving,' Dominic said calmly. The monks ignored his words and watched him hawk-like as he passed them by, their faces shrouded in shadow. Dominic paused as a couple of monks opened the gates for him and then he continued on his way. He crossed under the arch, leaving the sanctuary of the monastery for the harsh, bleak dangerous world outside. He walked as fast as he could until he reached the edge of the forest where he paused to collect himself – to think about his journey and get his bearings. He turned back to look at the grand monastery – his old home and sighed. He was alone now and his survival depended on his wit and intelligence. The comforts of a home, as cold and dreary as they had been, were gone. His exile had begun and even he didn't know if he would even survive the journey to the mythical city of Krinka.

*

Brother Dominic's journey was long and treacherous. He crossed many lands, trekking across the bleak moors and barren fields of England. It was a solitary journey and Dominic had never felt so alone and vulnerable – he was on his own and the world was against him. He had to hunt to find his own food and cook it on fires that he made himself. He had to find streams to get water and even the basics of survival were tough in the alien environments.

For days he trudged on and on across England, heading south and when he reached the waters edge he built a boat to sail across the channel to the land at the other side, only to have to walk further through foreign lands where he could not understand the language spoken by the natives that he came across. Luckily, language seemed not to matter. He was well looked after when he stopped at inns in far off towns and villages when his hosts realized that he was a man of the cloth – a man of God and somebody to be respected; a Cistercian monk in the land where his Order originated from. Thankfully here it was not known that he was in exile – that he was supposedly a host of the Devil, himself.

His path across France was the first major step in his foreign adventure as he walked through the countryside and many vineyards, passing churches, mountains and chateaus until he came to Italy and as he moved further down south towards the equator, the weather vastly improved. It became warmer and the architecture and culture of each place seemed to become more distant to anything he had seen before – it was exotic and exciting.

He eased into the adventure and began to enjoy his travelling. He could see the world in all its beautiful glory and it was in Italy, when he stopped off in a monastery for a few days with Brothers of the Benedictine order that he realized, though their ways of life were different, like their language; their beliefs and goals were the same. They all wanted a peaceful life and to worship God.

The Brothers treated Dominic welcomingly and made sure that he was as comfortable as possible. They fed him well and made sure he had as much comfort as possible and it saddened him to leave after his short break. He had enjoyed walking the grounds and listening to the beautiful chanting and prayer in the foreign tongue of the monks but as much as he loved this place, he knew there was something even better out there: The City of Krinka.

Dominic walked on and on, trudging through the breathtaking country of Italy that astounded him with its sheer size.

Their architecture was stunning and when he reached Rome he couldn't help but stop off at an inn and take the opportunity to explore the city. It amazed him and almost side-tracked him but he kept Krinka in mind and told himself that it would be a place to rival even this city of splendor that he found himself in now.

He continued his journey, passing through more countryside and small towns and settlements. He walked through mountains and struggled on and on, facing exhaustion but never gave up. Eventually he reached the waters edge where he paid a travelling merchant a copious amount of gold to take him across the ocean to the continent of Africa.

It was here, that finally, after months of travelling Brother Dominic reached his destination. Krinka; an impressive city fashioned from sandstone, surrounded by a high wall. On one side - the edge of a harsh and cruel desert and the other was the edge of a sheer cliff, which overlooked the clear and tranquil turquoise ocean.

As Brother Dominic sailed towards the enormous cliff that rose up like a rocky giant, he noticed that buildings had been erected down the side of the rock-face to the waters edge and there was a small harbour filled with small boats tied to a rickety wooden jetty and a steep, gravel path led up the side of the cliff side to the main gate. There were only a few buildings perched on ledges on the side of the cliff but they were all connected with bridges between eroded gaps in the cliff face and stony walkways and tunnels inside the rock. Dominic felt nervous as he drew nearer to the imposing sandstone city.

The sea was calm on the day that Dominic arrived and the salty waves lapped gently at the bottom of the cliff – everything about the place was dreamy. It was like heaven.

He sailed across the bobbing water and into the peaceful harbour at the foot of the cliff where several other wooden boats had already been moored. The captain of the ship anchored the boat and they bid their farewells. Dominic shook the man's hand vigorously, unable to put his gratitude into words. The captain smiled toothlessly and patted Dominic on the back. They waved goodbye as Dominic jumped off the boat, watched it turn and begin to sail away.

It didn't take him long to notice just how hot the climate was and just how different it was to the world he left behind. He stared up the hill towards the battlements that stood at the top of the twisted, rocky slope and summoned the last of his energy to begin the ascent.

Dominic struggled on up the narrow path as he sluggishly trailed up the steep, gravelly hill. He forced himself to keep going despite how he sweated in the sweltering heat and felt like he could collapse. He was there now – so close he could sense his new life waiting within his grasp but his exhaustion had grown so much that it almost got the better of him. He could barely move in the intense heat. He hadn't eaten properly for days and had only had stagnant water to drink but the promise of the conclusion to his journey spurred him on and he fought against the fatigue that wearied him.

When he finally reached the top of the cliff he followed the path closer to the imposing city. As Brother Dominic drew near to the high outer wall he could see the enormous gate that looked like a monstrous mouth that would swallow him when he entered. It was engraved with figures of people and demons all fighting. Intrigued by the intricate designs on the gate Dominic knocked gently as to not disturb the piece of art before him too much. He was greeted with silence for a few moments and just as he raised his hand to knock again, somebody stirred at the other side.

'Who is it?' they asked sternly.

'It is I, Brother Dominic. I seek refuge and was told that your city would welcome me,' Brother Dominic responded, his heart pounding as a combined result of his tiring climb and anxiety.

'Brother Dominic! Yes, you may enter. We have your sanctuary ready for your arrival. We have been expecting you,' replied a strong, yet kindly voice from behind the gate in an unusual accent.

A deafening creak filled the air as clanking chains were pulled and the enormous wooden gate heaved up into the air, allowing Brother Dominic inside. Behind the gate was a long tunnel, made from sandy brick which was lit by beams of light that entered through small, square holes.

'It is nice to meet you again, Dominic' said the voice and Dominic took a moment for his eyes to adjust to the change of light. He squinted, trying to make out who was speaking. 'It is I, Danko and it is an honor to have you in our presence,' Danko said welcomingly, holding out his hand to Dominic and he gasped as his vision cleared and his eyes latched onto Danko – he was definitely the same man who had visited him at Rievaulx. He was young, well built and handsome. His hair was short and dark and his eyes that were the deepest shade of green twinkled in a friendly way, standing out against his olive skin.

'Are we not all equal in the eyes of God?' Brother Dominic replied, shaking Danko's hand firmly.

'Very true, old friend,' Danko laughed and dimples formed upon his cheeks 'Now if you would kindly follow me and I will show you to your sanctuary. It is not so far away,' Danko said and beckoned Dominic to follow him.

Brother Dominic strode side-by-side with Danko through the long tunnel, relishing the coolness of the shadow after the blistering heat in the sun. Eventually, they exited the tunnel and out into a large square courtyard surrounded by high walls, like the battlements of a castle.

The grassy cloister was shaded by giant palm trees which grew in its center and Dominic felt refreshed to be standing on the ground underneath its canopy of fresh green leaves that cast a shade over him and Danko.

Underneath the trees were many types of beautiful, strong smelling plants that were all the colours of the rainbow and more besides. A massive stone fountain at the center sent a jet of water high into the air and as it splashed down the water sprayed all over the plants. Birds sang down from their nests in the trees and a couple of cats lazed by the water.

Dominic eyed the water greedily, as if longing to just dive in to relinquish himself of the heat that burned his body under his thick robes.

'You may take a drink, you look like you need it,' Danko said, nodding towards the fountain and Dominic bowed his head in thanks as he fell to his knees beside the stone basin, reached his hands into the cool, refreshing water and splashed it over his face. He sighed in relief and cupped his hands, scooped up water, lifted it to his mouth and gulped it down. Danko beamed at Dominic as he sat down, leaning against the fountain.

'Tell me Danko. Is this Heaven? Did I somehow die on my treacherous journey to my true destination? I cannot believe that this is Krinka,' Dominic gasped breathlessly as he stared around in awe, water trickling down his face like beads of crystal. 'Surely I have been blessed by the Almighty Creator to be allowed to take refuge in a place such as this.'

The journey had definitely been worth the trouble and Dominic found it hard to take in. Danko chuckled warmly but said nothing. Dominic climbed back to his feet and the two monks stood in silence, admiring the scenery for a moment, until Danko turned back to Dominic.

'Come, Your sanctuary is nearby.'

Danko led Brother Dominic down the narrow, peaceful streets of the city that led off from the courtyard. Each street was lined with small, sandstone houses. All of them adorned with rough wooden doors and holes for windows, most of which were covered from the inside by bits of wispy white cloth.

It was so basic but so peaceful. Dominic was used to living a very simply life but this was simplicity in paradise!

Brother Dominic felt as though he was in harmony with the city already. It was the most stunning place he'd ever seen and it was now his home – even better than Rievaulx Abbey from which he had been exiled.

Danko led Dominic down a narrow alley and up a flight of uneven, stony steps. They walked along another cobbled street and up an almost vertical hill, climbing a set of steep steps at either side, which, despite being so uneven (some steps even reaching knee height) were easier to climb than the hill itself.

At the top there was a cloister, just as exotic as the courtyard by the entrance, except the fountain here wasn't as impressive. It didn't work and was hidden in one of the back corners, covered by dominant ivy vines that twisted around the stony structure, rendering it useless and almost hiding it entirely from view. Had Danko not motioned towards it, Dominic would not have noticed it at all. His attention, instead, had been taken by an enormous tower which rose high into the air from the centre of the courtyard.

This tower was Krinka's beacon. If an enemy was to invade, the watchman would ring a bell and set his fire to warn of the attack. In the commotion all of the citizens would awaken and prepare to defend against the enemy.

'Do not fear, the watch tower hasn't been used for over a hundred years. Krinka is the safest place on Earth, after all,' Danko explained pompously 'From the top you can see for miles around – perfect for meditation. Up there you can be at peace with the world.'

Danko began to ascend the stairs and Dominic followed. As they ascended, Dominic felt claustrophobic in the tight, narrow space. Missing bricks substituted for windows here, just like everywhere else in Krinka, a faint trace of fresh air trickled in, keeping them cool and letting in small beams of light that split the almost darkness of the spiral staircase.

The climb to the top seemed never ending but when an exhausted Brother Dominic emerged into the sunlight once more, he realized that it was worth the long, tiring journey to the top. A colossal bell hung some twenty feet above them, a thick rope connected to the bell dangled down and the view between the hefty pillars that held the domed roof in place, was astounding.

Below them the walled city of Krinka spread out like a giant maze, its long, winding streets looked smaller and narrower from the high viewpoint. A few monks could be spotted wandering around in their white habits, looking like mice, scurrying about their business and even from here Dominic could see the magnificent fountain in the first courtyard blasting its jet of water into the air, sending a cool spray over the shady oasis. It was the most spectacular sight that he'd ever seen – one that took his breath away and rendered him speechless.

From one side a vast ocean stretched far out over the horizon, its waves gently lapping against the cliffs far below. But from the other side of the tower all that could be seen was sand. A vast expanse of desert stretched across the land like a giant, sandy blanket with dunes rising and dipping as far as the eye could see. There was no sign of life in its wilderness – only the strange pyramid structures that were scattered all over the dunes. They were made out of the same stone as the city walls and looked quite majestic.

Dominic knew that even though they looked small from where he was, close up they would be at least ten feet high. Dominic frowned, curious as to why they were there but then at his side Danko stirred.

'I see you've noticed the pyramids,' he said airily.

'I was just wondering, is it really *possible*?' Dominic replied, more to himself than to Danko.

'Is *what* really possible?' Danko replied, his voice catching in his throat as if he was trying to cover something up.

'I've heard that the pyramids were the ancient ways of dimension travel, used by our ancestors to maintain peace and order throughout all worlds,' Dominic whispered, barely able to believe what he was saying. It seemed crazy that he could actually talk about these things – that someone could understand and not call him a witch and try to kill him for it.

'Brother Dominic, why are you here?' Danko asked simply. He turned to the monk and looked at him solemnly, a knowing gleam in his eye.

'Because I can travel through the dimensions,' replied Dominic faintly. 'But I've only ever been able to use a travellers' token and that's gone now - destroyed. I've heard the stories about the great pyramids but thought it was only a legend.'

'Well, what if I told you that the stories you heard were not legend – they were *truth*?' Danko said and Dominic expected to see a smile on his face or for him to say that he was joking but Danko's expression remained neutral and pensive.

'You mean the Nazakan really *did* take them over and that was why we were stopped from using them?' asked Dominic in disbelief.

His eyes didn't shifting from the pyramids spread across the sand dunes far below.

'I'm afraid so. The Nazakan come through regularly. There was no way to stop them until recently. I was researching the pyramids in the city's archives and I found a way,' Danko said austerely, his eyes cold and steely as if he were hiding something.

'Why hadn't anyone found it before?'

'It wasn't written. It came in the form of a verbal warning. A fellow Brother appeared and told me of an ancient spell, one that was lost in the great earthquake many, many years ago. Before you or I were born,' explained Danko intensely. 'He said that a certain magic can stop them, or at least keep them at bay for so long… It may not sound like much but it's better than nothing. Worth a try at least,' Danko laughed forcibly, his voice wavering as he scanned the landscape below, his eyes glazed almost trance-like.

'So, is that why we're here, to protect the pyramids and stop the Nazakan from running free?' Dominic asked fearfully. A cold shiver shot through him and the hairs on the back of his neck stood on end. What had he managed to get involved with?

'In a way, you are right, dear Brother,' Danko laughed, turning away from Dominic to hide his anxious expression.

'What do you mean "In a way?"' Dominic snapped rudely.

'Krinka was created by the Almighty Creator who placed us here to watch over the dimensions. He created many of them, one on top of the other, trying to create the perfect world. When he failed, he just built another world on top of the last. Some were lost in time, some were kept hidden – not even reachable by the pyramids or travellers' tokens while others prospered and became more and more powerful; others began to breed terrible monsters or fell victim to plagues and darkness,' Danko said grimly, as Dominic nodded in understanding. 'Each Dimension was left to grow and develop naturally and some became, in time more advanced whereas others withered and died. Eventually, as a monk of the honorable Cistercian Order, I was placed here to make a sanctuary for banished Brothers of all Orders, who had also found out the secrets of travel and teach them all they needed to know for their mission –'

'What mission? I was under the impression I'd been summoned here, to a safe place, to live in peace. Nobody told me I'd come here for a mission,' Dominic snapped, irritated by the real reason he had been brought to Krinka.

'We here are united to keep the travelling community safe and Krinka is the heart of that operation,' Danko said, his voice stern and imperious. Dominic knew not to argue but his frustration only spurred him on. 'But you are here for something else entirely. There was a prophecy-'

'What?' Dominic gulped. This was the first he had heard about this.

'It is written that a warrior with hair of flame and eyes of ice will lead us to battle and defeat the Nazakan.'

Danko's expression was deadly serious as he looked right into Dominic's cold, blue eyes.

'That's why you brought me here?' Dominic said, slowly finding the words. 'You think I'm a warrior?'

'Hair of flame and eyes of ice,' Danko repeated.

'You brought me half way across the world because of my hair and eyes?'

'You have been watched throughout your travels. You showed promise.'

'You tricked me. I want no part of this. I don't want to fight. I want peace!' Dominic argued. He trembled, a mix of both anger and fear and he felt his knees almost buckle beneath him.

'We all want peace,' Danko replied. 'And you could be the one to bring it. Imagine. You. Bringing an end to the Nazakan.'

Dominic felt sick. He had come all this way just because Danko thought he might be the subject of a prophecy. It was ridiculous! It was outrageous! How many times had he almost died on the journey? Countless times. He had risked everything...

But had he not come here, where would he have been able to turn. He would have still been exiled. He would have been homeless and alone and vulnerable. The image of him begging and stealing on the streets crossed his mind and suddenly, whatever Danko had planned didn't seem so bad.

'You must be tired,' he said, his eyes lingering on the black bags under Dominic's eyes. 'Now that you know the truth, I will take you to your new home at last,' Danko continued kindly, as he turned away and began to descend the spiral staircase with Dominic following close behind. They didn't speak. Dominic was too confused – too angry. His whole world was crumbling around him and there were no words to express that. He felt scared – betrayed.

The sky was darkening now and the first dim light of the stars were beginning to show through the twilight that crept over the horizon. An icy chill blew through the air as Danko led Brother Dominic back down the stairs of the tower, across the cloister and down a small flight of steps to another courtyard.

Houses were built into the walls around the edges and every single one had a deep stone basin full of water by the side of its door. There were only a few trees in this courtyard and in the middle, rather than a fountain, there was a pyramid. Dominic eyed it suspiciously, staring up in awe at its pinnacle that pointed high in the air. It was a magnificent creation but the longer Dominic stared at it, the more he began to feel uneasy – if what Danko had told him was true, the Nazakan could come through at any time.

'You're perfectly safe here. There's no need to worry,' Danko insisted as he led Dominic to a decrepit sandstone shack in a dark corner.

'What can you tell me about this prophecy?' Dominic asked, summoning the courage to enquire.

'Please, let us not do this now.'

'You tricked me!' he raged 'Tell me!'

'Let this wait until tomorrow.'

'I want answers!'

'Tomorrow. I promise,' Danko insisted.

'We have time now.'

Danko looked angry and Dominic wondered whether he should dare push him anymore. He had been kind enough to invite him and take him in. Waiting until tomorrow wasn't much to ask.

Danko suddenly stopped walking.

'Here we are. This is your home. Sleep well and I shall see you tomorrow,' Danko said kindly, bowing to Dominic who bowed respectfully in return before turning to enter his new home.

'Thank you,' Dominic said politely, bowing his head in respect to Danko.

From the outside the shabby hut looked small but inside it was rather spacious. A roughly hewn wooden table with a couple splintery stools pushed up against a wall at the back. In the centre of the stony floor was a pile of twigs surrounded by a metal frame – a fireplace of sorts and finally there was a small bed tucked away in a corner near a window through which drifted a pleasant draft.

Dominic sank onto the bed and slipped instantly into a deep sleep that night as he lay on his hard bed beneath thick, itchy, woolen blankets but it was the best night sleep he'd had since before his exile. It felt strange to have finally reached his destination – to have reached safety. No longer did he need to worry about setting up camp where wolves might find him – no more fear of being found by bandits in the night. There was just peace...except for the niggling panic in the back of his mind – a whole host of questions that he could not wait to be answered in the morning. Perhaps there was no real reason to worry; maybe he shouldn't be so angry with Danko. He would have to sleep on it and wait to see.

He had no idea how long it had been since he fell asleep – it could have been minutes or it could have been hours. There was no way of telling but an almighty roar and a series of crashes came from outside.

In the depths of his sleep, Dominic thought it must be a dream. The screams and roars – the sounds of panic and clang of metal on metal awoke him instantly, wondering what was happening. Shrill shrieks pierced the air and then after a violent crack there was silence. Dominic jumped bolt-upright, wiping his bleary eyes to try and see clearly. He brushed the flimsy, white material aside and peeped out of his window to see a ghostly green light illuminating the courtyard. A couple of monks sprinted down a dark street yelling for help and Dominic's heart sank. He was consumed by fear. What should he do? He grabbed his walking stick for protection and ran out of his house to help the victims of the attack.

'DOMINIC! DUCK!'

Dominic dropped to the floor as a fist swung for his head. He felt the disturbed air above his head and heard the swish of the forceful punch that just missed him.

He looked back to see a creature taller than himself. It was pale and had short, sharp teeth. Mutant growths like warts and puss-filled boils on its face hid one of its eyes but the visible eye was lilac and flashed threateningly – it was not a creature of this world. Dominic scrambled to his feet and ran but the monster pursued him, roaring ferociously and baring its tiny, needle sharp teeth. Dominic grew tired. His legs burned, his heart was fit to burst and his breath caught in his throat. He knew he couldn't outrun it much longer. He heard its growls and grunts getting closer so he swung around and hit the creature forcefully in the face with his walking stick. It recoiled and roared as Dominic ran blindly, his legs burning and his lungs on the verge of collapse. He could barely breathe but he had to run. A figure dressed all in white appeared from around a corner just ahead.

'Go! Turn around and run! There are monsters!' Dominic shouted at his fellow monk. The man lowered his hood to reveal himself. It was Danko.

'Come Dominic, to the beacon tower!' Danko shouted; his face contorted with terror. He shuddered with fear and his eyes were dull in comparison to their gleaming state, earlier that day. Something was wrong.

Before Danko could speak or Dominic could even react, the creature dived at him, taking advantage of his moment of confusion. It grabbed the monk and flung him like a ragdoll onto the hard cobbles. Dominic hit his head hard. His vision swam dizzyingly and he tried not to succumb to the blackness trying to swallow him. He struggled to fight off the monster that thrashed so violently and clawed at him, tearing through the thick robes and into his flesh.

Dominic screamed. Everything was just a blur of limbs and claws and teeth. His entire being existed in a state of agonising, stinging pain; his body wet with hot, red blood but then the creature was pulled back. Dominic felt its weight taken off him and it felt like freedom, he felt like he was lighter than air – floating.

Dominic gasped for breath, his hands flying over his body, his fingertips dabbing his wounds. More harsh, stinging pain like knives driving into him. There was a loud *swoosh*, a *crack* and a *THUD*.

The crazed monster's head fell to the ground and rolled away over the cobbles, leaving a trail of thick, black blood oozing from the neck. Danko wiped his sword on his robes and sheathed it once more before helping Dominic to his feet.

'Are you alright, brother?' Danko asked, concerned.

'Fine.' Dominic lied. His whole body ached from smashing into the cobbles under the force of the creature. He had been torn to shreds by its claws, his heart was fit to burst and his head throbbed with adrenaline but he was alive and all thanks to Danko.

Dominic wiped a trickle of blood from his forehead and struggled to catch his breath.

'We have to go,' Danko demanded. He pushed Dominic ahead of him and they took off at top speed towards the tower.

They ran as quickly as the could and gathered all the other fleeing monks that they could on their way.

'The gateway at the bottom of the hill has been breached,' a man shouted desperately, his voice wavering as he tried to catch his breath.

'The south gate has been broken. The Nazakan have breached the city!' another monk shouted as he ran up to Danko and the others with a companion. He swayed on the spot and almost collapsed as he tried to catch his breath but his companion steadied him supportively.

Together the group of monks rushed down the streets that glowed pale green in the pyramids' ghastly light as more Nazakan

THE HAUNTINGS OF FATE

emerged, catching their first glimpse of prey dashing past. They gave chase to their targets - Danko and Dominic and the others as the tumultuous racket of fighting and screaming rent the air.

Eventually, they reached the tower and jumped through the door. An angry growl confirmed that they were still being chased. They slammed the door shut together and held all their weight against it as the creatures from outside barged into it repeatedly, trying to get in while Danko locked it with the wooden bars. It wouldn't take long to break through but had at least bought them a few more precious moments. They sprinted up the stairs, ignoring the stitches in their sides, ignoring their gasps for breath and their aching legs. This was life or death now, such small things didn't matter if they were to survive – if the Nazakan got through, they were cornered and not one of them stood a chance of survival.

Eventually, gasping and spluttering, they reached the top and took a moment to catch their breath as they looked back.

Chaos unfolded in the city below. All of the pyramids around the city glowed in their deathly green colour, like otherworldly beacons casting an eerie light over all of the poor people who still ran for their lives.

One man rushed down the steep hill, only to have a creature catch up to him, pick him up with a bloodcurdling screech. The onlookers were powerless to help as the creature snapped him in half then threw the bleeding, crumpled heap to the floor and moved on to another victim.

Over on the battlements around the edge of the city, a monk put up a valiant fight against one of the creatures. He swung his sword at the monster and skewered it right in the heart but with its final lease of energy, the creature shoved the unsuspecting monk. He stumbled backwards, losing his balance after being taken by surprise and toppled over the wall into the freezing sea below; his fragile body breaking upon the sharp and jagged rocks.

It was a heartbreaking scene as the miniscule figures - monsters and men ran, chasing each other and being fatally wounded, or for the lucky ones, murdered swiftly.

Monks ran for the front gate of the city, trying to break out of their sanctuary – to escape to freedom. An effort that was futile against the speed and agility of their attackers.

Dominic tore his eyes away from the dreadful scene but looking away didn't stop the screams ringing through the air like the final bleats of a slaughtered lamb and a tear of remorse streaked his cheek. He was still in a complete daze. He had woken up to a real life nightmare and had been running on pure adrenaline – the scenario hadn't yet completely settled in his mind.

There was a loud bang, followed by an ear splitting *crack* that brought Dominic and the others back to the harsh reality. They were trapped at the top of the tower and soon the Nazakan would break through the door and be upon them.

'They're trying to get to us. There's only one thing that we can do,' Danko said, looking worried, as though he'd being expecting this to happen, but not at that time. 'We have to resort to the ancient magic laws. All join hands!' Danko commanded. His face was solemn yet blank.

'Are you going to tell me what's happening?' Dominic interjected. 'You promised.'

'There's no time.'

'Please.'

'It doesn't matter anymore. I'm sorry,' Danko hissed.

'What do you mean?' Dominic was suddenly very concerned. There was a look in Danko's eye – a fear that Dominic had not seen in him before.

'Just hold hands,' Danko commanded and the tone of his voice told Dominic not to argue – there was something strong and triumphant about it. 'Trust me.'

Everyone joined hands and gathered in a circle, around the beacon in the middle of the tower. Their arms slowly raised into the air, touching by their fingertips.

'Close your eyes,' Danko dictated. There was an odd, resonating quality in his voice that echoed in their minds. Every single monk in the tower blindly followed his orders, trembling with fear as the banging grew louder and there was another *crack*.

There was complete silence except for the rushed, panicky breathing of the monks as they tried to concentrate and Danko muttered words in a foreign tongue. It seemed inevitable that the creatures had got in – that was the thought that had crossed Dominic's mind when the silence had fallen. However, he reminded himself to remain optimistic as his body felt a sudden surge of tranquility and calmness despite the situation – a sensation of floating.

*

Edgar awoke with a start. It had been the floating sensation that had woken him. It felt like he had been lifted from his body – that his soul was floating away from the shell of his living being. It felt like how he had always imagined death.

The covers stuck to his sweat-drenched body and had wrapped tight around him like bandages around a mummy. He fought his way free and lay rigid with fear, staring up at the glow-in-the-dark stars and planets on his ceiling, breathing heavily. The dream had felt so real. He had been there, witnessed the events through Brother Dominic's eyes and felt the panic that had afflicted the monk's fevered mind.

Edgar sighed a breath of relief as he sat up, re-adjusting to reality and took a moment to collect himself. He cast his eyes across his room. Star was curled at the bottom of the bed, her paws and whiskers twitching as she dreamed silently. Edgar smiled to himself but that quickly faded when he saw the figure in the doorway – a tall shape of a man. It flickered and rippled in the shadow, his hood covering his face and as soon as Edgar's eyes met the ghost it faded into the darkness. Though the glimpse was only fleeting, Edgar knew that it had been Brother Bradley watching silently over him from the shadows.

– CHAPTER FOUR –

GONE

The next week dragged on and on. However, there was one thing to keep Edgar struggling on - one thing to keep his spirits up so that he felt as though he could live through that week of boredom. He thought of it like a lighthouse in the dark. It was a symbol of hope. Edgar knew that there was a re-enactment to look forward too soon - a weekend where he could live a life as close to that of a time-traveller that he would ever manage. He could immerse himself in the medieval ways and see friends that he only got to see every summer at the special events.

Ever since he was a child he had been taken to the events all over the country by his mother who believed living in a tent and learning to survive in a world with no modern comforts would benefit him in some kind of obscure way, but somehow, it really had. Over the years he had learned the skills of sword fighting and above all, archery. Not to mention basic survival, making camps, finding water and cooking but of all his abilities, it was Edgar's skill with a bow and arrow that was unmatched by anyone else of his age. In fact, it was well known among their friends that the only person who came anywhere near to matching him was his friend Alvin who was nearly eighteen.

When the week was tough, and hit its slowest points, when boredom set in, it was this thought of escaping to a life of simplicity – to a carefree existence, if only for a weekend, that was welcoming and he knew that it wouldn't be long until he was back with his closest friends who he only ever saw for a handful of days each year.

Desperate to make plans and keep himself focused on the upcoming events, Edgar decided to call Alvin but he was too busy to talk and simply mentioned something about saying goodbye to Vicky because she was leaving on a mission. Under normal circumstances Edgar would have thought this was odd and questioned whether his friend's sister were some kind of secret agent but he knew they were Mormon so her mission meant that she was going to travel and spread the word of the Mormon religion across the world.

Edgar had never been religious, nor did he take to kindly to religion in general. In his opinion it caused more trouble than it ever sorted but Alvin and his family were cool; they respected Edgar's beliefs, so in return, he respected theirs.

Of all the people in the world Vicky was the most likely to go around the world as a missionary. She cared for everyone and everything. One time a couple of years ago, an annoying child called Oliver had been trying to kill a slug; he'd poured a circle of salt around it, so that in order for it to escape it would have to die. Vicky caught him, gave him a swift slap, picked up the slug and returned it safely to a bush, away from the horrible child who was the only thing in the world that Vicky wasn't entirely keen on.

'Who are you talking to?' asked a voice in the background on the other end of the phone.

'Edgar,' Alvin replied. 'And do you have to eavesdrop all the time?'

'I'm your sister, it's my job.'

It was Charity. She was only twelve but for as long as Edgar had known her she had done nothing but live up to her name. At every re-enactment she would assist the people looking after the horses or help in a shop at the market, selling anything from books to weapons. She helped anybody with anything. She was small compared to Edgar but what she lacked in height she made up for in personality. Alvin, Vicky and Charity were all very obviously from the same family when they stood together. There was no mistaking the black hair, green eyes and hooked noses; they all even had the same kind, caring nature and it hurt when Edgar thought about how much he missed them.

'Hope you're ok, Edgar!' she said.

'Yeah, I'm good thanks...can't wait to see you all soon!'

'It can't come quick enough. Conisborough castle is always fun.'

The event in a few short weeks still felt like a lifetime away and Edgar couldn't wait. He told Alvin to wish Vicky luck from him, which he agreed to do and then, as quickly as the conversation had started, it ended and Edgar was left in the silence of his bedroom once more but little did he realise he wasn't truly alone. Brother Bradley stood guard, like a sentinel by the door, watching silently.

*

Later that week, Edgar and his few friends from school had arranged a day where they could meet to go a picnic at the castle together. They all met bright and early outside the museum, where Priscilla happened to be working again.

There was short, bubbly Ophelia Dykes with her blonde pigtails. She was Edgar's old girlfriend and now best friend; everyone named her Feely D for short. Next was outrageous, outspoken Sybill Laurel; Paul Barker – Edgar's best friend with his watery blue eyes and wiry red hair; Merle King, the jolly giant who despised his real name, Merlin, and Lilith Santos – tall, thin and with skin like pale, frail porcelain whom had been nicknamed Raven for her love of Victorian writer Edgar Allen Poe and her sleek, raven black hair that fell to her midriff.

'I'll only be a few hours at the most,' Edgar told his mum as he saw his friends gather outside the museum, waiting for him.

'Are you sure you'll be alright?' Priscilla asked, making an embarrassing fuss of him.

'Honestly, we'll be fine, mum. There are loads of us so it's not like we're going to get murdered or anything,' Edgar snapped eagerly.

Priscilla sighed and grabbed him before he could duck away. She planted a kiss on his cheek and released him. Without a second glance, he turned and sprinted outside to join his friends.

The walk was pleasant. The sun glinted amid a cloudless sky and the friends chatted amongst themselves as they wandered along, basking in the warmth. When they came to the end of the foreshore Edgar led the way, trudging up the steep hill to the grassy path that led to the gates of the castle when his mobile phone started to ring loudly. The monotonous ring tone echoed in the silent area of grassy ditches and banks around the castle dykes. He knew immediately that it was his mum, and one look at his phone screen confirmed his suspicion; she probably wanted to moan at him for something or other. What had he forgotten to do? What did she want him to bring back from town?

'Hello,' he sighed wondering what could be important enough to disturb his day out.

'Edgar, something's happened,' Priscilla said. There was something about the tone of her voice, the way it cracked and she sniffled that told Edgar she was crying.

'What's wrong? Are you okay? Do you need me to come back down?' Edgar asked panicking. 'Has someone tried to break into the museum again?'

What had happened? Was everything all right? Edgar began to think these things and as he did he became more and more worried. The last time he'd received a phone call like this, a group of drunks had come into the museum, tried to steal some of the artifacts and assaulted Priscilla when she tried to stop them. She had only suffered a few bruises but was badly shaken.

It wasn't even a second, but time froze and Edgar awaited what felt like eternity for a reply. His heart sank, his head spun dizzily, legs turned to jelly and he felt like he could collapse. Something had obviously gone wrong – he could tell by his mother's serious, wavering tone. He sat down on the damp grass before his weak-knees gave way and his friends stood behind him looking confused.

'It's Betty,' Priscilla said urgently.

'What about her? Is *she* okay?' Edgar asked, his throat seizing up so it was almost impossible to speak past the lump.

'No.'

There was silence for a moment as Edgar let that one tiny word register. He couldn't even comprehend what it might mean and a distant buzz of static filled his head. 'She's dead,' Priscilla replied quietly, sniffling and Edgar could tell she was crying.

Dead.

He heard the word – understood it, even, but it just would not process: *Betty. Dead.* The two words wouldn't connect. It was impossible. She had been fine not so long ago. *Dead. Betty.*

No.

'No...' Edgar gasped, in a hoarse whisper, his throat suddenly dry. 'Why? How?'

'You can come back here if you want, or you can stay with your friends,' Priscilla replied, struggling to hold herself together.

The shock took Edgar unexpectedly; all he wanted to do was cry but the numb disbelief wiped away his ability to do so. He couldn't quite get his head around it. Betty was so nice, she'd always been kind to him. She'd often bring him a bar of chocolate and slip it into his hand when his mother wasn't looking. She'd tell the best stories the world could ever know- most of which stuck with him since his childhood. She had been there since he was a child. For years, since before he could even remember – since he had been a baby in a cot. Perhaps Betty had been a friend of his mother's before he was even born. It was just a fact that Betty was a close family friend – so close that she might as well have been family and now she was gone – taken from this world too soon. Why did she have to die? She was fine a few days ago. It wasn't fair. It didn't make sense.

'It's okay. We can have the picnic another day, I'm on my way back down,' Edgar answered. He hung up, and slipped his phone back into his pocket.

'I'm sorry I can't stay,' Edgar said numbly. He couldn't even look his friends in the eye as he struggled to hold back the tears. 'Go. Have the picnic and I'll see you later to explain everything when I understand it better myself. One of my close friends has...' Edgar choked on the word: 'Died.'

And that was when it hit him hard. He had said the word.

Betty had *died.*

Betty was dead.

DEAD.

The tears came without warning, flooding like a hot stream down his cheek. The pain that had hit him before, numbed by the shock suddenly seeped through the every single pore of his body. Every cell buzzed with grief – a helpless sadness. His chest constricted. He could barely breathe. He gasped and wheezed, sobbing. There was nothing he could do. Nothing he could have done and now she was gone.

'Oh my God. You'd better go, darling,' Lilith gasped.

She grabbed him and hugged him tightly; a flicker of a sad smile crossed her lips.

'Bye,' said the others waving Edgar off, not knowing what else to say.

'I'll catch you all later,' Edgar said bravely as he waved and turned away from his friends, walking back towards the museum leaving his friends in a stunned silence, staring after him as he stumbled away, tears streaming down his face.

*

When Edgar got back to Priscilla she was sitting on the doorstep of the museum waiting for him. Edgar ran up the steps to greet her, not knowing what to say. He knew how much Betty had meant to her so words would not be enough to shake away the hurt of her passing. Priscilla looked somberly at him, her eyes red and puffy from crying. Edgar sank down wordlessly onto the step next to her. As they sat on the step in front of the door, staring out onto the sea, framed by the spa bridge there was total silence – every sound drowned out by the questions and thoughts buzzing around his head like angry bees.

'What happened to her?' Edgar asked suddenly, looking sadly at his mum's forlorn expression.

'Pardon?' Priscilla replied, taken by surprise by Edgar's sudden words that shattered the silence.

'How did she die?' Edgar asked, staring down at his feet, unable to believe that Betty was gone.

'I don't know. Nobody knows,' she answered blankly. 'Doreen came in just after you left and told me the news. Betty's coat was found on the beach yesterday. It was wet and covered in sand. Her body was never found. She was most likely swept into the sea or something,' Priscilla explained, a tear trickling down her cheek.

Edgar stared past her to the sea beyond the arches of the Spa Bridge. The water was the most beautiful blue and the bright sunlight reflected off it making it shine and sparkle as if diamonds bobbed up and down on the waves. It looked so beautiful and calm as the waves gently lapped at the shore. How could something that looked so tranquil and serene kill someone so innocent? The sky above was cloudless and bright. The golden sands stretched alongside the clear, almost tropical water and ships sailed silently under the seagulls flying overhead squawking and swooping down into the sea to catch fish, while swimmers and surfers enjoyed the water as much as the sunbathers enjoyed sprawling on the golden sand.

A coach load of tourists pulled up on the main road and the old folks all disembarked; an aeroplane flew overhead, full of people heading to some exotic location for a holiday.

Suddenly the world was noisy again; so deafeningly loud and so much was happening. Wasps and bees buzzed around the beautiful bright flowers on the rockery in front of the museum, a ladybird crawled up the wall and a woodlouse scuttled across the path. People passed by chattering and laughing. *Laughing!* They were unaffected, their lives untouched by this immeasurable loss. How dare they laugh when everything was so wrong?

But that was it. *Life.*

Life carried on. It was confusing and unfair and it hurt. Betty was gone – her life taken and yet here, on this plain of existence, life carried on. Billions of people on the planet who were still there, living and breathing and going about their lives. Most would never know that Betty was gone. She meant nothing to billions of people. She was nobody to them...but she had been everything to Edgar and Priscilla and Doreen and the others who knew her.

This was the cruelest thing about life and death. We all live. We all die and when we go, we fade from existence with the smallest of impacts. Few will care, few will mourn and for that reason, Edgar refused to believe Betty was truly gone.

Denial.

One of the first steps of grieving. Betty wasn't gone. She couldn't be.

'Well, that proves nothing. It might not have been Betty's coat. Anybody could lose a coat,' Edgar said, his head still spinning '*Anybody could lose a coat*,' he told himself again building up hope in his mind.

'Betty's purse was in the pocket with her ID and everything,' Priscilla replied quickly, shooting Edgar a sad look and his hope came crashing down all around him. 'We've been invited to the memorial service, you know?'

'We'll go. It's the least we can do to pay our respects to her,' he said, smiling. 'She's done so much for us. She's always been around to help out – babysitting me when I was younger, helping you with money when you were stuck and I needed school stuff,' Edgar said, staring out at the glorious horizon.

Priscilla agreed, nodding her head slowly.

'She was a wonderful woman and if you only knew the half of what she'd been through in life,' Priscilla sighed heavily as she glanced across to Edgar beside her. Her eyes swam with tears and she removed her glasses to wipe them away.

'She always seemed happy to us,' Edgar replied, unable to believe that Betty could have had a hard life. 'She seemed so happy in general.'

'Adults don't like to talk about problems in front of kids,' Priscilla said sternly. 'You have no idea.'

'I know she got you through the tough times without my dad. She was the one you could talk to about stuff that you couldn't talk to nanna about, wasn't she?' Edgar said plainly, turning to smile weakly at his mother. She nodded, lifted her glasses and wiped a tear from her eye.

'You always knew?'

'Yeah,' Edgar admitted solemnly. 'You adults might like to keep the kids out of the way but I think we always know, deep down. I mean, I only realised when I was a bit older but I always knew something wasn't right...'

'Don't.' Priscilla said, her voice wavering and she began crying again.

'Sorry. I didn't want you to worry about me,'

Without a word, Priscilla wiped the tears from her eyes, put her arm around Edgar's shoulder and pulled him in tightly. He rested his head on her shoulder, trying to force back the tears. It was bad enough that Betty had been taken from life in such upsetting circumstances but seeing Priscilla upset – that diamond-hard, strong woman, a role-model to many; his own mother, was what broke him.

'I love you, mum.'

'I love you too.'

They sat in silence just holding onto each other and in that moment, the world, as harsh and scary and upsetting as it was, seemed a little easier to cope with. They still had each other and knew they always would.

'I hope she's happy now, wherever she is,' Edgar muttered, breaking the silence.

'I'm sure she is,' she paused, not knowing what else to say. There were no words. She took a deep breath, as she noticed a group of tourists heading towards the entrance. She climbed back to her feet. 'Well, back to work. Life goes on.'

Priscilla patted Edgar on the head and ruffled his hair before hurrying off back into the building to put on a brave face and greet the tourists who wandered into the building, smiling and chattering amongst themselves without a care in the world, unlike Edgar and Priscilla who both felt that their world had been torn apart.

– CHAPTER FIVE –

LEGACY

It felt like he was flying, soaring over the vast green forests beneath him which spread across the sprawling countryside, creeping up the mountains at either side of the valley. In the distance the forest ended and harsh, wild moors spread across the horizon, burning in the bright, blinding sun. He was an eagle, his eyes sharp and keen, taking in every detail. There was a clearing in the trees below and he swooped down. As he came closer he could see a giant, black structure that gleamed as if it were made from marble. A giant monastery with a huge tower, ornate and ancient standing atop a rocky outcrop above a waterfall that cascaded into a lake below. The spray of the water left a rainbow hanging in the air and despite the deafening crash of water, this haven was peaceful.

He glided down towards the monastery and towards a circular pattern above the heavy oak door; it had once been a window but the glass was now gone. He slipped through the gap and flew down the long, dark corridors that glittered in the half-light of the flame torches that hung in sconces on the walls. It was like a maze but Edgar seemed to know his way. Eventually he came to an open door which led into a library stacked high with hefty wooden bookcases, filled to bursting with ancient tomes and scrolls. Long wood tables filled any empty floor space amid the maze of bookcases and a rainbow of colours spread across the room as the sun shone through the stained glass window at the end. It was like no window Edgar had ever seen. Instead of Jesus and the crucifixion, it showed demons and pyramids; monks and magic:

A quiet voice echoed through the hall, it's words a mere whisper:

"Every second has a meaning,
Day after day, the world still spins.
Great barriers act as invisible pins;
All holding the fabric of time and space
Relatively in the very same place.

How would you cope,
Armed with nothing but hope to
Ready you for the dark times to come?
Over the barriers you will go,
Living your life, to help other's lives flow.
Deaf you will be to the Raven's crow."

Edgar glided around a maze of bookcases and found the source of the voices.

There was a man dressed from head to toe in white robes, his face hidden beneath his hood and he stood behind a child, his hand on the child's shoulder. Edgar stared at the child who keenly pored over a mass of books and maps sprawled across the table before him. It was unmistakable that the small, red-haired and blue eyed child was himself.

'What's this?' Edgar said, quietly.

'Patience.'

'Can't you tell me?'

'You'll see, Edgar,' Brother Bradley replied. It was the first time Edgar had ever seen him as a man and not a distorted ghost. 'In time, you will understand.'

Suddenly, Brother Bradley turned as if he sensed Edgar's presence. He looked right at him and lowered his hood slowly to reveal his face.

Edgar screamed. He was not greeted with the usual, handsome features he had expected, but instead a half-rotten skull. The decayed and blackened skin was taut around the bone, the sunken eyes were milky white and the monk reached out a cold, skeletal hand.

'You must save us, Edgar,' he rasped. 'You are the one.'

With a gasp of horror, Edgar jolted awake and his eyes darted around his room, terrified. It was dark and through his bleary eyes he could see that he was alone, drenched in sweat and tangled in his bedsheets.

*

Thursday arrived - the day of Betty's memorial service. The past couple of days had been a blur and Edgar had tried to convince himself that Betty wasn't dead – that she would just walk into the museum and greet him with her usual cheeky grin and sit down for a chat, alas, he was wrong. The museum seemed colder and emptier without her warm personality to keep it lively and slowly, her death began to sink in. It was real. It happened and there was nothing Edgar could do to change it.

With his head in a daze, Edgar walked up to the church at the end of his street which overlooked the sea; the long, jagged line of the coast stretched out to the horizon along the edge of the sea. The small graveyard housed many grim, grey tombstones which stuck out of the earth as reminders of all the people who had been buried there over hundreds of years; all of them ancient and covered in moss with faded engravings.

It was upon the Garden of Remembrance - a small patch of grass, bordered by rose bushes under the shadow of the church, that a small wooden cross had been erected among many others others. Bouquets of white lilies, Betty's favourite flowers, lay around its base and a small plaque read:

In loving memory:
Elisabeth Anne Tordoff
1938-2005
Lost but not forgotten.

Edgar stared at the cross and the floral tributes in front of it. The wind blew wildly threatening to whip the gorgeous flowers away and the trees swayed violently, looking almost as if they were about to be ripped out of the earth.

The vicar, a short, hunched man, shuffled out of the church and took his place upon the grass of the garden of remembrance amid the wooden crosses. He looked at Edgar and Edgar looked back at him. There were no other people around, not a single soul. The vicar waited a moment and Edgar felt awkward as he stared at the cross – all that remained of Betty's life on this earth.

A figure appeared at the end of the path and a short, hunched woman shuffled towards them, carrying a big shopping bag over her shoulder. Her eyes were fixed intently on Edgar. She didn't mean to stare but she always wore a constantly startled expression as if somebody had just crept up behind her and scared her. She was wrapped up in a giant wooly jumper and a fleecy coat with a sun hat perched on top of her head that threatened to blow away in the wind. She leaned on a wobbly walking stick and looked up at Edgar who towered over her.

'Doreen!' Edgar exclaimed, he made his way towards her, linked arms with her and helped her along the uneven cobbles towards the Garden of Remembrance.

Doreen smiled weakly at Edgar and he could see her eyes were red behind her round glasses. She had been crying. There was no need to exchange words. Just being there for each other was enough. The unspoken silence was worth more than any words.

When they reached the garden, it became apparent that they were the only two people there and that broke Edgar's heart more than her actual death. Out of the billions of people in the world, only two showed up to remember the remarkable woman who had so much to give.

'Just two of us?' Edgar asked and the vicar nodded solemnly.

The service began and the vicar started his speech in a quiet, frail voice. Edgar listened carefully to the vicar's long talk about Betty going to another place where she would be happier and how the Almighty God had saved her soul but the words just didn't seem to sink in.

He wasn't a religious person but for the first time in his life, Edgar found himself hoping and praying that there might be a God out there – that Betty really had gone to Heaven and that she would be happy in a life after death. It was something he had never thought of – never believed in. To him, death was death. It was an end to life and once the heart stopped beating, the lungs stopped breathing and the body turned cold and rigid there was nothing left.

Edgar believed there was no soul but instead the function of a body which was controlled by the brain and the nervous system. It was a matter of cause and effect, then, when that ceased, so did everything…but now he wished so strongly that he might be wrong. He hoped beyond hope that Betty really could be living a peaceful life in a world beyond, in some kind of Heaven.

It seemed strange to think in such a way after always refusing to believe in such things, after spending his whole life disbelieving. It was the re-appearance of Brother Bradley, a ghost, that had changed Edgar's perception on life and death. When Brother Bradley disappeared and never returned after the night when he stole his teddy bear as a child, Edgar had come to believe his mother was right in saying the ghostly monk had only ever been an imaginary friend and put the strange circumstances of the teddy's disappearance down to his mind playing tricks on him.

Now though, he had evidence that there was something after death – there was an afterlife and ghosts really did exist and they really did haunt people.

Edgar listened to the vicar and remembered Betty as the little old lady he had thought the world of and tried not to cry even though the tears burned in his eyes until they found a way to escape and the Vicar's words drowned out – just a barely audible sound over the thoughts racing through his head. He took Doreen's hand in his own and they held tightly to each other for support. It wasn't much but it made it a little easier.

*

The service ended. Betty was dead and gone and not even her body could be found. Wherever she was, Edgar didn't want to think. The sea had taken her so all that would be left of her remains was a sight he didn't want to think about, though it was one that had crossed his mind in dreams and made his gut twist sickeningly as he woke sweating and screaming.

He could see her floating – cold and still. Her frail, wrinkled skin tinged with blue. Her body broken and battered against the rocks at the bottom of a far off cliff where she would never be found – a place where she would rot away and decay - food for the fishes. Edgar cringed as this thought once again crossed his mind. His stomach turned and he was almost sick but instead, tears swam in his eyes and began to fall silently again. Betty wouldn't have wanted him to cry.

Unable to take any more, Edgar turned to walk away from the graveside but amid the whistle of the wild wind, he heard something that sounded like a voice. It was so distant he almost thought he had imagined it.

'Edgar!' Doreen said, her words like a whisper on the tumultuous wind. She tapped him on the shoulder and Edgar turned. 'Sorry, I was in my own little world. How are you feeling?'

'It's okay, I'm okay,' she said, her eyes drawn to Betty's memorial. 'But, for months now, Betty has been saying that when she's gone, she wanted you to have something. She was getting on in years you see, and she had her plans sorted. She said it was *very* important,' Doreen said with the air of a messenger delivering important news.

She reached into the enormous bag and pulled out an old oak box, with rusty brass hinges. On the top there was a carving of an arcane symbol – a pentagram with two crossed swords in the centre, surrounded by a wobbly line. It was the exact same symbol that Edgar had seen on the bottom of his boots and Betty's slippers – the symbol he had wanted to question her about the last time he had seen her.

Doreen handed Edgar the box and he held it tightly – it was a reminder of Betty – something she wanted him to have so he would keep it close to his heart.

'Don't lose it. She made it very clear that it was important for you to have it.'

Doreen sniffed and dabbed at her teary eyes with a lacy, white handkerchief and Edgar's fingers traced the etching as his mind began to wonder what it could possibly mean.

'Thank you,' Edgar said politely giving Doreen a friendly hug, wondering what was in the box. It was very heavy for its small size. He considered it closely and frowned – that symbol, yet again. What *did* it mean? Surely this was beyond a coincidence now.

'Thank you for coming. I'm glad I didn't have to be alone,' Edgar said, his eyes welling with tears too.

'If I hadn't had to give you this, I don't think I could have come myself. I've got nobody now.'

Doreen's words pulled at Edgar's heart and in the whirl of emotion that he already struggled with, it became even worse. He didn't know how to react. It was clear now that Betty's death had been a cataclysm that had torn more than his own life apart.

'If you ever need anything, you know where me and mum are,' Edgar said kindly.

Doreen stopped and turned to him. The corners of her wrinkled mouth turned into a slight smile and she nodded.

'Thank you,' she replied hoarsely, holding back her emotion and then carried on her way. She made her way down the slope towards the brick arches that framed the steps at the end of the path.

Edgar was alone and it saddened him to think that Betty's memorial service was over so quickly and now that it was done, she was left to fade into memory. With that he crouched down, kissed the tips of his fingers and then planted them on the cross, whispering to himself:

'Goodbye Betty,' before he left the graveyard, ignoring the small tears trickling down his cheeks.

*

Edgar returned home from Betty's service and stalked into to his room, his heart still heavy with emotion. Priscilla had been unable to take time off work and was out the museum so now was the perfect time to examine the box that Betty had left for him.

Edgar put the box on the floor, sat down next to it and slowly lifted the lid eager to see what was inside. It was light and opened easily with a slight creak. Black velvet lined the inside, a soft bed for the neatly folded pieces of old paper. The smell of musty paper struck Edgar's nose and he sniffed deeply. He had always loved that smell, but still couldn't help but feel disappointed. He had been expecting something exciting within the box and all he had found was pieces of paper. He pulled them out carefully, hoping they wouldn't fall apart because of their age. The top piece opened out, and as Edgar turned it over, his eyes lit up.

It showed, again, the arcane symbol of the pentagram with the crossed swords but unlike the etching on the lid of the box, or any others he had seen previously, this one contained numbers in each of the points of the star. Starting from the top point and going clockwise it read 5, 4, 7, 1, 18.

Edgar had no idea why Betty would want to give him these strange drawings but she must have had her reasons. He rummaged through the other pieces of paper which were very non-descript, just various sketches of flowers, people, and pyramids.

Underneath the papers, Edgar spotted several old photographs, long, narrow and sepia in colour, he plucked up the top of the pile. It showed a younger Betty doing archery at a re-enactment; the next one showed Betty with Doreen at the park in their younger years. Another showed an exhausted, middle-aged Betty standing at the top of a high cliff, among a cluster of long grass that swished around her knees. She looked down at the sea below, wearing a billowing black dress covered by a white overall and a black, woolen shawl over her shoulders. Her head was wrapped in dark material, like a hijab and she balanced a basket on it, while tall ships sailed across the horizon.

Edgar turned the photo and noticed the number 5 written in black ink by somebody with very neat handwriting. He slowly went through all of the pictures in the box, six in total until there was only a single piece of paper left in the bottom. Unlike the others though, this was newer. It was still white and hadn't aged since the day it had been put in the box. Curiously, Edgar took it out and held it in his hands. It was a letter, and although it was short and written in large but neat, flowing handwriting, it had an aura of great importance.

Edgar began to read, enthralled by the mystery Betty had left behind – perhaps her words in this letter would give him some answers:

Dearest Edgar,

I am afraid that if you are reading this letter I have gone to a better place. As I write this I know my life here is almost over. I know that by giving this box to Doreen, you will receive it when the time comes. We have been good friends since I was young and I trust her most deeply because it is of utmost importance that this box reaches you...and only you.

The world is in danger, Edgar and it seems that you are the only person who can help. I know this may come as a shock and I wish I could say this is all a joke but alas, it is true.

I understand you must have questions. There will be many.

I promise you that soon, you will find the answers that you seek but first you must find the artifact detailed in the drawings. I have included the relevant information as to its whereabouts in this box. I'm sure you will be clever enough to work it out.

I'm so very sorry it has come to this. Please, don't mourn for me.

I hope you are well.

With all my love,

Betty xxx

Edgar sighed and shook his head. This must be a trick, he thought. He was just a normal person – nothing special or interesting ever happened to him. He was just the boy who got bullied at school – the boy everybody loved to hate because he was so different.

He picked up the photographs again, turning them over so the pictures were face down and he saw the numbers scribbled on the back; two had the number 21 scrawled upon them, there were two pictures bearing the number 13, one picture with 5 on it and one with the number 19. It could be innocent but if that was the case, why did some numbers appear twice?

'What is this all about?' Edgar thought out loud, confused and frustrated. He sat on his floor staring at the numbers on the pictures that he had scattered orderly around him for over ten minutes, occasionally referring back to the letter and then he remembered...Betty had always told him about a secret code she used to use in the war. She had taught it to him when he was young and they would often write secret, coded letters to each other just for fun.

The Alphabet Code!

Betty had always taught him how to make letters into numbers, but in this cryptic message, the numbers needed to be translated to letters. Edgar quickly scribbled the letters of the alphabet and wrote the appropriate number next to them.

Quickly Edgar scrawled down a translation list in a notebook:

1-A, 2-B, 3-C, 4-D, 5-E, 6-F, 7-G, 8-H, 9-I, 10-J, 11-K, 12-L, 13-M, 14-N, 15-O, 16-P, 17-Q, 18-R, 19-S, 20-T, 21-U, 22-V, 23-W, 24-X, 25-Y, 26-Z.

Edgar's eyes scanned over the numbers until he found 21 paired with the letter U. Next he looked for 13, which matched the letter M. He traced his finger along the list for 5. This number was next to E. Finally he found the last number, 19 next to the letter S.

'STAR!' Edgar shouted in frustration at the little white cat who had decided to come in and walk all over the photos for attention. She purred loudly to herself and head butted Edgar lovingly. He shoved her aside in frustration but she kept coming back. Between the cat's affectionate advances Edgar wrote down the letters that he now had. U, U, M, M, E, S.

The letters were jumbled like an anagram and Edgar had never been very good at those. He sighed in frustration, wondering why he had even decided to play along with Betty's silly game.

'Why am I even doing this?' Edgar thought out loud to himself. 'Betty's gone. She left a joke behind to keep my spirits up.'

Edgar climbed onto his bed and lay there, staring at the planets and stars on his ceiling.

Two conflicting voices waged a war in his head, making him confused.

'Go ahead, do it,' one said. 'You wished for a more interesting life. What if there's some truth in this?'

'Don't be stupid, Edgar,' the other voice scoffed. 'Betty was an eccentric. She just wanted to have the last laugh after she died.'

Edgar screwed his eyes tight shut and tried to block his thoughts before they drove him to insanity. He wished there were a simple option and the letters swam around his mind, reforming and reshaping but he couldn't find a combination that made sense.

'Edgar,' came a quiet voice like a whisper.

Edgar opened his eyes, preparing himself to come face to face with the ghost of Brother Bradley once more. Though he had become acquainted with the man, it still made him anxious that he could see him when even his mother couldn't.

Edgar's eyes scanned his room and sure enough, the monk stood by the door, flickering and distorting.

'What do you want now?' Edgar sighed. 'Are you finally going to give me answers or what?'

'Good things come to those who wait,' Brother Bradley said as he strolled into the centre of the room. He stopped by the pile of papers and photographs and looked down at them. 'I see you have the box.'

'Yeah, it's just a joke,' Edgar said. 'Betty was like that.'

'You know that's not true.'

'It is. It's a joke. It's just a bit of fun,' Edgar insisted.

The ghost folded his arms and stared solemnly at Edgar; a cold gleam in his eyes. It was a withering glare that rivaled his mother's and made Edgar turn away anxiously.

'You want answers and you have them right here,' Brother Bradley hissed.

He pointed down at the papers strewn across the carpet.

'I wouldn't call that riddle an answer,' Edgar snapped irritably. 'Why can't you just tell me?'

Brother Bradley lifted a finger to his lips; Edgar jumped off his bed in frustration and crouched down beside him. He looked right into the ghost's deep, mysterious eyes. They were so close that Edgar could hear Brother Bradley crackle as his form stretched and shrank.

The ghost towered over Edgar; his height had always been intimidating.

'I cannot force you to believe, Edgar but deep down in your heart, something tells you that you should give this some thought.'

The ghost appeared sterner than Edgar had ever seen him before. Even as a child Edgar had never been afraid of him and though his visits had startled him, he had never been truly frightened. It was perhaps for this reason that Edgar knew he ought to trust his words – that somehow Brother Bradley was trying to help.

'So, if I stick with this riddle and solve it, then do I get some answers?' Edgar demanded as he picked up the notebook and scanned the hastily scrawled Alphabet Code translation.

'Yes,' Brother Bradley replied simply. Edgar opened his mouth to speak once more but the monk faded right before his eyes. Edgar reached out in a vain attempt to stop him but received nothing more than a cold shudder as a chilling tingle spread from his fingers, down his arms and into his chest.

'Right,' he thought out loud. 'Time to figure this out and find out why *he's* come back.'

Edgar picked up his translation sheet and scribbled down the letters that he had worked out: EMMSUU from the numbers on the back of the photographs.

As he began to move the letters around he came up with ESUMUM, *'not right,'* he thought so he tried again. SUMUME:

'Still not right,' he thought, beginning to feel frustrated that he couldn't do it. He tried a few more times.

For a further ten minutes he sat on the floor in his room trying to work out the anagram, staring at the letters and it hit him. He re-arranged them for the last time, before knowing that he was right. The letters re-formed into one word. A horrible word, describing a place of learning – a place where Edgar had spent most of his time with Betty - a place, which under normal circumstances, Edgar would love to visit but due to his mother working there, he'd come to hate the sight of this building in his town. The words unscrambled to say: MUSEUM.

Edgar looked at the paper, amazed by his unexpected intelligence. He'd worked out the clue, now all he needed to know was when his mum would be working next. He needed to get to the museum as quickly as he could but time had flown and it would be closed in ten minutes. He would have to wait.

*

'Mum, when are you at work next?' he asked as they sat watching TV together, that evening.

'Saturday. I've got tomorrow off,' Priscilla replied, raising an eyebrow quizzically. It wasn't like Edgar to be interested in her work pattern – usually he just avoided it and tried to get out of going with her. 'Why?'

'Just wondered,' Edgar replied trying not to act downhearted and arouse suspicion, finding it difficult to accept that he had to wait to be able to follow up on the clue that Betty had left in her box. Edgar's heart sank low into his stomach and he sighed.

He wondered if he should tell his mother about the box and the cryptic clues left inside but the stronger side of his conscience told him to keep it quiet – just in case it was a joke. He didn't want to look like a fool. Besides, Priscilla would only tell him exactly what he suspected – that it was nothing. This was something best kept as a secret.

– CHAPTER SIX –

THE TRAVELLERS' TOKEN

The next day passed in a blur of anxiety. Edgar spent every spare moment in his room examining the photographs and re-reading the letter over and over, wondering just what it could possibly mean. Each time he shuffled through the drawings he could feel Brother Bradley's eyes on him but every time he turned, there was nobody there.

The ghost was as silent as he had been for the last twelve years even though Edgar could sense his presence stronger than before.

Saturday came and Edgar tagged along with Priscilla. As soon as she unlocked the door, Edgar pushed inside, trying to keep his cool so that she wouldn't become suspicious.

'I'll go check the building and turn the lights on,' Edgar said, eager for an excuse to begin his search; a perfect opportunity to look around as there wasn't an inch of the museum that he could leave unturned.

He began on the bottom floor of each wing. Despite how closely he observed each glass display case, his eyes scouring every millimeter of the cases between the curiosities on display, there was nothing there that matched the object in Betty's drawing.

Part of him wondered why he was even bothering to look. He knew in his heart that it was all a joke. *Wasn't it?*

'Have you got anything for me?' he whispered quietly as he passed the Gristhorpe Man who lay, staring grimly into the ceiling through his hollow eye sockets. 'No, didn't think so.'

He continued his search desperately, hoping he hadn't taken too long but it was as he climbed the tight, spiral staircase into the central dome of the museum that he heard a shout from down blow.

'EDGAR, I NEED SOME HELP!' Priscilla yelled from downstairs. Edgar sighed, wrestling with the decision of postponing his investigation. He turned and slumped slowly down the stairs, a sudden feeling of glumness settled over him. As he reached the bottom of the stairs, he saw his mum peeking around the edge of the basement door.

'It's flooded,' she said rolling her eyes and turning back to the dark spiral staircase into the basement. 'A nice, quiet, easy day - that's all I wanted,' she muttered furiously to herself as she carefully climbed back down the stairs; a yellow, industrial torch in her hand.

Edgar followed her down the tight spiral stone stairs and into the cavernous basement. As he descended, he was hit by a foul stench and Edgar tried to hold his breath – it stank like sewage and permeated his every sense until his eyes watered and he coughed and spluttered, retching in disgust.

Priscilla stopped near the bottom of the stairs, flicked the switch on the torch and suddenly the light burst on brighter than sunlight to better reveal the long basement corridor that was flooded with filthy, brown water. Wooden crates covered with white tattered sheets were piled up against the walls and an old mannequin with no arms or legs was propped up against the wall on top of a pile of soggy cardboard boxes, staring at them with a blank painted face.

'I can't go down there,' Priscilla said, her face white as she covered her mouth and nose with her hand. 'Not in these shoes.'

Edgar looked down and saw her feet were shod in a pair of thin dolly shoes.

'I could go,' Edgar offered reluctantly. 'I've got my boots on.'

'Are you sure?'

'Yeah. I don't mind.'

Priscilla passed Edgar the torch and stood on the last step before the water. Edgar took a deep breath and took the torch, shone it down the corridor and stepped down into the stagnant water.

SPLOSH

The water splashed under his feet and Edgar winced as he wondered where the pungent liquid had come from. He carefully took another step down and then another until he was on the hard ground of the flag-stoned corridor. The water was up to his shins as he waded deeper into the dark, shining the torch ahead into the cavern of blackness.

'Be careful, Edgar,' Priscilla shouted, watching him advance further into the unknown. Edgar turned back, gave her a thumbs up and continued on his way. He hated dark spaces and basements. He had watched too many horror films.

When he came to a door at the end of the passage, labeled *Boiler Room,* Edgar pulled it open and stared into the black abyss beyond. He shone the light into the distance – beyond the brick arches that lined the edge of the room and spotted the source of the problem; a burst pipe. Even from such a distance it was easy to see that it looked as though the pipe had been split in half. Water spewed out like a waterfall, splashing to the ground. The smell didn't even register in his nostrils anymore and Edgar trudged closer to the pipe to get a better look.

He had always been scared of the boiler room. Ever since he had been a child, when his mother first began her job in the museum and he had sneaked down while exploring. It had been the darkness and the vast expanse of space – the feeling of conflict between the colossal space and pressing, claustrophobic dark – that had made Edgar feel like he had slipped entirely from the world and would never find his way back.

Now, with a torch it wasn't so bad but he couldn't shift the feeling that there were eyes on him at all times. He cast the torchlight left and right across the room, illuminating the wall and gleaming off the muddy surface of the flood water. The temperature dropped. Chills shot through Edgar and made the hairs on the back of his neck stand on end. Goosebumps erupted up his arms and when he looked around, a sudden sensation of terror gripped at him and made him want to run.

'Edgar,' said a deep voice of a man, reverberating through the darkness.

Edgar screamed as heart leapt into his throat and pounded in his ears. The echo of his name was drowned out by the sound of his own heartbeat. It was all he was aware of.

'Are you ok down there?' Priscilla's voice echoed down the corridor.

'Fine. Just scared myself,' Edgar shouted back as he turned on the slowly on the spot, shining the light all around him, searching for the source of the voice.

'I'm here, Edgar.' the voice whispered and Edgar shone the light to his right and it fell upon the flickering figure of a tall man, Brother Bradley. For a split second everything stopped. Time stood suspended in Edgar's sheer surprise. Brother Bradley always made him nervous and uncomfortable when he caught him off guard.

'What are you doing here?' Edgar asked, feeling his heartbeat slow back to a normal pace.

The ghost didn't reply. It merely pointed at the wall.

'I don't understand. Why don't you ever speak to me properly?' Edgar demanded. 'Why can't you ever just tell me what you want?'

The ghost turned his head and looked at the wall where he pointed a long, spindly finger, then turned back to look at Edgar. Edgar inched closer to the ghost, completely unaware of what it could possibly want.

'What are you trying to tell me?' Edgar asked as he came closer to the flickering figure that distorted and rippled eerily in the half-light.

He reached the ghost and his eyes followed the line of his arm. He looked at the wall – at the precise brick the ghostly monk's finger pointed at and he gulped. It stuck out from the wall slightly, as if it could be pulled out. He looked up to the friendly face of Brother

Bradley who winked at him; then, as swiftly as he had appeared, the ghost was gone and Edgar was alone once more.

Edgar's head spun, his knees felt weak and he had to lean against the wall. He took a deep breath and turned back to the brick that Brother Bradley had brought to his attention.

Upon this brick was the all-too-familiar insignia of the pentangle with the crossed-swords in the centre, faintly etched into the surface brick. Edgar reached out to touch the protruding brick. It felt rough under his fingers as he gripped the edge and pulled gently. It came loose without any effort and within seconds, Edgar held the brick in his hands and stared into the emptiness of the hole it had left.

Edgar slowly reached his hand inside, closing his eyes. He was reminded of so many films where characters had reached into dark holes and horrible things had happened. His heart hammered against his chest again and he took deep breaths, trying to remain calm. He felt something fine and sticky – a cobweb and as his fingers rubbed against the bottom of the hole.

Edgar cringed as he slipped his hand in further, his fingers brushed against a slimy (or was it just cold) object. He curled his fingers around whatever was in there and pulled his hand out and opened his eyes to look down at what he held in his hand.

It was round, slightly bigger than the size of a small medal and made of silver. There was a pentagram in the middle with several tiny holes and in the middle of the pentagram there were two crossed swords with a wobbly line that Edgar could only guess represented glowing light around them and in each point of the star, working clockwise there was a number next to the tiny hole: 5, 4, 7, 1, 18.

Edgar looked at the coin and smiled. Betty was right – after all his doubts, she had led him on a journey to discover this. It really did exist...but this was only half a battle won. Now he needed to figure out what it was – what it did.

A shrieking ring pierced the silence like an alarm. Edgar's heart skipped a beat and he looked all around for the source of the sound until he realized it was his phone. He reached into his pocket and answered it.

'Have you found anything?' asked the familiar voice of his mother.

'Yeah, there's a burst pipe. Water's spewing everywhere. I don't know if I can stop it. We need a plumber quickly,' Edgar replied as he stowed his discovery in his pocket. 'I'm on my way back.'

He kept the coin hidden in his pocket all day; frequently slipping his hand in there to feel the cold, smooth surface, making sure sure it was still there and every spare moment he had alone, he took it out of his pocket and looked at the etching of the strange symbol and rubbed his thumbs over it to feel the insignia under his fingers. He had no idea what he had uncovered but knew already that it was important.

*

That night he locked himself in his room again, not bothering to take his boots off. He looked at the coin trying to figure out what it did - if it really could do anything at all.

Maybe he was just being stupid to still believe Betty's story, but she'd led him so far into this mystery and had so much of it had been true, that he trusted her letter entirely. He took Betty's box from under his bed, opened the lid and leafed through the contents. He read and re-read the letter again hoping for some clarity and stared at Betty's drawing of the object.

If Betty's words were true, which they had been so far, then this coin ought to do something…but how did he activate it? How did it work? He tried rubbing it; that was how Aladdin's lamp worked…apparently not the case here. He tried spinning it, squeezing it, muttering absurd magic words at it. 'Abra Kadabra Alakazam!'

Nothing seemed to work.

'Work!' he hissed under his breath, staring at it until his eyes hurt. He screwed his eyes tight shut and wished really, really hard – so hard that he immersed himself in his full concentration until his head hurt.

'I give up,' Edgar sighed as he jumped to his feet and rolled the cold coin over in his hands, while pacing back and forth across his room. He glanced down at it again and checked the numbers in the points of the star.

The Alphabet Code! Maybe this would give him a clue on how to make it work. He picked up the piece of paper with the Alphabet Code translation on it, which he'd screwed up, thrown at the bin and missed. His eyes scanned the numbers and checked off the corresponding letters.

The numbers: 5,4,7,1,18 spelled *EDGAR* – his name in Alphabet Code. He couldn't get his thoughts in order. He didn't understand. What was his connection to this coin? It had his name on it, yet he couldn't even make it work. The frustration rising inside him was so intense that he threw the coin onto the floor, stomped across the room in a rage and as he paced back and forth, head in his hands.

In his fury, his foot accidentally crashed down upon the coin. There was a loud, unhealthy *crunch* as the object crumpled under the weight of his heavily booted foot.

'Ah crap!' Edgar thought. 'It's broken.'

He lifted his boot and looked down at the ground but he couldn't see the coin anywhere It had vanished.

The sickness hit him fast and hard. A terrible nausea swept over him and spread throughout his body. His stomach cramped – cold sweat drenched him and he tried to scream in agony but he couldn't even make a sound. Crippled by pain, Edgar fell to the ground, arms wrapped tightly around his stomach. His head throbbed until it felt like it could split open and his brain turned to cold mush. It was pain beyond pain. A strange, tingling sensation in his toes grew stronger and hotter until it actually burned and spread through his whole body like an internal fire. Edgar struggled to keep control and staggered across his room, trying to reach the door but it spun so dizzyingly that he couldn't bear it anymore. Just before him, Brother Bradley appeared. Edgar tried to muster the strength to call for help but the ghost merely watched him struggle until his eyes rolled back and his world turned to black.

– CHAPTER SEVEN –
THE UNSTERBLICHE

Edgar's eyes opened slowly. His vision was blurred and all he could make out were giant silhouettes against the blinding light. He lay, sprawled on his front and groaned. His whole body seared with pain; his ribs and his chest and his legs all felt as though they had been squashed by several tons of weight. Edgar rolled onto his side, noticing a tangy, metallic taste in his mouth. He spat out a gobful of blood and raised his hand to his throbbing head. A trickle of blood dribbled down his forehead from a cut sustained when he had hit his head on the hard concrete.

'Where am I?' Edgar asked himself out loud as he brought himself into a sitting position. His stomach churned, sending a dizzying shock of nausea through his body and suddenly, it hit him… all was eerily quiet – he was truly alone.

There were no birds singing, no sound of a breeze rustling through the trees, no cars rushing past. The air was still and peaceful, just a haunting dead silence that enveloped Edgar in its nothingness and filled him with a sense of escalating dread.

He rubbed his bleary eyes and took a moment to come around.

Whatever had just happened had not been pleasant. He felt awful.

Was this a dream?

Though he had no idea where he was, it certainly wasn't his bedroom.

Edgar stood up slowly, still dizzy and looked around him. The silver coin lay on the ground by where his feet had been so he picked it up from the pavement and examined it closely. There wasn't even a scratch on it...but he had heard it crack under his weight when he stood on it.

'Strange,' he thought to himself as he stowed it safely in his pocket.

The ground below him was paved with grey slabs of concrete and the road was coal black tarmac. A long yellow line, perfectly straight, ran along the road beside the curb and Edgar followed it, as if it would lead him somewhere.

'Follow the yellow brick road,' he thought, resorting to humour to try and make himself feel more at ease. It didn't work.

Edgar wandered slowly down the long, city street. Around him buildings stretched into the sky like giants, their windows glowing with the reflection of the setting sun which painted the cloudless sky gold. Glass walkways connected the skyscrapers like a gleaming web above him. It took Edgar's breath away.

He stared around in wide-eyed awe, excited by the new world he now found himself in. It was beautiful – so contemporary and so old at the same time. Ancient buildings fashioned from brick and sandstone with columns, statues, colonnades, gargoyles and porticos;

and the modern buildings of glass and steel dwarfed him as he walked along the deserted streets under their shadows.

His eyes scanned his surroundings in a vain hope of spotting some kind of life – one person who could help him – someone who could tell him where he was, but there was nobody there. In the middle of the vast city there was not one soul in sight.

'Where is everyone?' Edgar asked himself out loud. 'Great. Talking to myself – the first sign of madness.'

The fear struck Edgar hard. One minute he had been in his bedroom trying to figure out a way to use the artifact that Betty had left for him and now here he was God-knows-where and lost without a single person to turn to for help.

The loneliness was a frightening prospect – one that Edgar couldn't take.

'HELLO?' he shouted. 'IS ANYONE THERE?'

There was no reply; not even a whisper of the wind. Perhaps this was all a dream. Maybe it was in his head. Edgar nipped himself hard on the arm. Pain. He did it again, just to make sure and yet again, he felt the sharp shock of his nails digging into his skin.

'I'm awake?' Edgar muttered. 'But this can't be real.'

He looked around, gawping at the unfamiliar sights that surrounded him, half-squinting in the blinding sunlight that reflected in the gleaming windows of the many towers and walkways that all criss-crossed high above him from building to building, into the into biggest skyscraper in centre of the web of skyscrapers: *Arden Industries* was written across its front in giant letters. It reached into the sky like a proud spire of glass and metal with pinnacle that pierced the golden wisps of cloud that floated high in the sky.

Along the street, beyond *Arden Industries*, Edgar could see a sprawling expanse of grass; a park filled with trees. A high, iron arch stood over the entrance engraved with the words *Garden of Arden,* and beyond that, a jagged, rocky hill rose up on the horizon and a majestic castle stood atop it. Its turrets and towers were topped with copper roofs that had turned green over the years and hundreds of windows sparkled in the dying sun. Edgar's jaw dropped at the stunning sight and he stared for a moment, watching the final moments of the day as the sun sank below the horizon, casting deep shades of purple twilight over the land.

'HELLO?' he shouted again, desperate for a reply but still, he was greeted with silence.

A surge of nausea swept over Edgar, crippling him. He sank down to the stone steps in front of an ancient building, in the shadow of its columns. He needed to collect his thoughts, calm down and devise an escape plan. Wherever he was – however he got there, there had to be a way back. He took the coin from his pocket and stared down at it. The coin was heavy and cold in his hand. He twisted it between his fingers and held it up close to his face, surveying it through narrowed eyes as if that might somehow uncover its secrets.

'What are you?' Edgar asked himself out loud, gripping it like it was the only thing keeping him alive. 'Where did you take me… and how?'

A wave of nausea split through him again, his bleeding forehead throbbed and Edgar hung his head for a moment; squeezing his eyes shut to try and maintain composure. Sweat poured down his face and agony surged inside him – his whole body was in shock. Edgar opened his eyes again, but his vision began swirling fast as though he had been on the waltzers in a fairground for too long, and he couldn't see straight.

The pain in his head was unbearable, like his brain was in a vice and the handle was turning, turning, turning and squeezing tighter and tighter. To try and avoid being sick he spat another gobful of blood-tinged saliva onto the steps. The sight of blood turned his stomach – were his injuries serious? The shock and adrenaline had dulled all sense of pain but blood was a bad sign, right? In panic, he retched and a stream of vomit splattered upon the pavement by his feet. The discomfort only lasted a moment and when Edgar had finished bringing up the remainder of his last meal, he felt much better.

He stared at the chunks and felt his stomach grumble again. It was such a grotesque sensation that flowed through his entire body.

'I'm not going to get anywhere by sitting around,' Edgar grumbled to himself, tearing his eyes away from the steaming puddle. 'I need to find someone – find out where I am.'

Climbing back to his feet, Edgar stowed the coin back in his pocket and set off at a brisk pace, along the street. He kept moving for another ten minutes, becoming more uneasy as he explored the desolate city streets. It was too quiet, too empty, too clean; not even a single piece of litter lay on the concrete. The sky darkened rapidly and soon the twilight shifted to complete darkness. Stars twinkled in the night sky as Edgar found himself at the edge of the city and on a deserted suburban street. Whitewashed, wooden houses with quaint porches and picket fences bordering their neatly preened lawns lined the avenue.

Edgar shivered involuntarily. There was something about the pristine condition of such a desolate place that was deeply unsettling – as if those who had lived there had just vanished from existence – gone without a trace. Lights lit the windows of several houses but there was nobody to be seen; not even the slightest shadow.

'Surely people must live here,' Edgar thought and began to approach the nearest house.

He opened the gate and wandered along the cobbled path towards the porch. He anxiously edged closer to the house and peeked through the window; the curtains were open a fraction and he peered inside. He could see nothing in the lounge – just antique furniture that looked untouched and a chandelier hanging from the ceiling, its crystals sparkling from the light of the stumpy candles that were lit upon it.

A shadow moved at the edge of the room and Edgar pushed his face closer to the glass to try and see if anybody was there.

The face appeared from nowhere; ghostly pale and angular. It was a woman. There was no denying her beauty but her eyes were deep red and her lips pulled back in a snarl to bare a mouthful of razor-sharp fangs – suddenly the image of beauty was gone. She froze, staring through the window for a moment, her eyes burning into Edgar's.

Edgar tried to back away, but there was something in the woman's stare that held him fast. He could not tell if she had a hypnotic power or if it was his own fear that held him rooted to the spot. The woman's hands shot out and smashed against the windowpane in a rabid frenzy like an animal desperate to escape from a zoo enclosure, driven only by the impulse to devour the human on the other side of the glass.

CRACK. A web of lines splintered across the glass and still, she scrambled against it, her long spindly fingers and sharp nails tapping against the thin fractures. The window threatened to break under the force of her attack and Edgar pulled himself back to his senses with a shake of his head and stumbled backwards, unable to take his eyes off the woman.

What was this frenzied creature?

Edgar turned to run.

All along the street doors crashed opened and people stepped out onto their porches. Men dressed in pinstripe suits and bowler hats, carrying silver topped walking canes and women in stylish evening gowns flooded the road and sauntered towards him.

Tap, tap, tap. The men's canes tapped out a steady rhythm with each step. *Tap, tap, tap;* the same, pounding rhythm of Edgar's heart. He watched anxiously as more and more appeared, spilling silently from their houses, heading in his direction. He began to retreat but backed into the wall.

SMASH!

Glass shattered into a million pieces behind him. Edgar shrieked and ducked but before he could move away he felt long, cold fingers wrap around his hair and pull him back with inhuman strength. He yelled in pain. He fell into the wall, struggling and screaming as he tried to pull free from the grip of the raving monster leaning through the broken window. Edgar's neck bent backwards and he felt the sharp, jagged edges of broken glass that still clung to their place in the windowpane dig into his flesh. He daren't move. One slip and he could cut his own throat on the glass.

He was helpless as the woman's other hand reached out and he felt the cold, clammy fingers wrap around his neck, her long nails digging in hard. He heard her fast, grunting breath; felt the warm air brush against his face and a grotesque stench like death filled his nostrils. It was all he could smell. It consumed everything.

Edgar was powerless. He looked on at the other residents, so many of them, moving collectively with such grace that they seemed a single mass floating towards him. They approached from across the street, as if their curiosity was piqued and a morbid fascination drew them in like crowds to the scene of a tragic accident. Struggling and choking and flailing to no avail, Edgar panicked and tried to scream for help; help that he knew would never come but his voice couldn't escape his crushed throat. He spluttered desperately, his head feeling faint with the lack of oxygen.

His eyes widened and he thrashed around. A searing pain dug into the side of his neck – glass embedded in the flesh and tore it deeply as Edgar struggled. Fresh, warm blood trickled from the wound; his mind was spiraling out of control. What could he do? He tried to signal to the other people for help, though he knew deep down that this was a futile effort. Instead, the eyes of his voyeurs gleamed like the dying embers of a fire with a burning desire to see him suffer. It was as if they enjoyed it; that they revelled in his pain and for some despicable reason wanted to.

None of this made sense. Barely an hour ago Edgar had been in his room, safe, albeit frustrated as he tried to uncover the secret of the mysterious artifact that Betty had left behind. Now he had revealed its secret. It had changed the world around him...or transported him somewhere else. As the creatures glided towards him and he struggled to free himself, Edgar wished he had never followed Betty's clues.

In his terror, Edgar's mind raced through the consequences of rapidly approaching death – of the heartache his disappearance would put his family through. He could see his mother weeping with his grandmother and grandfather – his few friends who he had promised to see again soon would never see him again and nobody would know why. He could not give in. He had to fight.

He watched as the other vampiric demons glided towards him eerily, filling the whole street. There was no way he could make a run for it. There were simply too many. His mind was in a frenzy – there was no escape from this.

But maybe there was...

'I stood on it!' Edgar shouted out loud, suddenly realizing what he had to do.

Without thinking about it, Edgar reached for the coin in his pocket. He could not wait any longer – whether his suspicions were right or wrong, he had to try. He felt the cold metal against his fingertips – a gentle comfort amid the chaos. His fingers clasped around it but it slid out of his grasp and fell through a hole into the lining of his jacket.

Keeping one eye on the vampires (surely that's all they could be) Edgar shoved his hand deep into the hole and grasped desperately for the coin.

Creeeeeak.

The door of the house behind him opened and a figure emerged on the wooden porch. They were upon him; gliding out of the house and drifting up the garden path, gathering speed. Whispers of perverse heavy breathing filled the air as the vampires gained ground, almost upon him. There was no time to grab the coin. There was no time to just stamp on it and fly away – they would have him and tear him to pieces before he could even lift his foot.

Edgar spun on the spot, his eyes darting for an escape route but there were too many of those things and no room to maneuver between them. They were so close to him now – he could see their gleaming red eyes, like rubies. Their mouths were pulled back into hungry snarls and their long tongues licked their fangs; floating gracefully closer and closer. Edgar couldn't move. His legs froze with fear and threatened to give way beneath him. How could he escape? To run would be like playing a deadly game of tag but to stay would be to give in to the same fate.

Edgar took a deep breath and prepared himself. Running was the only option if he wanted to stand a chance.

BEEP BEEP BEEEEEEEEEEEEP

The car horn filled the air with its deafening sound. They stopped and turned. The advancing force fell as silent and as still as stone. Nobody had heard it coming or seen its arrival until now. Through the crowd of frozen, statuesque creatures, Edgar could see a long, black car, reminiscent of a 1970's Lincoln. The passenger side door opened and a man stepped out.

Wordlessly, the creatures fell to their knees, facing the man with their heads bowed as if in prayer. Edgar remained standing, looking out over the sea of kneeling bodies. A cold shiver shot down his back as the man who stepped out of the car turned to him and pointed right at him, his face hidden by the shadow cast by the peak of a large trilby hat and a black cloak, trimmed with brown fur hung over his shoulders, fastened across his front by a silver chain with an ornate clasp.

'You!' the man exclaimed, his accent rang with an almost Russian twang. He took off his hat and held it across his chest. 'You are the one.'

'I'm the what?' Edgar asked anxiously. 'I don't understand what's going on. If you could just help me-'

'My child, it is I who need your help.'

The man had an air of importance about him. Not only in the way these people seemed to worship him, but in his posture – the way he stood tall; upright and assured in the way he addressed Edgar. There was a kindness about him – something the others didn't have. He smiled with his eyes and his voice was soft.

'Who are you?' Edgar demanded, keeping his distance.

'Edvard Dardanoss,' the man replied with a smile but even his apparent friendliness couldn't hide the vicious fangs.

'And what do you want?' Edgar demanded, remaining cautious, slowly backing away.

'You,' the man spat viciously, his eyes suddenly alive with fire 'Your blood.'

The words hit Edgar like a lightning bolt.

'Vampires…' Edgar gasped out loud. 'I knew it.'

'We prefer *The Unsterbliche*,' Edvard replied matter-of-factly. 'And we want…'

'My blood.'

Edgar shivered as he repeated the words.

'Your blood.'

Edgar's mind swam in circles. None of this made any sense.

'It is what called me here; such a sweet, sweet aroma. I could smell it right from Kastell Deuathac itself. Thought I must have been imagining things. The hunger does that, you know? Drives you mad.'

The vampire's eyes flashed wildly. He licked his thin lips and stared at Edgar, reaching his hand out towards him. His gaze held Edgar transfixed and he shuffled forward a few involuntary steps towards the man.

'Come to me,' Edvard hissed and Edgar's small, tentative steps turned into a confident stride and all the while their eye contact never broke. 'Come to me, sweet child.'

Edgar's mind was empty. There was no fear, no anxiety; everything had been washed away. It was like he floated along effortlessly, pulled by a tether. The vampire's voice was like a light in the fog calling him, guiding him.

'That's right. Come. Come into my arms. Come to death. I am so hungry.'

Edgar reached the end of the garden path. His eyes were still fixed upon Edvard's and he carefully negotiated his way through the gaps between kneeling worshippers and reached out his hand towards Edvard's.

Their fingertips touched and Edvard grabbed Edgar's hand tightly. He pulled him in close, their eyes still locked. Edvard moved in and sniffed at Edgar's face. The cut on his forehead still trickled a steady stream of blood and Edvard inhaled deeply. He held his breath a moment, savouring the smell. He closed his eyes and rolled his hand, like a wine-taster sampling a fine wine. After a moment, he exhaled with deep, satisfied sigh.

'So sweet, so fresh,' he muttered madly, taking another deep, rattling breath to savour the smell of blood. 'I shall eat well tonight.'

He leaned down and ran his tongue along Edgar's face, lapping up the trail of blood that trickled down his cheek from his forehead. Still, Edgar gazed blankly, his mind lost in the haze. Edvard moaned with perverse pleasure as the tip of his tongue followed the congealed blood to the fresh open wound.

A shock of pain split through Edgar's whole body as the vampire pressed his tongue into the cut. The stabbing sensation jolted Edgar from his stupor and he screamed, remembering nothing of how he ended up in the vampire's grasp.

With a sudden surge of adrenalin he pushed Edvard away, turned with a stumble and began to run. He dodged around and dived over the kneeling vampires who filled the street like statues.

'GET HIM!' Edvard roared and the swarm of vampires launched back into action, reaching out for Edgar and clawing at his ankles as he darted past.

Edvard slid back into the car.

'Drive, Vladimir.'

The driver nodded and accelerated. Edgar heard the wheels spin with a chilling screech and the car horn tooted loudly into the night as the car engine roared and gave chase.

Edgar ran as fast as he could, tearing through the suburban streets. Everywhere looked the same – every street identical to the last. He felt trapped like a rat in a maze going in circles again and again. On every street more and more Unsterbliche joined in the chase.

As he sped along, Edgar saw them emerge from their houses and join the crowd but he kept his eyes forward, ignoring those speeding at him down their garden paths from all sides. Vampires ran at full pelt and dived at him, their long clawed fingers reaching out, trying to get a grasp of his clothes.

BEEP BEEP!

The horn blared but Edgar kept running. He couldn't turn back – he could feel them close behind him, only steps away. More and more spilled out of houses from all sides. Several filed out of homes ahead of him and rushed at him, their red eyes glowing with malice.

Edgar's eyes darted from side to side hoping to find somewhere to run. There was a turning just ahead. The vampires ahead approached fast. There was no way to avoid a collision. They would surely get him before he could reach the next corner.

Every step Edgar took, they seemed to take three. Their snarling, slavering mouths filled with needle sharp fangs unsettled him. If he was caught, those same fangs would tear the flesh from his bones.

Edgar pushed himself to move fast. His legs could barely cope with the strain but something deep inside kept him going – a need to survive. He could not and would not die here. What would happen to his family? What would they think if he never returned home?

That was reason enough to fight – to see them again. Edgar stared right into the eyes of his attackers and with a burst of adrenaline, he sped up and ran right around the corner onto the next street, almost tripping over as he turned sharply. He grabbed onto the sign post at the corner of the street in order to keep balance and kept running.

Edgar chanced a look back to see the Unsterbliche close behind him, gaining ground as they sprinted at superhuman speed.

Screeeeeeeeeeech.

The brakes squealed as the car swung around to take the corner and almost spun out of control. Edgar couldn't see it behind the sea of Unsterbliche that gave chase – just a blur of vicious, animalistic faces.

The car engine revved dangerously behind them.

BEEP BEEP BEEEEEEEEEEEP!

The angry horn blasted and only made his heart race faster by knowing it was gaining on him. The army of pursuers parted to let the car zoom between them. Edgar had nowhere to run, the car sped towards him and the street ended in a cul-de-sac; it was a dead end.

There were no houses at the end of the street – just a steep grassy hill that led up to a tree lined ridge. Perhaps it was a forest: a perfect place to hide. Edgar's legs burned from running and he could barely catch his breath. He glanced back – the car approached fast. It gained speed and he could see Edvard in the passenger seat beside a gaunt, thin-faced driver.

Edgar reached the hill and began to tear up it as fast as he could. It was a steady slope at first but it quickly became steeper. His legs ached as he tried to keep up the speed.

The gradient of the slope was almost impossible to negotiate now and Edgar had to stop for a moment. The top part of the hill was so steep that it was practically vertical and he was out of energy. He gasped and spluttered, his heart pounded in his ears and he thought for a moment that he might pass out.

Behind him, the cars breaks slammed hard.

Screeeeeeeeech.

Edgar glanced back. The car skidded to a halt below him and so did his pursuers. Edvard climbed out of the car and removed his stylish black glasses. Edgar avoided eye contact with him, fearing to fall under his thrall again.

'Come back, my child!' Edvard bellowed. 'You won't even feel a thing.'

'I'm not stupid!' Edgar shouted back, laughing nervously. 'I'm not going to let you kill me.'

'Who said we would kill you?' Edvard replied. 'You can become like us. Immortal. Forever young and eternally beautiful.

You need never grow old, you need never suffer from disease, you need never die.'

'Vampires always die,' Edgar scoffed, shaking his head. 'Find me a stake, some holy water, a crucifix or some sunlight and I'll prove it.'

'Legends! All of them. There is no truth in these tales,' Edvard retorted, laughing off Edgar's threats. 'Now come, join us! We must feed!'

The many Unsterbliche that surrounded Edvard muttered and nodded in agreement as they eyed Edgar hungrily. He kept slowly making his way up the hill, keeping his eyes firmly on them as he retreated, constantly pushing to put more distance between them and himself.

'There's so many of you though and only one of me. Who will get my blood?' Edgar demanded, already suspecting that the answer might be quite brutal and bloody.

'I shall take you and then they can fight over whatever is left,' Edvard laughed while his followers nodded feverishly, not taking their hungry eyes off Edgar. 'A King always comes first.'

The loyal subjects that surrounded Edvard nodded and spoke in agreement. They clasped their hands together and bowed their heads momentarily and Edvard smiled.

'Do you think any of them are so stupid?' Edgar shouted. 'You'll take all my blood. You'll kill me and drain me before you'd let them even get close.'

Edvard's smile faded and he shook his head.

'No, no, no. I will keep my promise.'

'I don't trust you,' Edgar shouted. He looked to his side where the almost vertical hill rose another twenty, maybe thirty feet to the trees at the top.

'Bring him to me,' Edvard bellowed, pointing a long, leather-gloved finger at the hill.

'Come on, Edgar. You can do this,' he thought out loud, daring only to take one more moment of rest.

He glanced at the hill and considered climbing the rest of it, then back at the vampires below.

As soon as he saw them, he wished he hadn't looked back. The Unsterbliche writhed in such ways that were painful to watch. They emitted high-pitched shrieks of agony as their bodies contorted into horrible shapes. The clothes on their backs began to ripple and ripped at the seams as the flesh beneath mutated, swelling rapidly.

Great, black, leathery wings burst from their backs and long horns unfurled from their foreheads. The faces of the creatures had twisted into a bat-like shape; their noses flattened and their mouths stretched wider into sinister grins that displayed their rows of long, jagged, razor-sharp fangs.

Edgar watched the metamorphosis in horror, unable to move. The Unsterbliche had been monstrous enough before but now they had changed into a purely demonic form he had no idea what to do.

He turned to face the hill, climbing as fast as he could. His feet slipped on the uneven ground and he grabbed onto chunks of grass to help aid his ascent. This was impossible but still, he pushed onwards out of sheer desperation. He scrambled up and up, not even daring to look back at the creatures that he knew would be back on his tail.

Whoosh, whoosh, whoosh.

Edgar felt the breeze brush against his face as something beat the air like a fan. He glanced over his shoulder and yelped. They were flying, their monstrous wings beating the air as they flew towards him, sneering and dangerous – just a mass of wings, bubbling flesh, red eyes and teeth.

They swooped at him, reaching out to grab him with sharp talons. Edgar braced himself for their attack and kicked out. His foot hit the vampire's face but another grabbed his leg. Edgar thrashed his leg hard trying to shake off the beast. As he struggled he clung to a bulky tuft of grass for dear life but it snapped and Edgar fell. He felt the spindly fingers release him and he began to slide back down the hillside towards the vampires that waited at the bottom.

Instinctively, he reached out and grabbed hold of more chunks of grass; each time they snapped and Edgar screamed as he slid further and further towards the horde awaiting him at the bottom – a mass of fleshy bodies, leathery wings and sharp fangs and claws – a deadly sea of creatures that would tear him apart.

His fingers clasped around more long chunks of grass but he was sliding too fast. He couldn't keep hold but then, with one final burst of desperation and a scream of defiance, Edgar reached out one last time and grabbed tuft of long grass. Its strong roots remained planted in the ground and it stuck fast. Edgar stopped falling and miraculously found his footing again. He began to climb once more.

Faster and faster. He glanced back to see the creatures below howl in frustration and turned back to his climb.

Edgar ignored the sound of beating wings and forced the grunting, rattling breaths of the vampires out of his mind and focused instead on his grim determination to escape. His sole objective was to survive. Not just for himself, but for his family and friends. Betty hadn't led him this far for nothing – there had to be something in this. He hadn't given it much thought until now. Betty intended for him to be there – for him to find the coin and for him to find out how to use it. Come to think of it, Brother Bradley had aided him too – the two of them surely wouldn't have led him into such danger for nothing. Whatever he was supposed to do, he couldn't let them down.

In his mind he could see Betty's face; her smile that made her emerald eyes narrow – the little wrinkles in the corners. He could hear her laugh and her voice telling him he would be fine, telling him to fight:

'Go on, Edgar. You're better than this. Don't give in. Fight. You're a survivor.'

'She's right,' Edgar thought as he clawed his way up the slope. The trees appeared closer than ever now. He was nearly there. Climbing, reaching, forcing his way onwards. The Unsterbliche all around him just an inconvenient blur. He couldn't focus on them or he would risk losing his cool and endanger himself. Climbing. Climbing. Climbing. Focused wholly on each hand and foot hold.

He did it. His hand reached up to the solid ground and he hoisted himself up onto the ledge where he rolled onto his back and stare up at the velvety dark sky above him. The pinprick stars and giant, milky moon the only light from above, occasionally blotted out by black silhouettes of the Unsterbliche darting across the skyline.

There was no time to waste. The creatures circled, spiralling ever lower. Soon they would spot him and who knew what would happen next. Edgar glanced over the of the hill and saw many Unsterbliche clawing their way up the hill behind him while the others circled in the sky above. The city sprawled across the horizon, glowing in the dark, illuminated by the streetlights. He could see all the way across the neat square blocks of the city to *Arden Industries* reaching high into the sky in the centre of the city, to the castle on the cliff beyond and the sprawling park near the castle gates.

Edgar scrambled to his feet and turned towards the thick forest standing before him. Without thinking of what dangers may lurk within, Edgar sprinted towards the border of the trees, hoping that in the darkness he could find some sanctuary.

– CHAPTER EIGHT –
THE HOUSE OF NATHANIEL

Edgar sprinted into the trees, his heart pounding in his throat and his mind reeling in confusion, freefalling in fear. He struggled to breathe as he passed over the threshold of the forest and dashed past the thin spread of trees that grew thicker and thicker as he ventured further into the dark tangle of trees that reached high above him. With each pounding footstep, the darkness enveloped him rapidly until he was completely consumed by it.

In the pitch black, Edgar could see nothing and for a moment it felt like the world had ceased to exist and everything, even his own tired, weary body were gone; everything had disintegrated around him, reality had unravelled, time had stopped and he was nothing but a floating consciousness suspended in the black heart of nothingness.

Edgar raised his hand to feel his way forward – he stumbled onwards, crashing head-on into low branches and tripping over dangerous rises and dips in the ground. He fell into the sharp-barked trunks of the trees all around him.

Eventually, as his eyes adjusted Edgar could make out colourless shapes in the shadows and he ducked and dived under low branches and around the twisted, gnarled trunks. His whole body screamed in shock and he needed to rest or he would surely pass out. For a moment, he paused and leaned against a tree, panting wildly.

His lungs were on fire and his legs threatened to give way beneath him.

'What am I doing?' he muttered furiously to himself. 'I can't stop. I have to keep going.'

Edgar moved on blindly in the darkness, hoping to lose the creatures that he could hear close behind. He rushed onwards but slowed to a steadier pace. He had to keep the noise to a minimum or they would hear and be upon him before he could have chance to escape.

Edgar stopped for a moment and looked back as he caught his breath once more. He saw humanoid shadows approaching fast in the far distance and he ducked around the tree and set off again at a sprint, hoping to put as much distance between himself and the Unsterbliche as he could.

Sniff. Sniff.

'We will find you,' The voice was raw and guttural and too close for comfort.

Edgar froze momentarily, suppressed a scream and forced his way onwards, his legs weak in fear. He dared to turn back and saw the shadows of the monsters closing in. He took off again at a steady jog, zig-zagging to make sure there was plenty of tree cover between him and them. Eventually, he took another brief moment to catch his breath. With his back pressed against a thick tree trunk, he gasped and choked for oxygen. His head spun from being so alert and driven by impulse. His legs were weak and the ground felt like it could be torn from underneath him at any second.

Scratch, scratch scratch.

The sound came from close by. Edgar's eyes widened, as if somehow he might enhance his lack of vision. Unblinking, he looked all around, sensing danger nearby. His eyes stung and began to water from his determination to not blink, the hairs on his arm stood on end; he knew they could see him but he could not see them. He poked his head around the tree, expecting to come face to face with a snarling monster, saliva dripping from its razor-sharp fangs, its eyes burning red like the fires of hell itself...but the creatures that had been so close behind him were gone. They had disappeared into the darkness of the forest – perhaps they had lost his trail.

Scratch, scratch, scratch.

It was only a faint sound but it was close. Edgar pressed himself against rough bark of the thick tree trunk, squeezed his eyes tight shut and held his breath.

Scratch, scratch, scratch.

A droplet of water landed on his hair.

'Great. It's starting to rain,' Edgar thought irritably, as if being chased by the Unsterbliche wasn't bad enough.

A quiet rattling breath. It shook Edgar's bones and sent a chill to his heart – they were near again. Edgar prayed that it was just the wind rustling through the bare branches but he knew he was wrong. He peeked around the trunk – nothing there; nothing but solid blackness interspersed with the silhouettes of other trees. Where were they? Had they surrounded him while he had been distracted? What was going on?

Another heavy drop landed on his face but this one was hot and slid down Edgar's cheek leaving a slimy snail-trail across his skin. Edgar wiped it away with the back of his hand; his stomach turned at the sight of the clear, stringy liquid. The stench was unbearable and Edgar's mind raced – was this substance what he thought it was?

Scratch, scratch, scratch.

The sound was closer than ever and accompanied with a rattling breath. The hairs on the back of Edgar's neck stood on end. A tingle of cold shot down his back like a sixth sense warning him of danger. He was just about to move when something tangled in his hair. Edgar tried to pull away but he was caught. His hands shot up to untangle himself but instead of touching the rough bark of the tree his fingertips brushed against something cold, clammy and smooth. His whole body tensed as he realised what was happening and he lifted his head up to look into the snarling face of the Unsterbliche. It hung upside down in the tree above him, naked and pale and gripped his hair with its long, clawed fingers. Its teeth were bared hungrily, saliva swinging from them in glistening streams.

Edgar forced himself not to scream, determined not to draw attention to himself as he twisted in a futile attempt to break free. The creature held on tightly and swiped its claws at Edgar as he tried to escape.

Far above the almost leafless canopy of twisted, bony branches, Edgar saw several shadows fly past: Vampires in the air, scouting the ground below for any sign of him. He wondered if they might have night-vision sight or some kind of heightened sense that would make him easier to find – Edvard had mentioned being able to smell him – was that how they had crept up on him in the trees? He knew it must be true.

Edgar thrashed around as if he were trying to wipe invisible spiders off his body but the Unsterbliche remained undeterred. As Edgar twisted, and struggled it finally let go of his hair and dropped calmly to the ground before Edgar. It towered over him – easily eight foot tall, its muscular body was pale and strong; its wings outstretched so that Edgar's path was blocked – just a shape, drained of all colour in the darkness.

Edgar froze, unable to move in sheer terror. There was a strange, horrifying beauty to the creature before him – the way that solid muscle clung to its giant frame, every single sinew visibly stretching and contracting as it moved. The snail-shell pattern of its curved horns was crisp and clean; the squashed snout and wide, razor-toothed grin were so reminiscent of a bat that all human features were lost. Its wings looked so soft and leathery that Edgar would have just reached out and touched them had he not been so afraid.

Edgar stood hypnotised by the Unsterbliche. It stalked towards him, long legs bowed and back arched to keep low as it stalked forwards, keeping its head level with Edgar's. He stared into its burning eyes, so full of fury, of vicious brutality and Edgar knew this creature before him wanted him dead. It had chased him like a cat after a mouse and now he was cornered. This was it. The game was over. It was end of the road.

The terrifying demon snarled, its voice rattled low and deep. It sniffed loudly and reached out a long claw towards Edgar's cheek.

'I can't die,' Edgar told himself defiantly. 'I won't die!'

He ducked under the monster's arm and dashed past, pushing its strong wings out of the way. For a moment he didn't think he would make it but the shock of his sudden bolt had stunned the Unsterbliche. It turned and reached out for Edgar, screeching in a deathly tone that shredded Edgar's eardrums but he fled, not looking back.

Another cold, hoarse shriek pierced the air behind him and he knew that the Unsterbliche was calling to the others – rallying them to its position, warning them their prey, Edgar himself, was nearby. He had no other option than to keep moving and not look back. Footsteps pounded after him, the sound of scratching and scraping in the trees above him and a series of cries as if the creatures were communicating with each other and sending commands for the hunt.

Edgar glanced back. They were onto him – running on foot, climbing through the trees and leaping through the skeletal canopy above with the speed and agility of demonic monkeys. There were so many of them.

'Run, run, run, run!' Edgar muttered under his breath as he dashed onwards, trying desperately to lose the creatures.

Soon the trees filtered out and Edgar found himself in a large clearing. Out of the gloom a large, bulky shape appeared. It was huge and square and as Edgar approached he noticed it was a house – a stony building in the middle of the woods. He sprinted towards it – towards safety.

'A place to hide and vampires can't cross a threshold unless they're invited,' Edgar told himself, thinking back to the old stories he had heard about where vampires couldn't enter buildings without invitation and he hoped the legend applied to these creatures he found himself running from right now.

He was almost there. The closer he came, the more details jumped out from the front of the house. Ivy crept up the walls, clinging to the cracks in the ancient stone and through the shattered windows. A hefty wooden door hung off its hinges. It looked as though the house hadn't had a resident in years.

Edgar reached the door and he skidded to a halt, staring into the blackness inside.

His gut twisted and his brain ached with a sharp pain – a sense telling him that danger lurked ahead.

'I might be wrong. What if something worse is inside?'

Edgar looked back. He knew they were right behind and despite being nowhere in sight, he knew they would soon be upon him. Perhaps they were planning some kind of trap?

'I only need a moment. Just enough time to get that stupid coin out of my pocket and stamp on it like before. It's my only chance.'

Another grotesque shriek pierced the night.

They were closing in.

Edgar dived inside without giving it another thought.It was his only option.

He rushed into the dusty hallway with stone walls and tried to push the door shut behind him.

It scraped on the hard wooden floor, then, with a *CRACK* and a *SMASH* it fell off its hinges and landed hard on the ground.

Edgar's heart skipped a beat – hopefully the noise hadn't given him away. He turned and moved quickly down the corridor, steadying himself against the damp, mossy wall, as he shifted through the dark. The wooden floor thudded softly beneath his feet, only softened by the patches of grass that grew from between the floorboards.

A doorway to his right led into a large room with a stony fireplace. A plaque bearing a dusty coat of arms hung above the hearth and broken furniture littered the hard wooden floor – leaning tables with splintered legs, smashed chairs and cupboards with loose doors.

His hands were already in his pocket, his fingers digging deep into the hole in the lining, trying to clutch the coin. Edgar peeked through the shattered glass in the windowpane and saw the creatures approaching slowly.

The Unsterbliche stalked closer, just pallid white ghosts advancing on him, their posture upright and tall, their gait a strong stride. Edgar ducked down. His fingers locked around the coin and he pulled it out from his pocket. He stared down at it in his hand. Edgar breathed a sigh of relief and kissed the coin, laughing to himself.

He stood up and something appeared in the corner of his eye – a shape. Edgar turned and screamed out loud. A face grinned at him through the hole in the shattered glass, its fangs dripping with saliva and eyes glowing red – the only light in the pitch black that consumed him.

'The house is surrounded,' the creature hissed. 'There is no escape.'

'But you need to be invited to get in,' Edgar scoffed. He wasn't entirely sure he was right but his confidence was admirable. 'I'm safe.'

Outside, the air was rent with the harsh laughter of the vampires.

Thump thump thump.

The sound came from within the house. Steady footsteps. Surely they were inside.

Edgar turned and his fingers loosened on the coin but before he could drop it, a blurry shape darted across the room, screeching once more in a horrible, piercing tone.

It was small, only up to Edgar's chest - a child and it ran full pelt towards him. Before Edgar could move the child dived and knocked him backwards. Edgar cracked the back of his head on the floor and the coin slipped from his grip and rolled away. He reached out to catch it but narrowly missed and it dropped into a gap between the floorboards like a penny in an arcade machine.

'NO!' Edgar shrieked. His heart sank as he struggled to fight off the child who pinned him down, scrabbling at his face with its claws. His only chance of escape was gone.

Edgar felt the pain as the child-like creature sliced at his flesh, leaving deep cuts on his cheeks and in the chaos he caught a glimpse of the face. Behind the demonic eyes that burned wild with rage; the fangs short and sharp and the waggling tongue, trying to lap up the blood that poured from the wounds they had inflicted on Edgar, was a little girl. Her long, dark hair was matted and tangled and fell into Edgar's face like rats tails.

Edgar wrestled with the child, trying to throw her off. He couldn't hurt her – vampire or not, she was just a girl but her strength was immense and her jaws snapped inches from his face like a hungry dog, spraying him with stinking saliva.

Edgar's strength was fading.

He couldn't keep it up much longer. More heavy footsteps thundered through the house and he knew he was done for – the horrendous chase, the desperate and valiant escape had all been for nothing. His arms weren't strong enough to keep the vampire child at bay and they gave way.

She fell on top of Edgar and the weight winded him. He screamed out, terrified, knowing that his end had come. He looked up into the demonic eyes and saw her face move like lightning towards his neck. He waited for the pain – for the searing agony as she bit into him and tore his throat apart…it seemed like eternity; like the world was running in slow motion.

Thud, thud, thud.

Footsteps, closer now, pounding like Edgar's heartbeat. Laughter and hideous shrieks from the other vampires filled his brain.

'Please let this be over quickly,' Edgar wished as his eyes rolled back and he almost lost consciousness.

CRASH

The child flew backwards, her arms outstretched, still reaching for Edgar, screaming and screeching as she soared through the air.

A woman appeared in the gloom, glowing white like an angel in the pitch-black. She reached out a dainty hand to Edgar who lay on the floor, staring at her; his whole body tense. She was beautiful. Her skin was fair and her long, blonde hair fell in curls but her glowing eyes gave away that she was one of them.

'We're here to help,' she said in a gentle voice tinted with an Irish accent. She reached closer to Edgar. He took her soft, cold hand and she helped him to his feet. 'You need to get out of the way. Hide and don't come out until I say it's safe.'

'What's going on? Where are they?'

'They're coming for you,' the woman replied in a hushed whisper and in the distance Edgar heard voices muttering and a voice shout out:

'Get them!'

The collective roar shook the foundations of the house and told Edgar he had no time to question his saviour. He glanced through the window and saw the horde of Unsterbliche surge towards the door of the house. He heard their feet pounding the wooden floorboards in the hall as they swarmed in and the very ground trembled like an earthquake under the weight.

The woman darted to the doorway and Edgar noticed she was not alone - several others crowded around the door, protecting it. They stood defensively, while another man, his face hidden behind a mane of long black hair, pinned down the little girl who convulsed like a possessed child and spat in his face, clawed at him and screamed in a pitch so high that Edgar had to cover his ears.

'Bryony, stop!' he bellowed desperately at the child. She didn't react and so he slapped her across the face but it only angered her. 'BRYONY!'

'I'm hungry!' the girl cried, her voice hoarse. 'SO HUNGRY!'

'I know, I know.'

In an instant the girl calmed and burst into tears. Her deafening wails and heart-wrenching sobs drowned out the sound of approaching footsteps and the man took her in his arms.

While everyone was distracted, Edgar ran to the spot where the coin had fallen through a thick crack between the floorboards, flung himself to his knees and tried to reach inside. He couldn't see a thing and his fingers wouldn't fit in the gap; he cursed under his breath and made another futile attempt.

Edgar looked up and saw the group by the hall door fighting against the Unsterbliche who tried to enter but there were too many. They were outnumbered.

Edgar tried to ignore the screams of agony and the clouds of dust as the creatures exploded.

He watched in horror as the creatures flooded in, barging past the guards who tried to fight them off. Edgar stood rooted to the spot, eyes wide as he saw one of the Unsterbliche grab a man and tear his head clean off his shoulders. There was a splash of blood and then *poof;* The body crumbled to dust and his remains fell to the ground, leaving nothing behind but the shell of his old clothes. Through the cloud, the murderous vampire stormed towards Edgar like a tank ploughing its way through a battlefield.

Edgar trembled as the creature stomped towards him. It hissed and a long, black tongue slid out from between its teeth. Suddenly it stopped dead in its tracks. Its hand shot up to its chest and its eyes widened. It opened its mouth but before the words could come out, it crumbled to dust. A man stood behind him with a sharp wooden stake in his hand. He winked at Edgar who nodded a wordless thanks.

'Hide. NOW!'

Edgar didn't need to be told again. He dashed around the room looking for somewhere to duck for cover. The guards were just about managing to hold the vampires off at the door but there was a deafening *smash* and a tinkle of broken glass. Edgar shrieked in surprise and dived aside to avoid the sharp rain of glass shards. Within seconds bodies flung themselves at the open windows and began to scramble through.

'Over here!' shouted one of the house's guardians as he ran over to the window to stop the flood of Unsterbliche but the creature was already inside. This one was bigger than the others – his horns curved up instead of down and his eyes glowed with bloodlust, anger and deception. He plunged his clawed hand straight into the guard's chest, fumbled around and pulled his hand back out, clutching a still beating heart within his talons. The guard crumbled to dust, his clothes falling to the floor.

'How many more have to die?' the creature rasped.

The guards by the door turned, caught by surprise upon hearing the deep, rattling voice behind them. Seizing their opportunity, the Unsterbliche in the hall burst through and filled the room.

The monstrous demon raised the heart in his hand to its mouth and bit a chunk out of the bleeding organ as if it were an apple; a plume of smoke billowed off his tongue with a hiss and the black flesh bubbled as if the other vampire's blood were a toxic acid. The heart crumbled to dust in his hand and trickled like sand between his fingers.

'We will take you all unless you just give us the boy,' the creature snarled, its teeth sharp and treacherous.

Edgar slipped into the shadows, ducked under a half-collapsed table that sat against the wall beside the fireplace and buried his head in his hands. The man who cradled the young girl in his arms jumped to his feet and made a stand. For the first time, Edgar caught a glance of his face – he was handsome with deep-set eyes and a scar on his cheek; his long, dark hair hung loose and untidy.

'You know we can't do that,' he said defiantly with his arms folded. His accent was distinctly Irish, just like the woman's. 'He's innocent.'

'He is, is he?' the Unsterbliche laughed hoarsely. 'And you dare to defy your Lord and King, Edvard Dardanoss, Ruler of Deuathac?'

'I've done it before and I'll do it again.'

'And I let you live only because of the agreement arranged by the merciful Lord Aldous Arden, the first Ruler of Deuathac, may he rest in peace.'

Edvard sneered dangerously.

Edgar stared at the towering demon, unable to believe this was the same being that had once taken the form of a human – the same man who had chased him earlier.

Edvard advanced towards the man who stood, unflinching. From where he hid, Edgar could see his scarred face twist grimly as if he knew his fate. He reached out long, slender fingers and caressed the man's face. The man closed his eyes and took a deep breath, refusing to appear intimidated.

'You ought to watch your mouth. I might just tear it off,' Edvard hissed, gripping the man's chin with his claws.

'Cormac!' the angelic woman screamed. She made a dash for Edvard and launched herself at him. 'You said you'd leave us alone! The agreement says we will come to no harm from you!' the woman sobbed, violently thumping her fists against the vampire's solid body but he didn't even flinch.

'That was when Lord Arden was Ruler of Deuathac, but now I am your king and I see you for the scum you are,' Edvard spat, leering down at the woman who pummelled him repeatedly.

'Caoilinn, back off,' Cormac warned, but the woman glared at him coldly.

'We were promised safety but tonight they've stormed in, wrecked out home and killed our friends. We can't sit by and just let that happen, brother,' Caoilinn hissed, casting her eyes back upon Edvard who shook his head in disagreement.

'And we'll make sure they didn't die for nothing, but please stop, it's not worth it.'

'Your brother speaks wisely,' Edvard replied. 'Touch me one more time and I will tear your head clean off your shoulders.'

Caoilinn glowered defiantly and clenched her fist. Edvard raised his brow as if daring her to test her.

She sighed, unclenched and turned away and from his hiding place, Edgar saw something drop down the long sleeve of her dirty, white robe. Her hand grasped around a sharp, wooden point.

'Your sister is wise, Cormac. Now give me the boy or we will take him from you and those who try to stop us will die,' Edvard snarled venomously. He licked his fangs and his eyes swivelled around the room. 'Enough lives have already been lost, we need not lose anymore.'

Edvard's fiery eyes landed on Edgar and he pushed himself further into the shadows, hoping to vanish from sight to no avail. He wished he could shrink – that he could just disappear but he wasn't so lucky. He had no super powers and instead he resorted to turning away, refusing to make eye contact with the monster and hoping it wouldn't see him even though its eyes had already locked on him.

'Hello again, my child. This game of hide and seek is over. Come out, accept your fate,' Edvard hissed his voice tinged with that sickly sweet, dangerous tone once more. 'I promise there is nothing to fear.'

Edgar didn't reply, resorting to his attempt at pretending to be invisible but he knew it was too late – he had been discovered and he froze, not knowing what to do.

'I can see you down there, child. Your blood is mine, and I shall enjoy it. It is always sweeter after a chase...all that adrenaline,' Edvard chuckled coldly and he began to skulk towards the table where Edgar hid.

Edgar pressed himself further back into the shadows, his back against the cold wall behind him and he whimpered in terror. Edvard inhaled deeply as he crouched down and looked into Edgar's eyes; his thin lips spread into a wide grin.

Behind Edvard, Edgar could see Caoilinn inching closer, her jaw clenched and her eyes burning with fury.

'Come on, my boy. You can't fight this,' Edvard said to Edgar, staring him right in the eye. Edgar felt his mind fogging as the vampire exercised his hypnotic grip over him.

'Edvard, please. We can bring you more blood – just let the boy go,' Cormac pleaded suddenly and Edvard turned to him as quick as lighting.

'More of your frozen, congealed dirt?' Edvard snarled darkly, towering over Cormac with a manic gleam in his eyes. 'Why would I want that when I can have it fresh and warm from the veins?'

'The poor boy doesn't deserve this.'

'The boy is but a fly in a spider's web,' Edvard chuckled. 'He is our prey.'

'NO!' Caoilinn shrieked. She pounced and landed on Edvard's back, wrapped her arms around his neck and plunged the stake deep into his heart.

Edvard groaned and with an unnatural strength, he flung Caoilinn to the ground, the wooden stake still impaled through his chest.

Caoilinn landed with a heavy thud. She groaned in pain and crawled backwards away from Edvard who stalked closer, towering over her. She whimpered as he glowered down at her, his jagged fangs bared. Edgar watched in horror and for a moment his eyes bore into Caoilinn's. He could see the fear in them – the desperate look of a woman who had seconds left to live – the flash of realisation that she was about to die.

'Please…'

Edvard laughed and shook his head mercilessly.

He crouched down beside the beautiful woman and took her head in his hands as if to comfort her. She sobbed and a red tear streaked her cheek – blood.

'Shhh, fair lady, shhh,' Edvard said gently, his voice eerily soothing.

'You don't have to do this, my lord,' Cormac blurted, his voice breaking with terror.

Edvard ignored Cormac's plea and leaned right in towards Caoilinn. He kissed her on the forehead as another bloody tear fell down her pallid, fragile cheek.

'Please…' she whimpered.

Edvard made a movement as fast as lightning. There was a crack and a pop as Caoilinn's neck broke and her head was torn from her body. The sound made Edgar sick to the stomach as he watched in disgust, unable to tear his eyes away. He slunk further back into the shadows, fearful that he might meet the same end, should he be caught, but he could not erase what he had seen.

Edvard held Caoilinn's severed head high by her long, golden locks and it disintegrated in his hands. Her body dropped to its knees and crumbled to dust, leaving behind only her white dress and the ashes of her very being.

'Your kind do not deserve being blessed with our gift. You are not worthy of becoming Unsterbliche.'

Cormac and handful of remaining guards stared open mouthed, unable to believe what Edvard had just done. He merely chuckled and his followers joined in the eerie chorus.

'Give me the boy or I will not hesitate to kill the rest of you,' Edvard demanded venomously; his deep, authoritative voice sounded harsh and threatening. 'Or I could just take him and have you all killed anyway. It matters not to me.'

'The boy is innocent. He has done nothing to you.'

'His blood is fresh. He is a mortal, untainted by our affliction. How long must we hunger for fresh blood?' Edvard said coldly.

Cormac didn't reply but he nodded, a solemn expression of understanding crossed his sharp features and for a moment, Edgar caught him turn to look at him, a hungry gleam in his eyes and he licked his lips. Had he just sided with Edvard?

Edvard turned to his followers who waited obediently, as still as statues, ready to fight and then, with a flick of his hand he muttered flippantly:

'Kill them all.'

The command hadn't even left his lips before the creatures leapt into action. The little girl who had attacked Edgar leaped into action and fought bravely alongside Cormac and the others who had guarded the room. It was chaos. The sound of snarls and roars filled the darkness. Shrieks of agony and eruptions of dust as the vampires from both sides met their demise.

Edvard rushed towards Edgar, leaning forward as if to give himself more momentum as he sprinted. He flung himself to the ground and reached under the table, grasping for Edgar who screamed, his voice lost amid the tumultuous racket of the battle raging around him.

He pushed himself against the wall and thrashed out, kicking at Edvard. Edgar noticed the wooden stake still sticking into the Unsterbliche's chest and with one hard kick he shoved it further into the flesh, deeper into his chest. Edvard screamed and fell backwards, writhing in shock.

Seizing the opportunity to escape from his cornered position, Edgar crawled from under the table and lifted a broken door from a cupboard that lay on the floor. He brought it down hard and flat onto Edvard's body, hammering the stake even harder into his heart. Edvard screamed and exploded into a cloud of dust as the stake pierced his cold heart. The fighting stopped abruptly as the cloak Edvard had worn floated to the ground and came to rest atop his pile of ashes. It was as if his followers were attuned to him, as if his death was felt by them all and stunned them.

The man who had driven Edvard's car ran forward and fell to his knees by the pile of dust and clothes. He was still in human form and had been stood by the side lines, just watching until now.

'Master!' he bellowed.

Tears of crimson blood streaked his cheek as he picked up Edvard's cloak and buried his face in it. His heaving sobs turned into angry groans and they slowly transformed into roaring, triumphant laughter. The other enemies froze, their attention on him.

Taking advantage of the momentary distraction, Cormac rushed to Edgar's side and put his arm around his shoulder.

'Are you alright?'

'I...I...I...killed him,' Edgar gasped, spluttering his words. The adrenaline pumped fast through his body and everything seemed to move faster. His gut clenched and had there been anything left in his stomach he would have thrown up again. Did this make him a murderer?

'We need to get out of here,' Cormac whispered, casting his eyes around the room, nodding discreetly to his allies. They nodded back, noticing his motion. 'You've bought us some time, but not enough.'

Edvard's chauffeur got back to his feet, turned to the others who had frozen in the shock of leader's sudden demise.

He swung the cloak over his shoulders and fastened the clasp.

'Kneel,' he hissed. 'I am your new Lord and Ruler. The rule of Edvard Dardanoss is over, and now begins the age of your Third King, Vladimir Gorganov!'

They obeyed immediately. They dropped to their knees and bowed their heads – all except Cormac's allies who skirted deftly out of the way without Vladimir noticing as he gloated over his power, looking down victoriously upon his new followers – his people, his puppets. They were his to control now.

'Quickly, we must go now,' Cormac demanded, steering Edgar around. A grumbling, scraping sound echoed behind him and as he turned, he saw the allies crawling through a hole in the back of the fireplace.

'I lost something. I can't leave.' Edgar muttered but Cormac didn't hear and pushed him towards the fireplace.

'Where do you think you're going?' Vladimir roared, rounding on them. 'You dare to commit treason by not bowing to me?'

'You are not my Lord and Ruler. We follow the path that the Almighty Creator laid before us. *He* is our Lord and Ruler. We will never bow to false gods,' Cormac said as he stood protectively in front of Edgar who froze, his eyes flicking between Vladimir and the secret crawl-space in the fireplace.

Everyone had gone through now – all except him and Cormac.

'You insult me and try to steal my fresh blood. You will pay for this crime,' Vladimir snarled as he stormed towards Cormac.

'GO!' Cormac yelled and Edgar realised he had no choice – he couldn't go for his coin which still lay somewhere in the foundations of the house underneath the floorboards.

Reluctantly, he turned and crawled quickly into the hole in the wall. Cormac backed up and followed Edgar along the low, narrow tunnel. Cobwebs tangled in his long hair and fat spiders crawled along the walls, so close to his face. Edgar tried his hardest not to pay attention to them – he hated spiders, they made his skin crawl. Instead he focussed on the dim orange glow of light in the distance, trying to block the sounds of screaming behind him as the fight began once more.

Edgar reached the other side and climbed to his feet. He frantically wiped the webs off him and plucked a spider off his shoulder. Just ahead there was a stone staircase lit by a flaming torch. He waited for Cormac to emerge, not knowing where it would lead.

After a moment, Cormac appeared, his scarred face pallid and pitiful in the dim, flickering light cast by the flame. Long, clawed hands shot through the hole after him and Edgar screamed but Cormac began to tug at a chain on the wall until a portcullis began to descend...but the Unsterbliche kept crawling through.

'Come on!' shouted the little girl from half way down the flight of steps.

The clang of the chain and the screech of metal against stone rang in his ears painfully. The first Unsterbliche managed to climb out and rushed towards Cormac in a frenzy.

'We have to stop them,' Edgar said to the girl and ran back up the stairs.

'It's me you want,' he bellowed. 'I'm the mortal.' The creature turned and stared at him. Without hesitation it dived upon him and Edgar dodged out of its way, noticing another Unsterbliche was almost through.

Cormac continued to pull on the chain and the portcullis dropped down on top of the vile monster. The creature writhed and screamed in agony as the sharp spikes dug into its back; blood poured from the wound and it burst into a cloud of dust and ash. The portcullis reached the ground with a solid *CRASH*.

Edgar turned to see the Unsterbliche dive at him again and once more, he ducked out of the way. He grabbed the flaming torch from the wall and held it out at arms length, swishing it around as if to frighten the beast and keep it at bay. The Unsterbliche recoiled, holding its arms up to its face.

A face appeared at the portcullis – its snout twitched and its mouth was wide, baring its horrible fangs. Its hand shot through a square hole and waved desperately, trying to grab Edgar's ankles. He swung the flame at it and it screamed, crawling away into the darkness.

'Pass me that,' Cormac demanded, striding forwards and snatching the flame torch from Edgar's hand.

His face was twisted with fury and rage as he stormed towards the Unsterbliche that retreated, terrified of the fire. Cormac was close to it now and thrust the torch right at the creature. It screamed and burst into flames, writhing and squealing. It lashed out at Cormac and Edgar who dodged its dangerous attacks and began to head down the stairs.

'But it –'

'It will die,' Cormac assured Edgar, as if he had read his mind; his red eyes gleaming with triumph.

Cormac took Edgar's hand and led him down the stairs quickly, the torch held aloft to light the way. Edgar glanced back, still hearing the roars of the dying Unsterbliche who screamed and writhed, a mass ball of flame. It appeared at the top of the stairs and raced towards them and Edgar's stomach churned. The smell of burned flesh was unbearable and the sight of its face; of its flesh, peeling and melting was enough to give him nightmares. It ran down the stairs after them, arms outstretched. In its haste, it stumbled, fell face first and bounced down the hard stone steps, crumbling into ashes and dust. There was nothing left glowing embers like the remnants of firewood in a hearth at the bottom of the stairs.

Edgar sighed a breath of relief as Cormac encouraged him to run onwards.

'I'm sorry you had to see that but there was no other way,' he said softly, his Irish accent tinged with concern.

Edgar didn't reply.

His eyes were wide with catatonic horror as he let himself be led down the stone staircase and along a brick-lined tunnel.

Somewhere far back from the portcullis the voice of Vladimir rang echoed after them.

'This is not over! You will pay with all your lives!'

At last, Edgar hoped he might now be safe; he could rest, but his heart told him not to trust his saviours – they were Unsterbliche too, judging by their glowing eyes and fangs. The young girl had already tried to kill him and maybe they weren't interested in protecting him at all – maybe they wanted him for his blood like the others but it was a risk he had to take. They had proven themselves trustworthy so far and Edgar knew he needed to take all the help that he could get until he could retrieve his coin and use it to escape again.

– Chapter Nine –

Underground

They moved in silence and at a steady stride, following long, dark tunnels where water dripped down the mossy stone walls and pooled on the floor.

Splosh. Splosh. Splosh.

Their echoing footsteps were the only sound. The light from the flame torch cast just enough light to see a few metres ahead and behind but everything else was consumed by blackness. Edgar shivered as they descended a slope so steep that steps ran up either side of it and the brick arch of the tunnel was so low they had to bow their heads to move through it.

It seemed that the further they went in, the narrower and smaller it became. This combined with the darkness and being in the company of the Unsterbliche who could turn on him at any moment made Edgar feel anxious. He wished that he had taken something – a splintered table leg or anything he could have kept as a weapon but it was too late to turn back now. He had to trust that he would be safe. These people had done their best to protect him so far and he had no other options but to trust them.   'Where are we going?' Edgar asked, his voice sounding much louder than he had expected in the silence as it echoed along the labyrinth of tunnels.

Cormac didn't reply. Neither did the girl, Bryony.

'I don't know where I am or what the hell is even going on. Can I just get some answers?' Edgar demanded, growing more frustrated. 'Please.'

Again there was no reply as Cormac and Bryony continued to lead him along wordlessly.

'I dropped something before. A coin. It fell through the floorboards back there and I need it. It's important.' Edgar insisted. Unsurprisingly, he didn't receive a reply again.

Edgar stopped walking and folded his arms across his chest. Enough was enough. He was tired, hungry, angry. He was hurt and bleeding and he had been pushed to breaking point – he had almost accepted that he might die. It was wrong. It wasn't him – he wanted home and his cat and his mother. He wanted home cooked food and his bed. He wanted safety and comfort but most of all, he wanted answers. *What did this all have to do with Betty?*

'How do I know I can trust you anyway?'

Cormac stopped dead in his tracks and turned slowly; his gaunt, scarred face, half-hidden under long straggles of greasy dark hair, appeared more treacherous in the flickering amber light of the flame torch.

'You can't know,' he whispered in a quiet, hoarse tone that made Edgar shiver. 'But I could have left you out there to be torn apart by the Ältere'

'What? I thought they were Unsterbliche?'

'So are we...all our kind are...but our society is split. I'll explain later, now keep it down and keep up.'

Cormac turned and continued to walk with Bryony by his side. Edgar took a deep breath and quickened his pace to keep up with them.

It wasn't long until the tunnels widened and in the distance Edgar could see a hefty wooden door. It stood slightly ajar and through a gap, a light shone: the light at the end of the tunnel.

Edgar followed Cormac and Bryony over the threshold and someone slammed the door shut behind him. He turned with a quiet gasp of surprise. He was trapped now. The remaining guards who had survived the attack on the house stood around solemnly or slumped on the ground, heads in their hands; their new company caught their attention and in an instant, all eyes were on them.

The room was small. Torches in sconces flickered away to light the dark and benches lined the wall. Aside from that, there was nothing except another door ahead.

Silence fell upon the group – a dense, solemn quiet. The injured and exhausted fighters seemed tense and stared at Edgar in a way that made him feel uneasy, their cheeks streaked with crimson tears.

'My friends,' Cormac said softly, his voice splitting the quiet like a knife. 'We suffered a great loss today but those who fell did not fall in vain. The bravery and loyalty shown by you all – your sacrifice for a world of peace and order will be remembered. The Ältere may not show their fear but they are afraid. Their Lord and Leader, Edvard Dardanoss was killed right before their eyes by this mortal boy and they will not forget it. Tonight, I join you in mourning, I share your pain for my own sister Caoilinn stands among the dead, but aside from our loss, this was a victory none of us will ever forget and so we must understand...balance has been restored.'

The allies remained as still as statues, their glowing eyes dangerous and filled with fury and sadness for the lost but Cormac's words struck a chord.

'I understand, brother, that we have had our vengeance and we have finally destroyed the dictator, Edvard, but Vladimir has taken his place. We're no further to peace than we were before nor will we be until we murder every single one of them.' The voice, again, tinged with a strong Irish accent came from the shadows and a man stepped forward into the light. His thin, pallid face looked like wax; his sharp cheekbones were streaked with crimson tears and his mouth curled into a grimace. The features were familiar – he was absolutely, undeniably one of Cormac's family.

The only real difference was that while his brother's hair was long, his was short.

'Eoghan, no,' Cormac said, shaking his head in disapproval.

'Caoilinn was my sister too and her loss cannot be simply swept aside.' Eoghan hissed venomously. 'She was one of us. She was our flesh, our blood. We were family! How dare you dismiss that?'

It was tense. Edgar glanced between the people, wondering what he had been caught in the middle of.

'I don't dismiss anything. Caoilinn was brave and her loss will haunt us, but do you not think she and those who fell tonight were done a favour?'

From the many that had been in the house, there were less than ten of them now: Cormac, Eoghan, Bryony and four others.

'Brothers, please,' another man stepped forward. He looked just like Cormac except his handsome face was scarless and his steely eyes weren't quite as sunken. 'Not while we have company.'

Silence fell and it was clear that Cormac found it hard to hold his tongue. He glowered at Eoghan and turned to face Edgar with the others. They seemed to turn in unison, their eyes slowly drifting over to him as if he had caught them by surprise and they stared.

Edgar tried to shake off the feeling of unease, of the sensation that he was shrinking before them to the size of an ant. There was something in the demonic, glowing red eyes that frightened Edgar. They were unnatural and it felt like they could see inside him, into his very soul. He could feel them tearing into his mind, into his deepest secrets and darkest fears. He wanted to speak out – to question everything, but when his mouth opened his voice stuck in his throat.

'Who is the boy?' asked a pretty woman dressed in tattered rags. 'Why did you bring him down here?'

The ripple of suspicion spread across those gathered in the room and all eyes burned into Edgar, devouring every inch of him.

'This is family business, I urge the rest of you to leave,' Cormac demanded.

'But who is he?' the other man asked.

'A traveller.' the woman said. 'The travellers' know not to come here. They haven't even tried to help us for at least a century and those few who get lost are killed before they could even run. This one though, he fought. He killed Edvard.'

The woman eyed him with keen interest; Edgar felt his heart skip a beat and his face flush red. He had only acted on his instinct – he hadn't meant to cause this trouble. He hadn't meant to spark this friction in the group.

'The boy is special. And that is something we need to discuss in private.' Cormac insisted, his tone wavering on impatient.

The others grumbled among themselves and then someone spoke out.

'He took away our chances. If one of you had killed Edvard, you'd be Lord and Leader but he did it; a mortal.'

The frustration bubbling inside reached an intense level. He couldn't stand it any more. So many people talking about him, about what he did and why and making assumptions. It was time to say something:

'Excuse me, I don't understand,' Edgar said, finally finding the courage to speak.

Cormac turned to the others.

'Please, leave us.'

They looked annoyed.

'Bryony, you too,' Cormac said, pointing to the door.

The little girl grumbled to herself and folded her arms defiantly.

'I'm not a child,' she said angrily, her eyes flashing dangerously.

'Bryony. Please.'

'We are all centuries old, brother. I am not to be treated like a child.'

'Very well, you may stay,' Cormac decided instantly. 'The rest of you, go. Leave us, this is family business.'

The handful of others obeyed immediately and left the room through a small wooden door in the back, all except Eoghan, the little girl and the other man.

'Now to business,' Cormac said darkly, a quizzical eyebrow raised, 'Who are you? You're a traveller, I can see that but like Clarissa said, your kind stopped coming here over a century ago and though there's the odd slip up, they don't live long enough to tell the tale – I doubt they'd even known they were here before the Unsterbliche attacked and murdered them.'

Edgar stood, rooted to the spot; his eyes scanned the room for a way to escape. There was nothing – just a door in front and a door back to the tunnels behind. Edgar remained resolute. He held his tongue and stared at his captors, biting his bottom lip nervously.

'We don't want to hurt you, if that's what you're worried about,' Cormac said gently, confirming what Edgar had known deep down. 'Now what is your name?'

Still, Edgar didn't speak but it wasn't because of a reluctance, it was out of sheer terror. Not fear of the company he found himself in, more of the horror of his situation. One minute he had been at home and something impossible had happened. He remembered standing on the coin, hearing it crack. He remembered how he had passed out but when he woke, he had been transported here, wherever here was. He had been weak and scared but he had fought and whatever had happened, he knew had happened because he had stood on the coin but now that was lost beneath the floorboards of the house above.

'What is your name?' Cormac requested again, this time with more urgency.

Edgar's silence was not a sign of disrespect. In a way, it was a sign of ultimate respect because here, with these people, he could pause. He could relax for a moment and try to come to terms with what he had faced since his arrival without having to plead for his life.

'I'm Edgar,' he muttered eventually. 'Edgar Harold.'

'Okay, Edgar Harold, come with us. We need to get you bandaged up,' Cormac asked kindly. He strode over to Edgar, put an arm around his shoulder and directed him towards the door that the others had gone through moments before.

Edgar's heart sank. In the heat of the moment, the adrenaline surging through his body had made him forget all about his injuries but Cormac's words made him crash back to reality and suddenly he was very aware of the sticky blood that trickled from his stinging cuts; his body ached with bruises and he felt terrible.

'There's nothing to be afraid of, you're safe here,' Cormac smiled. Edgar gazed blankly at him, still feeling uneasy about the mouthful of needle sharp fangs.

'Come,' he repeated, opening the heavy door and gesturing for Edgar to enter.

Despite feeling cautious, Edgar knew he had nothing to lose and his feet began to move without him even thinking. As soon as he noticed, a tiny part of his brain held him back so his footsteps were tentative but he passed through the door, over the threshold into the next room and his jaw dropped.

He stood inside a giant stone chamber with an arched ceiling with long tunnels spreading off in all directions and lit by flaming torches held in rusty iron sconces. Water trickled down the slimy, mossy walls and deep trenches cut across the ground, full of dirty water.

'This way,' Cormac said, taking Edgar's hand gently to lead him. Cormac's skin was soft and cold to touch; his firm grip was reassuring and a rush of warmth spread through Edgar and for the first time in this world, he knew for absolute certain that he was safe.

Cormac led the way along with Edgar by his side and the others following close behind. The steady *drip, drip, drip* of water echoed down the tunnel mingled eerily with the heavy footsteps.

Finally they came to another door and Cormac held it open, ushered Edgar inside and waited for the others to follow. The room was small and dark. Cormac rummaged in his pocket, pulled out a box of matches and struck one. The flame flickered, casting long shadows across the stony walls and Cormac lit a candle on the bedside table.

Once they were all inside, Eoghan, the last in, slammed the door shut. Cormac took Edgar's arm and sat him down on a small bed. It was hard and uncomfortable but Edgar wished nothing more than to lay down and pass out. He was exhausted by everything – the pain, the panic, the sheer terror of what he had just endured.

'So,' Cormac began as he rummaged through an old wooden chest at the foot of the bed. 'How did you come to be here?'

'I-I-I...' Edgar began, 'I don't even know. It was something to do with the coin. I stood on it by accident and I passed out. I woke up on the streets of the city and then they – those vampires – they chased me and I had to hide in the house but I dropped the coin and it fell through the floorboards but I need it. I have to get it back. I have to go home.'

His words flew from his mouth so fast and with no breath so he could barely control them. The sounds slurred and mingled into an unintelligible mess. Cormac pulled out an armful of medical supplies and crossed over to the bed.

'Oh.'

Cormac sat beside Edgar and poured a strong smelling liquid onto some cotton wool which he began to dab on Edgar's wounds. It stung sharply and Edgar cringed.

'We need to go back for the coin. Please, you've got to take me back.'

'But you killed Edvard,' Bryony squeaked excitedly. In the half-light she appeared reminiscent of a porcelain doll. 'You killed the strongest of all the Unsterbliche. Not even we could do that.'

'I had to do something. I didn't even mean to do it it if I'm honest...but I had to try. He would have killed us all,' Edgar replied as if it were nothing, gritting his teeth as Cormac continued to bathe his wounds. 'Please, listen to me...we have to go back. I need to get out of here. I can't stay – it's too dangerous. I need to go home.'

'You murdered the Lord and Ruler, Edvard Dardanoss and you will suffer the consequences of your actions,' Eoghan snarled. He leaned against the wall casually, his eyes narrowed in discontent. 'We all will.'

Edgar's heart skipped a beat. Was that a threat?

'I'm sorry. I thought I was helping,' Edgar said, his voice struggling to push past the anxious lump in his throat – something about Eoghan made him feel unsure about the company he found himself in.

'Now they will not rest until they have revenge on all of us, especially you,' Eoghan snarled viciously. 'If they catch you here again, they will tear you to pieces and lap your blood from the walls, floor and ceiling. You have crossed them and they will never forget your face; and by helping you escape, their hatred for us has been stirred.'

Eoghan was not happy. His tone was sharp and his brothers seemed to have picked up on it.

They looked nervously at him as he walked over to Edgar and crouched face to face with him.

'You have as good as killed us all.'

Eoghan's crimson eyes flickered treacherously and his jaw clenched tight. He cracked his knuckles and Edgar shivered, not knowing what to expect – was Eoghan going to attack him?

'That is why I need to get my coin and go home. I can't stay. If they find me, I'm as good as dead.'

Again, Edgar's pleas seemed to fall on deaf ears as Eoghan continued rambling, full of his own self-importance. His eyes fell upon the clumps of cotton wool, stained red with Edgar's blood. He opened his mouth to speak but found himself distracted, as if the sight of blood hypnotised him and overtook every one of his senses. He inhaled deeply, a dark grimace spread across his lips and his hand reached slowly for the cotton wool but Cormac grabbed his hand and twisted it backwards so far that it looked as though it might break.

'I don't think that's a good idea, brother,' he snapped in a voice barely louder than a whisper.

'Please,' Eoghan gasped and suddenly Edgar pitied him. The pathetic expression on his once sharp, strong face; the Hunger blazing in his eyes and the desperation that filled that one, simple, wavering word. It was clear he struggled to keep himself together, after all, blood was sustenance to his kind and he had gone without for so long.

'Colum!'

The other man who had remained silent stepped forward.

For the first time Edgar saw him properly. He looked just like Cormac but his face was less scarred and his features were slightly softer.

'If you want blood, there are plenty of rats, Eoghan,' Colum said, his Irish accent undeniably the same as his brothers.

He stepped in to pull him away but Eoghan struggled as his brother dragged him from Edgar. Colum slammed him into the hard wall with a *thump* and held him there by the throat but it didn't phase Eoghan. Instead he just laughed a cackling, manic bark that sent chills down Edgar's spine.

'There are ripples spreading across the city of Arden, right now. Small at first, just whispers and plots of revenge but those ripples will turn to waves and Vladimir will make sure we regret this night. You made history tonight, Edgar Harold, and what the consequences will be, none of us know. But one thing is certain. They will impact all of us.'

Edgar's eyes widened in fear. Eoghan's words struck terror into his heart like the wooden stake he had driven through Edvard's during that fateful moment in which the future of this world had changed – that pivotal moment that he had shaped.

'If only you had let me do it. I could have been the Lord and Leader. I could have brought in a new age of peace across our world,' Cormac sighed, as he began to cover Edgar's neck with a thick, soft bandage; his tone tinted with sadness at what could have been.

'But how could you? It was passed on to Vladimir,' Edgar said, bewildered. 'We saw it happen.'

Cormac smiled and shook his head. He muttered something quietly under his breath and turned to Edgar once more.

'By our customs the one strong enough to kill the Lord and Leader takes his place, but if a mortal were to ever succeed, the first sired by the deceased would take the role. Nobody ever thought it could happen, that a mortal would strike down the Lord and Leader of Deuathac, but you did and Vladimir was Edvard's first.'

'And so dawns the new age of dread,' Colum sighed, still holding onto Eoghan whose laughs had turned to sobs, the gravity of the situation weighing heavily on him. Colum let him go. 'Vladimir was close to Edvard and he will not take this lightly. Of course, he has power – a power he spent his entire life jealously searching for but now he has it, his word is law and he will never forgive you...or us.'

'Sounds like he should be grateful. Without me, he wouldn't have that power now,' Edgar said darkly, hoping that in some strange, roundabout kind of way, Vladimir might spare him in respect of his inadvertent aid in his rise to power.

'I'm afraid not. If anything, I fear Eoghan is right, you have doomed us all,' Colum said, speaking up. He sighed. 'We should have never come here.'

'But we did,' Cormac replied. 'It's done.'

'The Ältere outnumber us, they make our lives hell. This is no existence!' Colum snapped as he began to pace rapidly, his frustration growing. 'Look what's happened to us? It's us and them. It always has been ever since-'

'Ältere?' Edgar probed. He had heard the word before mentioned in passing but still had no idea what it meant. Nobody had explained to him.

'Oh, of course. Sorry,' Cormac replied kindly. 'Our kind are the Unsterbliche. We are all infected with the Unsterbliche Affliction, a virus-'

'A virus?!' Edgar exclaimed, slowly backing away from the others around him. He needed to be as far away as possible – he didn't want to catch this disease – to be infected with whatever it was that would make him become one of those creatures.

'It's harder to catch than you'd think,' Colum jumped in, sensing Edgar's fear. 'There's no need to panic.'

'How is it caught?' Edgar asked 'Just out of curiosity.'

'It takes just one bite to become infected but the virus is not triggered until the infected subject ingests Unsterbliche blood.'

'So you have to willingly become...what you are?' Edgar said, shocked. He glanced around those who surrounded him, wondering just why they had chosen this life when they seemed so opposed to it now. Maybe things had once been different. Perhaps, it had been the only option – that or death.

'Yes.'

'What made you choose this life?' Edgar blurted, unable to stop himself. His face flushed red as soon as the words had left his lips and covered his mouth as if he were unable to believe what he had just asked – it had been, perhaps, too personal.

'That is not a story for now,' Eoghan interjected, his tone sharp. 'But, back to the point; to answer your question, the Ältere are a line of Unsterbliche dedicated to following the laws and customs set by the first Unsterbliche: Aldous Arden.'

'And I suppose his laws were bad?' Edgar laughed uncomfortably, already knowing the answer.

'You've seen them in action. You understand. The Ältere were always brutal in their actions. Deuathac – our world – fell within months. The last humans struggled to survive but they were no match for the Ältere's overwhelming strength and numbers and soon, they fell. With no human blood the Ältere began a period known as "The Hunger." Luckily for them, lost travellers' like yourself would often appear but they would be snatched up and their blood harvested but sometimes, in the heat of the moment, accidents happened and these travellers were turned.'

'Do you think they would have turned me?' Edgar asked, his voice creaking, almost ready to break as he considered what might have been.

'They would have torn you to pieces and let you die. The Hunger has taken its toll for too long,' Cormac replied, his expression stony as he watched Edgar shiver nervously. He took a deep breath as he finished putting the last bandage around Edgar's arm. He patted Edgar on the back and sighed. 'All done.'

Edgar smiled weakly at Cormac.

'Thanks.'

'Glad you're all patched up. You'll be better in no time.'

And then it hit him. *"You'll be better in no time,"* Edgar squealed in excitement as the idea hit him.

'You said this Unsterbliche thing is a virus, right?' he began. The others nodded blankly, unable to grasp where this was heading. 'Every virus has to have a cure!'

He was greeted with silence and stony expressions. Cormac shook his head in dismay.

'Unfortunately not this one,' he sighed. 'Did you really think we hadn't already tried?' Eoghan spat.

Edgar felt stupid, his face blushed bright red and he shrank inside.

'Aldous Arden was the founder of Arden Industries – the leading corporation in pharmaceutical research. He could cure anything but even he couldn't cure this,' Bryony said matter-of-factly. Edgar had almost forgotten she was there, watching sheepishly from the corner, keeping quiet.

'But Aldous Arden was the first of the Unsterbliche. What if he never wanted to cure himself? What if he never even tried to make a cure?' Edgar insisted. 'There has to be a way!'

'How?'

'I don't know...but there's got to be something.'

'What would you suggest? We start brewing deadly concoctions and use our own kind as guinea pigs?' Eoghan hissed, his anger rising once more.

'But what if there was a way? You wouldn't have to suffer anymore.'

'There is no cure. Rumour has it that Aldous created the Unsterbliche Affliction as a cure for something else and one doesn't cure a cure.'

Eoghan's words echoed in the pressing darkness. The single candle on the table flickered and the long shadows flitted around the walls in its orange glare. The cold, pallid faces of the vampires appeared much creepier in the half-light and Edgar began to feel uneasy.

'What could be so terrible that someone would create...*that* as a cure?'

'That's the thing,' Colum said quietly. 'He called it a cure for mortality.'

Edgar's jaw dropped and his gut twisted nauseatingly. He frowned, unable to comprehend Aldous's motives – wishing he could understand why someone would actually make a willing decision to live the way the Unsterbliche did.

'It was a cure for death?' Edgar said, making sure he was right. 'He created it so that people wouldn't die?'

'Or so the story goes. Personally, I think there is so much more to it.'

'But death is a natural part of life. Everyone has to do it-'

Colum shot Edgar a cold look that made him stop. There was silence for a moment in which Edgar couldn't find the words to say. It was awkward...until Cormac spoke again.

'In the early days there were many of us: The Verstossen, they called us. It meant the outcasts.'

'Were?' Edgar said, hoping he wouldn't offend by pushing his questions further – the questions brewed in his mind and he couldn't help but blurt them out. 'What happened to you all?'

Colum, Cormac, Eoghan and Bryony looked at one another and their eyes gave away a great sadness which made Edgar feel terrible for intruding.

'There was a war. The Ältere decided their elite master race had gone too far by allowing those who were not of this world to become like them. We lived among them, as part of their world until they had enough and attacked. We fought and most of the Verstossen were killed, yet some of us survived long enough to make a pact and sign a treaty, promising that as long as we remained underground, never to be seen or heard, we could live. If we broke that agreement, the price was the life of one of our own – this time, the cost was too high. So many of our kind, including...our sister...Caoilinn...'

Colum told the story so dramatically, every single word fraught with emotion – such anger and hatred towards those who had forced him into this life.

'So you're not from here either?' Edgar asked, his curiosity piqued.

'Correct,' Colum nodded. 'We-'

'Enough!' Eoghan interjected, his voice raised. 'He already knows too much.'

'But-' Colum spluttered, trying to find the words to stand up to his brother.

'Eoghan's right. That's another story, for another time,' Cormac replied sternly.

Colum looked hurt, as if he had been waiting for a reason to tell his family's tale.

'I despise this place, I despise this life! What kind of existence is this? Trapped underground like animals, forced to drink the blood of rats,' he raged, kicking a chair. For a moment it seemed his anger and frustration might get the better of him but he managed to keep hold of himself and calmed. He slumped against the wall and slid to the ground, head in his hands.

'If you don't like it, why don't you end it. I could always do it for you!' Eoghan barked angrily and a tense silence fell over the room.

After all he had seen in the last hour or so, something told Edgar that Eoghan's temper was always this fiery and he wondered if this was possibly a common conversation and it made him feel awkward to overhear it.

'What's it like, immortality?' Edgar asked curiously.

'Like torture,' Colum said, his voice on the verge of breaking. Then he snapped and began to sob; crimson tears streaming down his cheeks.

'Then why suffer?'

'Because immortality comes with a price.'

There was silence again. The family looked around at one another, their expressions grim as if they were looking to one another for permission to explain further, none of them really wanting to be the one to talk about it as if there were a terrible, dark secret.

'Your soul,' Colum replied eventually. His voice was quiet and timid.

'Your *soul*?' Edgar repeated, confused.

'You don't understand, do you?'

Edgar shook his head.

'Every mortal retains a soul. The soul lives on after death – you can welcome the afterlife, you live on, but we cannot.' Colum explained solemnly. 'Our disease, the Unsterbliche Affliction, it eats away at the soul until there is nothing left. Once we die, we are gone forever. No chance of an afterlife, no ghosts for us.'

'But that's horrible.' Edgar whispered quietly, suddenly coming to realise just how sad that could be. Until recently he would have questioned the idea of the afterlife but he had seen enough ghosts to know there must be something out there – some kind of echo of a life after death.

'And that, Edgar, is why I fear death. That is why we all fear it.'

'I can understand that.'

Silence fell over the group. Bryony took Colum's hand gently and held it reassuringly. He smiled down at his little sister and hoisted her up into his arms. She wrapped her arms around his neck and rested her head on his shoulder.

'Speaking of ghosts,' said a stern voice, as if it were distant but right in his ear at the same time. 'I think you'll be needing this.'

Brother Bradley slowly faded into view, his translucent form flickering and stretching and shrinking in that strange, ghostly way. Edgar blinked in surprise and the monk glided towards him, hand outstretched, holding out the coin.

'Brother Bradley,' Edgar said, taken by surprise; his eyes fixed on the ghost.

'What?' Colum said, looking confused.

'Brother Bradley, can't you see him?'

'No.'

'And you're supposed to be scared of ghosts,' Edgar laughed.

'Take it,' Brother Bradley handed Edgar the coin. It was the exact same one he had lost between the gaps in the floorboards. The one he thought he would never get back.

'But how-?'

'I will not be around to help you forever, Edgar. Next time, do not be so careless.'

The ghost's words echoed in his mind, a quiet, sharp whisper. Edgar rolled the cold coin between his fingers and then, with a kindly smile and a wink, the ghost was gone.

'Who were you talking to?' Colum demanded.

'Just a ghost,' Edgar said as he held out the coin to show them. 'He's a friend. He brought this back for me. I can go home now.'

'There was a ghost here?' Bryony whimpered, clinging tighter to Colum.

'He's gone now. He came to help. He's kind.' Edgar replied, trying to ease Bryony's fear, except it didn't quite work so simply. The Unsterbliche's fear of ghosts was evident among all of them, but poor little Bryony the most of all.

Their expressions were grave and slowly dissolved into anger.

'He brought one of them right to us!'

'I didn't do anything! He came to help me!' Edgar snapped back at Eoghan.

'I think it's time you left,' Eoghan hissed viciously. 'We confess to you our greatest fear and then moments later, you deliver that same thing right to us.'

'But you didn't even see him, it caused no harm!' Edgar argued. 'And besides, it's not like he's bad. He came to help me.'

'I don't care,' Eoghan said.

Edgar looked anxiously from the coin in his hand to Colum and gave him an apprehensive look. From the looks on the faces around him, he knew he was in trouble. It was time to leave before Eoghan turned on him even more. Even the cold expressions from Cormac and Colum who had been nothing but kind weren't particularly friendly anymore.

'Thanks for everything,' Edgar said gratefully. 'Wish me luck.'

'I'm sure we'll meet again,' Colum said 'But for now, take care.'

'Thank you all again. I owe you.'

Before the family could reply, Edgar dropped the coin on the floor, thinking back to what he had done the last time and stamped his heavy, black boot onto it. He gritted his teeth and screwed his eyes shut tightly, awaiting some sort of signal to let him know it had worked.

It began almost instantly; a tingling sensation in his toes, which gradually grew into a burning fever that crept up his body, warming him up. As the warmth reached his chest there was a falling sensation that Edgar had only experienced before when he had nodded off then jolted awake again but this time, rather than waking up, all turned black and Edgar fell unconscious yet again. He had no idea where he was going to wake up, but hoped and prayed with all his might that it would be somewhere better than here – somewhere he might meet somebody who could help – someone who cared.

– CHAPTER TEN –

MR. GRIFFITH

Edgar landed with a solid *thud* that jolted him back from unconsciousness. His whole body hit the ground as if he belly-flopped from a diving board into a swimming pool. He groaned in pain and struggled to breathe with the wind knocked out of him.

Edgar slowly opened his eyes but it was pitch black.

'I'm blind,' Edgar gasped out loud in panic. 'I can't see!'

He lay still for a moment, frozen in terror; his eyes open so wide and unblinking that they stung and began to stream with water. Hot tears trickled down his cheek; he wiped them away but after a moment of staring wildly, shapes began to emerge from the darkness – vague outlines of what could only be boxes and shadows cast by objects in the room.

'Where am I this time?' Edgar wondered to himself as he fumbled around on the ground, feeling for the coin. His fingers brushed against its cold face and he picked it up, stowed it in his pocket and tried to get to his feet.

As he climbed up, the sickness and dizziness hit him hard again and Edgar wondered if the horrid side-effects of travelling would ever ease. He lay still, waiting for the nauseating, stomach-churning sensations to pass.

Eventually, feeling confident that he was well enough to get up and look for some kind of way out, Edgar pulled himself to his feet and took his first uneasy step forwards.

It began without warning; the deafening, shrill siren. It split the air all around him, rising and falling so loud that Edgar thought his eardrums might burst. He screamed as his heart leapt into his throat and he almost tripped over his jelly-legs.

'Please remain calm. The police are on the way,' wailed a calm, almost robotic female voice.

Edgar swore under his breath, cursing the voice that came intermittently over the siren.

Edgar covered his ears and stumbled in the darkness but nothing could block the irritating sound and he couldn't see a thing. Hastily, he moved through the blackness, unable to even see his hand in front of his face. He staggered around, bumped into boxes, tripped over something on the floor and fell into the wall. He put his hands out to protect and support himself. Quickly, Edgar slid along the solid wall, feeling for a door or any way out.

'Please remain calm. The police are on the way,' said the chilling voice again.

After what felt like an eternity of panicked fumbling in the pitch black, eventually, he found it – a door handle. He twisted it and the door opened. He found himself in a dark room. It was pitch black save for a red flashing light that split the blackness in time to the wailing alarm and cast a blood red glow over everything. Edgar groaned as the light washed over the room and he saw it was a long corridor filled with glass-fronted display cabinets filled with curiosities: ancient pottery, leather-bound books, spiky dangerous-looking implements and an assortment of other strange things.

'It's a museum,' Edgar thought to himself. 'But this isn't the Rotundra.'

He set off along the narrow corridor at a run.

Edgar followed the path which twisted and turned as if the whole floor of the museum had been turned into a maze of cabinets and displays.

Edgar moved cautiously, hoping there was nobody in the building and rounded a corner. He groaned as the red light lit up the space before him. *Hall of Historical Costume* said the neat words on a plaque beside the arched doorway. Beyond the open door, wax dummies in costumes of various time-periods stood around the room, their lifeless faces staring out with forced smiles and dead, glassy eyes.

Edgar froze and stared at the mannequins dressed in traditional garbs from each period of history – everything from Neanderthals to Egyptians; Medieval to Victorian, trying to build the courage to move through them. There was no other way. The only path was to pass them...to walk between them.

Edgar's heart pounded and he shivered, a cold sweat ran down his forehead. He had always been scared of wax dummies. There was something menacing in their blank faces – something about the imitation of life in an inanimate object that looked as though it might actually be alive. It was something that unnerved him deeply – something that seemed even scarier as the flashing light washed over them, creating long shadows that made it seem as if they were moving.

'You've just escaped from vampires, you can do this,' he told himself and took off at speed, holding his hands up to shield his eyes from the dummies that posed either side of him; their ancient, waxy faces pale and frozen into sinister smiles. Old, unbrushed wigs perched on their heads, looking like they might fall off; the costumes moth-eaten and dusty.

Before he knew it, he had passed the cavemen, the Egyptians and Romans, the Vikings and the medieval knights and ladies. He looked directly at the floor as he strode with purpose down the aisle. He followed the path around a corner and looked up to see how much further he had to go.

Ahead he could see the Elizabethans with ruffles around the neck, the pompous dandies of the eighteenth century and beyond them the Victorians.

'Hello?' shouted a rough voice in the distance.

Edgar froze. Had he imagined it?

'Hello?' came the voice again. 'Who's there?'

At the end of the hall appeared a hefty, wide shadow – from this distance it was impossible to make out any features but he knew it was a giant of a man from his deep, gruff voice and the sheer size as wide as he was tall. The red light continued flashing in time with the rise and fall of the shrill siren and Edgar panicked.

'The police are on the way, you know?'

The man turned towards the hall of historical costume and headed towards him at a sprint. Edgar's heart skipped a beat and he flung himself to the ground, ducking into an alcove behind a dummy of a woman in an Elizabethan dress.

'I know you're here somewhere! Just come out now and we can resolve this before the police get here.'

The voice was closer and as Edgar peeked around the dummy he saw the man searching the room. He looked around the back of the dummies and checked into alcoves.

'He's going to see me,' Edgar thought nervously and while the man was distracted at the other side of the room he crawled under the wide skirt and curled up underneath, his heart pounding in his throat.

'Where are you?' the man grumbled, his voice close.

As the blood-red light flashed, Edgar could see through the material and the shadow on the other side. The man came closer and crouched down. Edgar's heart fluttered. He held his breath and froze as still as the dummy he hid beneath. The shadow of the man's arm was long as he reached out and grasped hold of the skirt. He began to lift the heavy material and Edgar gulped hard. He brought his knees up to his chest and wrapped his arms around them and buried his head into his legs. The gap between the floor and the material began to widen as the man lifted it further.

'Jaspar!' shouted another voice and the man dropped the skirt. Edgar let out a quiet sigh of relief, unable to believe his luck. 'Did you trip the alarm?'

'No, sir.'

'You mean there's an actual intruder?' the other man demanded, an authoritative tone to his voice.

'Yes, sir.'

'You're meant to be my security guard, Jaspar!' The other man sighed in frustration.

'I'm sorry, sir.'

'You will...' the man's voice trailed off. 'I'm sorry. It's okay. Just help me find them.'

'And the police? Do we really want them trawling through here?'

'Tell them I set it off by accident. I came into work late. I was tired. I forgot the code.'

The large man nodded and with that the two men took off at a sprint, their footsteps thudding into the distance. Edgar let his breathing return to normal and he climbed out from under the skirt, uneasy on his wobbling legs. Suddenly, the dummies weren't as scary as they were before – not now he knew there were actual real people in the building with him - people who couldn't find him...what would happen if they did? Surely that could only mean trouble.

Edgar kept low and moved quickly, ducking in and out of the shadows until he reached the end of the hall and peeked around the door. It was quiet – nobody there. He stepped out and closed the door behind him. It wasn't as dark in here; a glass ceiling above let in the silvery moonlight from a full moon that hung in a cloudless, starry sky.

The pale light spilled over a long room filled with a myriad of plants, like a jungle. A wooden walkway with railings on either side, made a path through them and Edgar sprinted along, ducking around the leafy bushes and flowers that spilled out over the railings. In among them he caught glimpses of creatures – taxidermied animals leering at him with glassy dead eyes. Edgar sprinted as fast as he could, hoping to find a way out of the maze of plants and animals. He passed a pond and a small clearing with a bench; all the while, the rising, falling wail of the alarm like an air raid siren rang in his ears, fevering his brain and making him panic. The men could be anywhere in there with him and he needed to get out.

Eventually he reached a heavy wooden door at the other side.

He pushed it hard and found himself in a long corridor with a black and white tiled floor.

'This is just like the Brunswick Museum,' Edgar thought to himself, his mind wandering back to the other museum that his mother worked at in Scarborough. 'It's almost the exact same layout.'

The long corridor was dark and filled with glass display cabinets filled with curiosities: ancient cups and jewelry and books. Edgar rushed past doors on either side of the hall, hoping the men were nowhere nearby.

Still, the alarm rang and rang. Its horrible wailing tone had stopped now and it was simply a long, flat tone like a life support machine hooked up to a corpse.

'Please remain calm. The police are on the way.'

Edgar had lost count how many times he had heard the voice now. It had bellowed at him countless times as he rushed to find an exit in a vain hope of escape – a fire exit, anything and it did nothing but make him more anxious.

As he reached the end of the hall and looked out of the window the night sky was lit up with flashing red lights. Cars zoomed down a long, hedge-lined driveway to the front of the building and he knew the police had arrived.

He ducked, hoping the police wouldn't see him stood in the window and peeked over the edge of the window-pane. The police stopped and climbed out of the cars; swarms of men and women dressed in dark leathery armour with a spiky, metal badge on the breast. Upon their heads were black helmets with plastic visors that hid their faces from view and on the belts around their waists, he noticed holsters holding guns.

Edgar panicked. He was so caught up in his terror that he didn't even notice the alarms had stopped. Everything was silent as he stared out of the window, noticing his reflection, gaunt and anxious.

In the glass, a face appeared behind him. A face of a rugged man with rough ginger beard and short, red hair, flecked with grey; before Edgar could even turn he felt the hand on his shoulder and he yelped.

'So it's you who set the alarm off?' the man grumbled in a threatening tone. 'How did you get in?'

'I-I-I...' Edgar's voice trailed off. He couldn't think of anything to say.

'Who are you?' The man demanded dangerously.

Edgar glowered at him, refusing to speak.

'I'm Mr. Griffith. I own this museum,' the man said gruffly. 'You?'

'Ben Brown,' Edgar replied quickly. He knew wherever he was, his name wouldn't be known but giving a false name just came naturally.

'So, Ben Brown, I take it this is yours?' Mr. Griffith said, holding up Edgar's coin between his fingers.

Edgar didn't reply. His eyes focused on the coin – he had to have it back. He needed it to escape.

'It's yours, hmm?' Mr. Griffith demanded. 'How did you come across this?' the man demanded viciously.

Edgar refused to say a word and remained silent – partly out of fear but partly for refusing to dig himself into deeper trouble.

'I suppose you have a right to remain silent but the police will not treat you as fairly as I will,' Mr. Griffith hissed and for the first time, there was an almost gentle trace in his voice and as far as Edgar could see, he didn't have a weapon unlike the police outside.

Without a word, Edgar's hand shot out and reached to snatch the coin but Mr. Griffith pulled it away quickly, grabbed Edgar's hand and forced it back towards his wrist. It bent so far Edgar thought it might snap. He moved fast and twisted Edgar's arm behind his back, keeping his wrist bent too, with a strength that seemed impossible from that weak looking man.

Edgar gasped in pain as he felt his shoulder crack.

There was nothing he could do.

He was completely under Mr. Griffith's control.

'You're coming with me, Mr. Brown,' he snarled. 'I want some answers from you.'

'What about the police? They'll be in here any second. You'll never get your answers.'

'Jaspar will tell them it's a false alarm.'

Edgar didn't need to reply. He could hear in Mr. Griffith's voice that he was even more scared by the prospect of the police than he was.

He led Edgar along the corridor and through a door at the end.

They crossed the threshold and the man flicked a light switch on. A dim glow spread across the room and Edgar saw they were in an office. There was an ornate oak desk in the centre, filled with piles of paper under a small desk lamp; behind the desk was a wall of shelves filled with dusty leather-bound volumes. A green leather sofa sat along the side wall with a tall, bronze lamp beside it.

'Sit,' Mr. Griffith said, pointing to the sofa and Edgar obeyed, terrified of what might happen if he didn't. 'So, I'll ask you one more time and one more time only: How did you get in here?'

'I...I fell asleep and when I woke up, everything was locked,' Edgar said, thinking quickly.

Mr. Griffith frowned at him and stroked his stubble. His face was beginning to show signs of age with vague wrinkles and crows feet in the corner of his bright, youthful eyes. He got up and looked out of the window. Even from where he sat, Edgar could see the dark sky flashing with blue and red light.

'The police are still out there. I could hand you over to them,' he said sternly. 'But this intrigues me. It's certainly not from any of the museum displays.'

He lifted the coin up and studied it closely, before sitting down in the high backed chair at his desk. He opened a drawer, rummaged through it and pulled out a magnifying glass to examine the coin even more closely.

Edgar watched him in silence. His heart pounded and his head spun dizzily as he tried to work out what to do next. He needed to escape but he couldn't run – Mr. Griffith had his coin and he wouldn't make it past the police who had surrounded the building.

Suddenly, Mr. Griffith looked up at Edgar, frowning. He stared for a moment and shook his head. There was something in the way he narrowed his eyes and glowered coldly at him, that chilled Edgar to the bone; he felt himself shrink to a minute size under the cold gaze.

Heavy footsteps outside echoed loudly and Edgar knew the police hadn't believed Jaspar's story.

'They're coming. You should hide and I'll take care of this,' Mr. Griffith whispered hoarsely as he glanced back out of the window.

Reassured by Mr. Griffith's defence, he jumped to his feet and searched for somewhere to hide. He could see nowhere to go – everywhere would be in plain view.

BANG! The door of the room along the corridor crashed open and a few seconds later, someone shouted 'CLEAR!'

Edgar stood rooted to the spot, staring around. The man gestured towards the sofa and Edgar crawled into the gap underneath it. It was only a small place and he barely fit but he scrunched himself up as small as he possibly could and lay there, watching. It was dusty and uncomfortable, but Edgar knew he had no other choice.

BANG! The door burst open and several police officers stood there, guns raised and torches shining at Mr. Griffith who sat innocently at the desk. They inched towards him, guns pointing at his head.

'You could at least knock,' he spat defiantly.

'Sir, please stand up and put your hands where we can see them,' grumbled a deep, strong voice from beneath the visor of a helmet worn by a motorcyclist.

He obeyed.

'I'm the curator of this museum, you know,' he said and the police officer pulled a small electronic device from his belt. He pointed it at the man; a mechanical whirring sound was followed by several bleeps then a robotic voice confirmed:

'Mr. Lachlan Griffith, age forty-four, curator of the Scarthburg History Museum.'

'I do apologise, sir. Just a precaution.'

'I understand, but I find it particularly disconcerting when I come into work late to get some paperwork finished and you burst in here and treat me like a criminal,' Mr. Griffith snapped as he sat back down in his seat and folded his arms. 'Especially when my security guard has already told you it was an accident.'

'So it really was you who set the alarms off?' the officer asked; his tone suggesting he didn't believe him.

'Yes. I'm tired, I forgot the code to stop it – had to keep trying.'

'Then why come to work if you're tired?' another officer asked.

'This paperwork has to be completed in two days. Have you seen it?' Mr. Griffith replied hastily, gesturing to the enormously thick piles of paper on his desk.

'And you're alone?'

Mr. Griffith looked around the room, his eyes glancing at the spot where Edgar hid. Edgar didn't dare even breathe. His heart seemed to have stopped and that very moment froze. What if Mr. Griffith gave away that he wasn't alone? What if that quick glance had been to give Edgar away?

'Does it look like anybody else is here?' Mr. Griffith sneered. 'Obviously not, aside from Jaspar who is paid to be here. Now if you don't mind, I'd like to get back to my work.'

'I'd watch my tone if I were you,' the police officer snarled, cracking his knuckles. 'Wouldn't want anybody to get hurt, would we?'

'Get out!' Mr. Griffith demanded coldly, his eyes fixed upon the officers who stood before him.

The tension was unbearable and and as Edgar struggled to control his breathing his nose began to twitch. The thick dust under the sofa made his nostrils itch and he felt a sneeze struggling to burst out. He held himself together, shaking.

'It'd be a shame if someone were to accidentally pull the trigger on a man they thought was an intruder. Such an unfortunate tragedy,' the officer laughed, raising his gun and aiming it at Mr. Griffith's head. It was harder and harder to hold in the sneeze, it had become painful and Edgar trembled as he tried to keep still and ignore the itch.

'I won't say it again,' Mr. Griffith said, staring straight up at the gun, without a trace of fear in his voice. 'Leave.'

BANG!

ATCHOO!

The gun exploded, masking Edgar's sneeze and he wanted to scream. The sound deafened him and he screwed his eyes tight shut to avoid seeing the splatters of blood as the bullet split through Mr. Griffith's head.

'Next time, It'll be through your brain,' the police officer said coldly. He turned and stomped out of the room with the others, leaving the door open behind them. Their footsteps dissipated as they moved further down the corridor.

Edgar slowly opened his eyes and saw Mr. Griffith sat at the desk as still as a wax dummy; his face drained of all colour. Edgar didn't dare move – half-expecting the police to rush back into the room and put a bullet through Mr. Griffith's head and then his once they discovered he really had been there. The man slowly climbed up from his seat, crossed the wooden floor and closed the door, twisted the key in the lock until it clicked.

He turned to the sofa and looked down at the gap underneath it.

'You can come out now,' he said. 'It's safe.'

Edgar scrambled from the tight space in which he had wedged himself and brushed the dust from his clothes.

'Now you see why I couldn't hand you over to them,' Mr. Griffith said quietly as he passed Edgar and sat back down at his desk.

'Thank you,' Edgar said, his voice catching in his throat as he thought about what might have happened had Mr. Griffith not been so kind.

'You don't need to thank me,' Mr. Griffith said coldly. 'You'd be no use to me dead.'

He stared at Edgar with a dangerous gleam in his eye and in that instance Edgar thought that perhaps he was about to be met with a fate worse than a bullet through the head.

'I-I-I...'

'This doesn't belong to you, does it?' Mr. Griffith snapped, holding up the coin.

'It does. It was given to me by an old friend,' Edgar replied.

'If that's the case, Ben Brown isn't your real name, is it?'

Edgar opened his mouth to reply but paused. Should he lie again or just tell the man the truth? He didn't know. He struggled to find the words but the conflict in his mind caused him to choke.

'That's my name,' he spluttered, eventually.

Mr. Griffith eyed Edgar suspiciously and shook his head.

'You're a terrible liar.'

'What does it matter what my name is?' Edgar demanded.

'I don't like liars,' Mr. Griffith said, his eyes narrowed and his voice was tinged with malice.

'If I tell you my name, will you just let me go?'

Mr. Griffith looked thoughtful.

'If you tell me that and why a bleeding, bandaged boy is in my museum in the middle of the night with no explanation then I might just consider it.'

Edgar felt uneasy. He wondered whether he could really trust Mr. Griffith or if he was just trying to extract information and as soon as he got it, he would be disposable.

'You can trust me,' Mr. Griffith said, stroking his beard and watching Edgar through his narrowed, icy eyes. 'I don't want to hurt you.'

'Okay,' Edgar said cautiously. 'I can't tell you how I got here. I'm not sure myself.'

'Did it have something to do with this?' Mr. Griffith asked, holding Edgar's coin up.

'Yes. It...it's crazy, you'd never believe me.'

'I've seen lots of crazy things over the years. Try me.'

'Well, I kind of stood on it and it...it reacted...to my boots or something. It brought me here.'

'Your boots? May I see?' Mr. Griffith asked curiously and Edgar nodded. He lifted his foot up to show Mr. Griffith the worn down soles with the perfect imprint of the traveller's token in it.

'Now the coin slots into that indentation. It fits perfectly. The metal hooks hold it in place. Try it.'

Mr. Griffith reached out for the boot and looked as though he were about to slot the coin into place. Edgar's plan was working. Soon he would be out of here – hopefully back to safety.

'So you mean it made you appear here?'

'Yes!'

He retracted the coin.

Edgar's heart sank as he stared at it while Mr. Griffith rolled it between his long fingers. He had been too smart to fall for Edgar's trick.

'And what *is* your name?'

Edgar stared back at him through narrowed eyes, his brow furrowed as he tried to figure out whether he truly could trust the man.

'Come on, I'm Lachlan Griffith. You know my name.'

Edgar took a deep breath and exhaled. Surely his real name didn't matter here. Wherever he was, he was a stranger. He technically didn't even exist.

'Fine. I'm not Ben Brown. I'm Edgar...Edgar Harold.'

He wasn't sure if he had been heard. Mr. Griffith had turned towards the window, distracted. He looked outside where the flashing lights still lit up the dark.

'They're still there,' Mr. Griffith said solemnly.

'I need to go,' Edgar replied. 'I need to find my way home.'

Mr. Griffith turned back to Edgar, his eyes scanned him up and down and he smiled sweetly. There was something in the way he looked at Edgar that made him smile in return – a warm kindness that seemed much more genuine than the vampires whom he had been convinced would have torn him apart for his blood had they been a little weaker-willed. This was something authentic; the faint wrinkles of the crows feet in the corner of his were proof that he smiled with his eyes as much as his slightly lopsided mouth.

'Promise you'll be careful out there, Edgar,' he said and his tone was severe. 'Get yourself away from here and somewhere safe.'

'I promise,' Edgar said. 'I've seen enough already. I just want to go home.'

'Really?'

'Yeah. You wouldn't believe me.'

'After all that's happened tonight I think I'll believe anything.'

'There were vampires and-'

Edgar's words were cut short. Mr. Griffith held a finger to his lips and Edgar stopped speaking, listening hard. Footsteps were coming. Mr. Griffith dashed across the room and peeked around the door of his office then ducked back inside quickly. He slammed the door shut and pressed his back against it.

'What's the matter?' Edgar whispered.

'They're coming back.' Mr. Griffith gasped, his face drained of all colour.

'The police?'

He didn't have time to answer.

The heavy *CRASH* was enough to confirm their return. The door shuddered under the weight of the smash and then again *CRASH*.

'Let us in, Lachlan! We know you're hiding someone in there.'

Mr. Griffith held the door tightly shut, pushing against it with all his might.

'Edgar, you need to go!'

'What about you?'

'I'll be fine. Just go!'

Edgar dashed around the room looking for somewhere to hide.

CRASH.

CRASH.

CRASH.

With each blow the door weakened and Edgar still had no idea where to hide. Mr. Griffith's face dripped with sweat as he barricaded the door.

'You need this!' he said quietly, pulled the coin from his pocket. Edgar's eyes lit up and Mr. Griffith threw it to him. Edgar reached out but missed. It landed on the floor with a tinkle and rolled towards the window.

Edgar dived for it but...

SMASH

He was flung backwards by a heavy force as two armed police officers smashed through the window clinging onto ropes that they had abseiled in on. They formed a barrier between Edgar and the coin – a barrier he needed to cross. He tried to duck around them but they spread out wide like someone confronting a bear in the wild.

One of them pulled a strange electronic device from his holster and pointed it at Edgar. It whirred and then pinged.

'Subject unknown. Please try again.'

CRASH

The door burst open, sending Mr. Griffith flying to the floor.

He hit his head hard and the police officers stepped into the room to observe the chaos.

Then came the strange mechanical whir and the metallic ping.

'Subject unknown. Please try again.'

'He doesn't exist, boss.'

'He's one of them!' the officer snarled through gritted teeth as he pulled his visor up and grabbed his gun from his holster. He took aim at Edgar.

CRACK.

The shot only just missed and Edgar screamed as he dived to the ground, covering his head with his hands and scrambled between the legs of the brutish officer before him. Sharp splinters of glass ripped his clothes and tore his skin deeply as he reached out for the coin.

He cried out in pain but it didn't matter. This was better than being shot – this pain reminded him that he was alive. His fingers slipped around the cold metallic surface of the coin.

CRACK.

The second shot just missed too and instead smashed a vase on the desk.

Edgar quickly got to his feet and stumbled around. He saw Mr. Griffith on the ground, unconscious. There was nothing he could do...he had been so kind to him. He had helped and been a genuine friend but he hadn't been able to give any answers. He was a poor, innocent man caught up in the middle of something that even Edgar didn't know what it was. Both he and Edgar were victims of circumstances far beyond them.

Edgar turned to the officer who aimed the gun at him, his face twisted with hatred and anger. Edgar dropped the coin back to the ground as he pulled the trigger one final time.

Time slowed.

STOMP.

Edgar felt the familiar crunch of the boot contacting the coin.

The speeding bullet didn't slow down.

A warmth tingled in Edgar's toes and spread up his leg. It reached his chest quickly and he fell to his knees, struggling to breathe. The warmth turned to a searing, agonising pain. Edgar looked down, his eyes wide in terror as the dreadful realisation washed over him. Blood poured from a wound and seeped through his t-shirt. The bullet had hit him square in the shoulder.

The officer grimaced as he strode over towards Edgar. The slow motion was horrific, like the world was slowing down and coming to an end – to his end. He was dying and this was his mind trying to compensate, trying to hold on to those final few seconds of life.

Mr. Griffith stirred and he looked up, feebly. His hand reached out for Edgar.

'Edgar!' he muttered, blood running down his face from a gash on his forehead where he had hit his head as he landed on the floor. 'I'm so sorry.'

'Help...' Edgar croaked, the word barely making it out of his mouth.

The officer pulled Mr. Griffith to his knees and pointed his gun at him. He held his hands up in surrender Edgar screamed out loud but it was no use. *BANG.* The sound of the gun reverberated all around. Thankfully he never saw the bullet impact or the splatter of blood. Instead he felt a hard jolt like a sudden drop and everything turned black.

– CHAPTER ELEVEN –
THE STRANGLED FOX

The scream split the air and roused Edgar. A salty stench mixed with rotting fish infiltrated his nostrils that flared at the unexpected smell. A gentle breeze ruffled his hair and he realised he was alive. The scream came again – shrill and piercing. It was so loud that it made Edgar's ears hurt. He lay flat on the hard, bumpy ground, unable to move. Nausea swirled in his sharply cramping gut and his head spun in circles. He opened his eyes wearily and his vision blurred. He looked around trying to focus, weak and unable to move at all. All around him were shadowy figures. He couldn't make out who they were and he blinked repeatedly, trying to clear his sight. His eyes were hazy, his body bruised and sore but he was alive at least.

Then he remembered...the bullet. His hand reached for his chest but there was no wound. How that was possible? Edgar had no idea. It was a miracle. He glanced down at his body; his shirt was still covered in blood and there was a hole where the bullet had hit him but beneath that torn fabric, the flesh was shriveled and soft like scar tissue. Edgar wondered if perhaps he were truly dead and this was all in his mind but that was when the voices came through the fog of his inner thoughts and brought him back to reality.

'He just appeared there. Fell out of the sky, he did,' said the hoarse voice of a woman as more people joined her side and gathered around Edgar. They stared, whispering amongst themselves and pointed at the stirring body sprawled on the cobbles beside the canal.

Edgar scrambled to sit up and rubbed his eyes until he could see.

'Y'alright, darlin'?' a woman asked in a rough Cockney accent. Edgar looked at her, his head still spinning dizzily.

She crouched down to become level with him but kept her distance as if he were a rabid animal that might attack at any moment. She wore a filthy, soot-covered dress that appeared to have ripped and frayed over many years judging by the various patches which made it look more like a patchwork quilt than a dress. Her youthful face was afflicted with the onset of aging – the small creases of wrinkles and scars across her face. She reached a hand out towards Edgar and he took it in his own. It was rough and well-worked; her fingernails were chipped and jagged.

'I'll be...' Edgar's voice trailed off before he could say *fine* as a surge washed through his body and he fell forward and vomited a stream of bile all over the dull, grey cobbles.

The crowd shrieked collectively and retreated a couple of steps.

'Where am I?' Edgar asked groggily, wiping the slimy residue from his chin.

'Poor dear, 'ave you been drinkin'?' the kindly woman asked again, shuffling closer to Edgar and put her arm around his back. 'One too many down The Strangled Fox, eh?'

'No…I just…'

'You've dropped this, pet,' the woman said, holding out the coin in her hand.

Edgar snatched it from her and stared at it. He turned it over in his hands, staring at the symbol imprinted on its shiny metal surface.

'Thanks,' Edgar replied, 'do you know what this symbol means?' he asked hopefully and the woman looked suspicious.

'No,' she said. 'Never seen it before.'

The crowd simply stared and Edgar scowled back. All of them were dressed in shabby old-fashioned clothes: the men in crinkled flannel shirts and woolen waistcoats with flat caps and baggy trousers; the women in dirty patchwork dresses and their long, greasy hair tied up with rags. Every single one of faces around him, caked in grime carried the distinct look of having led tough, working-class lives like the people in old photographs from the Victorian Age.

'What's going on?' Edgar said, shuffling backwards in retreat from the sinister crowd.

'You tell us!' a man exclaimed and Edgar noticed that there were many gaps between his stubby yellow teeth. 'You's the one what dropped out the sky.'

'I didn't…I can't have…'

'Well you did. We all sawed it with us own eyes,' the man replied and the crowd around him muttered in agreement, nodding and looking to one another for support of their claims.

Edgar remained silent, his heart in his throat.

'Watch out. 'E might be an angel what was no good and got chucked out of 'eaven. Why else would 'e fall from t' sky?' a wizened old woman warned, her face was so wrinkled that her beady eyes were hidden deep beneath the folds of skin on her brow.

'No, no I'm not an angel!'

Edgar laughed at the absurdity of the accusations but he still felt rough – his head ached and his brain felt like icy mush. His whole body was stiff and rigid but his legs were like jelly so he couldn't stand. His stomach turned again. He took a deep breath, inhaling the chilly, salty air that was tinged with rotting fish.

'What's that you got, lad?' a scruffy man in rags asked, leering at him as he reached out and grabbed Edgar's wrist. His grip was strong and all Edgar could do to keep his coin safe was to wrap his fingers tight around it.

'It's nothing,' Edgar protested.

'You gots money, I know it,' the man snarled and Edgar shook his head defiantly.

'I haven't. I haven't got anything.'

'Come on, spare a coin for a poor old man,' he growled aggressively, pressing his face right up against Edgar's, baring his blackened teeth. His breath stank of stale beer and up close, Edgar couldn't help but notice the man's eyes were bloodshot and red. There there were crumbs of bread and various other rotting morsels of food caught in the bristles of his tangled, graying beard.

'I don't have anything to give,' Edgar demanded and the man snarled, his hand gripping Edgar's wrist ever tighter.

'Stop him, please...' Edgar begged to the people in the crowd who just watched like this was some kind of street performance and the whole event, merely an act.

'*Get off me!*' Edgar insisted, trying to break free of the man but he was still too weak.

'Give me your money and you can go,' the man hissed and Edgar shook his head. 'You got silver. That's enough to buy me ale for a day or two.'

The tramp let Edgar go and muttered to himself under his breath. He turned away and reached deep into his jacket pocket, fumbled for a second and then, before Edgar could even react, he spun back round and knocked Edgar flat to the ground. The man jumped on top of him, pinned him down under his heavy weight and held a sharp blade at his throat.

The people in the crowd screamed and dispersed without a care for Edgar, only fearing for their own safety.

'Please,' Edgar gasped, barely able to breathe under the weight of the man pressing down on him. He didn't know what to do. He thought he'd faced the worst when Spencer used to corner him and beat him up at school but he had never been held at knife point before. He had, however, been chased by blood thirsty vampires and shot by corrupt police yet somehow managed to survive. This would not be the end.

He lay there, his whole body tense with adrenaline as he stared up into the fiery, mad eyes of the crazed man. He wanted to cry for help but knew if he did, the man would kill him there and then. There was nothing he could do but lay there and try to relax.

The hard cobbles beneath him dug into his spine until it hurt and Edgar took deep, wavering breaths to calm himself.

'Help an old man out, or I'll take your money from your corpse.'

As the man spat his words, flecks of spittle sprayed over Edgar's face and the bitter stench on the man's breath overwhelmed him. Edgar's stomach flipped and he retched.

'Don't you even dare.'

The man pressed the blade harder against Edgar's throat. He felt the cold, sharp tip dig into his flesh and for a moment he worried that it might already be too late – that it might have pierced the skin.

The man laughed madly as he brought the tip down to Edgar's shoulder and gently slid the tip of the blade down his arm to his wrist.

'Open your hand before I open your veins,' the man commanded, digging the knife into Edgar's wrist.

Edgar gasped, screwed his eyes tightly and shivered. His fingers clenched defiantly around the coin. There was no way he could let the man take away his only hope of escape. He just needed to buy time – to keep the man talking until he could muster the strength to break free and escape.

'You have 'til the count of three,' the man said.

'One,' he pressed the knife harder against Edgar's wrist and Edgar winced. He didn't know what to say.

'Two,' he increased the pressure and Edgar screwed his eyes tight shut – there was no time to think – no time to make a plan. It was now or never but he didn't know what to do.

'Wait-'

He stabbed the knife into Edgar's wrist before he had even counted *'three'* and Edgar screamed. The sharp, agonizing pain pierced through his whole body and his fingers flexed open instinctively. He tried to keep them closed but the pain was too much to bear. The man snatched the coin from Edgar's hand, jumped to his feet and rushed away.

'No!' Edgar shrieked, scrambling towards the wall to hoist himself up to his feet. He reached out for the rough, soot-blackened brick to steady himself and saw his injury.

A stream of claret blood streamed down his arm from the wound on his wrist. He ignored the pain, his entire attention focused on finding the man who had stolen his coin.

Edgar rushed along the side of the canal, stumbling over his boots as he moved along in the direction that the man had taken off in. He followed the path, half leaning against the crumbling soot-blackened wall to keep himself upright. The pain in his wrist was intense and he could feel the blood trickling down his hand and dripping from his fingertips, leaving a trail behind him.

Small boats sailed down the canal, filled with boxes and steered by bulky men who barked commands at one another.

'Help!' Edgar shouted, leaning over the rusted railings at the side of the canal. 'Please, I'm hurt. Help me!'

The men looked at him but turned back to their jobs and ignored his pleas. Edgar continued to run after the man who had vanished from sight. He had already lost him and could only guess his direction. As he came closer to the centre of the town, more canals crossed paths and joined each other, bridged by rickety wooden contraptions.

The air was thick with smoke billowing from giant chimneys in the distance and settled in the streets. Red brick shacks and houses, dirtied with years of grime and factory smoke lined the streets and haphazard wooden stalls were set up along the roadside. Rats ran among them, scavenging crumbs of bread and left-over bits of fish while skeletal people, no more than malnourished living corpses behind the stalls reached out as if begging for Edgar to purchase their filthy, rotting wares.

'I need your help, please,' Edgar said, holding out his arm. The blood flow was dangerously fast and he felt himself growing weaker with fatigue as life ebbed away. With every second his head spun more viciously. He couldn't go on. The stall-holders screamed at the sight of blood and even Edgar's pleas for help couldn't keep their attention. They shielded their eyes and turned away.

Edgar staggered down the street, reaching out and begging for people to help – becoming as desperate as those who had reached out for him. People shoved him aside and shot him cold looks of disgust. Nobody would help. To those around him, he was no better than one of the tramps on the streets – as far as they assumed he may as well have been injured in a bar brawl.

It was no good. The blood streamed faster his panic only made him feel dizzier.

'Stop,' he thought to himself. 'Just stop.'

He paused, leaned against a wall for a moment and took a second to calm down and think.

'Hold your arm up to your shoulder,' he told himself. *'It'll slow the blood flow. And stop running. It's making your heart beat faster – making you bleed out quicker...and above all. Stay. Calm.'*

He was impressed with his own advice but it was hard to follow. How could he not run when he needed to find the man? How could he stay calm when he could have gone anywhere with the travellers token?

Just as he was becoming desperate, Edgar noticed a crooked building on the corner. Its door was open and a lantern was lit in the boxy bay window that stuck out over the street. The rotting corpse of a fox hung over the door with a noose around its neck. Its orange and white fur was matted, its eyes were milky white in death and its pink tongue lolled out of its open mouth between sharp teeth. Edgar knew that this place was his only chance. A name, *The Strangled Fox,* was written faded gold letters on the black paint of a long wooden board above the window

The woman had mentioned that she thought Edgar had been drinking at *The Strangled Fox* and the man had stolen his coin to pay for his ale – the pub must be the place. It had to be. Edgar stumbled over to the window and peeked through the thin glass. The inside was intimate with small booths around the edge of the room and a few tables and chairs set in the middle. The wooden rafters hung low and the long bar at the back was deserted save for one man.

He stood there, talking animatedly to a beautiful young girl with long, wavy black hair and a pale, pointed face. Edgar had to look twice to believe it wasn't his friend Lilith – she looked just like her except a little older. She seemed angry; a frow etched across her brow and arms folded across her chest.

The man slammed his hand down on the bar and turned around, huffing furiously and Edgar saw the face – a face he would never forget. It was the man who had stolen his coin but he was armed and dangerous – there was nothing he could do. He was already weak and the loss of blood only contributed to that. In his heart, Edgar knew he was in a race against time until death caught up with him.

He slumped down against the wall, his head in his hands and tears streamed down his face. He was going to die and there was nothing he could do. After all he had faced since he had become lost and this would be what tipped him over the edge; nothing exciting or supernatural...just a disgustingly simple, human injury. A slit wrist. What a boring way to go?

But it wast not just that - his death was going to come in a place far from home, a place that seemed out of time. He knew his only hope of healing and home was with the power of the artifact that the man had taken from him when he had slit his wrist and placed this death sentence on him. If he died here his mother would never know what happened to him – he would just be another of those teenagers on the news who vanished and were never found. It would destroy her – first his father and then him…that was why he had to fight. Family. He would never give up for their sake. He had to get home. He had to retrieve the coin and he had to do it quickly.

There was only one thing he could do. He had to take back what was his and he would do whatever it took. The man had almost killed him – for all Edgar knew, he might still die. Desperate times called for desperate measures. Warm blood trickled down his hands and rage and fear swelled inside him, burning in every cell of his body as he imagined the face of the man who had done this to him. He didn't know what he would do but he had to do something – every second he wasted on feeling sorry for himself brought him a second closer to death. The time to act was now. After all he had been through over the past few hours had changed him. He would no longer allow himself to be a victim. He would become a fighter. A warrior.

Edgar glanced around the street and spotted a stall nearby where a woman was busy gutting fish with a sharp knife. The woman eyed him shiftily as he loitered, pretending not to watch her, while she continued to gut the fish and throw the innards into a bucket by her side. She was distracted for a moment by a flock of seagulls that swooped down and squawked, trying to steal her wares. She dropped the knife onto the counter, waved her arms feverishly and chased the birds away down the street.

While the woman tried to shoo the squawking birds away, Edgar marched over to her stall, his body pumping with adrenaline – the only sustenance that kept him going and grabbed the knife, before vanishing back into the crowd before she returned.

With the knife in his hand, Edgar stumbled back towards *The Strangled Fox*, his head spun and his heart hammered against his chest. He couldn't comprehend how in a matter of moments he had armed himself and decided to take such drastic action. He was scared – this wasn't him. It wasn't his nature.

'An eye for an eye,' Edgar thought to himself as he stumbled through the door of *The Strangled Fox*. A bell tinkled as it opened and he slumped through, holding one hand against the wall to steady himself. He gasped for breath and shuffled his feet, coming further into the pub. All eyes fell on him – on his wrist and the blood streaming from the wound, dripping onto the wooden floorboards around him. He gripped the knife a little tighter, scared by just how far this had gone.

'You can't pay with that,' insisted the beautiful woman behind the bar. 'I won't tell you again.'

'It's silver, innit?' the man snarled in a vicious, drunken slur. 'And at' end of t' day, silver is silver. Now get me my ale, wench.'

He grabbed the woman's wrist, pulled it towards him, prized her fingers open and thrust the coin into the palm of her hand and curled her fingers around it.

'*You!*' Edgar sneered, his weak voice broke in terror as he spoke and his legs turned to jelly. He raised his arm and pointed the blade at the tramp. 'That coin is mine and I want it back.'

The man turned slowly. His red, puffy eyes fixed on Edgar and looked him up and down as he lifted his hands into the air as if to surrender.

'It's money, lad. It comes and goes and belongs to nobody.'

'It is *mine*. And you stole it from me,' Edgar whispered hoarsely, his voice barely audible in his rapidly declining weakness.

'I will not have no brawling in my pub!' the woman shrieked from behind the bar. Edgar froze.

'I'm sorry, but please, you have to help me,' he said, his voice suddenly softer as he turned to the woman, appealing desperately for her help. 'This man stabbed me and he stole my coin. I'm bleeding. It won't stop.'

The woman looked down at Edgar's wrist – at the blood trickling down his hand and leaving a trail of crimson droplets on the ground behind him. She gasped in shock and covered her mouth with her dainty hand.

'MARTIN!' she screeched, her shrill voice splitting the air. 'MARTIN!'

Thundering footsteps sounded from somewhere above and in a matter of moments the door behind the bar burst open. A handsome young man rushed out dressed in black frock coat with gold trimmings and big brass buttons. His hair was combed back and tied into a ponytail and his trousers were tucked into a pair of big black boots. His wealth was apparent.

'Nessa? What's wrong?' he asked, springing to the woman's side.

'This boy needs help,' she said, pointing at Edgar and Martin raised an eyebrow curiously. 'He's bleeding. This man attacked him.'

'I gave him a chance to give me the money but he wouldn't. He was asking for it,' the tramp replied as if he had a legitimate defence.

Martin scowled at the man and then looked at Edgar who retreated a couple of steps, keeping the knife raised and pointing at the man who had attacked him.

'Put that down, son,' Martin said, nodding at Edgar; his eyes fixed on the blade. 'You don't want to do this.'

'I don't know what I want to do,' Edgar replied, jabbing the air between himself and his assailant with the sharp blade. 'I just want to go home. Whatever it takes.'

The man looked at Edgar, his eyes wide with fear.

'You wouldn't,' he laughed. 'Put it down.'

'Just like you wouldn't hurt me?' Edgar bellowed, raising his other hand to show the wound on his wrist. The blood stained the whole side of his body now. He could barely hold his arm up – the strength required was too much. This blood loss was dangerous – thankfully the cut wasn't too deep and had missed the main artery or he would have already been dead. 'An eye for an eye, I say.'

The tramp rolled his eyes.

'Time I just finished-'

He never ended his sentence. As he dived at Edgar, reaching for his own knife, a CRACK rang through the air and a shower of blood splattered Edgar's face. The man fell face-first to the wooden floorboards with a dull thud.

Edgar squealed and covered his eyes with his hands, smearing the blood over himself and he peeked through his fingers.

Martin stood behind the bar, arm straight out and the flintlock pistol aimed at where the man had stood.

'That's gonna take some cleaning,' Nessa sighed, her eyes wide in shock.

'You shot him...' Edgar gasped, staring at the body with the bloody hole through the back of its head.

'You're safe now,' Martin said kindly. He lowered the gun and jumped over the counter as Edgar sank to the floor, shaking.

It was too much. He had been pushed too far. His fight or flight instinct had taken its toll in the most unexpected way and Edgar wondered if he even knew himself anymore.

'I believe this must be yours,' the lady, Nessa, said as she came over to Edgar and crouched beside him with Martin. She pressed the cold coin into his hands.

'It's okay, now. He's gone,' Martin said, his gruff voice sounding as kindly as it could.

'Thank you,' Edgar whispered, barely able to force his voice to work. 'But I still need help. I'm hurt…I need to get home.'

'Nessa, grab a cloth, quick,' Martin commanded and the woman rushed off. She vanished behind the bar for a moment and returned with a dirty cloth which Martin took from her and wrapped tightly around Edgar's wrist. 'You need to keep it elevated.'

Martin took Edgar's hand and placed it against his chest, just above his heart. Edgar knew that this would only help temporarily. The damage had already been done – he was slowly dying. He knew the only way to save himself was to travel. Maybe, just like last time with the bullet, his wound would heal by magic…but he couldn't flee so quick. He owed his saviours. At least he had the travellers' token now. He could leave whenever he wanted. Another moment here couldn't hurt.

'This'll do,' Martin said as he finished wrapping the bandage. Nessa patted Edgar on the back. Her deep dark eyes locked onto his and she wiped a strand of her long, raven black hair out of her pale, elfish face. She smiled and Edgar returned it. There was something enchanting about the woman – just being in her very presence held him transfixed and made him forget that he was injured.

'Thank you, again,' Edgar said, unable to portray his gratitude to his saviors. 'But you didn't have to kill him.'

'You looked like you were going to kill him yourself,' Nessa said, her Cockney accent jarring with her stunning appearance. 'If Martin hadn't done it, would you?'

Edgar froze. The question hit him hard; just a few hours ago he had been sat comfortably on his bed at home and now he had faced so much adversity in so many hostile environments. He was alone, he was in danger. It was fight or flight and Edgar just wanted to survive. It had been him or the man and Edgar thought about how far he had been pushed to survive.

Edgar's forehead wrinkled as he thought deeply and he shook his head solemnly.

'Do you really think you would?'

Edgar thought again, struggling to find an answer.

'I wouldn't have,' Edgar lied. 'I couldn't. I only did what I had to do – just wanted to scare him.'

'We all have to do that here, my dear,' Nessa said and Martin nodded in agreement. 'It's survival of the fittest and unfortunately, sometimes, people die.'

'I didn't want that though. He was just a poor man, trying to survive too,' Edgar replied. His words were not sincere and didn't fool anybody. He just knew that he wanted to retain what little humanity he had left – or at least pretend to.

'You don't have to lie to me. I understand,' Nessa laughed and she winked darkly.

'Okay...maybe I would but I only wanted my coin back.'

He held the coin in his uninjured hand and squeezed it tightly between his fingertips. He looked down at it and rubbed the etched symbol, feeling safer to have it back in his grasp. He kept his other hand above his chest and the cloth wrapped around his wrist was so tight that his hand had turned numb but perhaps that was from his injury; either way, it didn't feel quite right. The cloth had absorbed some blood and turned red but the worst of the flow seemed to have stopped.

'Must be some special coin to chase after a man like that in your state,' Martin said, looking quizzical and Edgar merely nodded. 'Mind if I ask why?' Martin probed and Edgar held it out to show him.

'You saved me so I guess I can trust you,' Edgar decided after a moment of thought. 'God knows I need some friends out here.'

Edgar held the coin out and showed it to Nessa and Martin. They looked down in awe and then turned to each other. They nodded slightly and Edgar noticed the look of surprise between them. They beamed as they turned back to Edgar and he continued to explain.

'I was left a trail of clues that led me to this when my old friend died. I stood on it by accident and passed out. I woke up in some...place...and there were vampires and I barely escaped. I ended up trapped in a museum and got shot by the police and I ended up here and that's when that man cut me and took it. This coin is my only way home.'

'You're a traveller?' Nessa squealed. There was excitement in her voice and she clapped her hands together gleefully.

'A traveller?' Edgar asked curiously.

'A dimension traveller!' she said, looking at Edgar as though he were mad for not understanding. 'You can travel through the dimensions with that coin – it's a travellers' token.'

'Oh,' was the only quiet sound that Edgar could muster. His head spun dizzily again as he remembered his vivid dream about the monk, Brother Dominic and his exodus to the City of Krinka. He had been a dimension traveller too...but he was also a monk. Did that mean Brother Bradley was also a traveller? Was that why he had returned after all this time – because he knew Edgar was about to embark on this journey?

It made so much sense now; and his father had left him the boots that made this possible. Did that mean that he had been a traveller as well? And Betty! She had left Edgar the trail of clues – her obsession with finding a coin to go home...had she been a traveller? Perhaps she had kept watch over him since he was a child to ensure that he would become one too...but why him?

It hit Edgar with such a hard force that he felt it impact on his chest as his heart hammered against his sternum and he could barely catch his breath. It was too much to take in. It was incomprehensible that this moment had been in motion his entire life

– that everything leading to now must have been carefully planned for him.

'So you're new to all this, then?' Martin asked and again, Edgar nodded, trying to clear his head and think straight.

'I just need to get home. I don't belong here,' Edgar said. 'I don't suppose you could help me get back, could you?'

'I unfortunately don't know how to use the tokens. I only know of the legends that speak of travellers' and having met a few over my years of living and working in his pub,' Nessa said apologetically as he looked at Edgar.

'Can you at least tell me where I am?' Edgar asked desperately. 'I have no idea.'

'You're on Alpha Island. The main continent of Merimalima,' Nessa explained kindly and Edgar frowned, her words meant nothing to him. 'This dimension is called Merimalima. It is a world of oceans and seas patrolled by pirates and monsters. There are islands spread out over its waters and Alpha Island is the biggest, most important. Our trade and industry is based here in our factories and workhouses.'

'Wow,' Edgar gasped. He had seen the factories outside – industrial giants across the skyline.

'Do you know anything else about Dimension Travel or any of the other dimensions?'

Nessa opened her mouth to reply but was interrupted by the gang who burst through the door, their mouths covered by black bandanas tied around their necks and their eyes glinting dangerously under the shadow of their tri-corn hats.

'We 'eard there were trouble,' said a gruff, angry voice of their leader and Edgar shuddered. The men looked down at the wooden floor where the old tramp's body sprawled with a hole in his head and a pool of blood around him.

'We had to. He tried to kill this lad,' Martin said, sensing the danger as the leader of the gang reached for a holster tied from his belt and drew his flintlock pistol.

'He tried to kill me - stole my money and slit my wrist for the trouble,' Edgar explained quickly, hoping his answer would diffuse the situation.

The man curiously studied Edgar's anxious expression for a second, still keeping his distance. Edgar held up his wrist bandaged in the bloody cloth so the man could see he was injured but instead of showing sympathy, he just laughed.

'That fella had a hefty bounty on his drink-addled head. The same head you put a bullet in, so we're going to have to return the favour. You know the law. You take our bounty, you take their place.'

The gruff man shuffled forward and aimed his pistol at Martin.

'You have to leave,' Martin whispered to Edgar out of the corner of his mouth.

'I can't leave you like this.'

'I can look after myself,' Martin assured Edgar, a gleam of solemnity in his dark eyes.

Edgar nodded slightly.

'Make it look like an unfortunate tragedy – the outcome of a vicious brawl,' the leader said as he strode closer, his pistol still pointing at Martin's head. 'I'd say I was sorry but it's your own fault.'

The group of bounty hunters strolled further into the pub and jumped over the bar where they began to smash glasses and spill beer over the floor.

'Time to count your last seconds of this life,' the leader grumbled. 'Take it down from three.'

'Three,' Martin said, there was a defiance in his voice – something that told Edgar he had a plan as he stared up at the barrel of the gun.

'Two,' Edgar froze in sheer terror, his eyes wide and unblinking.

'One!'

The shot rang out and it happened in slow motion.

Martin dived, charged into his assailant and the bullet missed him. It smashed through the floor and Nessa squealed. The leader turned and tried to take aim at Martin again but Nessa dived on him from behind and managed to restrain him for a moment.

The other men reached for their guns and began to shoot blindly in their panic. Edgar screamed as bullets whistled past his head and narrowly missed him. He dropped his traveller's token to the ground and stamped down hard. There was a familiar tingling sensation in his toes and then a warmth that spread through his whole body. The heat hit his head and he collapsed, leaving behind the screams and echoes of gunshots as he fell into darkness.

He had no time to think or hope for safety. It was apparent there was none in this dangerous life. All he could do was think about getting out of there – of escaping to somewhere quiet but most of all, the realisation of what he truly was – a traveller – weighed heavily on his mind. All he could think was: *Why?*

– CHAPTER TWELVE –
INTO THE ICE

Edgar landed with a soft *thump* and an icy, cold shock shot through his body, causing him to jump up in surprise. The bright sun hung in a glorious blue sky and blinded him but he screwed his eyes up tight and held his hand up like a visor and his vision improved. Suddenly, he could see everything and he gasped in delight.

The view was astounding and despite his anxious feelings, Edgar smiled to himself with a quiet chuckle as he observed the vista with awe. He had landed at the peak of a mountain. It was rocky and half-covered with a blanket of powdery snow. He looked down at the imprint his body had left, like a dying snow angel and squinted in the bright sunlight. Across the horizon were more mountains, all of them covered in snow, pure and white and glistening.

A long, crooked path made of loose pebbles and crumbled chunks of rock led down the mountain side, curving and zig-zagging down steeply. Before he moved, Edgar looked down to the ground where he expected to find his travellers' token but it was nowhere to be seen. A pang of fear split through him and twisted in his gut but he lifted his foot and looked underneath the boot in desperation. It was still in place, hooked in with a metal clasp. Edgar unhooked it and held the coin in his hand.

'Where have you taken me now?' he asked out loud.

As he glanced down at the coin, it suddenly struck him that the pain in his arm was gone and when he looked at his wrist, he was surprised to see the wound had healed just like the wound in his chest had healed over from the bullet before, but now was not the time to try and understand the miracle. He had to find out where he was – find some help so that he could return home.

It seemed unlikely that he would find any people up here in the mountaintops but it was so beautiful that he couldn't resist exploring. He could leave as soon as he wanted, all he had to do was stamp on the coin. That much was clear now and that was one of many mysteries solved – at least he had one answer.

The sun burned down on Edgar, intense and relentless. He was taken by surprise by just how hot it could be at the top of a mountain – he had always expected that it would be freezing because of the snow but he was wrong. Instead of biting chill, he felt like he was burning alive and sweat trickled down his face uncomfortably.

The pebbles beneath his feet were loose and slid under his boots and as he reached the edge of a steep dip down, he could see far down below where lakes of clear turquoise water spread for miles and tree-covered hills spread across the horizon – just forests for miles and miles as far as the eye could see.

Taking a deep breath, Edgar began to navigate the steep hill, sticking to the path made from dull red and shiny silver stones. Chunks of white marble-like rocks, covered in moss jutted out from the side of the uneven surface beneath his feet; tiny plants with pretty royal blue petals grew along the side and water from the melting snow trickled down in a narrow stream beside him, towards the lakes at the bottom of the mountain.

The heat was too much and it was hard to keep going. It was only then that it hit him just how long it had been since he had eaten or had a drink. It was a thought that came at the wrong time and since it crossed his mind, it rooted itself there and refused to move until it made Edgar dizzy. He wiped beads of sweat from his face and continued, hoping to find a source of water before he passed out from dehydration. He thought to turn to the stream but it had gone now and taken a different path straight off the side of the mountain.

Buzz. Buzz. Buzz.

The sound came from nearby, quiet at first but growing louder and Edgar turned around, trying to spot what caused the horrible noise. The mountainside shimmered like a mirage in the heat and Edgar thought that he saw a shadow of a person stagger across the brow of the hill but he looked again and it was gone, along with the buzzing sound.

'I'm going mad,' he told himself. 'I just…need…water.'

He lumbered on, the exhaustion of his previous adventures finally catching up to him. His mind wandered back to the Unsterbliche – to the Nathaniel Family and the situation he had inadvertently caused there. He had killed their Leader, Edvard. Did that make him a murderer? The moment had gone and passed so quickly it felt like a blur and he couldn't even remember it clearly but the shock hit him hard like a speeding train.

'I killed someone,' said the voice in Edgar's head and he stopped walking and stared ahead blankly. *'I killed Edvard. It was me who finished him off.'*

'But he would have killed you. It's not even like he was a person. He was a monster,' he argued with himself, trying to justify his horrendous actions.

'It doesn't matter. I killed him.'

'You've killed bugs and flies and spiders. It's no different.'

'But he was a living thing – he had been, at least...He *had* been human once upon a time.'

'Mr. Griffith was shot and you did nothing. You would have killed that tramp in Merimalima. Both were living, breathing people. You are a murderer. Their blood is on your hands. Who are you, Edgar Harold? What have you become?'

'I became a survivor.'

'You became a monster.'

'I did what I had to do!'

'And who decided that you had to?'

'I did! Okay, *I* did!'

Edgar slumped down against a boulder for a moment, trying to ignore the thoughts in his head. Now was not the time to have this conversation with himself. His stomach turned at the thought of what he had done to ensure his own survival. He had dropped into these people's lives and caused nothing but chaos and destruction. Caoilinn had died fighting for him alongside so many other, nameless Verstossen and Ältere. Mr. Griffith had taken a bullet for him so he could escape and he had just fled from *The Strangled Fox*, leaving the innocent proprietors, Nessa and Martin, in danger. He was like a bad omen, a curse. With a heavy-hearted sigh, Edgar wondered if life would ever be okay again because there was no going back from this.

Why had Betty chosen him to inherit that box? Why was he so important? He was the bullied kid at school – the one who was always last to be picked in P.E. He was the punchline of every joke. He wasn't made for this sort of life and he regretted ever wishing for change on that shooting star in the churchyard on the night Brother Bradley had returned.

A quiet dripping sound suddenly pulled him from his moral dilemma. The snow atop the rock beside him was melting slowly and dripping to the floor. Without thinking, Edgar held out his hands, caught the water and lapped it up.

The cool refreshing liquid made him feel alive. It cooled him down and alleviated a little of the torturous heat. When he had drank enough, he picked up a handful of snow and rubbed it on his face to cool down. The icy snow melted on his skin and ran down his face, making his whole body tingle pleasantly. It was only a temporary solution but it was better than suffering from heat stroke and he wondered why he hadn't thought about that simple solution before.

Buzz. Buzz. Buzz.

The sound came back. It was louder than before and when Edgar looked around, he saw a black mass heading towards him, floating in the air like a small cloud. As it came closer, the sound grew angrier. It was a deadly swarm.

He didn't need to think twice. Edgar jumped to his feet and ran. The path grew narrower again and steeply dropped down the mountainside. Edgar jumped from rock to rock, his feet slipping on the loose stones underneath. He looked back over his shoulder. The swarm had almost caught up with him – hundreds, if not thousands of tiny flying insects buzzing and humming as they advanced, showing no signs of slowing down.

Edgar turned back to face the path ahead. It was hidden beneath a layer of snow that had cascaded down the side of the mountain; he had no idea how deep it might be but he had no choice but to keep going. His first step into the snow sank almost to his knees but he kept going, forcing himself to move. It was hard work, trying to navigate the snow but the buzzing swarm was close. It was almost on him and the irritating sound rang in his ears, rendering any other thought impossible – the *buzz buzz buzz* was the only thing in his head.

He stumbled and slipped; he began to slide down the side of the mountain on the snow but he grabbed hard and dug his fingers into the ground. He caught hold of a rock and pulled himself back to his feet. His hands were numb with cold, he suspected he may have frostbite from the bitter chill that gnawed right through his flesh to the very bone, so cold that it burned hotter than the heat of the sun.

He stumbled onwards, slipping in his haste but he could not outrun the swarm. Within seconds, before he even had chance to turn around, they were on him; spiraling and circling and buzzing in his ear. It was like being inside a dense, noisy cloud and Edgar tried to shriek, to swat them away with his flailing arms but it was no use.

The tiny yellow and black striped hornets landed on him and crawled on his skin, up his nose and into his ears. Edgar screwed his eyes tight shut and held his breath. He tried to stand still and hoped they would go but more only began to crawl on him. He waved frantically to swipe them away and tried to move, slowly and carefully with his eyes still shut but he slipped and he fell.

Suddenly, he was aware of a falling sensation. He felt the snow moving beneath him and he opened his eyes. He slid down the side of the mountain, gathering speed. He tried to grab at the snow but his fingers couldn't grip and only left long track marks. The swarm was far above him on the path and only a few insects remained, clinging to his face. Edgar screamed as the edge came closer. He took one last look at the stunning mountain scenery that surrounded him before the snow thinned and rocks protruded through the surface, catching at Edgar's flesh leaving long, deep cuts. He reached out to try and grab them but he was sliding down at such speed they just cut his hands.

CRACK

His finger smacked against the side of a boulder and bent right back. Tears filled in Edgar's eyes instantaneously. The pain was unbearable and there it was. The edge. He screamed – a mixture of pain and terror and anger – *why did it have to end this way?* He shouldn't even be here. Betty had chosen wrong and he was suffering for her mistake. This was it...he was as good as dead.

Only metres away now.

Closer.

Closer.

Closer.

Far below, the giant, turquoise lakes glimmered peaceful and serene. It was a spectacular scene – one hell of a final view but it didn't stop him screaming as he slid further towards the edge; harsh rocks still tearing him to shreds, battering him from side to side as he passed them, trying to grab a hold. His voice echoed through the empty mountains and he screwed his eyes tight shut. He felt his body tip over the edge and free fall. He was almost weightless. His stomach tied in knots, his voice cried out and despite it all, his mind was blank. He knew this was the end and he couldn't bring himself to look.

Falling.

Tumbling.

Spinning through the air.

THUD

Edgar landed hard, his impact softened by a blanket of snow. He felt his whole body crumple and he groaned in pain, suspecting that he had broken several bones. He lay still for a moment, not daring to move; eyes still tightly shut. He focused on his body – on feeling every inch of it. There was pain but nothing intense – just the burning ice that cut right through him, a heavy ache and a throbbing in his head. What was this? Another miracle? Surely a fall from that height should have killed him.

Slowly, Edgar opened his eyes. His vision was blurred but slowly, his surroundings became clearer. He stared up at the sky, dazzled by the sun. The mountainside towered over him, rocky and treacherous.

He had only fallen a short distance - enough to have survived and remain relatively uninjured. He was lucky. He sat up slowly and checked that he was fine. Everything was good except for his dislocated finger which bent at a crude angle from the middle knuckle.

He knew what he had to do but he didn't like it. He had seen it done on television and films countless times but couldn't bring himself to do it. He knew he had to crack it back into place...but what if he did it wrong?

He stared at the finger and only made himself feel worse. The tip had started to turn blue and he knew that wasn't a good sign – if he didn't want to lose it, he had to act quick and take a chance. Taking a deep breath, Edgar stared down at his finger and tried his hardest not to panic. He touched it gently and screamed in pain. It hit him hard and seared through his whole body. Nausea twisted in his gut and he restrained himself from being sick.

Another deep breath and a sigh, and he took the end of his finger firmly and yanked it downwards without sparing a second thought – he wasn't sure if that was right, but it would have to do. There was another *CRACK* and he screamed out obscene language, while trying to maintain his composure. Hot tears streamed down his face, warming him momentarily. The pain slowly subsided and while it was still horrific, it felt better than before.

He tried to help himself back to his feet, clinging to rocks and boulders to aid him but the ground was too slippery and it was impossible to get his balance. His legs slipped in opposite directions and he collapsed. Edgar fell to the ground again face first. It was ice.

CRACK.

The ground beneath him splintered; Edgar groaned and the ice beneath him creaked.

CRACK

The loud sound echoed in the silence and Edgar tried to crawl away but his hands covered in cuts couldn't grip at the freezing ice. He slipped and skidded but he could not move, shivering and shaking. He was too cold.

CRACK.

He didn't even have time to react – he couldn't even scream.

BANG

The ice gave way beneath him and Edgar fell again. Not too far this time. *THUD*

He landed on something soft – snow - but began to slide. The twisting tunnel spiraled deeper and Edgar could only go limp as his body tumbled downwards; rolling and flipping and crashing into the hard, rocky walls. It wasn't far, only a matter of seconds, but it felt like an eternity until he hit the bottom and flew out of the mouth of the tunnel into a freezing pool of water.

The agony hit instantly. The water temperature must have been subzero and Edgar knew he had a matter of seconds to get out. The shock of being submerged so fast, hit him so hard that he gasped and filled his lungs with water. In sheer panic he flailed limply but his arms and legs were numb. Still, he fought against the impossible, focusing every ounce of energy on moving his body properly. He tried to exhale the freezing water in his lungs but it made him splutter and need another breath which in turn made him inhale another gulp of water. His head felt hazy, his vision growing darker. He had survived the fall but...

He had survived the fall.

That was all he needed! He had already survived the impossible.

With a final burst of strength he forced his way up and he broke the surface of the water. He spat out the remainder of water and greedily gulped down air. The oxygen hurt he inhaled, coughing and spluttering. The numbing cold sent his body into spasm which only made it harder and that was when Edgar remembered that he wasn't out of the woods just yet. He had only seconds left until the water would become deadly.

He swam as best he could, the short distance like an eternity. His body numb, all his muscles contracting so that it was unbearably painful to move, his lungs hardened, unable to breathe in the cold. He summoned up all of his inner strength and kept going towards the edge and scrambled out. He lay there, on the solid rocks by the edge of the pool, panting; his clothes were soaked through and his hair clung to his face in soggy clumps. He stared up, breathing heavily, amazed he had survived. The chill gnawed through his clothes, through his flesh and bit at his very bones. Edgar couldn't move. He was paralysed.

'Perhaps I haven't survived after all,' Edgar thought to himself as he tried to will his body to move, to no avail. *'Hypothermia will finish me off.'*

The icy walls of the cavern shimmered in the most beautiful blue hues to match the crystal clear water he had just pulled himself out of and as he lay there. He stared at the walls of his tomb, wondering again if this might be how it would all end. The familiar thought of fighting through to see his family again, to not just become another missing person who would never be found wasn't strong enough to help him pull through.

He lay there, hyperventilating and teeth chattering. He clung to himself, as if trying to warm himself with a hug from his own arms but it achieved nothing. There was no way out of here. He was trapped...but something caught his eye. A narrow tunnel; a thin slice through the icy wall. It glowed in an eerily green light as if something shone through from the other side and something unknown called to him – a feeling, an instinct. It told him that he had to find the source of the light.

'I am *not* going to die,' Edgar whispered to himself..

He struggled to roll over; his whole body going into shock and his teeth chattered violently, almost to the verge of biting his tongue off. His skin had turned a dark hue of blue and he feared the worst. Slowly, he managed to get onto his front. The rocky ground beneath him was hard and jagged. 'Keep moving. Moving will make you warm,' he told himself.

And he forced himself to crawl, slowly at first but then gathered speed as he gained momentum. When he reached the narrow crevice, he used the wall to steady himself as he got to his feet and Edgar squeezed in sideways. He shuffled along slowly, the bright green light coming closer. His breath hung in the air like a cloud and the cold nipped at him, growing more deadly by the second. He felt it gnawing deep inside him now, freezing his insides and soon they would be as icy as his surroundings. He didn't have long if he intended on surviving.

When he reached the other end of the tunnel he emerged into an enormous cavern. Its high ceiling was as tall as a cathedral, held in place by columns and pillars of ice. Sunlight split through cracks above him, lighting the cave. The ground was slippery under his feet and he took slow, tentative steps over the treacherous ground but caution wasn't enough and Edgar fell flat onto the ice and groaned in pain.

He lay on the freezing ground for a moment, struggling to find the strength to get back to his feet. His body was too cold to work. He could feel it beginning to shut down. He could hardly move.

'How the hell am I getting out of this one?' he muttered to himself, his words a weak stutter and his head fell onto the ice.

The cold seeped through his skin and skull to his brain. He was as good as frozen and as he stared into the depths of the cavern ahead of him, unable to move, his breathing quick and shallow, he noticed a bright green light again in the distance; perhaps it was all a trick played by his dying mind. The ethereal light shone through the ice, making it glow like emeralds...and there were silhouettes in the ice...a shape of a giant pyramid. It was from this structure that the light shone and all around it, interspersed in the ice were shapes of distorted figures.

'Hello?' he called out weakly. 'Is anyone there?'

The shadows against the light were humanoid in shape and size, so much so that Edgar was convinced they were people but as he came closer he noticed that they were not human at all; and they were not on the other side of the ice. They were inside it. They were trapped.

Tall, ugly creatures – at least fifty of them spread around the walls of the icy tomb like a forgotten army. Their naked, leathery bodies were twisted, bent and broken. Their faces squashed and rotting with cold, dead eyes. Their skin covered in sores and growths.

'What are you?' Edgar asked himself as he forced himself to his feet, leaned on the icy wall and inched tentatively closer, shivering – a combination of both terror and the biting cold.

The creatures appeared like ancient mummies trapped in the ice, preserved in time. Whatever had happened to them can't have been pleasant. Had they suffered some kind of disease?

Edgar was face to face with one of them now. He stared into its wide, open eyes, horrified but enchanted by it. It blinked. Edgar stumbled backwards in surprise. Had he imagined it? He was so cold, so tired...his mind was susceptible to playing tricks in this state. He looked around, feeling uncomfortable. Eyes watched him from all over the tomb.

He turned back to the creature beside him with its squashed nose, lopsided smile and narrow eyes...they blinked again.

'They're alive,' Edgar gasped, trying to pull himself together.

He turned and glanced around. Silence. Perfect still.

Back to the monster. His eyes scanned the length of its malnourished, naked body that seemed so thin the bones threatened to rip through the flesh. A finger twitched and a quiet sound broke the silence. A low, guttural growl. The creature blinked once more and its head tilted to the side slightly as if it were intrigued by Edgar's presence and it snarled, baring its sharp, crooked teeth.

There was a low rumble in the distance – a small avalanche cascading down the mountain above. No doubt Edgar had caused that disturbance when he fell. The sound grew louder and louder. The tomb trembled and a mixture of rock, snow and ice fell down from above. Edgar stared at the chaos, unable to move. His body was too weak and he was too scared. Instead he simply curled up in a ball. It was all he could do. His only plan was to ride it out.

The cracks in the ceiling widened and golden sunlight streamed in, lighting up the clouds of snow that crashed down from above with the heavy debris. In the middle of the disaster, the tall pillars that held the tomb intact began to split and the creature before Edgar began to wriggle, its movements becoming larger until:

CRACK

Edgar looked up.

A line fractured through the ice. The creature clenched its fist and punched its way through in one blow.

Sharp shards of solid ice flew through the air and Edgar rolled aside. The creature roared loudly, its voice hoarse and resounding with a bloodlust that chilled Edgar to the core. It was hungry.

It took a slow, clumsy step as it warmed up from so many years of being frozen and turned to its victim: Edgar.

Edgar couldn't even muster a scream. Silenced by fear, he forgot all about his condition and pushed himself to his feet. He could barely stand but that didn't matter, his whole body was running on adrenaline. The creature roared and began to advance on Edgar.

CRACK

The others were waking, struggling and clawing at the walls of their tomb; throwing themselves against it in desperate need to break out. Their voices were deafening and grating like nails on a blackboard. Edgar stumbled on, skidding across the ice beneath his feet. He chanced a glance back over his shoulder to see the monster giving chase.

It slipped and struggled to keep its balance. It fell and crawled closer, screaming. It was relentless in its pursuit. Edgar paused and watched it pitifully. He was scared but there was such hatred in its desperation – a fury that burned deep inside it like a zombie driven by a pure need to feast on human flesh. Was that its only desire?

CRASH

The walls crashed down around him.

Edgar had almost forgotten about the others and now they were free. So many of the monstrous things climbing from their resting places where they had been trapped and starving for so long. Their hunger was apparent and they began to advance on Edgar, arms outstretched. One of them dived at him but Edgar dodged and it missed. Another came at him but again, Edgar dodged. The creatures began fighting each other – a mass of flailing limbs and skinny bodies entangled ripping and tearing each other apart; black blood splattered the ice and Edgar made a run for it.

His legs were so cold that they didn't want to move, his body weighed down with soggy clothes but he pressed on as quickly as he could...but it was too much. He slipped and slid over the ice and his legs gave way. He fell to the ground hard and cracked his head.

Edgar shouted out in pain and the creatures turned. With their attention redirected to Edgar they gave chase, shuffling and stumbling like the undead; their bodies frozen stiff from being entombed in the ice for so long. *How could they still be alive?*

WHOOSH!

A towering, human figure appeared from nowhere. It just faded into existence a few feet in the air and dropped to the ground where it landed on its feet between Edgar and the monsters. The figure caught sight of the creatures and turned around. It spotted Edgar and for the briefest second, Edgar saw that it was a man. He was tall and muscular, dressed in medieval style clothes – a green doublet, brown woollen trousers and black boots that resembled his own. A black bandanna emblazoned with a white symbol was tied around his head.

'Edgar?' he asked urgently 'Edgar Harold?'

'Yes,' Edgar replied weakly.

'You need to come with me right now,' the man said, reaching his hand out for Edgar's.

Edgar eyed him suspiciously. A strange man had appeared from nowhere, looking for him – that was not normal. Could he be trusted? He noticed that the symbol from his coin was printed on the man's bandana and that he wore boots similar to his own.

The creatures shrieked once more, their gravelly, cold voices just a horrifying sound echoing through the cave as they lumbered towards them. Edgar shivered, a mixture of the cold and his indecision.

'There is no time Edgar. Come with me and you'll get all the answers you're looking for.'

The creatures were coming fast. He had no choice. It was a split second decision – no time to weigh up pros and cons. The man might be a traveller too – he had the boots and the bandana. Edgar reached out to take the man's hand and as they connected a static shock smacked Edgar hard. With the sound of bloodcurdling roars and demonic screaming everything turned black.

– Chapter Thirteen –
The Burning at the Shrine of Saint Margarette

Light...and chirping birds. There was warmth in his blood and Edgar stirred with a groan.

The man sat on the twisted tree trunk beside Edgar scrambled over to him and crouched down beside him. He took his hand in his own.

'What the hell just happened?' Edgar grumbled as he came around. He was aware that he felt warmer – that the biting cold that had chilled him to the bones was banished and though he was still damp, he had dried off considerably.

'You travelled,' the man said, rolling his eyes.

'Obviously. I meant in the cave!' Edgar sat up and looked around. He was in a forest of tall, spindly trees with short, spiky branches that looked like ladders up to the canopy of green leaves above.

'You woke the Nazakan. You set them free.'

'Nazakan?' Edgar repeated, feeling as though he knew the name from somewhere.

'The Nazakan. Those monsters. You're lucky that Devi saw it.'

'Devi?'

'A friend. She had a vision,' Edgar looked incredulous and his rescuer, noticing Edgar's disbelief continued. 'She's a witch.'

'Oh...so a witch had a vision about me?' Edgar said, hardly believing the words on his lips. 'That's not normally good, you know? How can I trust you?'

'Are you serious?'

'This could be a trap. You might be luring me into a false sense of security,' Edgar theorised, his voice strained with worry. 'You're working with a witch, afterall!'

Something inside made him want to trust the man. He seemed warm and friendly. He had saved his life and he wore boots just like his and the bandana on his head with the travellers' insignia must have been a dead giveaway that they were on the same side...but too much had happened. Too much had changed and now it was impossible to trust anyone. If Edgar wanted to survive he had to question everything, rely on his gut and something told him that he could not completely trust the man. Not yet.

'We've been waiting for you, Edgar. We were worried. We thought you should have been here by now. That's why we made her look,' the man said sympathetically. There was a kindness in his steely eyes but Edgar still felt uneasy.

'You've been waiting...for me?'

'Long story. I'm Charles by the way.'

He extended his hand. Edgar reached out carefully, worried the same might happen as last time and he would be zapped with static shock and be whisked away to another far off location, but it was a needless worry. He shook Charles' warm hand, thankful to feel heat again and Charles set off ahead. Edgar stopped in his tracks, thoughtful.

'I'm meant to follow you?' he asked stubbornly. 'You drop out of nowhere, bring me to a strange place and start talking about witches seeing me in visions? How do I know you're not gonna lead me to a gingerbread house and chuck me in the oven?'

'Come on, Edgar. It's not like that.' Charles laughed. 'Devi is a white witch. Without her, you'd be dead in that cave.'

'I still don't trust you,' Edgar decided, a cold gleam flashed across his icy eyes and Charles couldn't help but laugh.

'Then stay here and go nowhere then,' Charles replied, a hint of sarcasm in his light tone. He didn't even wait for a reply and simply swaggered off. He turned back to see Edgar looking torn. 'If I wanted to kill you or harm you, I'd have done it already.'

'Prove it.'

'I'm on your side,' Charles said seriously and pointed to the bandanna on his head. The insignia of the coin – a pentagram with crossed swords was stitched upon it. He was right. Edgar was being stubborn, scared to let his guard down. It was understandable, but he knew that was all he needed as proof. Charles was an ally. He was was somehow linked to all of this strangeness. He had promised answers – maybe he was right after all.

'And you promise I'll get answers?' Edgar demanded, pulling himself together.

'Promise,' Charles said kindly, his smile irresistibly charming.

Edgar stopped, looked thoughtfully at Charles as if considering every inch of him. He looked innocent enough, his face was fair but strong and when he flashed that cheeky smile, Edgar couldn't help but trust him. He was right. If he had wanted to harm him, he would have done it by now.

'Ok, then. I'll come with you!' Edgar sighed.

'We need to head this way,' Charles said, leading the way through the dense trees.

Edgar followed him, snapping twigs and stumbling over the uneven ground; nearby the steady trickle of a stream wound its way through the undergrowth of the glorious forest. It was beautiful – like something from a fairytale, an idyllic place marred only by the sour stench of wild garlic that turned Edgar's stomach.

They strolled through the forest for what seemed like forever and Edgar felt anxious about where Charles might be leading him but he had no real choice other than to follow him. He had promised answers and a safe haven and that was good enough reason to stick by his side.

The journey was quite unremarkable and quiet – most of it was spent with Edgar trying to keep up with Charles' giant strides but when they reached a wide clearing where sunlight streamed through the branches and lit a giant, rocky structure like a spotlight, Edgar began to feel uneasy.

'What's that?' he asked, feeling like he already knew the answer. He had seen identical structures in a recent dream and one in the ice cave. He remembered the ethereal green glow and the Nazakan bursting through the rough wooden doors and the slaughter that followed in the fall of Krinka.

Up close and in real life and without a barrier of ice there was something even more foreboding about the architecture. It rose up, a good ten feet high; its sheer, smooth sides reached up at an almost vertical angle to the pinnacle where the insignia of the pentagram with the crossed swords in the centre was engraved and a hefty wooden door was set into the stone.

'The pyramid?' Charles said, heading over towards it. 'You don't know about them?'

'I've seen them...but...I don't think we should be here,' Edgar mumbled, anxiety taking hold. 'The Nazakan might-'

'We're fine,' Charles said. 'If they were here we'd know about it.'

Edgar knew that much was true. If the Nazakan were there, they would be dead.

He stared at the pyramid in absolute awe. Despite it being such a symbol of danger, there was something enchanting and beautiful about it – something that made Edgar want to stand and stare until the Nazakan came to send him running, and even then he might not have moved.

He reached out and touched the stone which was like nothing he had ever seen and it was like silk beneath his fingers. It was hard, but so smooth and warm that Edgar was taken aback by surprise.

There were no cracks nor any lumps or bumps in its surface – it was just completely pristine but there was also something that made the hairs on his arms stand on end, it sent chills through his body and numbed his heart. It was some kind of evil energy and Edgar switched from being enthralled to wanting to run for his life.

'It hasn't weathered,' Edgar murmured to himself; Charles overheard and nodded.

'And these pyramids have existed for longer than anyone can remember. They were built to last, and they did. Not that we can use them anymore.'

'The Nazakan?' Edgar knew the answer without having to ask.

'They swarmed the pyramid system and now it's under their control. We could use them but it's not worth the risk,' Charles replied solemnly and Edgar nodded in understanding. 'Let's get moving.'

Edgar didn't need to be asked twice. He knew what the Nazakan were capable of and he didn't want to be around if they were to break through. Charles began to walk once more and Edgar merely followed.

Eventually the trees began to thin out but the undergrowth and bushes remained as thick as ever. In the distance, the quiet, still air was disturbed by the racket of voices shouting and jeering and singing. Edgar couldn't tell whether they were friendly, angry or a mix of both.

'Stay back,' Charles whispered, holding his arm out as if to keep Edgar back. He took the bandana from his head, folded it and slid it into his pocket. He smoothed down his messy, sandy hair with his hands but it didn't help.

'What's going on?' Edgar asked anxiously, ignoring Charles as he crept forward side by side with him.

'It's the villagers,' Charles began, his voice hushed.

'I can see that...but what's happening?' Edgar interrupted, peeking out through a gap in the bushes at the crowd.

'They hate our kind – think we're all witches. They don't understand our customs or traditions. They don't understand that we're the ones keeping them safe and thanks to us they can sleep safe at night.'

Edgar peeked between the branches and watched as the horde of people gathered around the hill where a steep flight of stone steps led up to the statue of a young man clad in armour, kneeling, head bowed with his long hair covering most of his face. His arms were outstretched to the heavens and long, chunky ropes dangled from both wrists. Around the base of the statue was a pile of firewood and long, thick sticks tied together with ropes.

'Who's he?' Edgar whispered.

'Who?'

'The statue,' Edgar replied quietly.

Charles turned and stared at him open mouthed. His eyes wide in shock as he shook his head in mock disgust.

'Seriously?' he hissed.

'Seriously,' Edgar muttered solemnly.

'That, Edgar Harold, is not a *he*. It's *she*. It's Saint Margarette!'

'And of course I know who what is...' Edgar replied sarcastically. He had never heard of her and why should he have? He wasn't from here – he hadn't the faintest idea about the saints of this world.

'Saint Margarette!' Charles repeated. 'Only the most important traveller in our history. Her adventures were legendary! She shaped everything we are now!'

'Oh...right.'

It meant nothing to Edgar but he guessed in time he would end up learning more about the iconic woman.

Charles opened his mouth to speak but he was cut off by a piercing scream that split the air, followed by an eruption of noise from the jeering crowd that gathered at the foot of the steep steps, looking up at the shrine of the ominous Saint Margarette atop the hill.

'Let me go! Get off me! I'm innocent!' a girl screamed, her voice muffled inside a hessian sack that covered her head. She was dragged violently by a tall, muscular man through the crowd which parted to let them pass. He pulled her up the steps and she fell down, shrieking. 'I can't see where I'm going!'

The man continued climbing the stairs and just dragged her after him. She struggled, trying to get back to her feet but the man was too fast and she couldn't get her footing. Her body impacted each step like a ragdoll and she screamed in pain as the sharp stone cut her skin and a trail of blood spilled on the ground. Still the crowds cheered, enjoying the brutality.

'What is he doing to her?' Edgar gasped, unable to believe what he saw unfold right before his eyes.

'You don't want to know,' Charles murmured, turning his back.

'HELP! HELP ME PLEASE! SOMEONE!' the girl screamed, reaching out to try and grab hold of something, anything...and the man stopped in his tracks. He turned, kicked the girl in the face and heaved her up over his shoulder. She thrashed around, kicking and punching but to his giant muscular frame her attacks must have felt like a tickle.

When they reached the top of the steps he dropped her on the ground where she landed in a heap and he took a rope, one hanging from each of the statue's outstretched hands and tied them around the girl's wrists. She continued screaming, sobbing and trying to fight him off but her attempts were futile. The crowds cheered and whooped as he pulled the ropes tight and hoisted her into the air so she dangled between the statues arms, her tip-toes reaching for the ground but finding only thin air.

'Charles...what's going on?' Edgar asked again but Charles ignored him and crouched down in the bushes, keeping low and out of sight. 'Charles!'

'Turn your back.'

'What are they going to do to her?'

'They think she's a *witch*,' Charles said darkly and the emphasis on the word witch hit Edgar hard and his stomach back-flipped. Suddenly the arrangement of firewood at the base of the statue made sense. He had been through his fair share of horrifying ordeals since he left his home but this was by far the worst – an innocent human being, faceless and anonymous about to be burned alive.

'We have to-'

'There's nothing we can do,' Charles sighed sadly.

'We can't let them!'

Charles shot Edgar a dark glare.

'Then let's at least get away from here. I can't stand this.'

The screaming was only getting louder – so shrill and agonising over the booing and jeering crowd who may as well have been screaming at the actors on stage at a pantomime.

'Our path leads right past them. We can't go out now. We have to wait.'

'They're going to burn her! We can't just sit here.' Edgar argued.

'We have to. Cover your ears, close your eyes. It might make it easier,' Charles said solemnly but Edgar couldn't comprehend.

'Confess,' said a deep, harsh voice. It was the man who had dragged her up the stairs and tied her up 'Confess your sins and judgement will be swift.'

'I have nothing to confess,' the girl snapped, her voice still half-lost beneath the thick, itchy material of the sack.

'You are one of them!' the man shouted and the crowd booed. 'You are a witch!'

'I'm not a witch! I promise. Please...'

'Let us look upon the face of a demon! One who would threaten us all with her magic!'

The man strode over to the girl and pulled the mask away from her face. The crowd gasped and some screamed as the sack was torn away and they gazed into her eyes...but none were as shocked as Edgar. The face burned into his eyes and even when he blinked in disbelief, it was all he could see like a light that had branded itself into the back of his eyelids. The girl dangling above the firewood was none other than his best friend, Alvin's sister. It was Vicky.

Edgar's head began to spin and he rubbed his eyes as if trying to erase the scene playing out before him. It couldn't be her – it had to be someone else! It was impossible. Her emerald green eyes glistened with tears as she stared out at the crowd. Alvin had said she was going on a mission...but he had assumed he meant as a missionary. This was impossible but Edgar would know that face anywhere. The soft, elfish features, the steely eyes and the long, braided black hair...even the voice was identical.

'Charles! I know her!' Edgar exclaimed in shock.

'You can't.'

'I do! We have to do something!'

'There's at least a hundred villagers out there and two of us,' Charles said, his words were the voice of reason that Edgar needed to hear, despite being the exact opposite to what he wanted.

'But she'll die!'

'So would we and there's bigger plans for you, Edgar.'

'What do you mean bigger plans?'

'You'll find out as soon as we get back to the campsite but let's just say, you're worth so much more than burning right here,'

Charles insisted, his tone sharp and serious. 'If you even think of trying something I'll have to stop you.'

Edgar sighed in frustration. What were these *"bigger plans"* that Charles mentioned?

'Please!' Vicky begged weakly, her voice cracking as she burst into heart-wrenching sobs. 'I'm innocent.'

'Then explain THIS!' the witch hunter bellowed, holding up a coin much like Edgar's. 'You are one of them! Confess.'

'One of them?' she sobbed, 'What do you mean?'

'One of the Devil's Daughters,'

The witch hunter ignored Vicky and approached the mound of wooden logs, a flaming torch held ceremoniously high. Slowly, he lowered it and Vicky began to scream, tears of terror rolled down her cheek. She was helpless, Edgar was helpless. There was nothing he could do unless he wanted to be tied to a stake and burned alive too.

'By the powers granted to me as Lord Protector of our village. I hereby condemn you to be put to death by the purifying flames,' the Witch Hunter announced to a tumultuous round of applause and wolf-whistles from the excited audience.

'Now, by the Shrine of your sacred Saint Margarette, you will meet your fate as will all others of your kind who pass through here.'

Vicky had fallen silent now. She appeared to be muttering words under her breath – a prayer as if she expected it to bring her some reprieve, her wide, terrified eyes on the flame in the man's hand.

'BURN THE WITCH! BURN THE WITCH! BURN THE WITCH!' The crowd chanted.

The Witch Hunter stared at Vicky in disgust, a flaming hatred flashed in his eyes and, then, without any warning he just tossed the torch onto the pile of wood.

It quickly caught on fire and soon the smoke rose into the sky, thick, acrid and choking. Vicky struggled to escape, wriggling in her restraints as she dangled above the bonfire, arms outstretched in the crucifix position. Her legs kicked furiously as the flames grew and danced around her toes. The intense heat rose rapidly and sweat rolled down her face. Vicky screamed and kicked harder, trying to create enough of an air current to extinguish the fire but it only seemed to make it worse. The flames grew taller as they consumed the firewood and soon Vicky couldn't lift her legs high enough to escape them.

'BURN THE WITCH! BURN THE WITCH!'

Her legs flailed uncomfortably as the flames licked at them, burning and cracking her fair skin; her agonising screams filled the air. Edgar closed his eyes tight, unable to watch. He glanced over to Charles who sat with his back turned to the event, his hands over his ears. Edgar placed a gentle hand on his shoulder and Charles turned, smiled weakly and took Edgar's hand in his own.

Edgar had never felt so powerless. He couldn't cope. Until now it had been him in danger and he could take control – he could will himself to survive but this was different. This was someone else and he was unable to do anything for fear of the same thing happening to him. He could run out and cut her down and save her...but how? There were so many villagers; a huge, angry horde baying for blood and the more the better.

He would stay with Charles, hidden in the bushes and simply watch. Vicky's death was on his hands – his inaction was as good as murder and he knew that he could never forgive himself but Charles was right. There were bigger things waiting for him and he would never see them through if he ruined it all by running out now.

The choice was too simple but was it strength or weakness? Edgar's heart pounded, his head reeled and his breath caught behind the lump in his throat as he decided to do nothing. It was Vicky or him and after all he had been through he wasn't ready to die yet – and what did it matter? She had her God. Edgar didn't.

It was hard to see through the tears in his eyes. He clenched his jaw tightly and squeezed Charles' hand as Vicky's screams became hoarse and shorter *How had he been able to watch for so long?* Shock. Disbelief. Denial.

His selfishness disgusted him – what kind of monster was he? Perhaps it was the shock of finding her here in this far off place that made it feel as though it wasn't even real – just a terrible nightmare from which he would soon awaken? He hoped so, but the pain he had endured himself told him that this was all too real.

Edgar's eyes were blurred with tears so he only saw the vague outline of flames catching Vicky's dress and spread rapidly until she was completely engulfed, suspended over the bonfire like some kind of hellish angel, shrieking like a banshee and forsaking all of those in its presence.

Edgar wiped the tears from his eyes and gritted his teeth, focusing his mind on anything but this – focusing on finally getting home, on seeing his family again...but going home would soon mean seeing Alvin again and how could he face his friend after this? How could he look him in the eye knowing that he made the callus decision to let his sister die rather than to risk his own life? The answer: he couldn't. It was the sickly stench of burning flesh drifting towards him, carried on the thick, white smoke, that knocked Edgar back to his senses. He retched, unable to bear it – the screams, the smell, the whole situation was deplorable and he wanted it to be over. He could barely see her through the smoke now – just the orange glow of the fire and the silhouette of Vicky's dangling body, limper than it had been.

'Don't think about it, don't think about it,' he whispered to himself, rocking back and forth. Charles shot him a weak, encouraging smile which Edgar returned and he let himself drift off into his head, blocking absolutely everything else from existence. *'You'll get through this. It's not your fault.'* the voice in his head continued, even though he knew for a fact that it was his fault – this was entirely his fault...but he could always pretend.

Soon the cries faded out and Edgar knew she had passed. A shiver shot down his spine as he thought about how his friend had just died before his eyes in the most agonising way and he had done nothing.

The ropes that held her suspended had frayed and the body fell down with a lifeless *flump*, still burning; her skin raw, peeling and blackened; her dead, glassy eyes staring into the abyss of death before her.

'What have I done?' Edgar whimpered, unable to tear his eyes from the scene before him; the mob began to cackle and cheer as if they had just witnessed something wonderful.

'Edgar...'

'I let her die. It's my fault...I...I...'

'Edgar, it's alright,' Charles said, keeping direct eye contact in an attempt to reassure him. 'There was nothing either of us could have done or we'd have joined her up there.'

'I could have done something. I should have.'

'It's fine. It's-'

'It's *not* fine!' Edgar hissed quietly, trying to keep his voice down as to not draw the attention of the crowds just meters away on the other side of the trees. 'None of this is fine, Charles. Since I've been out here, travelling all I've seen is death and destruction and pain and if that's what this thing is all about, I don't want it.'

Edgar's hand reached into his pocket and he felt for his travellers' token but it wasn't there.

'Looking for this?' Charles held the token up between his fingers and then stowed it back in his pocket.

'That's mine!'

Charles chuckled and rolled the token through his fingers.

'My token. Give me it – send me home and don't ever bother looking for me again,' Edgar demanded fiercely, attempting to snatch it back. 'Give me it.'

Charles shook his head and retracted his hand.

'You really want to come with me, Edgar,' he said plainly.

'You don't know what I want. You can't tell me what to do!'

'I know you'll thank me if you just come back to the campsite. Please, trust me,' Charles insisted. There was a steely gleam in his eye that told Edgar he was never going to back down.

'Your people are burned at the stake as witches! How do I know I can trust any of you?'

The question seemed logical in his mind but when he said it out loud, he realised it seemed a little harsher than he had meant it.

'We're your people too, Edgar.' Charles said softly. He reached out to take Edgar's hand in his again but Edgar's retracted as if Charles' were a hot flame.

'No!' Edgar spat. 'You're not. I don't know you, you don't know me! You can't just assume these things!'

'You need to trust me, Edgar.' Charles tried softly. 'I saved your life and I need you to believe me when I say that you need to come with me to the campsite.'

Edgar took a deep breath, collected himself and nodded in agreement.

'I'll come but after that I'm going home,' Edgar insisted.

'We'll see.'

It felt like forever waiting for the crowds to disperse and leave embers of the glowing bonfire with the blackened remains of the charred body.

Once it was safe, Edgar and Charles crept out, keeping low. Edgar rushed over to the shrine and stumbled up the uneven steps to the bonfire at the top. He looked up at the cold, stony face of Saint

Margarette and then down to Vicky's body that lay upon the crackling embers.

'I'm sorry, Vicky.' Edgar whispered, his voice breaking as he struggled to speak.

'Come on, we don't have time,' Charles shouted from the bottom of the stairs. 'We have to go.'

Edgar ignored him. He had to take a moment to pay his respects.

'I'll make this right, I promise,' Edgar thought choking on the tears that welled up in his eyes.

'I had to save myself but I'll make that mean something. I promise,' he said out loud, his voice catching in his throat.

'Edgar!' Charles repeated impatiently and Edgar glanced over, nodded and got back to his feet. He took one last look at the burned corpse, his stomach twisting in knots and then he joined Charles once more as they set off towards the campsite.

– CHAPTER FOURTEEN –
NIGHTMARE CREATURES

It felt like a long journey back to the camp and was spent mostly in silence – neither really knew what to say to each other after what they had just witnessed. Charles made a few attempts at small talk:

'It's warm isn't it?' he had tried, followed by an awkward silence to which he added 'Those clouds look a bit dark in the distance. Hope it doesn't rain later.'

Edgar had been too preoccupied with his thoughts to really care about clouds or the heat and in fact, he thought a bit of rain might actually be refreshing. The smell of burning flesh lingered within his nostrils and would not leave. It clung to his clothes and his whole body– perhaps a shower of rain would wash it away and he might be free of it...but he still wouldn't be free of the guilt that weighed heavy on his shoulders, making each step a burden, like he carried the weight of the world. Nothing could wash that away.

Still the anxiety of telling Alvin what had happened to Vicky played in his mind – a million conversations, a million outcomes, each one so different from the last but none of them any more reassuring. It hurt his dizzy head. Everything that had happened since he had first left home on this ridiculous adventure, if he could even call it that, had been so intense – a blur of moments blending into one hurried rush of panic. It was as if death sped towards him but he kept dodging it narrowly, as if they were dancing together. One mis-step, one slight slip of a miscalculation and it would all be over.

'Stop!' Charles hissed. He held his hand up and clung to the twisted trunk of the tree next to him. He peeked around its side and beckoned Edgar closer.

'What's wrong?' Edgar whispered, his voice automatically coming out quiet. He knew there was danger. He could sense it.

'Over there,' Charles whispered, pointing into the trees.

Edgar looked in the vague direction of Charles' finger and it took him a moment to see what he was pointing at but there it was as clear as day. It was almost camouflaged in the bushes – a tall, skinny creature with sagging, rotten flesh hanging from its skeletal frame, as loose as the tattered rags that gave it only a slight bit of modesty. It groaned and gasped, like a zombie and it reached its arms out, waving and scrambling. It kept walking but went nowhere, as if it were trapped behind an invisible barrier.

'What the -?'

'Can you tell me what that is?' Charles said, pointing to the creature.

'I'm not sure. It's like one of those creatures from the cave...the Nazakan.'

Charles nodded solemnly.

'Correct,' he said as he stepped out from behind the tree and moved cautiously towards the Nazakan.

'Charles! Don't!' Edgar squeaked as he tried to grab his friend's hand to pull him back.

The Nazakan's burning eyes caught sight of Charles and it worked itself into a frenzy. It snarled and spat, its jaw snapping as desperately as its flailing arms. It stumbled on the spot, its footsteps growing faster and faster but it simply could not move an inch closer.

'Come here,' Charles said, waving Edgar over. He stood so close to the Nazakan that its broken fingernails barely missed his shirt. It screamed hungrily, growing more and more frustrated that it could not reach its prey no matter how hard it tried.

The shrieks echoed through the thick forest, surrounding them. Edgar worried that there might be more around, that they could be ambushed at any moment and he took a few slow, tentative steps towards Charles and the creature.

'It's safe,' Charles assured him but Edgar still remained cautious. 'Come on.'

Edgar moved as close as he dared. He was near enough to Charles now, just a couple of inches behind.

'What's wrong with it?' Edgar asked as he surveyed the Nazakan, looking it up and down. 'Why can't it get us?'

'It's a long story. But you need to see this, Edgar,' Charles said sternly. 'This is our enemy. The Nazakan.'

The monster screamed at them in a long lost language that neither could understand. It looked at Edgar, its eyes burning with fury and hatred. It launched itself against the invisible wall violently. It was more frenzied than before, as if it had been overcome by a madness – as if Edgar had driven it over the edge.

'Why is it trapped though?'

Charles turned to Edgar and opened his mouth to speak.

AROOOOOOOOO

The howl was nearby.

It was too close for comfort.

The screams that followed told Edgar that whatever it was that made the noise was much worse than the Nazakan they faced here.

'No!' Charles spat under his breath. 'Quick. With me.'

He grabbed Edgar's hand and pulled him away from the manic Nazakan and further into the forest. They ducked and dived under the low hanging branches and jumped over narrow streams of water. It was such a beautiful place but there was no time to admire it. Their feet padded over the carpet of golden leaves and squelched through the soggy mud patches until they came to the end of the woods and the sunlight split the horizon as they ran towards the last trees, as if they were sprinting towards the edge of the world.

Eventually they broke out from the shade of the forest and stood on the side of a large, open field packed with tents and a few wooden caravans. In the near distance, a group of black horses grazed in long grass, the paddock secured by a crudely constructed wooden fence. The surroundings reminded him strongly of somewhere he'd visited before and that was when he realised that it looked like a re-enactment that he had been to when he was young but he couldn't quite recall where it had been.

'Where is everyone?' Edgar asked but Charles didn't answer. 'Charles? Is this where the screams came from?'

The silence was uneasy considering the size of the campsite – why was it so quiet? Moments ago there had been screams and now it was as silent as a graveyard. *Were the tents now tombs and caravans mausoleums?* Edgar shivered to think. He had faced enough death.

'Charles? Where are we?' Edgar tried again.

Charles stopped in his tracks, held up his hand and Edgar froze. Charles' expression twisted with anxiety which only made Edgar's nerves more jittery.

'It's too quiet...' Charles whispered, a fearful tremble in his usually strong voice. 'They must still be here. Stay low.'

Edgar followed his commands but as they crept towards the campsite he couldn't help but worry. What if Charles had lured him into a trap? Anyone could just jump out and attack.

'What's going on?' Edgar whispered as they arrived at the edge of the campsite and began to duck between the tents, crouching down as low as they could.

'I'm not sure. Could be an attack.'

'An attack? It's a bit quiet for an attack,' Edgar said. 'What if everyone's dead?'

'We need to get you to that caravan,' Charles replied, his eyes gleaming with determination. 'You'll be safe there.'

He pointed towards an old gypsy caravan that stood almost in the centre of the camp by the blackened remains of a fire circled by a ring of logs. It still burned away by itself. The whole campsite was eerily dead as if the occupants had just suddenly vanished and left everything behind exactly as it was.

A low, rattling sound like someone close to death and struggling for breath came from nearby and Edgar's heart sank. It was a sound that stopped him in his tracks, a sound so bloodcurdling that he shot Charles a furtive glance as if to ask if he had heard it too.

'Did you hear that?' Edgar said, his voice quiet as his ears strained to hear the sound which came again, closer this time.

'Stay down!' Charles whispered, gesturing for Edgar to remain crouched low.

He took Edgar by the hand and dragged him so forcefully that he almost fell flat on his face. Charles led Edgar between a rows of tents and a low growl rumbled nearby, mixed with the soft padding of footsteps across the grass. A giant, shadowy, humanoid figure appeared at the end of the aisle between the tents but before Edgar could get a good look, Charles dragged him inside a tent.

'Do. Not. Move,' he hissed.

'What was that?' Edgar whispered but Charles merely lifted a finger to Edgar's lips and he knew to be quiet.

They crouched in the tent, listening to the soft *pad, pad, pad* of footsteps on the grass; a low growl hanging in the air as the creature passed by. Edgar could see its towering, gangling form creep past. It walked on all four of its long limbs, its sharp ears stuck up on the top of its head from which a long, snout protruded.

The monstrous shape outside paused, lifted its snout to the sky and the front legs followed until it was raised on its hind legs, and Edgar could hear the deep *sniff, sniff, sniff* as it tested the air, hoping to catch a scent.

AROOOOOOO

It howled a terrible howl, so frightening that it made Edgar's blood run cold. He clenched his fist and held his breath, trying so hard to not make a noise, to not be scared – could it smell fear? Might he give away their position if he let the creature unnerve him. He felt a tiny squeak escape as he struggled against the urge to scream and he shoved his hand over his mouth as if it would help.

Edgar turned to Charles and he, too, looked terrified. There was some comfort in knowing that he wasn't alone in his fear, that they were both in this together. Edgar had grown so used to being alone and facing the terrors of dimension travel by himself, of having only himself to rely on but now he had Charles....and he didn't like it. Alone, he was in charge and solely responsible for his own survival; Charles, however, was just something else to weigh him down – a risk that could get him killed.

If the monster knew they were there, what could Edgar do? Should he run and not look back or should he try and help Charles escape too? He knew the correct answer but Edgar had changed over the course of the last few hours and now the choice between what was right and what was wrong had become a choice between life and death. It was every man for himself – his choice was an obvious one.

A scream in the distance brought Edgar crashing back to reality and as he snapped back, he saw Charles dive out of the tent.

'Help! Please! Someone!' a distressed woman shrieked somewhere nearby.

'Charles! What are you doing?' Edgar hissed, peeking between the tent flaps.

'Norma!' Charles bellowed, ignoring Edgar, and he began to run.

AROOOOO

AROOOOO

AROOOOO

A chorus of howls erupted from across the campsite and Edgar's heart sank. Suddenly it was painfully clear that there were more than one of those creatures and Charles was out there alone.

'Charles! Wait!' Edgar shouted and, setting off at a run, he left the safety of the tent.

Edgar had just, moments ago, been contemplating how he would leave Charles and save himself should he need to but now, in the heat of the moment, when disaster struck, Edgar revealed his true nature. He was not a cold, uncaring person. He was a hero.

Edgar sprinted after Charles. He was ahead and he was fast but Edgar spotted him zigzagging between the rows of tents.

He followed as fast and as best he could. He rounded a corner and Charles was gone.

Pad, pad, pad.

AROOOOO

Edgar froze. He knew the creature was close and as he turned slowly, he could sense the monster behind him. Before he could see it, the creature lashed out and pushed Edgar to the ground with such force he was instantly winded. Struggling for breath, he tried to get to his feet but the creature, dived through the air, landed on Edgar and pinned him down. It was bigger than he was and so heavy he couldn't move. The blinding sun caused him to squint and he could hardly makeout the features of the shadowy monster's face but as it moved its head to block the sun, Edgar got a full view that he wished he could unsee.

It was a dog – the ugliest dog he had ever seen. Its black skin was leathery like a bald bear and clung tight to its skeleton as if it were malnourished. Tufts of matted grey hair sprouted from its ears and its eyes, milky white, were eerily blank and dead; its teeth crooked and yellow but as sharp as razors. The dog-creature snapped at Edgar's face with its powerful jaw but Edgar pushed against it with all of its strength and kicked it off of him.

He scrambled to his feet and began to run again – not even caring about the direction. He just wanted to get away. He glanced back and saw the giant dog get back to its feet. It stood, once more, on its hind legs and howled to the sky before giving chase. Edgar stumbled onwards and turned away, not daring to look back.

He tore through the campsite, squealing internally, trying his hardest to find Charles. Suddenly, another monstrous Hound charged at him from the right, this one pink-skinned with blotchy patches of discolouration, and cut off his path. He turned left and sprinted down the path between the tents. There were more than one of the monsters. That was the only thing on Edgar's mind. Just how many were there? He had to get away – he had to escape from them.

A scream in the near distance reminded him that Charles was nearby. He had to find him.

Edgar sprinted as fast as he could, sensing the *pad, pad, pad* of paws behind him. He glanced back over his shoulder to see three now giving chase. They split up, taking different paths among the tents. Edgar rounded a corner and there was Charles.

He rushed to his side. A young woman with dark, braided hair lay on the ground, her pretty face drained of all colour. She was in shock and trembled uncontrolalbly.

'You'll be alright, Norma,' Charles insisted, clinging to her hand. 'I love you. You're safe. I'm here.'

Norma gasped for breath. She tried to speak but no words would come out.

AROOOOOOOOO

Edgar turned. They were there again, joining together. The pack of Hounds advanced on him, walking on their hind legs, towering above them. They snarled dangerously, saliva dripping from their rabid jaws. Norma lay on the ground, Charles beside her, arms wrapped around her for protection. She buried her head into his shoulders and sobbed. The creature stalked closer and Edgar could tell it was smiling sadistically by the way its thin lips curled.

'Stay away!' Edgar commanded but the Hound paid no attention. It merely licked its lips and continued closing in. It held its sharp claws up, ready to attack. Edgar looked all around, hoping to find some kind of weapon to fight with. By chance, he spotted a weapons rack filled with swords and pole-arms. He dived over, grabbed a long pole with a sharp metal spike on the end and held it out defensively.

'Get her to safety!' Edgar commanded to Charles who simply nodded, got up and slung Norma over his shoulder before dashing away.

Edgar faced the monstrous creatures alone. They stalked closer and he could tell they were working together in the way they forked off. One to the left, one to the right and the third staying straight ahead. He was surrounded and they stalked closer. He swung the pole-arm at them, hoping to scare them into backing off but it was useless. They kept advancing and he had to swipe the heavy pole around to keep all three at bay. If he turned his attention from one of them for too long, that could mean death. He had to be careful – be aware.

The Hound straight ahead howled and sprinted straight forward. It leaped through the air and Edgar moved quickly, held the pole out and the Hound landed straight upon it like a skewer. The force of gravity ensured the blade cut right through its skin and flesh and bone and popped out of the other side with a spray of black blood. It thrashed around, screaming in agony, growing limper by the second. It swiped its claws at Edgar but was not strong enough to do any real damage. He dropped the pole and backed away, horrified. His stomach turned. He had just killed that creature. Again, yes, it was evil and wanted to kill him, but he had killed. He was as much a murderer as that monster.

Sensing his momentary weakness, the other two Hounds pounced and knocked Edgar to the ground. He hit his head, hard and for a second, he thought it was all over. He couldn't move – all he could do was curl into a tiny ball, knowing that even that was no protection against their sharp claws and vicious jaws.

AROOOOOOOOO

Edgar tensed and scrunched his eyes closed. He had only seconds to live.

This was it. The end....again.

THE HAUNTINGS OF FATE

'Get away from him!' shouted a sharp voice.

Slowly, Edgar opened his eyes and peeked through his fingers. A shadowy figure stood nearby, swimming in a dizzy haze. The Hounds rounded on them instead. Edgar wanted to help but as he tried to climb to his feet, he fell flat on his face and hit his head hard on the ground again. The soft grass was still not enough of a cushion to protect his head. His vision blurred and eyes heavy.

'Come and get me then!' shouted the voice. It had a soft Scottish twang – or at least Edgar thought so. It sounded familiar and echoed in his head as he drifted off into unconsciousness and the cold darkness enveloped him but that warm, kind voice reverberated in his mind, making him feel safe despite the surrounding danger.

– CHAPTER FIFTEEN –
THE SHAPE OF DESTINY

Edgar came round slowly. He was aware that he sunk into a comfortable, soft surface – a bed - with a thick, grey blanket wrapped around him and several colourful cushions under his head. The smell of incense hung in the air and someone sat next to him on a chair holding his hand in theirs. The soothing sound of violin music drifted in through an open window with the bright sunlight and Edgar felt at peace.

'There you are,' said a soft voice. 'You've been through the wars. I was so worried.'

The voice sounded distant and swam in and out of focus but it was familiar and tinted with a gentle Scottish accent. Edgar blinked several times to clear his eyes and looked into the face of the person who sat by his bedside. It was a friendly face – wrinkled with bright, emerald eyes and a mop of curly, white hair.

'Betty!' Edgar gasped, his voice frail.

For a moment Edgar wondered if despite his best efforts the Nazakan and its Hounds had defeated him. He hadn't stood a chance against them and he stared into those bright, gleaming eyes and found himself more confused than ever. Those eyes he had never expected to see again, at least, not in this life and it was this that sealed his expectations.

He was dead, there was no other explanation.

'Take your time, I'm sure you've a lot of questions,' Betty said quietly, her finger tracing a small circle on the back of Edgar's hand. He didn't know why, but it felt comforting and calmed his panicked mind.

Edgar couldn't reply. There were so many questions.

'I'm...dead?' Edgar whispered hoarsely, completely believing his words.

'I'm so glad Charles found you,' Betty beamed. 'You had us so worried.'

'I'm *not* dead then?' Edgar gasped. '*You're* not dead?'

Betty remained solemn.

'Of course I'm not dead. I'm here, aren't I?'

'What did you do to me?' Edgar asked, his voice catching in his throat. 'Why did you leave me that box?'

'Now that's more complex than you could ever understand right now,' Betty said and Edgar knew she was keeping something from him. 'But in time-'

'You *owe* me answers. Now!' Edgar demanded, his strength returning rapidly.

He sat up and propped himself against the headboard with the soft cushions behind him.

'I suppose I do,' Betty began. 'But I believe it's best to begin with me and my side of the story.'

Edgar nodded, half in understanding and half willing her to continue.

'See, when I used to say I needed to find a coin to go home, I assume you now understand I didn't mean any normal coin,' Betty chuckled as she held out a coin identical to Edgar's. 'I was searching for a travellers' token so I could return here – to Grindlotha – to *my* home.'

'Grindlotha?' Edgar whispered, more to himself. He was sure he had heard the name before. *He had!* In the dreams he had as a child! Dreams of white monks in a grand, black, marble library, reading from ancient tomes and maps.

'This world's name. You see, there's more than just your world out there, which I suppose you know by now.'

'Yeah...there's Merimalima and Deuathac too...and one with psycho police.'

'I'm sorry you had to experience Deuathac. My intention was always for you to reach me before you'd ever have to see that dreadful place.'

'I almost *died*,' Edgar spat viciously. 'Several times. I'm lucky to be here – in fact, I don't even know how I did it. Are you *sure* I'm not dead already and this is all in my imagination?'

Betty stifled a smile as if she were trying to hide the fact that she was enjoying this.

'I'm glad it's not-'

'But you would say that if you're my death dream.'

'You're not dead, Edgar. You are as alive as I am.'

'But in my world, you're dead,' Edgar argued. Despite the evidence of his quick beating heart and shallow breathing, things of which he was suddenly very aware, he absolutely could not bring himself to believe that he had survived yet again.

Betty looked stern, her usually bright face was tinged with sadness and Edgar stared at her, struggling with his feelings but as furious as he was, he couldn't stay mad. After everything, Betty had survived. Just like him. And here she was alive and well in another world.

All that pain and the tears and the hurt that had torn Edgar apart had been for nothing! He had grieved and mourned for what had felt like an eternity but here she was in front of him acting like it was all nothing...but it was! She was here all along; flesh and blood, living and breathing...and it had only just hit him. He laughed out loud and couldn't stop, not even when he struggled to breathe and the tears rolled down his cheeks. He dived at Betty and wrapped his arms around her. Her body was warm and Edgar buried his head into her shoulder, sobbing in relief.

'It's good to see you again, Edgar. I'm sorry-'

She couldn't go on. Her voice crackled as it forced past the lump in her throat. Tears rolled from her eyes too and they embraced in silence, heaving and shaking, unable to let go.

'Now is not the time for this madness,' Betty muttered to herself as she pulled away and wiped the tears from her eyes. Edgar quickly tried to pull himself together too but he couldn't stop the flow of tears of relief, of joy, of frustration and confusion. 'I assume

Charles told you there was a reason he needed to bring you back here.'

'He might have mentioned it,' Edgar murmured, struggling to remember what Charles had actually told him – it had all been a blur: their meeting, Vicky's death, the attack on the camp and then this.

'Good,' Betty said.

Silence fell over them. Neither knew quite what to say and outside Edgar could hear that the person who had been playing the violin was playing another tune now; this one was a long, sad melody.

'So I guessed from reading your letter that you seem to think I'm some kind of *Chosen One,*' Edgar said eventually, breaking the silence and somehow managing to remain serious even though the words he just spoke sounded utterly ridiculous. 'Why me though? You could have picked anyone to follow your silly clues but you chose me and look what happened. I nearly didn't even get here. You picked the wrong person.'

The more he thought about it and the clearer things became in his mind, the angrier he became. Fire writhed in his belly and his brain. Betty had endangered his life and she didn't even seem to care!

'I'm afraid you're wrong, Edgar. You were the only person I could have chosen,' Betty replied simply. There was an edge to her tone that told Edgar not to cross her and her emerald eyes flashed.

'But why me?' Edgar demanded. 'I'm not special. I'm not anything. I'm not a hero or a chosen one. I'm a...a nobody and that's how I get through my life. I keep my head down. I'm not meant to-'

'*Edgar Harold!*' Betty interrupted furiously. 'Look what you've been through and what you've survived to get here. You are *somebody*. You're brave and clever and resourceful. You are a hero and I believe you are the hero we need.'

Edgar rolled his eyes.

'Maybe I am...but it's not like there are ancient prophecies foretelling my heroism or anything.'

Silence fell and Betty coughed quietly to clear her throat. She turned away and crossed the caravan, unable to look at Edgar. He got to his feet slowly and took careful, weak steps after Betty who apparently couldn't bring herself to look at him.

'You mean there are?' he asked quietly and Betty turned around. She only came to his shoulder and she looked up into Edgar's bright blue eyes, so full of curiosity and desperate for answers. 'You know, if there *are* prophecies about me I think I deserve to know.'

'I'm sorry,' Betty whispered, her voice catching and she quickly moved away from Edgar and sat down on a stool beside the table. She pulled another out and patted it gently, offering for Edgar to join her. He did.

'So. Answers?' Edgar said sternly as he sat down. 'No more hiding.'

Betty nodded and took a deep breath. She muttered something under her breath and couldn't bring herself to look Edgar in the eye.

'Answers,' she said quietly.

'Am I the Chosen One?' Edgar demanded, not sure he wanted to know the answer.

Betty remained silent, still unable to look at Edgar and the longer he waited, his eyes transfixed on the poker-faced old lady, awaiting his answer, the more his heart hammered against his chest in pure terror. Betty sighed, closed her eyes and nodded solemnly.

'I am?' Edgar whispered, his voice hoarse.

'Yes and no,' Betty replied quietly. 'I mean to say, yes...there is a prophecy - a legend of a warrior with eyes of ice and hair of flame.'

'Yeah, I've got blue eyes and ginger hair. It doesn't make me the warrior that you think I am!' Edgar snapped in frustration but Betty didn't appear shaken.

'It very well might, Edgar. See, I've not been entirely honest with you all these years.'

'I can see that! You're a bloody dimension traveller. You never cared to tell me that!'

'I know. I'm sorry. But the problem with this prophecy is that it has been misinterpreted before and might be again. I could be wrong about you,' Betty said, eyeing Edgar as if sizing him up.
There was something in her voice that gave away she wasn't entirely confident in her choice – she wasn't confident in him.

'Misinterpreted?' Edgar raged.

'Well-'

'So you drag me into all of this when I might not be the person you need? What happened to the people before who were *misinterpreted*?'

Betty remained silent, staring down at her clasped hands. She knew she deserved everything Edgar threw at her.

'Well?' Edgar shouted. 'What happened?'

Betty didn't flinch. Her expression remained stony.

'You've dragged me in this far, you might as well tell me the truth,' Edgar insisted viciously.

Betty took a deep breath and her voice came out almost silent but Edgar could read the words on her lips:

'They died.'

The words smacked into Edgar so forcefully he felt himself recoil but despite hearing and understanding the sentence, it just simply wouldn't process. His heart skipped a beat, the world plunged into slow-motion and Edgar was surrounded by an all encompassing silence – there were sounds: Voices outside, birds tweeting in the trees, usual every day sounds but Betty's revelation changed everything. Today was no longer normal – not that it ever even had been. Those mundane noises meant nothing. They, just like the words Betty uttered, wouldn't process in Edgar's mind. He was numb. Terrified.

There was so much he wanted to say – so much he wanted to scream and shout and argue but they wouldn't come. He was in shock and simply gaped at Betty...until he found his strength to keep going on.

'Great. Thanks. So what gave you the right to drag me into this? Is that why you stuck around my entire life? You just thought I might be your perfect chosen one to fulfil a prophecy so you groomed me to become just that – so you could use me? I'm fifteen! I'm just a kid!'

Edgar couldn't stop.

The anger that twisted inside him was so intense like a flaming rage that consumed him, burned him alive from the inside out. He trembled and tears welled in his eyes as he thought back through the years – all the time he had spent with Betty. All the fun times he had enjoyed when really she had been twisting and manipulating him in a selfish attempt to shape his destiny.

'The Alphabet Code, all your adventure stories, your stupid anecdotes. It was all part of your plan to bring me here? I can't believe you. You are disgusting. You're selfish and I wish you really had d-'

He stopped before he finished the word but the damage had already been done. Betty's eyes brimmed with tears. She clenched her fist and bit hard on her lip, struggling to keep her cool. She glowered at Edgar, shook her head and got to her feet silently. She headed towards the door but Edgar, suddenly aware the power of his words, jumped up and grabbed her hand.

'I didn't mean that. I'm glad you're still alive,' Edgar apologised and Betty simply sighed again.

'I deserved that, Betty whimpered, choking on the tears that she struggled to contain. 'But I never groomed you to be who you are. You became who you are on your own, I simply had to prepare you.'

'Prepare me for what?'

'For what I have to ask of you. See, if you are the warrior we need, I am so sorry...'

'What do you need a warrior for?' Edgar spat incredulously.

'You've seen the Nazakan. You know what they're capable of.'

'Yeah. I wouldn't stand a chance. They nearly tore me apart.'

'They would have...without remorse, too,' Betty said heavily. 'They are our sworn enemies. Since the beginning of recorded history the Nazakan have ruthlessly slaughtered our kind. They swarmed the Pyramid network which we used to use to travel and forced us to devise a new way and that's when the idea of boots were created-'

'And how does it work? I don't understand how a coin can slip into the sole of a boot and make you travel through dimensions.'

'It's ancient magic. Powerful and secret. Not even I know the true answer.'

Edgar tried hard to comprehend it all but it just went straight over his head. None of this made sense – it was storybook stuff. This happened to fictional characters in books and films. Not him. Not in real life.

'Where were we?' Betty said to herself, frowning as she tried to remember where she was in the story. 'Yes, the Nazakan. They took the pyramids, we created the boots but still they came. We couldn't hold them back. A warrior was chosen – Brother Dominic.'

The name rang a bell in the back of Edgar's mind and he thought hard, trying to remember where from.

'Dominic travelled to the city of Krinka where he was to train with Father Danko, a renowned traveller and become the warrior we needed to defeat the Nazakan but it was too late. Before Dominic could begin his training-'

'The Nazakan attacked and they were trapped in the tower. Danko did something – a spell to keep them at bay. I had a dream. I saw it with my own eyes!' Edgar exclaimed. Visions of the dream flashed back into his mind and he could see it all vividly. The nightmarish attack on Krinka had been violent and desperate, he knew that all too well.

'And the spell worked...but at a cost. Everyone in that tower died in the process. Their bodies burned up on that tower-top. Their lives were sacrificed to create the magic and now the Nazakan can travel no further than half a kilometre from whichever pyramid they emerge from.'

'Which explains the invisible barrier...' Edgar whispered more to himself than Betty. She looked at him curiously and he shook his head as if to tell her to forget it.

'With Dominic and the strongest members of the Order of Krinka dead and the Nazakan merely held at bay it was only a small victory. Years and centuries rolled by, warriors came and went, none of them turned out to be the person of the prophecy and while we were waiting for our hero, the Nazakan retreated to their home where they created lackeys who could cross the magic barriers created by Danko and the Order -'

'The Hounds?' Edgar guessed.

'The Hounds,' Betty confirmed. 'And with their creation, their armies swelled and their power grew once more. This is why we need you, Edgar. If you really are the true warrior we've been waiting for, you will lead us to war against the Nazakan and the Hounds.'

'Me? Lead a war?' Edgar laughed. There was no other reaction for it. He could cry but he had done enough of that and it hadn't gotten him anywhere. 'I can't even lead my own life properly, never mind an army! I'm no leader.'

'You got here in once piece,' Betty smiled reassuringly. 'You're tougher than you give yourself credit for.'

Edgar couldn't think of the words to reply. He felt sick. The weight of the revelation was heavy on him. It was the fate of the world – of several worlds - on his shoulders.

They sat in silence for a moment as Edgar tried to make a little more sense of everything. He pinched his arm several times and doubted the sharp pain that he felt. This must be a dream just like the one about Krinka or the one in the library when he was a child. This couldn't be real. He had to wake up and he had to do it now. He struggled so hard, focused all his concentration on waking from his sleep but no matter how much he forced it, nothing happened. This was real. It was actually happening.

'There is one thing,' Betty said. 'One thing that makes me think I could be right about you.'

Edgar didn't reply. The pressure was too great – in an instant his life had changed and here Betty was, just piling more on him.

'The attack just now-'

'What about it?'

'That was something new, Edgar.' Betty said solemnly. 'They might be our sworn enemies but they don't come looking for a fight. Most attacks are opportunistic, just the odd lone traveller in the wrong place at the wrong time. Maybe once in a while they'll try their luck if we camp too close but this was a full scale attack way out of their way.'

'And how is that anything to do with me?'

'They can sense something is amiss. That's why they lashed out. It's the only way to explain such odd behaviour.'

Edgar thought for a moment. He didn't know a lot about the Nazakan or the Hounds but the reasoning behind Betty's logic seemed legitimate. *Could the Nazakan be reacting to him? Could the attack on the camp be all down to him?*

'I just want to go home,' Edgar said quietly. 'I want to go back and forget this ever happened. I can't do it. I'm sorry. I'm not the person you think I am.'

'Are you quite sure, Edgar?' Betty gave him a cold look and Edgar just gazed back, blank and numb.

Betty sighed. She reached out a wrinkled hand and took hold of Edgar's. Her touch was soft and calmed Edgar, he looked into Betty's eyes, a brow raised in curiosity. There was something else. Something on her mind, on the tip of her tongue – he knew it.

'Since we're being truthful it's time I told you everything.'

'You mean there's more?' Edgar asked nervously, his grip tightening supportively on Betty's trembling hand.

'I always knew you were destined for this life. You're not just randomly selected by a prophecy which may or may not be correct. This travelling life runs in the family. It's in your blood.'

'I don't understand,' Edgar said. 'My family have nothing to do with this?'

'It was your father who left you the boots for your fifteenth birthday, wasn't it?' Betty said imperiously and suddenly the realisation dawned on Edgar. His father, the man he never knew had been a traveller. 'Your father was a traveller.'

'But that's-'

'Why do you think I was always there for you and your mother?' Betty interrupted earnestly, still clutching Edgar's hand tightly. She looked into his eyes, her own brimming with tears. She tried to speak the words stuck in her throat. She coughed quietly and tried once more. 'I'm your grandma, Edgar. I'm your father's mother.'

Edgar was stunned. The world stopped spinning momentarily and his whole body tensed as the words slowly formed into a cohesive sentence in his brain. He stared into Betty's eyes. For his whole life had assumed she was just a close friend. He had never known what she truly meant to him. She was family. True family. His mother had known and she had kept it as secret as Betty had. They were both to blame! Why would they keep that from him?

Secrets.

Some things are acceptable to hide, others not. Everything comes out in the end and things like this were just too big to comprehend. It changed everything.

'My dad. Do you know where he is? Is he still alive?' Edgar asked, the words flying out of his mouth before he could stop them as he suddenly came round and everything came out all at once.

'I'd like to believe so. There's always hope, isn't there?'

'Did he ever find his brother?'

'He did but it was too late, I'm afraid,' Betty sighed sadly.

'And does mum know?' Edgar gasped, his mind flashing back to every single time his mother had mentioned his father – that sad look in her eyes. 'I'm sorry about his brother. I know he'd have been my uncle.'

'He was a good man. They both were. You really do look just like him, you know?'

'Yeah, mum said. Sometimes I worry that it upsets her. I can tell some days she can't even look at me.'

'Love can break people,' Betty replied sadly. 'She loves you very much.'

'So mum knows about the travelling and everything?'

'Again, I believe she does. Aidan told her everything – there were no secrets between them. They were the happiest couple and so in love. I'm sorry that you never got to know him. He would have been so proud.'

Edgar's heart swelled. His father was still out there somewhere...not that it would matter should they ever meet. He would never even know – what would he even say if he did know him? What could he say to the man whom he had never met?

'Why did you keep this secret?'

'The time had to be right. There was too much at stake.'

'I need to go home,' Edgar said. 'Can you help me get there?'

'I can, but first there is one last thing we need to do.'

Betty struggled to her feet and shuffled over to the door. She opened it wide and the sunlight streamed in. She stood by the open door, arm outstretched as if gesturing for Edgar to get up and go outside. The violin music still wafted through the air, thankfully a much jollier tune this time.

Edgar got up, crossed the caravan and stepped out into the blinding light. He shielded his eyes and felt Betty's hand on his shoulder, guiding him onwards. He climbed down the steps onto the grass and saw a group of people gathered around an unlit campfire on a circle of logs.

'Good afternoon, everyone.' Betty chirped and they all murmured in reply and bowed their heads in respect.

Edgar stared at the group, anxious about meeting such a large amount of new people at once. He always hated awkward introductions and felt far too shy to be facing this alone. 'I thought it might be nice to introduce Edgar to everyone here before he heads home.'

'Make sure he doesn't come back,' snarled a large, intimidating man.

'Now, Bardolph. We'll be seeing more of Edgar soon, so please be kind.'

'If I must, but what if we're getting our hopes up?' Bardolph snapped. 'Look at the state of him! All that blood...and that's before he's even supposed to lead a war. What if he's not our warrior?'

'Then that's a bridge we can cross when we get to it,' Betty replied deftly and Bardolph opened his mouth with another rude retort but Betty held her hand up and he stopped in his tracks.

'Right Edgar. This is Adolphus,' Betty said, pointing her finger at the man sat nearest to Edgar. A tall man with long, wispy hair turned around to wave with a long, narrow hand. His face was long and his sallow skin stretched so taught that his steely eyes bulged and his flesh looked like it might tear on his sharp cheekbones.

Next to Adolphus sat Marianne – a short, plump and round-faced girl with a cheeky grin and smiling brown eyes. She sat hand in hand with Fergus – a tall and broad man with long, wild hair and an equally untamed beard.

Then there was Ansé – a stern looking boy with sharp, angular facial features and piercing green eyes and fluffy, mousy hair with a white streak in his fringe. He nodded politely as Betty introduced him but his polite gesture didn't stop his solemn pout. Next to Ansé was Malachi – an old man who gave the impression of wisdom that suggested he must have been as old as, if not older than Betty. Next to him were Eartha and Kerridwen – two best friends who looked almost alike; both with long, curly hair.

Then Bardolph – brother of Adolphus. He couldn't have been any further removed from his brother, not only in terms of position around the circle but in terms of appearance. For what Adolphus was to skinny and skeletal, Bardolph was to large and solid; but this wasn't blubbery fat, this was solid muscle and though Adolphus appeared much older, Bardolph seemed to be quite a lot younger. Next, was Saldi - a cheerful lady with long blonde hair, a cheery smile and glazed over eyes. She rocked back and forth slightly, staring at Edgar in a daze as if she didn't really acknowledge he was there.

'Sorry about her, she's been on the wine,' Betty said, nodding at Saldi who just nodded and giggled to herself.

Next to Saldi was Mary Dandy – a kindly looking lady; and another who smiled with her twinkling eyes. Finally there sat Charles whom Edgar had already met and next to him Norma, a beautiful young girl with long dark hair that fell right down her back. It was tied in a weaved ponytail and she waved sweetly, looking Edgar up and down. There was a long cut across her face and Edgar recognised her as the woman Charles had raced to save earlier. There was something in her expression that made it clear to Edgar that her smile was false. Deep inside, the girl was sad – he could see it in her dark eyes that just looked blankly at him – they were devoid of light or life. She was empty.

It made Edgar feel a little more at ease to see the friendly smiles on the faces of so many strangers. They all stared, awestruck, as if he were some sort of celebrity but he couldn't help but feel unnerved by Bardolph's scowling. He had done nothing to deserve it!

'Hello, everyone,' Edgar said at last. 'I suppose it means a lot to you all that I'm here...especially if I really am your warrior. I'll try not to let you all down. I promise.' Edgar said, not quite knowing what he was meant to say to a group of people who had obviously all heard of him and waited so long to meet him.

'It's lovely to meet you, Edgar,' Mary Dandy began as she jumped up from her seat and kneeled before Edgar. She took his hand in hers and shook it vigorously and Edgar just smiled awkwardly.

'You too, Mary,' he replied and Mary jumped to her feet and scuttled off.

'He knows my name!' he heard her hiss as she vanished around the side of a tent, squealing.

Next he spotted Ansé walk forward, wrapped in a heavy white cloak with a giant red cross on the back. He carried a sword by his side, which he unsheathed as he knelt and jabbed the blade into the soft grass and leaned on the hilt.

'May it be my honour to fight by your side, Edgar Harold. May it be my honour to lay my life down for the one true warrior.'

There was a solemnity in Ansé's voice and Edgar looked a little perplexed. He wasn't used to this; back home he was the kid people bullied but here he could tell from the gawping expressions of everyone he had met that he was worshipped and revered, almost as a kind of God.

'Thank you,' Edgar replied, unsure of what to really say.

His words were cut short and drowned out by a tumultuous hubbub of chatter and Edgar spotted several people whispering behind their hands while they eyed him darkly and it made him feel uncomfortable – he felt naked, exposed and it wasn't helping the anxiety of what he had just learned about himself.

'Now you've met the boy himself, we've got business to attend to,' Betty said sharply and the chaos subsided. Silence fell but all eyes were still on Edgar, gleaming hungrily as if they were predators and he were their prey. Betty took Edgar's hand and led him back inside the caravan, slammed the door shut and pulled down the curtain over the window.

'Back to business,' Betty muttered. 'Your Token. Give me it.'

Edgar's hand reached for his pocket and as his fingers slipped in and brushed against the cold metal he felt a rush of relief. It was still there. It was safe. He pulled it out and passed it gently into Betty's hand. She lifted it up so Edgar could see it clearly.

'I assume you'll be wondering how it works?' Betty said and Edgar couldn't help but laugh.

'Talk about stating the obvious,' he thought.

'Well,' Betty began. 'Each point of the star has the little hole in it, right?'

Edgar nodded. There *was* a small hole in each point of the pentagram, right next to the numbers: 5,4,7,1 and 18 which he knew spelled out his name.

'Right, so each point of the star corresponds to a dimension.'

'Got it so far.'

'So the top point is Erathas, the place you call home,' Betty said, pointing a finger at the top of the star. 'The second on the right, Alternus Erathasus, the bottom right is Deuathac, bottom left is Grindlotha and the left is Merimalima.'

Edgar listened intently, trying to commit this information to memory.

'Erathas is home. Grindlotha is here. Deuathac is the place with the Unsterbliche, Merimalima is the one with the islands and

Alternus Erathasus...well, that sounds like Alternative Erathas, which would make sense why the museum was like the Brunswick.'

'Correct,' Betty excitedly clapped her hands together. She was so proud of Edgar for picking it up so quickly. 'Now, remind me which point corresponds to which dimension.'

'Erathas is the top, Alternus Erathasus is right, bottom right is Deuathac then Grindlotha and then left is Merimalima.'

'Correct again,' Betty beamed. 'Now that's the basics, never forget them. Never.'

'But how do I make it work properly? I thought I just had to stamp on it but if it's so precise, I guess that's wrong,' Edgar chuckled and Betty shook her head, laughing with him.

'Lift up your foot.'

Edgar did as he was told and placed his booted foot on the table.

'So, the metallic indentation on the sole has the same insignia as this travellers' token?'

'Yeah,'

'It fits into there and the little metal spike goes through the hole corresponding to the dimension you want to visit.'

Edgar nodded, sort of understanding what Betty told him. It made sense.

'Once it's set, you give it a little clockwise twist. Never anti-clockwise,' Betty noted warningly which only elicited a puzzled stare from Edgar.

'Why?' he asked, almost scared about what the answer might be.

'Anti-clockwise allows us to time-travel-'

'TIME TRAVEL?' Edgar bellowed, unable to contain his excitement. Betty shot him a dangerous glare, colder than Priscilla's and Edgar knew that this was not something to celebrate. He wondered why, time-travel would be a fantastic opportunity.

'We never use that unless in an extreme emergency,' Betty said darkly.

'Why? It could be-'

'One slight change in the past can alter the entire future. One slight mistake then BANG you're gone. You never existed, wiped from time. Gone.'

'But it would be hard to cause something like that – you don't just go back in time and make people unborn,' Edgar argued hotly. He didn't care what Betty said – he wanted to time-travel. There was so much history he had always wished he could see first hand and now he could!

'It's not just that. Your boots could break. You loose your token, you get hurt, trapped...what would you do then?'

Edgar couldn't think of a reply. Betty made a decent point, but it still didn't stop the curiosity.

'You've seen how dangerous it is out there as it is. There are darker times across all the dimensions, cataclysms, viral outbreaks, wars,' Betty began, her voice tense and passionate. 'And now we face our own war, Edgar and we need you. We can't lose you. It's simply too risky.'

Edgar could see what she meant but it wasn't fair! Why tell him he had this power then strip it off him?

'Not even one trip?' Edgar tested but Betty glowered at him and he knew he had pushed too far. 'Only joking,' he lied, hoping to make it right again.

Betty sighed.

'Ansé. That boy out there,' she pointed at the door. 'He was stuck in the crusades. Took a lot of fighting to get himself out of that mess, he won't really talk about it. All we know is that he got caught up with the Knights Templar and they made him do things. Bad things and he was almost burned at the stake for his involvement. It still tortures him.'

Edgar stared open-mouthed. He loved the Crusades – it was his favourite period of history. The Knights Templar were one of the most illusive cults in history, their origins and secret ways shrouded in darkness and hidden by lies. Edgar had studied them at school and become enthralled in the mystery.

'The crusades though!' Edgar shrieked excitedly, open-mouthed. 'Ansé was there?'

'Not worth the risk. You need to know where you want to be, need to see it, feel it. Most of us can only travel along our own time-lines as we know places and times better than anyone else. The stronger the connection, the easier it is to travel,' Betty explained and Edgar's eyes lit up.

'Can I sneak forward?' Edgar muttered 'See what happens in this war? If I really am your warrior?'

Betty shook her head solemnly.

'Nobody can go forward in time. According to the legends, Saint Margarette managed to but they're only stories. It wouldn't work because of the nature of *how* you travel, needing to know places, times, et cetera,' Betty scoffed. 'The same can be said, however, for simply travelling dimensions. Always have a place in mind, picture it, feel it, live it. If not, you'll be dumped randomly in that dimension which could end up with catastrophic consequences.'

'Okay...so recap?' Edgar said, pointing at his foot on the table. 'Clockwise to travel properly. Anti-clockwise for time-travel. We don't time-travel. The star points on the token match dimensions. The top is Erathas-'

Betty nodded and jammed his token into the boot.

'No! Betty! What are you doing?' Edgar shrieked, panic stricken.

He couldn't go home. Not now! He still had so many questions to ask – things he needed answered. He shivered and closed his eyes in anticipation of the agony to hit him. It wouldn't be long until the stomach ache and the sickening nausea started. He waited for his surroundings to turn black as he moved on but it didn't happen.

'I'm sorry, you've been gone long enough. We can't risk you being away too long. Priscilla will start to suspect something is amiss,' Betty explained calmly, while Edgar froze in terror. It felt different this time. 'I'll see you soon.'

Instead of passing out, a deafening wind blasted in and brought with it, thick mist flooded that enveloped him until the caravan was invisible and Betty faded away like a ghost.

Whoosh.

The wind whipped him upwards at a tremendous speed and Edgar couldn't help but scream. Why was it happening differently this time? He felt as though he was being dragged up towards the sky, like bungee jumping in reverse, gaining more and more speed as she fell upwards. All around him the cloudy mist darkened and as Edgar reached the apex of his flight; he broke through the cloud and dark into bright, blinding light. He stopped momentarily and went completely weightless, like an astronaut in space and then his stomach flipped.

That moment felt like an eternity, staring out at a vast expanse of pure, bright nothingness. It was beautiful and calm amid the fear and confusion that filled Edgar's heart...but it didn't last. Suddenly there was a jolt and it was like falling down a sheer drop on a roller coaster.

Edgar's hair whipped into his face, choking him as he screamed out; the sound hardly came out as the fall ripped the wind from his lungs and he fell and fell, feeling like it would never end and then Edgar's feet pushed through the cloud and they broke around him. He was falling down and down towards the Earth. It was gaining on him, or rather, he was gaining on it. The ground came closer and closer. He closed his eyes, screaming and crying.

What was going on?

Was this it?

After all he had been through he was going to die now.

He glimpsed bravely between his tight eyelids. The wind whipped him around and now he was upside down, falling face first. He recognised the place from above and he opened his eyes wide – if this were to be his last sight he really didn't mind.

The castle headland with the bones of the old settlement curling around the top of it, protecting the town from the expanse of the North Sea and the crooked streets of the old town – the long, glorious and golden beaches either side of the headland. He could see Oliver's Mount and all the way out to the neighbouring villages of Osgodby and Cloughton. He rushed towards it, closer and closer until he could see his house directly below.

Falling, falling, falling.

Screaming.

Flailing.

Scrambling.

Edgar twisted and turned in the air, trying to aim himself at the sea. At least if he hit water it might offer him a chance of survival...but what was he kidding himself? From that height, hitting water would be like landing on concrete; even if he did survive he would knock himself clean out and sink beneath the waves.

Edgar had faced death so bravely so many times now that his mind cleared with acceptance. He closed his eyes once more as he came closer and closer to the house beneath him – his own home. With one last deep breath and a nervous gulp, Edgar accepted his fate.

THUD.

Then there was nothing. Just darkness and silence.

– CHAPTER SIXTEEN –
A HIDDEN FORTUNE

Ugh.

Edgar groaned and stirred. First his fingertips, then his whole body. He was breathing, deep and slow. His veins pulsed with adrenaline. He was alive.

That journey had been terrifying; he much preferred it when he had passed out...but at the same time it had been exhilarating! *Had he gone through the same while being unconscious on his previous trips – why had it been different this time?* So many more questions despite him having only just gained some answers.

Edgar raised his head and glanced around. He had landed in the middle of his kitchen where sunlight streamed in through the window and pooled on the laminate floor around him.

'I see you've made it back,' said a severe voice before Edgar could even get to his feet. It was Brother Bradley, standing in the middle of the living room, framed by the door. 'And now you understand.'

'I don't understand anything. All I have is more questions,' Edgar spat in frustration as he stood up and leaned against the kitchen table, beside the little square window. 'I almost never made it back. I wouldn't have if it hadn't been for Betty.'

Brother Bradley stood in the middle of the living room, his giant frame flickering and distorting as usual.

'Yet you survived.'

'Yeah..but that's not the point. It was pure luck.'

'You're a stronger person than you think, Edgar,' Brother Bradley said. He glided towards Edgar, reaching out and placed his hand on his shoulder. It was cold like ice and made Edgar shiver.

There was a momentary pause in which Edgar looked up into the towering monk's eyes, hoping to find some kind of clarity in what he was saying; hoping to be able to discern whether it true or if he was just saying it to be kind.

'Am I the True Warrior?' Edgar asked nervously, still maintaining eye contact with the flickering ghost.

'Only time will tell,' Brother Bradley said solemnly.

'And what about the others before me? What about those who failed and died? What if the same will become of me?'

'Death is nothing to be afraid of, Edgar.'

Scratch. Scratch. Scratch.

The noise came from behind the kitchen wall. It seemed distant and quiet but it was distinct and Edgar fell silent, straining his ears to hear.

Scratch. Scratch. Scratch.

'What's that?' Edgar asked curiously, looking to Brother Bradley with a raised eyebrow. The ghost simply remained stony and still, just flickering.

Scratch. Scratch. Scratch.

Edgar crossed over to the back of the kitchen and pressed his ear against the wall. The scratching became louder. He could hear something scuffling behind the brick...but that was impossible. There was nothing but solid dirt behind the wall. There was an allotment behind the house but that was at roof level and could only be accessed by a flight of steps behind a gate half way down the street.

'Might be rats in the pipes or something?' Edgar guessed out loud but when he turned to Brother Bradley for reassurance, the monk was gone.

Star sauntered into the kitchen, mewed loudly at Edgar, rubbed around his legs and then settled down to eat her dinner.

Scratch. Scratch. Scratch.

Star stopped eating. She glanced over to the back wall and arched her back and began to make horrid, growling noises. Edgar crouched down to calm her but she hissed and attacked him.

'OUCH!' Edgar screamed as the cat sliced him to pieces; her sharp claws sliding through his flesh like butter.

Star bolted through the house, up the stairs and out of the small, square window in the bathroom that was always left open as a cat flap. Edgar tore through the house after her, stumbling on the stairs in his haste. He peeked out of the bathroom window and saw Star sat on the flat roof of the kitchen extension below. She mewed and jumped up to the back wall and disappeared over the other side into the allotments.

'You have no idea what it's capable of!' said a deep voice from somewhere nearby. Someone was in the allotment.

'I've never seen anything like it,' said another quiet voice, again, it was a man.

'They'll be coming soon,' the first man said. His voice was tinged with urgency. 'We've got to destroy it before they find us but I don't know how.'

'Set it on fire? Smash it?'

'It won't work. I've already tried.'

Edgar froze. He had no idea what these people were talking about but it didn't sound good.

'OI! Who's there?' he shouted through the tiny window, unable to see over the wall.

'Shh,' whispered the voice over the wall. 'Keep it down. Someone's there.'

'I dunno what you're doing but you'd better move along or I'll call the police!' Edgar bellowed and the voices muttered quietly among themselves. There was a *thud* followed by the sound of running footsteps, a click of a lock and the *WHOOSHING* gust of wind as a draught blasted through the house, then silence.

'What's going on?' Edgar shouted again but there was no reply. He waited a moment. Nothing.

Edgar turned and caught a glimpse of himself in the mirror that hung above the sink. He stopped. Stared. It was like an entirely different person stared back at him. The eyes were tired and sunken, this hair was tangled and messy. His pale skin covered in dried blood, his clothes tattered and torn. He had been through hell and back and it was starting to show.

He turned the tap and the water began to stream. He cupped his hands, caught the water and splashed it all over his face, wiping and scrubbing with his fingers until the blood came away. Crimson water washed down the plughole. That was better.

Quickly, he dashed into his bedroom and changed into clean clothes and hid the ripped ones under his bed.

BANG

The foundations of the house shook as the front door slammed shut.

'Edgar! Edgar, I'm home. Where are you?' It was Priscilla, back from work.

Edgar didn't reply. He ran down the stairs and hung on the corner, peeking down into the living room below.

'I just overheard someone in the allotment talking about smashing things up and setting stuff on fire,' Edgar felt anxious under the cold, scrutinous glare of Pricilla's narrowed eyes. She was suspicious and he knew it.

'Seriously, mum. I shouted and they ran off but what if they're still up there? We need to get in.'

'You know that it's impossible to get up there. Only George has the key to the gate.'

'Can't you call him and get him to let us in?'

'No, Edgar!'

'But *mum!*'

'Fine, I'll call him.'

Edgar couldn't move; his legs wouldn't allow him.

Perhaps it was that the exhaustion of his travels finally hit him but he stared at Priscilla, forcing a smile to hide all that was on his mind.

'Are you alright?' she asked, suddenly aware that her son wasn't quite himself.

'Fine,' he replied quietly as he slowly forced himself to shuffle down the stairs, his body still stiff and aching from his travels. Priscilla's eyes remained on him like a hawk. She frowned suspiciously and as Edgar wrapped his arms tightly around her and hung his head on her shoulder, she didn't quite know how to react.

'Are you sure you're alright?' she asked curiously. 'You're not on drugs are you? If you're on drugs, so help you God!'

'It's not drugs, mum. It's just-'

No. It was too soon.

Yes, there was a possibility that she would completely understand what Edgar was. There was a chance she would know what he had been through but there was something in his mind that held him back. A sharp fear that she wouldn't understand at all or that she would just deny all knowledge of everything. After all, it was this life that had cruelly taken his father from her and judging by his recent adventures, Edgar knew she could easily lose him too. No, It was not a good idea to tell her. He had to keep it secret, at least for now until he felt more confident and had wrapped his own head around his new life.

'You're being...odd,' Priscilla muttered as she broke away from Edgar and sat down in her armchair.

'It's been a long day...I missed you is all,' Edgar lied quickly.

Priscilla rolled her eyes. She would never understand him.

'So about the garden?'

'YES! I'll call George! If you'll just shut up. Now go make me a cup of tea.'

*

Later that evening they met George halfway down the street where a tall, black gate shut off an alleyway with a flight of steep steps leading up between two houses on either side to the allotments at the top.

'Sorry I'm late. I've been up town, shopping,' he wheezed.

George was particularly old and stooped over like a hunchback. His short, white hair was wispy and blew around even in the most non-existent of breezes. His frail, pallid skin was wrinkled like a prune and heavy black bags had developed under his watery eyes.

'Are you alright George?' Priscilla asked worriedly and George smiled toothlessly.

'Getting by,' he wheezed.

Priscilla looked sad, she didn't quite know what to say.

'I'm glad you called actually, Priscilla,' George continued, his voice raspy as is he struggled to get each word out. 'You know, I'm not well and I can't keep up with all this gardening, so I want you to have the land behind your house when I'm gone.'

'George, don't be silly,' Priscilla said, a tear welling in her eye. 'Don't talk like that.'

'I've been thinking for a while, but while I'm here, I might as well tell you and you can get a headstart on getting it up to scratch, I'll tell everyone else about their plots nearer to the time. It's only fair you all get your own land. Make it nice, enjoy it.'

George pulled a key from his pocket and handed it to Priscilla.

'Oh, George. Thank you,' she said gratefully. She hugged him warmly and he patted her on the back.

'You're a lovely lass, Priscilla and your lad is a good 'un. You've done a fantastic job of bringing him up all by yourself. Well, I'd better let you get on. No way I'll make it up them steps without a heart attack.'

'Are you sure? I feel dreadful getting you all the way over here just for this.'

'No, no. It's fine Priscilla. I'll see you soon.'

Priscilla unlocked the padlock on the high gate and it swung open with a creak. As she and Edgar ascended the steep, stone steps their footsteps echoed.

The steps up were crumbling and cracked with weeds sprouting through the holes in the concrete and when they reached the top there was an expanse of overgrown land with more weeds popping up out of every possible surface; stinging nettles hiding among them waiting for an unsuspecting victim to attack. In the rare sections of uncovered soil bits of broken brick, glass, old sweet wrappers and a few animal droppings of various sizes could be seen strewn all over as if it were an ancient dumping ground.

The plot of land behind Edgar's house wasn't too bad. It was full of overgrown grass and weeds but with a few days worth of solid, difficult gardening it would be up to scratch in no time. Edgar immediately wished to never see another overgrown garden in his whole life – he loathed gardening and it made him feel sick just looking at it.

Edgar and Priscilla wandered the whole length of the land checking among the bushes for any signs of people hiding. Edgar even braved peeking into the old shed at the far end of the allotment by the wall that separated it from the churchyard but there was nobody to be found. Whoever had been there was long gone.

'EDGAR COME HERE! I'VE FOUND SOMETHING,' his mum shouted excitedly as she stuck her head up from a red gooseberry bush a short distance away.

'What is it? Edgar shouted over to her.

She turned to show Edgar something in her excitedly shaking hands.

'This is fascinating; I've got to take it to work to show Patrick,' she squealed. 'He'll love it!'

Edgar rushed over to take a closer look. Priscilla held a small, black sculpture in her hands. It was shaped like a pyramid - like the one in the ice caves and the one in the forest. Edgar took it from her and turned it over in his hands. It was heavy for its small size and it was cold and smooth like marble. On the bottom, the pattern of the crossed swords and the glowing light from the travellers' token was etched into it as if somebody had faintly scratched it on and in the top point of the star was the number *18* – the other points were blank.

'Wow,' said Edgar taken back by surprise of having something so strange behind his house but at the same time wondering what it could possibly mean. Why was the same symbol from the token on this pyramid? It was all too much of a coincidence and Edgar couldn't work out what it could mean. Something like this couldn't have just been left laying so openly on the ground. Had the people he had heard dropped it when they fled? Is this what they wanted to destroy and if so, why?

'Patrick will definitely know what it is. He loves antiques and stuff, doesn't he?' Edgar replied as he passed the artifact back to Priscilla.

'I'm at work tomorrow so I can take it in then,' she squeaked excitedly, bouncing on the spot. 'Bloody hell. The ground sounds a bit hollow up here. Listen.'

Priscilla stomped on the soil and Edgar felt the vibrations through the ground and heard a dull *thump*.

'Weird,' Edgar muttered, more to himself than to Priscilla.

*

That night Edgar lay in bed, staring at the ceiling. He couldn't clear his mind and rest despite being so exhausted. He wanted nothing more than to drift off and go to sleep but too much had happened. He just couldn't forget it all and sleep.

The thoughts of his journey replayed again and again like a nightmarish loop right before his eyes. So much had changed so quickly and in a sense, Edgar just wanted to forget. He didn't want to be a warrior. He didn't want to lead a war. War wasn't something he believed in. It was too much trouble, too much needless loss of life and even if they won and he survived, another enemy would find a way to rise and the whole vicious cycle would start again. That's all that ever happened with war until someone brave enough could take a stand and say no.

That's what he wanted to do. He wanted to refuse – to stand resolute and unwavering in his reluctance. He had seen enough horrors already and he didn't care to see any more. The thought of the suffering he would inflict by agreeing to fight was too much to bear – those people who would agree to fight by his side and put their lives at risk for the sake of an ancient prophecy could die and it would all be on him. No. He wouldn't let it happen. Mr. Griffith and Martin and Vicky had already died because of him. No more. But if he didn't fight, if he didn't stop the Nazakan and their Hounds, what would happen then? He had seen them in action – seen with his own eyes what they were capable of and that terrified him. If he let them live, left them unchecked then what hell would be unleash on the world?

Perhaps the war was necessary.

It was too confusing to think and the thoughts clouded his head, spinning in circles until he was dizzy. He needed to weigh up the pros and cons – to balance his argument logically, to recount his experience, to put it all into the words that he couldn't say out loud. It was time to start a diary.

Edgar rolled out of bed and began rummaging through the drawers in his desk. He knew he had one somewhere...there it was! He pulled it out and sat down at the desk to begin writing.

As the words poured out, he began to feel as if the weight of the world were being lifted from his shoulders, like it was somehow relieving him of the burden he had to carry. He wasn't alone anymore. It was him and his trusty little book; his diary of secrets.

He recounted Betty's death in agonising detail, he wrote of how he inherited her box of clues and how he followed them to find the travellers' token and how Brother Bradley had helped lead him to it. He wrote about the terror of his encounter with the Unsterbliche – how he learned of the schism between the Altere and Verstossen; he wrote of his guilt over the death of Mr. Griffith in the museum and the corrupted police who ran amok in that world. He described his near death experience in Merimalima, his discovery in the ice tombs, the rescue by Charles and the burning at the stake – how he just sat there and let his old friend die...how he watched her burn alive and did nothing as she screamed out for help...and he finished the story so far with the revelation od Betty's survival and the discovery that he was supposedly a warrior who was meant to lead a war.

The pain he felt as the words came tortured Edgar but it felt good. It helped to make sense of the madness. Though he only scribbled down the basics, it was off his chest and with this little relief, Edgar climbed back into bed, clung to his pillow and slowly drifted to sleep, completely unaware of the ghost stood in his doorway, watching like a silent, eagle-eyed guardian as always.

*

Priscilla and Patrick sat down in the office at the heart of the museum, talking about the artifact that she had just shown him. Edgar had been told to wait outside but he sneaked up to the door and tried to catch a snatch of the conversation, relying on his stealthy eavesdropping skills to find out what was going on without being caught by Ida who skulked around and trying to weevil out any signs of mischief that were going on around the building.

'I've never seen anything *quite* like it,' he heard Patrick say, astounded.

'But you deal in antiques, you should know about these things.'

'But this is one of those things that seems rather rarer than those that I deal in and that's saying something,' Patrick said curiously.

Edgar peeked through the keyhole and saw Patrick pacing the office examining the artifact, turning it in his hands and studying it. He pushed his enormous glasses back up his hooked nose and brought the pyramid closer to his face, examining closer.

'Do you know anything about this symbol?' he asked and Priscilla shook her head.

'Well, instinct says it's occult, used for some kind of, possibly Pagan ceremony. Of course, I'm not certain but that's what I feel when I look at it,' Patrick said thoughtfully. 'I must admit, I've never seen anything quite like this etching. Not even in all of my research.'

'So you have no idea what it is then? Not even the slightest inkling?' Priscilla asked disappointedly as she sipped her coffee and Patrick shook his head.

'I haven't.'

'Then what should I do with it?'

'Would you be interested in giving it to the museum?' Patrick asked her 'For our collection.'

Edgar grew bored of the conversation and he couldn't be bothered to listen to Patrick waffle on about the museum collections...*again*. It was all he ever talked about and he had endured enough one-sidedly enthusiastic conversations with him about the collections over the years. Besides, Ida had just stalked around the corner, resembling a bird of prey as she peered down her beak-like nose at Edgar. She sniffed loudly and wandered past.

'Hi Ida,' Edgar said to her, trying to appear surreptitious. She nodded at him silently and took a seat behind the desk to wait for customers. There was no possibility of sneaking around anymore. He'd be in plain sight so he took advantage of the time he had left to wander the museum and enjoy the moment of peace.

When Priscilla eventually emerged from the office her eyes were sparkling with excitement and her whole body quivered as though she could burst. However, she managed to suppress her laughter until she'd reached the door.

Outside his mum let a hysterical, almost insane laugh and then a long, loud sigh of relief.

'What's wrong?' asked Edgar eagerly.

'Well, Patrick just said that he doesn't know what the artifact is but fact one; the land behind our house needs excavating and exciting fact number two; he's just paid me six thousand pounds for the artifact, which is going towards the museum's permanent collection,' she whispered, still shaking with excitement.

Edgar laughed with her. He couldn't remember them having that much money ever! They were rich. Not *really* rich, but rich enough and Edgar could hardly believe their luck.

The rest of the day passed quickly and Edgar's mind kept wandering back to the thought of the amount of money that his mum had just been offered for the artifact. He simply couldn't believe the small fortune that had been hidden in the bushes upon the allotment. He had spoken a lot of fate recently – perhaps this was just another reason to believe in it.

'Everything happens for a reason,' he told himself.

Edgar smiled to himself. Fate was a complicated business but it had finally thrown something worthwhile his way. That money – a whole six thousand pounds, could fix all his and Priscilla's problems. They could live comfortably for a while rather than scraping by on her meagre wage. It made a world of difference.

Fate was complicated but life was good.

– CHAPTER SEVENTEEN –
BROTHER BRADLEY'S WARNING

That night, Edgar lay in bed unable to sleep. He took the coin from his pocket and began to fiddle with it obsessively, staring down at the strange symbol etched deep upon its surface. His thoughts were on the pyramid object Priscilla had found in the garden – Betty had mentioned a Pyramid network of travel that had been compromised by the Nazakan. He had seen one for himself, seen the creature that had come out of it and it would haunt him forever.

He wanted to go back and see Betty with all his heart, but he was too scared. Whatever Betty said about him being a warrior and leading an army – she was wrong. It wasn't him. No way. He couldn't defend himself from bullies like Spencer at school so there was no way he could lead a war against the Nazakan.

With sleep slipping further from him thanks to anxiety, Edgar settled down instead to offload his fears and thoughts onto the pages of his diary but as he let his soul seep from the nib of his pen and flow over the paper, Edgar felt the pain strike hard once more.

The guilt.

The sadness.

The death.

Edgar had killed Edvard and it was true that though Edvard had been a monster, it still made Edgar a murderer. He had taken a life. He had considered taking another in Merimalima. He had let Mr. Griffith die and done nothing; the same thing he did when Vicky, one of his closest friends, was dragged up the steps and strung up to burn in the flames at the shrine of Saint Margarette.

The shouts, the screams, the pain and agony. The anger and the fear; it was like a cruel ghost that would never stop haunting him. The ghosts of those who died, whose blood was on his hands. They would never let him rest and that was why he could not sleep, even when he flung his diary into the corner, wiping the frustrated tears from his eyes and slumped into bed so exhausted he felt like he might pass out. He pulled the covers over his head and tried to close his eyes but was greeted with the faces of his personal ghosts.

Slowly, he poked his head out from under his duvet and sighed. He didn't notice the figure stood in the corner of his room again - the flickering shape of a man beside his wardrobe. Edgar lay there for a moment, staring up at the glow in the dark stars on his ceiling, numb and then he noticed him. He wanted to scream with shock but he really wasn't scared. It was Brother Bradley again.

'What do you want now?' Edgar sighed.

'I bring a warning.'

Edgar frowned.

'Why now? Why not before?'

'You deny Betty's choice. You believe you are not the true warrior of legends,' Brother Bradley said softly.

'I'm not. I can't be,' Edgar replied with a sigh. 'It's not me.'

Brother Bradley just stared incredulously.

'Why are you back after all these years? Why are you following me?'

'I never left. Your loneliness and your sadness brought me back,' Brother Bradley said solemnly. The corners of his mouth flickered into a sympathetic smile. 'I know you're bottling lots up. You can talk to me like you used to.'

Edgar felt a warm, salty tear fall. It was true – he couldn't tell his mother about how bad things had become at school; she would only worry or try and do something but only make it worse. It wasn't just that though, it was the burning anger inside Edgar's heart, the searing hatred of his bullies and then there was something else – something he couldn't explain eating away inside him like a darkness that even he didn't know what it was or how to control it, instead, *it* controlled him.

'So what do you have to warn me about?' Edgar asked, trying to avoid the subject of his mental health. He had put it all down to puberty – the teachers at school, his mother, his friends, had all said that growing up is hard and strange things can begin to happen: mood swings, frustration, anger all caused by hormones and the chemicals warring against each other inside his body and his brain. He had assumed it was normal.

It was, wasn't it?

'I cannot say too much but there is more going on than you know. Do you remember the words I spoke to you as a child.' There was some urgency in Brother Bradley's tone – something that told Edgar he had to take everything in.

'I still remember it,' Edgar said quietly, his eyes wide as his mind drifted back to his childhood.

"Every second has a meaning,
Day after day, the world still spins.
Great barriers act as invisible pins;
All holding the fabric of time and space
Relatively in the very same place.

How would you cope,
Armed with nothing but hope to
Ready you for the dark days to come?
Over the barriers you will go,
Living your life, to help other's lives flow.
Deaf you will be to the Raven's crow."

The ghost and Edgar whispered the words together in a perfect unison, as if reciting some ancient, powerful spell.

'I don't understand it,' Edgar sighed. 'I never did and I probably never will.'

'Oh, you will, Edgar Harold. Time will tell,' the ghost replied.

His tone was pointed and he looked at Edgar coldly, almost disappointed that he hadn't worked it out.

'It's about my life, isn't it?' Edgar guessed, slowly realising. 'It's about what I've got to do – dimension travel and stuff.'

Brother Bradley nodded slowly, still flickering and distorting in the half-light of the night.

'It is, but it means so much more,' he said gravely and Edgar looked confused again. '*First,* write it *down* like a *letter.*'

'What do you mean?'

Brother Bradley repeated himself in a dark tone and Edgar climbed out of bed, feeling embarrassed that he was only wearing a pair of boxers in front of the monk. He walked over to his desk, holding his hands in front of himself as if to protect his modesty and he grabbed a pair of jeans from the pile of clothes on top of the table. He pulled them on quickly and then took a pen and a piece of paper from a drawer.

He sat back down beside Brother Bradley who watched him intently.

'Your handwriting is still atrocious,' the ghost snapped like a strict school teacher.

'Yeah. I'm not a very neat person – just look at this room.'

The ghost didn't seem amused.

'Funny how I remembered this,' Edgar muttered. 'It's been so long. Twelve years since you vanished...and the last time I saw you, you-'

'I did *not* steal your Teddy and I shan't tell you again.'

'Then who did?'

Brother Bradley shrugged.

'So,' Edgar had finished writing the poem down. His eyes scanned over the words, trying to spot something that Brother Bradley had clearly insinuated was there.

'What am I looking for?' Edgar asked, puzzled.

'Seek and you shall find,' Brother Bradley said sternly, there was a waver in his voice as if he were holding back his frustration.

His face remained severe as he watched Edgar struggle.

Edgar spent what felt like an age scanning the words that made up the lines of the poem but he couldn't make any sense from it – all he could figure out was that it was about dimension travel – that was obvious. Perhaps it was something to do with *"the Raven's crow"* – he had no idea what that meant.

'Is it something to do with the Raven's crow?' Edgar asked, hoping he was right. 'I don't even know what I'm looking for.'

'Edgar, not all things need to be read from left to right,' Brother Bradley said with a wink to make the hint more obvious.

Edgar read the poem backwards but it still made no sense – there were no hidden clues...but then he remembered something from school. He had learned about acrostic poetry where the lines were read normally but the first letter of each line made a word when read downwards.

Edgar's eyes followed the first line down and to his surprise he found something he hadn't expected. He found a name – his own name: *Edgar Harold.*

'This poem was about me. It's always been about me – that's why you used to tell me it as a kid. You were *always* hinting, even way back then of what waited ahead in my future,' Edgar gasped, unable to believe what he had just discovered – his name with another blatant association with dimension travel.

'This is an ancient poem but it all links to your fate,' the ghostly Monk said severely, watching Edgar as he clutched his head, trying to get his mind around what was going on. 'Fate is the air we breathe and the food we eat and the water we drink and it seems the fate of the Warrior of Legends has your name laid all over it – strewn across many places until the paths meet at a crossroads and there you are.'

'Nice metaphor,' Edgar laughed. His face was screwed up and his forehead wrinkled as he tried to figure out what Brother Bradley had meant – it partially made sense.

'So my fate is haunting me?' Edgar sighed glumly – it only seemed that Betty's prophecy about him being the warrior to lead the war kept getting stronger. 'I can't run from it, can I?'

'Like my fellow brothers and I, you were called to your cause. Our lives are pre-planned by a greater force than us and we exist to humbly serve our purpose.'

'You expect me to believe that?' Edgar scoffed. 'I know you're a monk and religion is your thing, but -'

'I should warn you to not blaspheme, Edgar Harold. In time you will face the Almighty Creator,' Brother Bradley snapped in a pointed tone. His expression was austere and Edgar backed down.

'There were others like you, weren't there?' Edgar probed, curious to know more 'Like Brother Dominic and Danko?'

Brother Bradley could not hide his emotions. He winced as if the words physically hurt him. Edgar could see that he knew something – something dark and sinister; there was something in that pained look in his eye, the frown set on his heavy brow and the way he clenched his jaw that gave him away.

'I must leave now. You need some sleep and I think you need to be cautious from now on. It was not I who stole your teddy bear – this house is not as safe as it once was. Its defences are weakening so who knows what might break through in the dark. I shall keep watching you, Edgar Harold but I cannot assure your safety.'

'You didn't answer me. Did you know Danko?'

Brother Bradley smiled kindly at Edgar and hung his head as if in prayer. He walked towards the door and stopped, glanced back and then continued on his way. He stepped out onto the hallway and was gone.

'What about Krinka? Is that real?' Edgar asked out loud, speaking to thin air. There was no reply. 'Fine. Ignore me then,' Edgar grumbled as he shuffled under his duvet, trying to get comfortable.

He rolled over and came face to face with a man – a distorted, flickering face that stretched and shrank as if it were clay being moulded by an invisible giant's hand.

'Do *not* insult me, Edgar Harold,' Brother Bradley hissed.

'Oh sh-' Edgar stopped himself from swearing. 'I just want to know about Krinka and the other monks. Was that real?'

The nightmare of Dominic's journey across the world to the city between the desert and the sea had plagued him for so long now. He couldn't shake the story from his mind – the Nazakan breaking through, over-running the city. He had seen the monks fight, he had seen them die in the most gruesome ways possible and now here he was, stuck in his own horror story within the same universe as the dream. *How had he known? How had it all come to him before he even knew the truth?*

'For your rudeness, I shall not give you a proper answer but think of this,' Brother Bradley began viciously, 'Houses hold memories and echoes from the past. They are filled with emotions of those who have lived there before and can affect the subconscious mind. Your dream told was just a story. Somebody or something could have been speaking *through* the dream to give you a glimpse of Krinka's downfall, Edgar. Someone or something knew it was only a matter of time until you discovered who you really were.'

The monk spat the words venomously and Edgar lay there, fearful as the man climbed out off the bed and stood next to him, looking down at him with fury in his glowing, ghostly eyes.

'I'm sorry...I-I-I just want answers. Too much has happened recently and I know practically nothing. I just wanted some clarification,' Edgar apologised, still shaking in shock of the ghost's sudden re-appearance. 'I don't know if I really *am* this warrior that everyone thinks I am. There's all this evidence but it can't be me. It just can't.'

Brother Bradley shot Edgar an intense stare that told him to hold his tongue. It was more dangerous than Priscilla's glare of doom.

'One final warning, this house is not as safe as it once was. Its defences are weakening so who knows what might break through in the dark. I shall keep watching you, Edgar but I cannot assure your safety,' Brother Bradley said sternly. He winked at Edgar, then turned and walked once more from the room; he vanished into the darkness.

Edgar lay awake, his heart still pounding from the shock the monk had just bestowed upon him. His mind was reeling – what did he mean that someone or some*thing* might have spoken through his dream. *Did that mean he had been possessed or that the story had merely got into his subconscious mind?* It was late and though he couldn't sleep, Edgar stifled a yawn, fluffed his pillows, closed his eyes and tried to sleep. At last it happened and as he drifted off to sleep he began to sink into dreams of the horrific memories of his adventures replaying over and over.

Faces and places flashed in Edgar's mind but he couldn't escape them. He woke with a start, breathing heavily and drenched in sweat. Fearing the terrors that awaited behind his eyelids, Edgar lay awake, trying to rid the demons from his head. He had survived and that was all that mattered.

– Chapter Eighteen –
The Soldier in the Trench

The next morning Edgar slumped downstairs, yawning and struggling to keep his eyes open. He had slept terribly thanks to the horrible dreams that plagued his mind. When he reached the kitchen and began to pour his cereal into a bowl, however, he was not welcomed by the now strangely familiar sound of scratching rats behind the kitchen wall but to an unfamiliar banging and scraping; instead of squeaking there were voices shouting to each other and the sounds weren't coming from behind the wall, they were coming from the allotment.

Edgar abandoned his breakfast and charged through the house and down the street, leaving his front door wide open, and let himself into the allotments through the gate half way down the street which had been left unlocked. In the plot of land stood a huge congregation of people. They all carried shovels and spades, running backwards and forwards busily, shouting orders and whispering excitedly. Edgar walked among them, feeling lost and confused; wondering if he was dreaming as he wandered over to the land behind his house.

He tried the cliché of pinching himself but it hurt and he became even more confused. This wasn't a dream. His head was spinning and buzzing with blankness. He had no idea what was going on.

They were already digging, and plotting where their trenches were going to go with string. Edgar introduced himself and asked if he could help the archaeologists. They gladly accepted his offer, telling him that they'd been sent by Patrick after the discovery of the fascinating artifact and that had been found. Edgar had always been interested in archaeology and he'd wanted to try it out since he had been a child so this was a dream come true and he spent all morning digging with them.

His mother occasionally came up with cups of tea and coffee and plates of sandwiches which were quickly devoured by the hungry hordes. She stood around watching them digging in and eventually, after much persuasion, Edgar managed to get her to join in.

They dug wide, deep, trenches while the hot summer sun beat down on them and as the day wore on it became hotter and hotter. The sweltering heat made the work unbearably slower than they had all anticipated.

At eight o' clock that night Edgar went inside to do some of his holiday maths homework that had been set by Mr. Wise. The sun was still up and showing no sign of giving up and going down. Everybody was still hard at work in the garden and when Edgar finished his homework he went to bed, listening to the banging and shouting from the garden.

The next day was Friday and Edgar woke up to a completely different atmosphere to the day before. Yesterday had been swelteringly hot and everybody was working slowly, they all seemed to have been thinking that they wanted to be somewhere else but today, the archaeologists in the garden seemed excited. They seemed driven by their curiosity and the work was made easier by the skies being overcast and grey, cooling it down although threatening rain.

A young man with short, spiky brown hair, leaned against the roof with a sandwich in his hand. He surveyed the others and watched them dig while he enjoyed simply watching. He wasn't particularly old and was quite handsome. He was dressed casually in ripped jeans and a red and white checked shirt.

'Hiya, what's going on today?' Edgar asked as he approached him.

'Quite a lot. We're all really excited – found some great stuff,' the young man said, taking a bite of his sandwich.

'Really?'

'Yeah.'

Edgar looked over the fence they had set up around the plot of land and upon the soil lay a sheet of tarpaulin with bones, coins and bits of pottery strewn upon it.

'James, by the way. You must be Edgar,' the man said, offering Edgar his hand.

'Yeah. Nice to meet you,' Edgar replied, shaking James' hand firmly.

'You ain't seen the best bit yet. There's something you missed,' James said darkly with a cheeky smile that made Edgar wonder what he hadn't seen.

'Look, at this rock we found,' James said pointing at a large slab of rock that was lying on the ground at the bottom of a trench.

Edgar walked towards the edge of the deep trench and looked down into it. There was an enormous stone about the size of a paving slab, made of black marble rock that lay sparkling in the sun.

'Wow. What type of rock is that?' Edgar gasped as he crouched down beside James to take a closer look. 'I've never seen anything like it.'

'It's a rarity, that's what it is. We've never seen one like it either, your mum's just phoned some geologist friends up from the museum. We can't even move it in case it breaks or something,' James explained, beaming in excitement.

'Oi! You better not be taking all the credit for my discovery, cheeky,' said a deep voice from behind them.

Taken by surprise, Edgar turned around to see a man towering over them, his shadow cast them in darkness.

'Course not,' James laughed as he jumped to his feet and embraced the tall man who leaned forward, kissed James on the cheek and took his hand in his own and held it tightly.

Edgar didn't know what to say – it wasn't that he had a problem with gay people, he just didn't expect to see them be so open with their affection. At school even the suspicion of someone being gay was enough to have them persecuted and bullied for the rest of their lives. In a way, it made his heart flutter happily to see them act so comfortably and at ease amid the busy crowd.

'This is Damian,' James said, beaming. 'My boyfriend if you hadn't already guessed.'

'James, I can introduce myself, thanks,' Damian snapped, shooting a piercing glare at James who merely chuckled to himself. 'Yeah, anyway, I'm Damian.'

He extended a thick hand and Edgar took it, his own seeming small in comparison. Damian's fingers wrapped around Edgar's hand so tight they nearly crushed it and Edgar shook firmly, looking up at Damian's handsome face. There was something about the man, something other than his height that made Edgar feel like he was two feet tall. Perhaps it was the way that he looked – tall, bulky and intimidating or maybe it was because he looked like everything Edgar wished he could be. He was the very definition of masculinity – of physical perfection.

Damian's eyes were deep-set and despite being dark brown they shone brightly; his eyebrows were thick but neat and he had a kindly smile with gleaming, white teeth that was framed by tidy, black stubble and his short, dark hair needed no product to stay in place on the top of his head. Edgar wished he could be so lucky – his hair was always a mess.

Damian dressed fashionably despite being on an excavation site – a tight, black vest top that showed off his bulging muscles and a pair of khaki shorts that came to just below his knees…and then there were the boots; they caught Edgar's eye almost immediately. They were almost identical to his own.

'I'm Edgar, by the way,' Edgar said coyly, feeling inadequate beside Damian. 'This is my garden.'

'Ah, cool. Uncle Patrick said I'd meet you here. Your mum's Priscilla, right?' Damian said and Edgar noticed there was a slight, subtle trace of a southern accent. It wasn't too in-your-face but the accent hinted that he came from a well off family – it was gentle but his words were pronounced with such delicate precision that Edgar wondered if it was just natural to him to speak that way or whether he put it on.

'Yeah, Priscilla. You know her?'

'Of course I do. I met her not so long ago, when we had the introductory meeting at the museum after Uncle Paddy asked me to come and do some work with him.'

Edgar nodded, pretending that he understood. He had never really heard Patrick talk about his nephew before – let alone mention he was coming to work with them for a while.

'So, Patrick's your uncle?' Edgar asked, surprised to discover they were related. Damian seemed so far away from Patrick that he simply couldn't believe it. There was no kind of family resemblance whatsoever. Patrick was such a shrewd, old-fashioned man with his giant, thick glasses and his tweed suits and Damian was bold and young and handsome.

'Not quite…we're related. Distantly. But he's still Uncle Paddy,' Damian grinned and Edgar nodded, understandingly, still eyeing Damian's boots in awe. James caught Edgar looking Damian up and down, mesmerised by him and he coughed subtly.

'Back to work then,' James said suddenly, clapping his hands as if to try and be encouraging. 'Damian, you can't just stand there looking pretty all day.'

'Shut up, you.'

'Make me.'

'Don't tempt me.'

Damian punched James playfully on the top of his arm but nearly knocked him flying. It seemed that James' scrawny build was no match against Damian, even when he was being gentle. James laughed as he slapped Damian jokingly in the face. Damian gasped, jumped on James and pushed him to the ground where they both started to wrestle and play fight.

Edgar had to tear his eyes away to avoid laughing and distracted his attention, feeling quite awkward, almost like he was invading a private moment.

After a moment, James screamed for mercy and Damian let him go. James stalked off to the other side of the dig-site, constantly looking back over his shoulder at his partner.

Damian sighed and sat down on the edge of a trench, staring down into its depths. He lowered himself down and crouched on the dirt, his head disappearing below the ground as he surveyed the thick, black chunk of rock. It glistened in the light so that thin veins of silver and purple could be seen running along its surface.

'Are you okay?' Edgar asked, approaching the edge of the trench. Damian looked up at him and nodded but there was something in his sparkling eyes that told Edgar he was about to cry.

'You're not,' Edgar replied softly, sensing that something was amiss and Damian sighed.

'You're right,' Damian said quietly, his voice warbling as he verged ever-closer to tears. 'It's too much.'

'What's the matter?' Edgar asked sympathetically, jumping down to join Damian and offer his support.

'It's nothing,' Damian sighed heavily 'I'm sure it's just me being stupid but I don't even know anymore.'

Edgar remained silent, hoping Damian would elaborate. He didn't want to pry but something told him there was something deeper going on.

'So, I guess this is the stone they've all been talking about,' Edgar said, reaching out to touch its smooth, glossy surface. It felt cold and hard under his fingers – just like any other rock but there was something about it that made his whole body tingle as if static electricity tingled through his body.

'Yeah, it's weird, isn't it?' Damian replied thoughtfully, his voice breaking as he tried to focus on Edgar and put the things in his mind aside.

'I wonder what it is,' Edgar said, his fingers still pressed against it, following the swirling lines upon its surface.

'Don't know.'

'Damian, are you sure you're alright?' Edgar probed inquisitively. 'You seem really down.'

'I'll be fine.'

'Are you sure?'

Damian fell silent for a second. He looked at Edgar, his deep, dark eyes surveying him; almost as if trying to see inside, wondering if he could trust him. He sighed again and shook his head.

'I'm just one of those people. I rush into things without thinking. I mean, life is to be lived. You have to take risks but I've taken too many already in my life. I've made so many mistakes and I think I've made one more recently.'

Damian's eyes swam with tears and Edgar's heart sank. This man before him had everything that Edgar could have ever wanted – the looks, the body, the confidence and yet he was so sad when he should be the happiest man in the world.

'We all make mistakes, it's what makes us human,' Edgar replied, offering the only clichéd advice he could think of in an attempt to be supportive. He didn't like seeing other people upset because he was one of those people that it rubbed off on and if they cried, he cried.

'Then I must be super-human with the amount I've made,' Damian laughed, shaking his head as he wiped a tear away and Edgar forced a smile at his joke.

'You look like one,' Edgar said bluntly. 'You've got everything going for you. People like me envy people like you.'

Damian looked at Edgar soberly. Edgar's words had warmed his heart and made him feel a little better.

'Yeah, but when you've got everything going for you, everyone wants a piece of you. Everyone has expectations that you can't possibly fulfil,' Damian replied down-heartedly and Edgar didn't know how to reply.

He could completely understand where Damian was coming from and it seemed there was nothing else he could say to lift his spirits. His eyes stared down at the loose dirt beneath his feet thoughtfully and again, he caught a sight of Damian's boots. He glanced over his shoulder to see if anyone was around and then back at Damian. If he was going to find out if the man beside him was a fellow traveller, now was the time to do it.

'Your boots,' Edgar said. 'They're like mine. Almost identical. You're…'

'Ex-military,' Damian interjected before Edgar could finish.

It was such a relief that he hadn't been given chance to finish his sentence. That could have been very awkward.

'You were in the army?' Edgar said, and he didn't know why he was so surprised.

'Why else would I look like this?' Damian said, forcing a laugh and flexing his biceps.

Edgar chuckled, his eyes fixed upon Damian's bulging muscles. They were amazing, as if they had been crafted lovingly by a Greek sculptor. Edgar could only feel weak and scrawny and ugly in comparison.

'That's pretty cool. You're a real hero then.'

'Nah, that whole thing was a mistake. If I could take that part of my life back and change it all, I would in a heartbeat.'

'What happened?' Edgar asked out of interest and quickly regretted it. Damian shot him a dark look and shook his head silently.

'I'm sorry. I shouldn't have-' Edgar replied quickly, hoping he hadn't offended Damian. After all he had been through lately, Edgar could well understand Damian not wanting to talk about the army. He had clearly faced horrors, much like Edgar had – possibly worse. Edgar had fought monsters but Damian must have fought against people – other human beings and to Edgar, that was a lot scarier than any Unsterbliche. At least they were supernatural creatures but when it came to fighting people, others just like himself, that wasn't natural at all. However, Edgar had learned the harsh lesson in Merimalima about how far normal people can go when they are hurt and scared and pushed to the very edge. There was a darkness in him that would have allowed him to kill, a darkness that he knew must lay dormant inside every human being – a primal urge to survive.

Damian's face turned white and blank as he stared at the ground. He shivered in the cold, deathly silence that swallowed them, then he looked up, right into Edgar's eyes with a deep sigh.

'Couple of years ago I was out in Iraq. I was young and stupid; fresh out of college and looking for an adventure. I joined the army thinking it was big and clever, a guarantee to get all the boys. I was wrong. I ended up in one of the first British squads dispatched there when this war started up and was lucky to get home in one piece.'

Again, Edgar didn't know how to reply. He simply stared at Damian in shock. This handsome but seemingly normal man had been thrust into a living nightmare but he had survived and it was clear he carried the guilt and trauma of what had happened out there, across the sea.

'I'm sorry,' Edgar said after a long pause, searching for the right words. He remembered the news reports from that time. He had seen how bad it was and he had only seen the censored version that had been broadcast to the public; he couldn't even imagine what horrors Damian had personally encountered.

'Don't be. It was my mistake. War isn't worth the risk. All that death and destruction and chaos - the things I've seen and all the while, fighting for a cause I wasn't even sure of. I've done things that will give me nightmares 'til I die. We all did.'

'Is that what was bothering you?' Edgar asked anxiously, hoping he wouldn't provoke an angry reaction but Damian shook his head. His throat tightened and he gulped hard. Damian had fought in a war – the man he sat beside who clearly suffered had been through hell and back – something Edgar was expected to do too.

The weight of Betty's prophecy suddenly seemed much more real and Edgar shivered, his whole body tingling with goosebumps – if he survived would he become just as broken as Damian – just a numb shell of a person? 'Sorry, I shouldn't pry.'

'No, not the war stuff...it's James,' Damian said coldly, peeking back over the edge of the trench to check his partner was out of earshot. James was at the other side of the dig-site, talking animatedly to a woman and Damian turned his attention back to Edgar.

'Since I came back, I just wanted to escape the past; to meet a man and settle down but I've worn my heart on my sleeve and it's done nothing but cause trouble.'

Damian's eyes began to tear up again and Edgar's heart fluttered. He felt so sorry for Damian and didn't know what to do.

'Problem is, James is...well, he's quite...high maintenance and I just can't handle it,' Damian explained, looking at Edgar with a glint of sadness in his deep blue eyes that only made Edgar's heart sink. 'I like the guy but I want someone who will take care of *me* for a change. I'm not emotionally stable enough to support myself *and* someone else.'

Edgar nodded understandingly and Damian sighed again.

'Then you need to get rid of him. You need to wait for the right person to come along. He's out there somewhere, you just need to find him,' Edgar advised. 'I know it's hard after all you've been through and you want to settle into a peaceful life but just be grateful you've got home safe from Iraq and you've got a long, happy life ahead of you. There's plenty of time to find Mr. Right.'

Damian chuckled and narrowed his eyes as he surveyed Edgar closely.

'How old are you, Edgar?'

'Fifteen.'

Damian looked surprised, as if Edgar's answer had taken him by surprise. He knew he looked older than his age and always found it amusing when people were shocked by the revelation.

'You're so wise for someone so young,' Damian scoffed 'I wish I'd been the same – could have saved myself a lot of trouble.'

'It's never too late to start,' Edgar beamed and Damian grabbed him, wrapped his solid arms around him and squeezed so hard that Edgar could barely breathe. Damian's chest heaved as he began to sob and Edgar felt the warm tears on his neck.

Awkwardly, Edgar patted him on the back and Damian released him, tears streaming down his face. Damian reached for Edgar's hand and held it tightly in his own.

'You're a good kid, Edgar. If you ever need anything, you come to me, right?' Damian said, his voice certain and demanding. 'Absolutely anything. I'm here for you as a friend, as a brother,' Damian added as he wiped his tears away with his other hand. Edgar nodded, taken aback by Damian's reaction. All he had done was offer some honest advice.

'Thanks,' Edgar replied quietly, his voice catching in his throat.

'If there's one positive thing I learned in the army, it's that we all have to stick together. Friends are like brothers. We're family and we have each other's backs no matter what happens.'

'Yeah, thank you. It means a lot.'

Damian didn't reply, instead he leaned forward and kissed Edgar on the cheek. It was only a friendly gesture, nothing more, but it felt strange. The stubble tickled his cheek and though it had lasted only a second, the warm tingle of Damian's lips stayed upon Edgar's skin. He shuddered as warmth seeped through his whole body from the source of contact and he looked into Damian's eyes that were deep, dark and mysterious, not knowing quite what to say.

'I like your tattoo,' he said, noticing tattoo on Damian's shoulder. It was a snake, curled in a circle with it's own tail in its mouth.

'Cool isn't it?'' Damian said. 'It's the ouroborous.'

'I have no idea what that means,' Edgar replied.

'It symbolises a cycle in which we are all reborn; that we are eternal and infinite,'

'A bit morbid.'

'It doesn't necessarily mean in death. We're reborn in our lives. We just keep changing.'

'That's true.'

It was a beautiful way to think about life, as a constant change and rebirth but it was true – Edgar had recently been reborn when he discovered dimension travel. He was as different as he possibly could be from the person he had been mere days ago.

'DAMIAN!' someone shouted from nearby.

'I have to go now, see you soon, bro,' Damian said as he climbed slowly to his feet and vaulted out of the deep trench. Edgar nodded and waved goodbye silently, reaching up to touch the tingle that lingered on his cheek from Damian's kiss.

It felt like forever that Edgar mulled over his conversation with Damian. He pondered over the secrets that had just been revealed to him and how Damian had offered to help him no matter what. He had made a friend without even trying – something he seemed to be adapting to quite well over the past few days despite the enemies he had faced as well. Maybe he wasn't as big a loser as those at school would have him believe.

Moments later, Edgar was pulled back to harsh reality with a crash when he heard raised voices at the other side of the garden. He couldn't quite make out what was being said, but he knew that one of the voices was the familiar, thundering tone of Damian's.

Edgar peeked over the edge of the trench and saw James and Damian in the distance. Damian stood his ground, firmly rooted to the spot while James stomped around and hit him, screaming and shouting before he stormed away down the path, shoving Priscilla aside in his haste to get by. Edgar gasped and jumped out of the trench, running towards her and the people who followed. Anger flowed through him – nobody pushed his mother around like that.

'Don't you even-'

'Edgar! What's going on?' she asked as Edgar stormed past her, after James.

He wasn't aware of what he was doing – he wasn't in control but his fists were clenched and ready to hit him. Hard.

'OI!' snapped Priscilla as she grabbed Edgar's arm hard and stopped him in his tracks. 'What the hell is your problem?'

'Erm...I....I don't know,' Edgar replied, trying to cover-up the obvious breakup of James and Damian's relationship that he had instigated.

'You need to calm down, love. I've brought the team to check out the mystery rock,' Priscilla said and Edgar could see from the twinkling in her eyes and her wide grin that she was hiding something.

He glanced at the woman by his mother's side and as his anger dissipated; his vision cleared and his jaw dropped. As he let out a quiet squeak of excitement. She was a tall, strikingly beautiful lady with shaggy, shoulder-length blonde hair and pale grey eyes. She leaned casually against the wall wearing a black t-shirt and green combat trousers.

'LARA!' shouted Edgar as he launched at her and they embraced rightly 'I've missed you! It's been like three years! I've got loads to tell you,' he said happily, astonished to see her again.

'And I've got loads to tell you as well!' she replied excitedly.

'So what you been up to? Any adventures as usual?' Edgar asked with keen interest.

Lara always had great adventures when she was away and always loved to tell him about them whenever she came back. As a kid it had always been his dream to accompany her on one and to travel the world with her. There was no need for that now – he could have his own adventures and they weren't restricted to this world.

'I've been in America with some colleagues of mine and I got stuck with looking after Amelia, the new girl; very clever lass but a bit clumsy. She got into all sorts of mischief,' Lara said casually.

'That is so cool,' replied Edgar, staring at Lara with utmost respect and admiration. Lara told Edgar all about her time in America and the dangers and adventures she'd got into. Edgar took in every word. Lara told the most exciting stories, even the ones that seemed impossible like the story about accidentally driving into Area 51 and being chased away by helicopters thanks to her new colleague's map-reading skills; being invited to the White House to meet the President for outstanding geological work at the San Andreas Fault and how Amelia had spilled her coffee down him and not to forget dropping important equipment in the La Brea tar pits – again, Amelia's fault. There was something about Lara's stories that held Edgar enthralled. She was a masterful story teller and he hung on every single word.

Edgar and Lara chatted well into the afternoon. He considered telling her about his new adventures but didn't dare – he couldn't tell a soul, so instead he simply told Lara about his mundane school life and his being bullied by Spencer. Surprisingly, Lara gave the exact same advice as Priscilla had.

'Ignore them, they're all stupid and will never get as far in life as you will. You're already miles ahead of them, and they're all just jealous,' she said to Edgar sternly.

Aside from their conversation, the rest of the day passed in a rush of digging and shovelling. Various bits of pottery and silver were found although most of it was modern and Lara grabbed James to help her try and identify the strange type of rock by running special tests involving coloured liquids and swabs. There was still an obvious tension between James and Damian who kept their distance from one another but kept shooting daggers when each other's backs were turned.

Edgar felt guilty for being responsible for the hostility but surely it was better to have come sooner than later?

The day was fading to a cool, damp evening when Edgar's mum wandered up the garden path again with one last plate of sandwiches. She set the plate on the wall and everyone helped themselves again and thanked her for her kindness.

'Come on Edgar, we've got to go. We need to get to Conisborough by nine and it's already five o'clock, we'll be pushing it to make it there on time,' she said sternly and Edgar's brow furrowed.

Of course! He had forgotten that they were going to the re-enactment this weekend. It was only a little event and not much would be going on but the shops were always good and his friends were all going, so it was better than nothing – a chance to relax, enjoy the weekend and most of all, it was an excuse to run from him problems again.

Priscilla gave Lara the keys to the house. She pressed them into her hand and Lara took them and put them safely in her pocket.

'Make yourself at home,' Priscilla said kindly and Lara nodded. 'Just don't forget to feed the cat,'

Edgar rushed back up to the excavation site to say goodbye to Damian but he seemed pre-occupied talking to someone else – a tall, scrawny man with a strong chin and narrow jaw; his long fringe was streaked with blonde and covered half of his face, completely hiding one of his beady green eyes that were framed with thick square glasses.

There was something about him Edgar didn't like – something he couldn't explain. Maybe it was his rat-like features or maybe it was the way he looked at Damian and touched his arm in a way that didn't seem appropriate (it lingered just a little too long.) It could have been the obviously fake laughter that came out of his wide thin-lipped mouth; even his giant, buck-teeth and gums annoyed him because they didn't fit his mouth but the thing that annoyed him the most was that Damian paid him attention and didn't seem to notice Edgar stood there when all he wanted to do was say goodbye.

– Chapter Nineteen –
Secrets and Swords

The rest of that evening was spent speeding down the motorway. The sun shone weakly, eventually giving up and disappearing behind the thick, black clouds that hovered threateningly above. Soon, the heavy rain pounded down on the car, drenched the road and clouded the other cars on the motorway with a cloak of mist. The only sign of the other cars driving down the motorway with them was the occasional *WHOOSH* of a passing vehicle or the headlights glowing dimly in the mist ahead.

He stared out of the window, absent-mindedly tracing raindrops with his finger.

'You ok?' Priscilla asked, barely even taking her eyes off the road to look at him.

'Fine.'

But he wasn't fine. He hated the rain. He dreaded finally getting to Conisborough where he would have to put up a tent in it, especially knowing how Priscilla could become just as frustrated and angry with tents as he could. It must have been a genetic trait, something he must have inherited from her. It wasn't just that though, it was Damian. He had wanted to say goodbye – to see him one last time; his new friend – someone who genuinely cared for him...but he had been ignored. Who did Damian think he was to look right through him? Had he even noticed he was there? Did he really care as much as he pretended to? It made no sense why it bothered Edgar so much but it really, truly did.

The car sped along, weaving across the lanes of traffic and swerving through the spray like they were driving on a cloud. Before they knew it, the terrible journey came to an end. It had only taken a couple of hours despite the weather. The field was soaked and the car sank into the muddy grass as Priscilla drove through to the campsite.

'Mum, can't we just forget the tents and sleep in the car?' Edgar pleaded – he couldn't deal with the thought of Priscilla taking her frustrations out on him; that combined with being drenched to the skin in a matter of seconds was enough to make him want to cry.

'NO! It's character building, sleeping in the rain *never* hurt anybody did it?' she replied mercilessly and shot Edgar that icy cold glare that froze his heart and chilled him to the bone.

She climbed out of the car, stormed around the front and wrenched open Edgar's door forcefully. Edgar cowered from her and tried to move away from the open door but she grabbed him by the arm and pulled him out into the pouring rain. Within the two seconds he'd been out of the car he was soaked to the skin and his clothes stuck to him, making him shudder as the cold got to him but on the bright side, he couldn't get any wetter!

'You say the rain might not have hurt anyone, but it's sure killed them when they got pneumonia,' he sighed loudly and flopped out of the car angrily.

'DON'T YOU DARE GIVE ME LIP!' she yelled at Edgar, who decided to shut up and get on with it as she slapped him around the back of the head for his cheek.

Edgar threw all of the wooden poles onto the floor and then laid out the canvas material, before helping Priscilla set up the wooden framework inside the material so that it would stay up but it was no use. The tent almost blew away in the growing wind, acting like a sail on a ship and there was an unnoticeable hole above Edgar's head, which leaked a steady stream of water over him.

'I GIVE UP!' Edgar screamed, throwing the wooden pole that he was holding to the floor. 'I can't do it.'

'Yes, you can. Get this tent up, or you can sleep like an authentic archer,' his mum snapped sternly, giving him "The look" again.

'You wouldn't dare do that because you'd have to do it too and you wouldn't do it in this weather,' Edgar snapped argumentatively.

'Oh yes I would. It's character building and if it taught you a lesson I'd force you to do it any day,' Priscilla snarled angrily, stabbing the ground violently with a tent pole as if she was trying to stake a Vampire through the heart. She glared icily at Edgar again so he quickly shut up and put the rest of he tent up without complaint. He was *not* going to sleep on the muddy ground, using just a couple of twigs and his cloak as a tent. He was brave...but not stupid.

Eventually, after an hour of trying, the tent was finally up with everything laid out. The floor sheets were down; the sleeping bags were in place in both compartments, the blankets were thrown over the floor underneath and over the top of the bags. He took a moment to get changed into dry clothes and coyly apologised to Priscilla for his attitude while putting up the tent.

'Ed, is that you in there?' came a quiet, hesitant voice from outside.

'Who is it?' Edgar huffed as he pulled back the front flap of his tent to see who was there.

It was a tal,l young man with short, mousy hair and wide grey eyes. Fair, wiry stubble sprouted from his chin and he beamed, his signature hat complete with brown pheasant feather sat on his head and as he beamed excitedly at him, Edgar's heart sank.

'Alvin,' he said, stunned.

'Alvin, darling!' Priscilla shouted from the privacy of her compartment. 'Just getting changed, I'll be out in a minute.'

It had been so long since Edgar had seen his friend – in fact it felt like forever since they had spoken on the phone and discussed coming to this re-enactment. Even though it had all been planned it was a shock to see him here and it wasn't a pleasant shock. It was a horrible shock that made Edgar's stomach turn and twist in a tight knot.

'It's so good to see you again!' Alvin said. 'It's just me here this time though – Vicky's still on her mission and Charity's at summer camp.'

'What about your mum and dad?'

'Having a nap. It's been a long day.'

'Oh...' Edgar said. He didn't know what to say. Alvin didn't know about Vicky and that made him feel even more nauseous. He was the reason Vicky had died and now he stood there, face to face with her brother, knowing what he had seen, knowing he had done nothing.

'That's good. Shame the others aren't here,' Edgar said breathlessly, trying not to raise suspicion.

'We'll survive. I brought sweets.'

'Brilliant,' Edgar replied, smiling as he forgot about the trouble looming over him.

'Good to see you again, darling!' Priscilla exclaimed as she came out and embraced Alvin tightly.

The rain continued to pour down for the rest of the evening and Edgar remained in his tent, playing chess and eating sweets with Priscilla and Alvin into the night and when the rain finally stopped pounding down Edgar and Alvin decided to venture outside. The rain still fell in a light drizzle and the wind ferocious wind had settled. Edgar and Alvin walked up a hill and sat down on a tree stump under the shelter of the surrounding trees on the border of the small forest until the rain finally ceased for a short while to let the sun break through the gargantuan grey clouds for a brief time.

It was sunset now and dying sun cast its last golden glow over the landscape; the trees from the forest cast long shadows over the sparkling, dewy grass and from the hill they could see out over the whole re-enactment. They could see the authentic camp along the side of the path to the castle, at the bottom of the hill there was a sweeping lawn of grass and an enormous park full of trees and there in the distance, was a small boating lake in the middle of the grounds. One corner of the enormous lawn was dedicated to the plastic campsite where modern tents were camped, out of the view of visitors, under the shade of the trees and of course there, atop a high hill, stood Conisborough Castle surrounded by a tall, stony wall around the keep and the inner grounds, where people would have lived in medieval times.

'So what's been going on Ed?' Alvin asked casually.

Again, Edgar's heart sank. Vicky's demise crossed his mind in a violent flashback and he couldn't shake the awful feeling in his gut.

'Not a lot,' Edgar lied. It was easier that way. 'It's quiet without Vicky and Charity though isn't it?'

'Yeah. Charity's having a blast but we haven't heard from Vicky in a while,' Alvin replied down-heartedly. There was a trace of sadness in his voice, as if deep down he suspected that maybe something was wrong but daren't even think about it.

'Good, well that's alright then isn't it? She's probably enjoying herself so much helping the people there that she hasn't had time to write you a letter,' Edgar replied feigning some kind of optimism; his conscience making him feel severely guilty. All he could see were the flames and he could hear the screams and smell the burning flesh. It was all so clear, so vivid like he were re-living it yet again.

Edgar was distant and Alvin stared at him, knowing something was wrong. He sighed, shook his head and walked away. Edgar followed.

'Sure you're alright?' Alvin asked and Edgar replied with a quiet *'Mhmm.'*

They walked back to camp in the dark and silence. When they reached their tents they muttered 'goodnight' and went their separate ways at opposite ends of the field.

Alvin stalked off to his tent wondering about why Vicky hadn't got in touch and if Edgar's suspicions of her being busy were truthful or if something far worse had happened to her. He couldn't take it any more.

"She's fine and Ed was right," Alvin convinced himself as an unwanted tear streaked down his cheek. He missed his sister terribly and just wanted to know she was safe – not hearing from her was torture. What if something had happened to her and nobody knew?

Edgar looked back at Alvin walking slowly to his tent and realized that he was upset. Edgar felt awful that he'd had to lie to one of his best friends but he had to protect him from the truth – he wouldn't believe him if he told him and the story of Vicky's demise was too much to bear – the fact he was responsible, that her death was on his hands and he was as good as a murderer was too much to accept no matter how much he tried to come to terms with it. It was like a colossal black hole opening up in his stomach and slowly swallowing him from the inside. His heart was trying to escape from it by moving into his throat but it just made him feel worse. At least he'd given Alvin some hope. At least he had a spark of an idea that his sister was alive and well even though that was far from the truth.

Edgar couldn't deal with himself. He knew that he should have told Alvin the truth. He had the *right* to know, even more so than Edgar did. Alvin was part of her family and Edgar was stuck in the middle, feeling like an intruder on personal family affairs. With the weight of his actions crushing him down, Edgar trudged over to his tent and crawled into his bed, trying to clear his head of his guilty conscience.

*

'Edgar, get up! I'm going to buy you a new sword!'

Priscilla stood over him, already dressed in her blue medieval dress.

'What?' Edgar grumbled, slowly coming round.

He opened his eyes and rubbed them to clear his bleary vision. He had begged Priscilla for a sword for so long and she had refused because of the expense, so why the sudden change of heart?

'Get up and come with me before I change my mind. There's a good shop that's full of really nice ones and you can choose which ever one you want,' Priscilla demanded. She sounded certain and Edgar wasn't going to let the moment pass.

'Why... Why are you doing this mum?' asked Edgar, still confused. 'Swords are expensive.'

'Well, that money that Patrick gave me won't spend itself will it and you haven't had a treat for ages, now hurry up,' she commanded, her eyes twinkling kindly.

'Won't be a minute!'

Edgar jumped up with glee and quickly dressed into his pure white medieval kit: white shirt, medieval underwear that resembled a pair of modern three quarter length shorts and his brown hat; he could finish getting dressed properly later.

He ran out to the front of the tent to meet his mum and they walked together down the muddy track to the market place. It was a cloudy day and rain drizzled in a thin sheet that soaked everything but the sun shone weakly through the thick grey clouds making them feel hopeful that the rain would soon clear.

The market here was smaller than the one at the other re-enactments but there was a sufficient amount of shops to suffice for any needs. Unlike other re-enactments where the shops would spill out over the grounds with tables full of interesting items for sale, the shops here looked like normal re-enactment tents.

It was probably something to do with the rain and the hour being so early that the traders weren't quite ready to be open but there was one tent that was bigger than the others. It was the size of at least three normal tents and decorated with black and red stripes; its flaps were wide open and inside Edgar knew it was a trading tent.

'Wow, it's the biggest shop here,' said Edgar gasping for breath. He could only imagine what wonders would lay inside.

The tent seemed much smaller inside; probably because swords were mounted on every wall but despite all the weapons of different shapes and sizes there was nothing terribly exciting, neither were there any swords that caught Edgar's eye. There were replicas of claymores, scimitars, Roman swords and even artists impressions of Excalibur and others from ancient legends; in fact, every type of sword Edgar could ever imagine filled the tent. They were mostly ornamental but there were some that were for use on the battlefield but these were all ugly and plain - just a blade with a simple hilt, nothing fancy like he had expected and the few fancy ones that he could see just looked tacky and encrusted with plastic gems.

'Good morning,' said a voice in the distance 'I'm Drystan, is there anything I can help you with?' said the man at the counter in the far end of the tent. He was quite short, only about as tall as Priscilla; and just as portly. His hair was long, wavy and brown and he'd grown a goatee beard of the same colour. He reached his hand out and Edgar shook it politely.

'Edgar,' he said and Drystan smiled, nearly yanking Edgar's arm off as he shook his hand over-enthusiasticaly, his tight grip nearly crushing Edgar's fingers.

'Is there anything in particular that you're looking for? Anything that I could help you with?'

'Well, my mum's getting me a new sword and I don't really know what I'm looking for,' Edgar replied, his eyes still scanning the tent for a sign of anything that might catch his eye but the truth was, he really wasn't keen on any of them.

'You've come to the right place then, Edgar...'

Drystan trailed off and stroked his goatee thoughtfully as he surveyed Edgar with beady-eyed interest.

'He's fussy,' Priscilla chirped up. 'He's so particular about his weapons. He spent months searching for his bow.'

Drystan chuckled and nodded in agreement as if he completely understood.

'If there are none in here here that take your fancy there's always some in my secret store,' Drystan said with a sly wink. Edgar wondered if he knew him from somewhere – why was Drystan so familiar?'Would you like to see?'

Edgar nodded excitedly and Drystan led Edgar and Priscilla across the tent and through an almost invisible flap in the back into the secret room.

The room wasn't particularly exciting – upon first glance it would not appear to hold any secrets. Drystan's bed lay in the corner covered in fur blankets, a wooden chest sat at the foot of the bed and large sacks were stacked around the edge of the small space. Edgar hovered near the entrance, feeling like he was invading Drystan's private space.

'Come,' Drystan said, beckoning Edgar and Priscilla inside as he crouched down beside the roughly hewn wooden chest and lifted its lid.

Creak.

Edgar joined Drystan as he reached inside and pulled out several swords. He lay them over the rough hessian ground sheet and Edgar was surprised by the secret swords that Drystan had kept hidden in here.

These seemed to be much more ornate; their hilts were encrusted with real jewels, or engraved with ornate patterns but not in a way that felt cheap - these swords had much more gravitas behind them and as Drystan passed them to him, letting him hold them, feel the weight and examine them closely. Edgar couldn't explain what it was but he was filled with emotion. It was so confusing; he felt happy one moment but like bursting into tears the next. It was like each one had its own story and unique history and he could feel it, like he was in tune with them.

'Well, what do you think of my collection?' asked Drystan imperiously. He watched Edgar as he shuffled around the room, completely amazed by every sword that he examined.

'It's amazing. How did you get so many?' Edgar asked, turning over a hefty sword in his hands and examining the long blade that was engraved with runes.

'I've just acquired a lot of them over many years,' Drystan replied looking around at his collection, a proud expression on his face. 'I even forged some of them myself.'

Priscilla crouched down next to Edgar, as mesmerized by the collection as much as he was. She took one and examined it with awe.

'That's one of my creations,' Drystan said proudly. It was a short sword, Roman inspired but forged from a gleaming golden metal.

'Wow. What does your wife say to you collecting all these?' Priscilla asked jokingly and Drystan stammered.

'I-I-I don't have a wife at the moment,' he said quietly. 'I'm still looking for that one special woman who I want to spend the rest of my life with.' There was a sweet, dreamy tone to his voice and his eyes glazed as he stared thoughtfully into space.

'That's very sweet. There should be more men like you in the world,' Priscilla replied sweetly and Edgar blushed. Drystan's cheeks flushed red too and Edgar couldn't help but notice.

He looked awkwardly from Drystan to his mother, then back again and stifled a giggle. He was old enough now to understand flirting, not that he was good at it or had ever even really had chance to do it. His only girlfriend, Ophelia, had lasted a matter of weeks. He still felt ridiculously awkward whenever he thought back to it – they had been best friends and thankfully, remained so. However, when they had decided to get together it had nearly ruined everything. Edgar was too immature or too shy to even hold her hand, let alone kiss her. It wasn't that he hadn't wanted to, of course he had, but there was just something blocking him and he could never tell whether it had been some physical energy that simply repelled them or something in his own head that held him back.

'I'm sorry Edgar, I won't be able to afford these ones, but they're so beautiful aren't they?' Priscilla said softly, bringing Edgar back to his senses. She had been chatting quietly with Drystan as Edgar had handled the swords, distracted in deep thought about Ophelia, about his friends and how he hadn't seen them since the day of the picnic, since the day Betty had died...and then again, everything that had happened since. He kept trying to push it from his mind but it wouldn't budge. He couldn't escape it...and now here he was looking for a sword. This was his opportunity to arm himself for the war ahead – that brutal, terrifying war he didn't want to think about. He couldn't ignore it. He had to face it. Things were horrible enough and when Priscilla said he couldn't have one of these swords, Edgar's heart dropped into his stomach.

'But mum!' Edgar groaned. This wasn't a simple want. It was a need – a necessity.

'Edgar,' she said warningly, a cold glint crossed her eyes and Edgar knew not to reply.

'Now, if there's something you like, I'm sure we could reach an arrangement,' Drystan interjected and Edgar suddenly felt a little relieved but Priscilla didn't look too confident.

'Now you've had a little hold and a feel, have a swing of them,' Drystan said, offering Edgar a vicious looking sword with a jewel covered hilt and a big, spiky blade. It was weighty and when he swung it, the blade almost made him fall over. Edgar could feel that it was an angry sword and he didn't much like it.

'That's not right for you,' Drystan said expertly, taking the sword from Edgar and replacing it in the wooden chest. 'You'll be able to tell when you've found the right one. It will feel like an arm extension, when you swing it, you'll feel *different*, not like you've ever felt before,' he explained and Edgar just scrunched his face rudely and looked at the sword-seller as if he were insane.

Drystan grabbed another sword with a lion's head carved into the hilt. No luck. It was too heavy and much too clumsy. Edgar kept trying but every time was bad luck. The more he tried, the more he could understand what Drystan had meant. None of the swords were for him, they were all unbalanced in his grip and made him feel like he would swing and fall. He tried another dozen or so before admitting defeat.

'Here. Try this Katana,' Drystan said, offering Edgar a Japanese style sword with a short hilt wrapped in silk.

'No thanks, I don't really like those.'

'So, are there any that you liked?' Drystan probed curiously.

Edgar didn't get to reply. Suddenly nothing else mattered. His eye was drawn to a sword that he was sure he had missed before and he couldn't help but wonder how. Most people would have completely ignored the simple blade but there was something about this sword in particular that attracted Edgar like metal a magnet. It was a very basic design but he was hypnotised by its simplistic beauty. It had a black two-handed hilt, with a plain silver blade and pommel. The end of the hilt, where most swords had ornate patterns or jewels sunk into the metal, was just a silver octagon with a cross crudely indented in the middle. So dazed by his discovery, Edgar had no idea how he had made his way across the room to the sword but up close it was even more beautiful to him.

'I love it!' he exclaimed as he picked it up and examined it closely. It felt just like an extension of his arm, it seemed to attach itself to him, like some sort of symbiotic entity, and rather than feeling horribly clumsy when he swung it, it felt...right.

Priscilla and Drystan watched excitedly as he swung the sword around gracefully cutting the air with fancy twirls and slices of the blade.

Edgar knew this was the sword for him.

'Mum, I *need* this one,' Edgar gasped immediately, knowing the answer would probably be a solid *"No."*

'Okay,' she said, beaming. Edgar could tell by the look in her eye that she knew just how much he wanted it – that she could understand that it was the right sword for him. 'I'll see what I can do. I might have to get you it at another event.'

Edgar sighed. At least that was better than nothing but now he had connected with it, he didn't want to let it go.

'I'm surprised you spotted that one. It's very unassuming,' Drystan said curiously. 'It's nothing to look at, easy to miss. What drew you to that *one* particular item out of my entire collection, may I ask?' Drystan continued, eyeing Edgar with intrigue.

'It just jumped out, for some reason then when I picked it up it just felt like it *fits...like it* attached to my hand,' Edgar explained. It seemed odd – there was no real explanation. He had just seen it and liked it. He was drawn to it for no particular reason and the odd feeling it forged with him was impossible to describe. This was it. The one he needed if he had to fight.

Drystan beamed at him and nodded lightly as if he had figured something out in his mind but was reluctant to say it out loud.

'Ed, go next door and get us some beads, I've got to finish those rosary's off,' Priscilla ordered sternly and Edgar nodded before heading out of the tent. He lifted the flap that led into the shop, turned back to thank Drystan and left the tent, bursting with excitement. He was finally going to get his first sword!

In the craft tent next door, Edgar spent a while picking through the boxes, choosing some of the prettiest beads he could find. He took a mix of cedarwood and bone beads as well as some tiny, carved crucifixes so that he and his mum could finish making the rosary bead chains that they'd started making together at the last re-enactment in Poppleton. He had just finished paying when someone appeared behind him.

'Edgar,' said Priscilla's voice from behind him. He turned around and there she stood, holding the sword! She held it out and Edgar snatched it from her joyously.

'What made you choose this one?' she asked curiously, looking at Edgar with a dark gleam in her eyes.

'I don't know...I just liked it.'

'Ok...'she replied, almost silently.

'Thanks mum, but you said you couldn't afford it,' Edgar said, raising an eyebrow as if to will her to explain.

'Ah, well it should have been six hundred quid!' she exclaimed and Edgar gasped. Suddenly he was ready to hand the sword back – Priscilla couldn't afford to spend that much on him despite the large sum she had been given by Patrick.

Edgar's jaw dropped. It had been very pricey.

'No, it's fine!' Priscilla interrupted. 'Drystan gave me it for a hundred because you reminded him of someone who used to own it and he said you need it more than he did.'

Edgar couldn't reply. Drystan had been so kind – first by letting him see the secret swords that he stored in his chest, and now by reducing the price of the sword so drastically. *Could he have been right? Did Drystan know him somehow?* It should be impossible but Edgar had learned recently that nothing was impossible, just highly unlikely at the very most.

'You got it cheaper because you flirted with him,' Edgar sniggered and Priscilla's eyes popped out of her head. She stifled a laugh and instead snorted loudly so that a group of visitors wearing canary yellow cagoules looked around in disgust.

'*Did not!*' Priscilla snapped, but by the bright red flush in her cheeks, Edgar knew she was lying.

'He's a nice guy but face it, he's a hairy little hobbit. What were you doing, flirting with him?' Edgar laughed sarcastically.

'So?'

'He's not your type at all.'

'But he was sweet, that's what this world needs, more people waiting for true love and not just marrying anything that moves for the sake of it,' Priscilla said sloppily, her eyes as glazed as Drystan's has been in a misty, romantic haze. Edgar rolled his eyes.

*

Back at the camp Alvin had been waiting eagerly for Edgar to return.

'Hello, Edgar!' squeaked Mrs. Wright who sat outside her tent on a fold-out chair. Her voice was high-pitched and tinged with a Brummie accent.

'Morning!' Edgar replied politely.

Mrs. Wright was a sweet lady and very clearly the mother of her children with her rosy cheeks and constant smile that she had passed down to the next generation. Her grey hair was plaited into a long, ponytail and half-hidden under a floppy straw hat. Alvin sat beside her and there was no sign of Mr. Wright.

Seeing Mrs. Wright smiling and waving at him killed Edgar again. He usually loved hanging out with the family but now he couldn't – he wished the ground could just swallow him up so that he could vanish and never have to face them again. It had been bad enough facing Alvin but sweet, innocent Mrs. Wright was too much. It always made Edgar feel slightly uncomfortable how the family were extraordinarily chirpy. Would they still smile if Edgar dropped the bombshell on them about Vicky? Something told him *yes*, they'd probably find a way to smile through the pain of the loss. It wasn't normal. Nobody was ever that happy...except for the Wrights, that is.

'Come here, darling. I want a hug!' Mrs. Wright said and Edgar's heart sank. He couldn't refuse or they'd know something was up.

He moved over to Mrs. Wright, leaned over and wrapped his arms around her. She embraced him in return and he felt sick. They were so close. They practically treated him as family and he knew such a dreadful secret and could not bring himself to say a word.

He took a deep breath, glad that Mrs. Wright couldn't see his face as he hugged her. She couldn't see the turmoil in his expression – the tears welling in his eyes.

'We wondered where you'd gone!' Alvin exclaimed as Edgar broke away from the embrace. 'It's not like you to go on an adventure without me.'

'Mum got me a new sword!' Edgar exclaimed, brandishing his new weapon at Alvin who fell back in surprise. 'We can practice properly now that I've got my own!'

Alvin didn't even need to ask Edgar if he wanted to have a quick practice right now. He simply dived up, grabbed his own sword from the tent and came back out, prepared. They launched into their fight and as Edgar swung his sword, it felt light and the pain and anger that surged through him over Vicky's loss, the torture that

Alvin's mere presence caused him, he took it all out on his friend and for the first time ever, Alvin lost.

'Since when did you get so good Ed?' Alvin gasped in surprise, trying to catch his breath as they sat down on the thick, twisted roots of a nearby tree.

'I don't know. I think it was just luck that I beat you,' Edgar replied, shaking off his victory.

'But *how* did you get it though?' Alvin asked again, even more anxious to know.

'Well, mum found an artifact in our garden. She took it to work to get it identified and they gave her loads of money for it even though they didn't know what it was – must be something really rare,' Edgar explained smugly.

His mind wandered back to that tiny black, marble pyramid and wondered what exactly it was. It was odd that it had been just laying there in a bush – surely it ought to have been found before but it hadn't and once again, it seemed that fate had controlled Edgar's life and led to him getting the sword.

'There's got to be more to it,' Edgar thought to himself, deep in contemplation. He didn't know and didn't really care – all that mattered was that things were going his way, fortune worked in his favour and he now had a weapon for the fight ahead.

The day passed quickly and before they knew it, the day was drawing to a close and once again the sun was setting but the fine, misty rain showed no sign of ceasing. Alvin and Edgar strolled down to the lake and sat by the edge of the water looking into its murky depths, scanning it for signs of life, but with no luck.

'I wonder if anything actually *does* live in there?' said Edgar, staring into the dirty water.

'Don't know,' Alvin said. 'It seems too dirty, you might get a few Trout or something but that'd be it.'

He was an expert at fishing so Edgar took his word.

Edgar sat in silence, staring into the murky depths of the lake, his reflection staring back. He barely recognised himself after the events of late and felt like he was looking into the eyes of a stranger he was meeting for the first time. He looked at the soft features of the reflection with its long hair and bright eyes – so young and innocent but that was not him anymore. He was old at heart, broken and beaten but with a hard path still ahead. *What would that do to him in the end? How much further would he be pushed? How much more could he be tested?*

Edgar had no idea what was to come – of how much more pain and suffering he would have to endure but he could guess and it wasn't pleasant. He glanced at Alvin and could only see his sister's face in his angular features. The whole family were so alike that if it were possible Edgar would have thought them to be clones. If the guilt wasn't enough to kill him, looking at Alvin and Mrs. Wright and seeing them beaming, completely unaware about what had happened at the Shrine of Saint Margarette, seeing their faces so fair and so similar, it was like Vicky's ghost haunting him, torturing him through her living relatives and still he could say nothing. *How could he explain it?*

He couldn't.

'I'm heading back, you coming?'

Edgar shook his head, still enthralled the the glassy surface of the water, rippling with raindrops.

'Fancy going to see the Medieval Minstrels playing in the Beer Tent? I think your mum said she was going to meet Murdoch there.'

Again, Edgar shook his head glumly. He loved the Medieval Minstrels – the group of beautiful women with voices like sirens, who could pull him out of the darkest of moments – but not today. He had never felt so conflicted and twisted. From all he had been through, all he had seen and now he had to face Alvin and his family and just smile and pretend nothing had happened. It was exhausting. He just wanted to be alone. Alvin muttered something under his breath, got to his feet.

'Bye,' he muttered as he walked away but Edgar didn't even reply.

Alvin was gone, the gentle drizzle fell lightly leaving a refreshing hint of a petrichor on the breeze; the dying light of the day clung to the darkening grey skies and despite the glumness, Edgar found it quite beautiful.

Peace. He could breathe at last.

– CHAPTER TWENTY –
THE QUESTION DECK

The next morning Edgar woke up to find that the battle demonstrations had been cancelled due to the unsafe conditions with the ground being wet and slippery. He had really wanted to practise fighting with his new sword again and the worst thing was that they couldn't even go home early because the cars would churn up the mud and make the exit impassable. Edgar sighed miserably to himself as it began to rain heavily and a roll of thunder could be heard far off in the distance.

'Well,' Alvin said 'We could explore the castle and the market.'

Edgar agreed and the two of them ran off towards the market. They were drenched to the skin within seconds but what did it matter? They were going to get wet either way in this weather and at least now it was impossible to get any wetter. They sprinted along the gravelled path that wound around the hill and through the gates into the castle grounds. There weren't a lot of shops at Conisborough compared to other events but there were still enough, including Drystan's sword tent, an armourer, a fortune teller, a fletcher and a potter.

'Madame Samara's fortue telling?' Edgar exclaimed. 'Come on. It'll be funny,' Edgar mocked, trying to convince Alvin and beckoned him eagerly as he rushed off towards the purple tent that was covered in sparkly silver and gold stars.

'Fine,' Alvin sighed under his breath

He reluctantly followed into the dark tent – he hated this sort of thing. It was always a pack of lies drawn from a pack of cards or phoney rubbish made up by an old hag who wanted to scare people in Alvin's opinion.

Inside the stylish but also very unauthentic tent was a small round table piled with packs of cards, a crystal ball and a ceramic hand with thin black lines painted all over it. Incense sticks burned, filling the room with a dizzying stench. It was all very cliché. The inside décor was bright orange and gold and yellow veils of silk dangled from the ceiling to contribute to the air of mysticism.

'Hello,' said a mysterious, husky voice from the shadows behind the table.

'Hi,' Edgar replied nervously, feeling like he'd made a mistake going there to see a weird old woman make up things about his future. His future was decidedly uncertain after what he had learned from Betty and he wasn't sure if he wanted to know what lay on the horizon.

'Be seated,' she said sweeping out of the shadows and sinking onto her wooden chair. The mystery of the situation dissolved in the atmosphere when Edgar saw that she was just another re-enactor wearing normal re-enactment clothes.

374

He'd been expecting something scary or mystic like a witch, alas, he was wrong. He'd seen scarier plague victim costumes than this person in her red woollen dress and black shawl. Her tatty boots were and falling apart and her long, straggly ginger hair hung right down her back in scruffy locks and her obscure medieval style glasses made her already hard, wrinkled features look even sterner.

'Good morning young man. I am Madame Samara,' she said huskily as she rushed around the table, grabbed Edgar by the arm and pulled him towards a chair.

'I sense already that you are troubled. Yours is a heavy heart burdened with horror, betrayal and guilt.'

Edgar looked worriedly at Alvin as the woman made sure Edgar was seated and then spun around, grabbed Alvin and pulled him closer to Edgar so that he stood right beside him. Madame Samara swept around the table and sank into her seat with her hands on the table top and hunched low over it, eyes narrowed as she surveyed Edgar.

Edgar glanced from Madame Samara to Alvin and back not knowing what to say. It was all too awkward. He wasn't sure how to react to her – whether he should take her seriously or to ignore her as a fraud.

'Choose a pack of cards. Let your spirit lead the way,' she instructed, gesturing to several piles of cards that lay across the table.

Her eyes watched his every move eagerly.

Edgar felt suddenly unaware of his movements. He was not in control. His hand moved, unguided by himself, to a pack of face down cards.

'Ah, the Question Deck,' Madame Samara said mysteriously, looking Edgar in the eye, not breaking her eye contact which made Edgar feel uncomfortably nervous.

'What do I do?' Edgar asked worriedly, not knowing what to do with the cards he now had in his hand.

'Ask the cards anything and then let your spirit guide you to the answer in the deck,' Madame Samara explained airily, as if it were obvious.

Edgar thought and thought, racking his brain for a question – there was so much he wanted to ask but couldn't. He had to think of ways to carefully word his questions to avoid looking like a lunatic. Finally, after almost giving himself a headache one came out:

'Why does everything always happen to me?' This was the only way he could get around to mentioning his dimension travelling adventures in his present company.

He reached tentatively toward the deck, letting his soul guide his hand towards the card in the pile that would serve as his answer. *"Letting his soul guide him"* was just a pompous way of saying do it without looking, thought Edgar as he moved his hand around over the deck with his eyes closed. His hand shot towards a card and he pulled it out.

His heart leapt when he saw the picture.

The Nomad it said on the bottom of the card in curly black letters.

An old man dressed in white, hanging his head. He held a withered, twisted walking stick that was as tall as himself. The figure reminded him of the ghostly Brother Bradley Was it a coincidence?

'What does *this* mean?' Edgar asked curiously, studying the card again.

'Your affairs involve travel. Nobody knows where your journeys will lead to but it is certain that they will test you to your limits,' Samara said coolly, watching Edgar as his jaw dropped. He was soon aware of his over-reaction and quickly composed himself. 'Pick another.'

'Why did Betty trust me?' Edgar asked the cards confidently, getting the hang of the idea.

His hand reached out, hovered over the deck. His finger pointed towards a card. That was the one. He took it gently, anxious about turning it over to see the picture and title. He flipped it and looked at the title:

The Hero.

It depicted a man holding a sword above his head with both hands; a pure white sky was burning around him and a single bolt of black lightning shot down and touched the tip of the blade.

"This is weird," he thought to himself. The answers were too close to home but nothing yet had given him anything new – anything helpful he could really work with.

'Will it be alright? Will I get through this?' Edgar asked the cards again, his voice quiet. This time he closed his eyes and let his hand move over the deck until he felt ready to jab at a card and take it.

He pulled the card from the thick deck:

Victory.

A ferocious lion, mid-roar was the picture and Edgar suddenly felt a little more at ease. If there was any truth to the cards, then he would be alright. He stood a chance after all.

'Thank you,' Edgar said politely to Madame Samara. He had asked enough. He knew that he could be victorious against the Nazakan threat and that was enough for him.

'Go on. Take another card. You asked two questions,' Madame Samara said gesturing back towards the cards.

'I only meant it to be one,' Edgar replied.

'Take the card,' Madame Samara said coolly, her eyes burning into Edgar's.

He took the card: A distorted face, hidden half in shadow. *The Secret Enemy.*

'But *who's* my secret enemy?' Edgar wondered out loud, staring at the card in his hands. 'It can't be Spencer – he's my enemy but it's not exactly a secret. There are loads of people who don't like me but they're all so *open* about it. So who could my *secret* enemy be?' Edgar said, feeling like he'd picked a wrong card and his heart sank. Perhaps the cards weren't particularly accurate after all. Since when was *The Secret Enemy* a proper answer to *Will I get through this?*

'Take a card and find out,' Madame Samara said, with a suggestive wink. Her hands clasped together upon the table and her wide eyes stared at Edgar, magnified through her glasses.

Edgar closed his eyes and swayed his hand over the cards. Alvin gave him a funny look almost as if he thought Edgar was stupid for taking part. Edgar ignored him. Finally he decided to jab his finger at a random card in the deck.

He opened his eyes, wondering what amazing shock would greet them next. He pulled the card from the deck, his fingers trembling.

The Raven.

A stunningly beautiful, pale girl with long black hair that flowed right down to her backside stood by a willow tree with a raven resting on her shoulder. The tree above seemed to be covered in black leaves, but in fact the whole tree was full of ravens roosting in the bare branches.

'Can you tell me what this means please?' Edgar asked the wide-eyed woman who shook her head feverishly and flipped her hand to swipe her greasy ginger straggles out of her eyes.

'This card is bad. A raven is crowing. Someone you *know* or *will* know is deceiving or will deceive you. *Do you know who it is?*' Madame Samara whispered almost fearfully.

'Well of course I don't. I wanted to find out who my secret enemy is but instead all I find out is the same information I got before – some random person is out to get me and I didn't know who before and I don't know now. You know, I don't trust these cards. They've hardly answered my questions.' Edgar snapped.

'Who's to say they haven't?' Madame Samara replied darkly. 'The answers can be a lot more cryptic than you realise.'

'What's the point?' Edgar muttered to himself as he exhaled a long, sigh.

Samara simply pointed once more at the cards.

'I don't need to take another one!' Edgar retorted in frustration.

'A question was asked. An answer must be given.'

'Fine.'

He followed the procedure, except this time he didn't bother feeling for the right card and merely grabbed the first one he touched.

The Tower.

An ancient crumbling tower standing on a cliff high above the rough seas below. Lightning strikes hit the tower, flames burst from the windows and human shapes tumbled through the air, over the edge of the cliff.

Edgar knew from his vague knowledge of tarot cards that the tower was not a particularly pleasant card to come across. It was the card he had always feared finding, knowing of its dark meaning.

'The Tower,' Madame Samara said. There was a tone of sorrow in her voice, as if she were partly afraid and partly offering her condolences. 'I can see you know what that means.'

'Death, destruction, chaos,' he replied solemnly. It was enough to make him hope that the Question Deck had been inaccurate but the first couple of answers had been so true that it sent a shiver down his back.

'This might not be a bad thing. You asked *"What is the point?"'* Madame Samara interjected. 'Maybe this just means that you need to remain focused on the things important to you otherwise everything will fall apart around you.'

'But what if it doesn't?'

Samara gestured to the cards again but Edgar shook his head. He had had enough of letting a deck of cards give him answers to such big questions. Maybe Alvin had always been right – fortune telling was a waste of time. Life would work out the way it was meant to and there was nothing he could do about that. He just had to take it as it came.

'No. No more cards.'

Edgar climbed out of his seat and shoved Alvin down in his place.

'Go on then Al. Your turn,'

Alvin looked anxious but there was a flicker of a smile on his lips as if he had been looking forward to taking a turn, even though he knew it was all a hoax. He looked at the decks of cards that were lying on the table and took the same dilapidated deck as Edgar had and asked:

'How long will Vicky be gone?'

Edgar should have known his questions would be about his sister. He was absolutely devoted to her – the whole family were. They were so close that being apart must have been tearing them apart. He swallowed hard to try and dislodge the painful lump in his throat – he knew the truth and had not dared to say a thing.

Vicky had been away for a long time already and nobody was certain when she was going to get back. The length of her missionary position had been changed from six months, to one year, to two years, then back to six months. There had been no news from Vicky for a long time and Edgar knew why but he didn't want to tell Alvin. It would only upset him and then he would have to tell him everything about dimension travel which could only land him in serious trouble if he did so. Alvin would think he was insane! He would tell everyone and Edgar would likely end up in an asylum. It wasn't worth the risk...

However, at the same time his heart was telling him to do it. It felt like Edgar was trapped in the middle of a tug of war with his conscience and he was being used as the rope and suddenly he was back in Grindlotha, hiding in the scrub with Charles. Vicky was burning. She was screaming and crying and Edgar just crouched there.

He tried to move but his body felt like it were encased in concrete. Movement was impossible. The crowds were jeering and booing. The air was thick with smoke and the stomach churning stench of burning flesh. The crowd revelled in it and Edgar couldn't turn away.

The imagery was so strong – a traumatic memory that he could never erase. He could feel the tears welling in his eyes and he bit his lip hard to try and stop them. He couldn't cry. He couldn't give anything away.

Alvin waved his hand surreptitiously over the cards and jabbed one with his forefinger. He pulled out a card depicting a rather dramatic scene.

A young woman, dressed in a floating white gown lay on a large slab of rock while a young man knelt over her still body with his head in his hands. Behind him a tall black, silhouette of a demonic creature. Its thin, skeletal hand was on the man's shoulder and its red eyes glowed ominously.

Death.

'No,' whispered Alvin, hoarsely, a tear running down his cheek. 'She can't be dead.'

'Remember cards can be unclear,' Samara said desperately trying to convince Alvin 'And Death can represent new life.'

'But what about my sister?' Alvin asked in clear distress and Edgar looked on in horror, his jaw hanging open. It was impossible to hide the truth any longer. He almost spoke out there and then but remembered they weren't alone.

'I'm sorry, but I may not interfere with your family's personal affairs,' Samara sniffed sternly and turned her nose up, giving Edgar a shifty look, as though he should understand her doing this even though his face was contorted with confusion. *Did she know what he had seen? Did she really know the truth? Could she read his mind?*

Edgar had never felt so panicked in his life. His body trembled and his heart stopped momentarily. It was like the world moved in slow-motion, as if he had manipulated time. There was no way to avoid the inevitable – the moment where he had to reveal the truth was on the horizon and he couldn't hide any longer. He did all he could and put a warm hand on Alvin's shoulder to try and comfort him.

'Come on Al, we have to go,' Edgar prompted, wishing that Alvin would follow him. The tension had grown to such an amount he couldn't stand it and wanted to be out of there and free from it – he knew he had to tell Alvin what had happened but that was going to take time.

'Come on,' he said, trying a softer approach this time.

Alvin did not hear him and simply sat in his seat, catatonic. There were no more tears and he simply remained statuesque in shock.

'Alvin!' Edgar demanded, still there was no reply so he grabbed Alvin's arm, pulled him out of his seat and dragged him over to the exit.

'Edgar! I want to ask some more questions,' Alvin argued as he pulled his arm out of Edgar's grip and squared up to him, clenching his fist.

'You're upset,' Edgar snapped in reply, his eyes on Alvin's tight fist. 'But don't you dare threaten to hit me. I'm trying to help.'

'If you want to help then you can leave me alone,' Alvin snarled.

'Boys,' Madame Samara tried softly. 'Please refrain from fighting in my tent. It'll disturb my chakras.'

'One last question,' Alvin hissed, his face inches from Edgar's; he stared right into his eyes but Edgar refused to back down. He would not be intimidated. He clenched his jaw, blinked hard to try and stop the tears but nothing could prepare him for Alvin's final question:

'Is Edgar hiding something from me?'

The words hit him like a bullet. His breath caught in his throat, leaving him breathless. His eyes widened and he tried not to give away that the question had hurt more than Alvin could ever know.

'Is Edgar hiding something from me?' he raged again.

Edgar gulped. He could feel his entire body quaking and he had to stop. His eyes stared back into Alvin's steely gaze. He couldn't blink – that would show weakness.

The silence and the tension was so thick, so awful that any sudden movement, any sound could have triggered an explosive reaction. Like a bomb diffuser, Edgar knew he had to choose his words correctly. He gulped hard and tried to act cool but he couldn't. His wide eyes were full of fear and his jaw hung open.

Madame Samara simply sat in her seat, watching in intense shock. She daren't move or face the wrath of either of the boys.

'I don't need to pick a card to know the answer,' Alvin snarled. He pushed Edgar aside and stormed out.

As Edgar took off after him Madame Samara fanned herself with her hand and shook her head, unable to believe the display she had just seen before her.

*

The rain thrashed down and the sodden grass beneath their feet squelched with each slippery footstep.

'What the hell is your problem?' Alvin protested. 'What are you hiding from me?'

The marketplace was almost dead except for the odd figure darting from tent to tent and some public who sheltered under the tents, watching Edgar and Alvin in surprise as they stood in the centre of the market field, staring at each other, fists clenched, gritting their teeth.

'Look, Alvin, This is awkward - I know how you must feel... but...but....that woman was weird,' Edgar said rationally as he forced himself to remain calm despite the heat of the moment and tried to reassure Alvin. Now was not a good time to admit everything.

'It doesn't change the fact that you're not yourself. You're distant and you're acting strange and it only got worse when I mentioned Vicky in there!' Alvin raged, his face burning red and his tears lost in the raindrops that trickled down his cheeks in their place. The public still stared at them like caged animals at the zoo.

'No, you won't understand. That woman, Samara - she said that cards could be wrong and even if the Death card was right *"Death"* can mean *new life*!' Edgar snapped in his defence and stomped his foot to emphasise his point. 'Vicky's gone on her mission. She's on an adventure, it's changing her, made her a brand new person.'

'Stop changing the subject!' Alvin shouted; his emotion and paranoia getting the better of him. 'What is wrong with you?'

Edgar's mind whirred in over-drive. He needed an excuse. He couldn't tell him the truth – not yet, not here with so many people watching.

'Fine,' Edgar spat. 'I miss her too.'

'And?' Alvin laughed maniacally. 'That's no reason to act like a psycho.'

Edgar closed his eyes, terrified of the words that were about to come out of his mouth. How would Alvin react?

'I'm in love with her.'

SMACK.

The force of the blow to his face knocked Edgar off balance and he fell flat onto the soggy mud.

'Alvin...' Edgar pleaded. He hadn't expected it to go like that.

'So that's your secret?' Alvin snarled. 'That's what you've been hiding from me?'

Edgar nodded solemnly, his hand reaching up to the sore spot on his cheek where Alvin's fist had made contact.

'I'm sorry,' Edgar muttered. Alvin stared down at him, fists still clenched and a terrifying look in his wide, furious eyes. 'You wanted the truth...you got it.'

'You were meant to be my best friend.'

'I still *am,*' Edgar replied quickly, still unable to gather the strength to stand. Alvin towered over him and despite all he had faced recently – the Unsterbliche, the corrupt Police of Alternus Erathasus, the tramp in Merimalima and the Nazakan and Hounds - he had never been more scared. Alvin was his friend, a true friend and someone who cared for him when not many others did. He needed Alvin. He couldn't lose his friend and the thought of that happening tore Edgar to shreds even more viciously than the razor sharp fangs or claws of any monster.

'You only wanted to be close to me to get to my sister.'

'Where has this nonsense come from?' Edgar demanded, finding the strength to climb back to his feet. He glanced down at himself and was furious to see that not only was he soaked to the bone, he was covered in mud too.

'You! You brought it on yourself!' Alvin shouted, his voice wavering. He was so caught in the moment that he had not noticed the growing crowd surrounding them. His anger blinded him so that he didn't see the pointing and laughing. He was oblivious to the Japanese tourist recording Alvin on a video camera, giving a running commentary in his own language and he had no idea the crowd around them had grown so large. Edgar had noticed. He was aware of the eyes upon them, the spectacle Alvin had created. It made Edgar feel uncomfortable. This was private.

'GO AWAY! Leave us alone!' Edgar bellowed at them, losing his temper.

They ignored his request which only made Edgar's blood boil until he could hold it back no longer and waved his arms at the tide of tourists who'd gathered around.

'GO AWAY!' He shouted as he ran at them, shooing them away, like a kid scattering a group of pigeons.

'Rude child,' tutted an old woman in utter disgust.

'RUDE?' Edgar screamed. '*RUDE?* Look at yourself you miserable old cow! This is private!'

'Truly disgusting behaviour,' moaned a man with a young child, putting his hands over the young child's ears to block out the angry words.

'He's right though. It's none of your business, clear off,' said a loud, familiar voice. Whoever it was sounded fierce and the crowd dispersed as the person pushed her way through. It was Priscilla.

'What's going on?' she demanded, shooting the piercing glare at Edgar.

'Everything's fine,' Edgar lied, trying to cover up what was really going on as he looked bashfully at his mum who could obviously see right through his lie.

'Really?' Priscilla sneered sarcastically, giving Edgar the all-knowing look that *proved* that she knew he was lying. 'Why else would you be covered in mud? Why have a group of people crowded around, staring at you?'

'Stuff just happened,' Edgar said trying to hide Vicky's death. They were told the cards could have been wrong and Alvin still had a glimmer of hope for his sister's survival but Edgar knew that he was wrong to let Alvin carry on, blissfully unaware of the truth, still, he couldn't bring himself to say anything. If he had reacted that way to the lie Edgar had created, how would he react to the news of her death?

'Stuff happens all the time but *stuff* doesn't attract a crowd like that,' Priscilla said, digging deeper.

'It was just some fortune telling stuff,' Edgar said and Alvin shook his head.

'Oh, Alvin. You know those cards can be wrong. Let me guess, you used the Deck where *you* pick the cards and ask it a question,' she said looking kindly at Alvin who was still clearly traumatised and shaking as he tried to control himself – his face a mess of rainwater and tears. 'It's so open to interpretation, love. That's why they do it. Don't be upset over it.'

'It's not just that,' Alvin said darkly. His narrow eyes fixed on Edgar and he knew what was coming. 'Edgar just admitted he's in love with Vicky.'

The words hung in the air like an echo that would forever replay in his ears.

Edgar felt sick. He didn't love Vicky at all – he had never seen her in that way.

Why did he have to use such a flimsy excuse?

It had well and truly backfired and he was the only one to blame.

'Is this true, Edgar?' Priscilla asked, a flicker of a smile on her lips. 'Do you really?'

Edgar didn't reply. His heart thumped in his chest, his stomach churned and he felt sick. He had never thought about relationships with anyone after the disaster with Ophelia – let alone spoken about them...out loud...with his *mother!* It was mortifying. He had never really thought about *anyone* in that way, never mind Vicky. Even if he did like her that way their love would be doomed from the start. She, like the rest of her family, was Mormon, so it would never go anywhere.

'He only wanted to be my friend to get close to her,' Alvin sneered and Edgar's heart dropped.

What had gone wrong? Why had this happened? For once he wished he could consult the cards and find an answer – whether it would be helpful or not. Alvin had betrayed him and Edgar thought back to the answers he did have: *The Secret Enemy.* Could it have meant Alvin?

'You know that's not true,' Edgar muttered, his voice breaking as he struggled to hold back the tears. It was too much –

Alvin's betrayal, Priscilla's probing and the both of them believing he was in love with Vicky. It was as awkward as it was unbearable.

'Edgar...' Priscilla began softly. She could tell Edgar was upset and knew not to push him any further.

'SHUT UP!' Edgar bellowed and before he could stop himself, he sprinted along the path towards the castle. He was not in control. His body ran on autopilot, his legs scurrying as fast as they could, slipping and sliding on the wet grass and his feet stuck in the mud so that he stumbled.

'Edgar, please!' Priscilla shouted after him, hoping he would hear and stop but he didn't.

It was too much. He needed time alone.

As he stormed away from the scene, Edgar broke down. He couldn't handle the effect of the conflicting emotions and the adrenaline causing the chemical catastrophe in his body. Tears streamed down his face and his whole body shook as he struggled to breathe properly.

As he came closer, Edgar noticed that the castle was not very wide, but what it lacked in width, it made up for in height. The building was colossal and looked like a giant dominating the hilly landscape. Edgar raced up a steep flight of rickety wooden stairs to the gargantuan doors that stood open, awaiting his entrance.

He dived inside. It was dry and it was quiet; and though he was soaking wet and sobbing, he was alone and that was what he needed more than anything else.

– CHAPTER TWENTY-ONE –
GHOST STORIES

Edgar slumped through the castle, weighed down by his water-logged clothes. A hefty clap of thunder was accompanied by a flash of lightning and the thunder was so loud that the very foundations of the castle vibrated as it rumbled. He headed towards a narrow archway at the back of the hall and began to climb the stairs. Along the walls of the staircase were alcoves that cut into the walls containing narrow windows. Glimpses of murky sky and swirling black clouds could be seen through these slits and rain still poured down. Thunder and lightning waged war with each other overhead Flashes of light briefly illuminated the dark staircase in different shades of blues and purples and rumbles that shook the ground beneath his feet and shifted dust that fell in thin trickles from the ceiling.

He fumed as he charged up the steps at speed. Alvin's betrayal still played on his mind. He didn't know why it bothered him so much. Both Alvin and Priscilla thought he was in love with Vicky.

So what?

Surely it was better for them to think he was in love with someone than be a weirdo who wasn't in love with anyone. Love was a natural part of human life but for someone who had never learned what true attraction was like or made a real sexual connection, or even gone as far as a kiss, it was awkward and weird. His mind threw back, once more, to when he had gone out with Ophelia for a couple of days and he was too shy to even hold her hand – how he had tried and it had just felt wrong.

"Is there something wrong with me?" Edgar thought to himself. He had entirely forgotten that he was only fifteen. It wasn't the be and end all of his life but everyone at school had formed relationships. They had all kissed, some had even lost their virginity and liked nothing more than to brag about their sexual conquests. Compared to them he felt inadequate...like there was some basic fault inside him that prevented him from being able to function like a normal teenage human being.

"I bet Damian never has problems like this," he thought to himself. *"He's perfect."*

He wasn't quite sure what had reminded him of Damian but the more he thought about his new friend it didn't matter if Alvin had fallen out with him. He barely saw him anyway but Damian was closer to home. Edgar smiled as he pictured his perfectly symmetrical face and his deep, dark eyes that gleamed when he flashed a sparkling smile.

"Why can't I be like him? What wouldn't I give to be so strong and handsome and confident?" Edgar thought to himself glumly. And then it hit him.

"Maybe he could help me," Edgar thought. He needed help preparing to fight in the coming war so maybe he should start going

to the gym. A scrawny, young boy could never lead an all out battle and expect to win. He had to start doing something about it and if Damian could help him, as bad as things seemed now, at least he could look forward to having a true friend when he got home – one who wouldn't betray him or hurt him the way that Alvin had.

At the top of the stairs another room spread out into the darkness as a rumble of thunder echoed in the distance and the wind howled, growing stronger and blew a draft through the open holes in the ancient brick work of the Norman castle. Edgar felt uneasy in here – the hairs on his neck and arms stood on end, a chill tingled down his spine as if he had been charged with static. It was eerie, like someone watched from the shadows. Edgar sneaked into the middle of the room, looking around to check if he was alone.

It was unnerving. Perhaps it was the silence and the emptiness of the huge castle. Suddenly, being alone wasn't as inviting as it had seemed to be before and Edgar wished he had some company. He crossed to an opening in the wall, where a door would have been in the glory days of the castle; a couple of steep steps went up in the alcove and wound around to the side. He wouldn't have noticed it if it weren't for the light coming through from a gap in the wall where several bricks had broken away over the years and created a hole that was big enough to fall out of.

Edgar walked towards it and looked out; he saw how far down the ground was and nearly threw up – he hated heights and was at least eighty feet up in the air over a sheer drop to the ground. It was frightening but then his attention was drawn away because he felt as though something was around the corner. It made him shudder to think about what to expect to see but he knew deep in his heart that someone was there. He could sense them there as he peeked around the corner and nearly screamed.

It was a Monk. He flickered again leaving a faint buzz as he did so. His back was turned to Edgar but when he gasped the Monk turned quickly and put his finger over his mouth as if signalling for Edgar to be quiet.

'You're not Brother Bradley. What do you want with me?' Edgar asked, shaken by the surprise. The ghost ignored him.

Thud, thud, clatter.

'Edgar?' shouted a voice. It was Alvin.

'What do you want?' Edgar repeated in frustration but the ghost simply pointed over Edgar's shoulder, nodded and walked away through the hole and out into the sheer drop on the other side of it. Slowly, he turned to see what the ghost had pointed at. It was only then that he realised Alvin was standing behind him, giving him a look as if he thought Edgar belonged in an asylum. 'Why are you following me? Just leave me alone?'

'Edgar...' Alvin whispered, his voice catching in his throat. reluctant to speak to him. 'I know something's wrong. Something more than you're letting on.'

'You don't sound like you believe that,' Edgar replied, noticing that Alvin sounded as if he were reciting from a badly rehearsed script. 'Has mum sent you to spy on me?'

'No, I just want to make sure you're okay,' Alvin replied quietly.

'After you just smacked me in the face?' Edgar scoffed, pointing to his bruised cheek. 'How do you think I'm doing?'

Alvin looked sheepish and opened his mouth to speak but seemed to think better of it.

'You think we're friends after what you just did to me?' Edgar asked, raising an angry eyebrow and Alvin didn't reply again.

His former friend twiddled his thumbs and looked awkward.

'You're just here because mum sent you. Tell me I'm right?' Edgar thought out loud and Alvin grimaced. He didn't reply but the sheepish look in his eye gave him away. Edgar was right.

'I'm not in the mood. Do me a favour, piss off and go tell her to get stuffed. Whatever. I don't care anymore.'

Edgar pushed past Alvin and marched down the stairs. Alvin followed Edgar to the bottom of the next flight. Edgar wasn't sure which way to go and headed through the nearest archway – he could feel Alvin chasing after him but he remained strong and refused to look around. Perhaps if he could get away from Alvin, he would go away and leave him, but he wasn't so lucky.

Alvin followed him into a small, dark side room that was only just big enough for the two of them to fit into. The room was empty except for the hole where boiling oil or water would have been poured out of. Now it had a thick iron grate over it to stop people from falling out.

Edgar looked down through the gaps between the hefty bars and saw the ground and part of the authentic camp far below and he felt dizzy again. Alvin reached out and touched Edgar's arm.

'Get off me!' Edgar exclaimed furiously. He thought about pushing past Alvin but he was cornered. There was no way out. Alvin blocked the way, arms folded.

'I'm worried about you, Ed,' Alvin said calmly and for the first time, Edgar thought he might actually be telling the truth. His words seemed sincere and the look on his face was etched with uncertainty. 'Who were you talking to up there?'

'It's a long story. One I'd rather not tell,' Edgar replied. He wasn't ready.

'I'm sorry for before. The least I can do is listen to you now.'

Edgar hesitated. He couldn't tell Alvin the truth. An awkward tension surrounded them and Edgar tried to think of an excuse...but look where excuses had got him before; they had almost ruined everything. Perhaps it was finally time to be truthful. *If Vicky had been travelling, did that mean the Wrights were travellers too? Should he tell Alvin everything?*

Edgar took a deep breath to calm his nerves.

'Promise you won't judge?'

'Promise.' Alvin reached out and shook Edgar's hand.

Edgar took another deep breath, worried that this could ruin things even more than his previous excuses.

'It was a ghost,' Edgar said and the four words were enough to set Alvin off into hysterical laughter.

'No judging, remember.'

'But *ghosts?*' Alvin snapped. 'Ghosts don't exist.'

'They do! When I was young, just a toddler, weird stuff started happening. Everybody else just assumed that I just had an imaginary friend...but I didn't. There was this ghost in my house – a white Monk, because my house was built over the ancient foundations of a Cistercian Monastery. I understood when I was older, but as a child, it made no sense,' Edgar began to explain. Alvin was listening with great anticipation despite the incredulous expression etched on his face.

'Anyway, He used to talk to me but it was weird,' Edgar carried on, Alvin's eyes growing wider with interest. 'He used to teach me to read and I called him Biggy because he was really tall. He was nice and he was kind. There was nothing scary about him – nothing horrible or evil-'

Alvin let out a laugh, which he managed to discretely disguise as a sneeze.

'And what did a ghost teach you to read - ghost stories?' Alvin ridiculed rudely as he cut Edgar off to disrupt the story.

'You promised not to make fun of me. Now shut up or I won't tell you the rest,' Edgar said angrily. He should have never trusted Alvin. 'He taught me how to read anything, actually. He would literally pull the books off my bookcase and leave them all over the floor for my mum to find. She would never believe that Biggy did it.'

'This is ridiculous,' Alvin hissed furiously. 'Are you having a breakdown or something?'

'No, I swear on my life it is all true. Biggy did exist but there was one day he came to me and I didn't understand then – don't now and probably never will. It was the only time he scared me – the only time his visit felt...different. He whispered to me in the bathroom

THE CHRONICLES OF EDGAR HAROLD

while my mum was making my bed. At the time I thought nothing of it...he told me he needed to borrow something and that one day I would understand then while my back was turned he stole my teddy bear that was dressed up as a white Monk and then he vanished.'

'A teddy bear stealing ghost?' Alvin laughed, shaking his head in disbelief.

'Thing is, Biggy, or Brother Bradley, as he's really called, came back recently. He told me that it wasn't him that stole the teddy bear that night,' Edgar whispered darkly. There was a gleam in his eye – a look of a man desperate to solve a mystery. 'I don't know who or what it was in his place but I knew they didn't want to harm me. Who knows, maybe the day I understand will still come. I only ever assumed it *was* Biggy because of his robes but the way he didn't flicker – the way he didn't echo *and* he didn't mention the poem...' Edgar explained.

'What poem?' Alvin asked as he looked over to Edgar who sat in silence, almost in a trance-like state as his mind whirred in circles.

'*The* poem. The same poem Biggy recited every time we met. It was just something he said every time he left me:

"Every second has a meaning,
Day after day, the world still spins,
Great barriers act as invisible pins.
All holding the fabric of time and space,
Relatively in the very same place.

How would you cope,

Armed with nothing but hope to

Ready you for the dark days to come?

Over the barriers you will go.

Living your life to help others lives flow,

Deaf you will be to the Raven's crow."

'I don't understand it? Are you writing a book or something? Is this all a joke?' Alvin sighed, quickly becoming more and more sceptical about Edgar's story of Biggy, the further it went on.

'Honestly, cross my heart,' Edgar said as his hand shot up to his chest and crossed it. 'He always repeated the same poem again after our reading sessions. I never understood it, but it stuck in my mind for some reason,' Edgar explained grimly without a trace of mockery on his serious expression. Alvin frowned thoughtfully. 'Turns out it was an acrostic poem. It spells my name.'

'And what else did this ghost tell you?' he asked curiously, still unsure whether to believe Edgar or mock him again.

'He always told me that I'd see my dad again one day, that I was destined for great things and that one day I would understand – he said that a lot...'

Alvin looked perplexed and Edgar felt a weight off his shoulders. Whether Alvin believed him or not, it didn't matter – he had offered an insight to his crazy life and Alvin had just mocked him. That was enough proof for Edgar that the secret about Vicky was one he would have to carry around a little longer.

'I think you're mad but I want to believe you,' Alvin said quietly. 'Is this what's been going on then? Why you've been acting weird?'

Edgar nodded wordlessly.

'So about Vicky...?'

'An excuse,' Edgar replied, the feeling of relief washing over him. At least nobody would think he was in love with her now.

'Good,' Alvin laughed 'Or I'd have to kill you.'

'Are we friends again then?' Edgar asked coyly.

'We never weren't,' Alvin replied, shocked that Edgar would even ask such a question.

'You punched me in the face!' Edgar exclaimed, reaching to his cheek. The purple bruise was tender to the touch. Alvin didn't reply and Edgar knew it was because he felt too awkward. It didn't matter. It was over, it was forgiven.

*

The rest of the afternoon passed quickly and without any more signs of ghosts. Things seemed to be fixed again between Edgar and Alvin – their friendship had suffered a sharp blow but had thankfully survived, proving that best friends could never fall out for long.

Back at the campsite, Edgar got changed into clean, dry clothes and spent the rest of the afternoon in the tent avoiding Priscilla's awkward questions about his love life. She wouldn't let it go and Edgar retreated to his compartment for peace. He lay there, listening to the steady *pitter-patter* of rain hitting the tent and watching the droplets roll down the side. It was calm and exactly what he needed. Eventually, he drifted off to sleep. It had been a long, eventful day. He needed the nap.

*

'Ed, I'm coming with you!' Alvin announced loudly as he poked his head into Edgar's compartment.

'WHAT?' Edgar spluttered, in complete shock. He sat bolt-upright, taken by surprise by Alvin's sudden appearance.

'My parents have just had an important phone call and have had to rush off to see Vicky. Something's happened to her,' Alvin explained, his eyes were glazed over with shock as if the severity of the situation hadn't had chance to sink in.

Edgar's heart sank. He felt sick. Maybe he wouldn't have to tell Alvin after all.

'So why aren't you going with them then?' Edgar asked in horror. His very body and his mind went numb – he didn't know what to think or do or feel.

'They said I'm not allowed to go. I'm to stay here,' Alvin said, holding back the tears that were sparkling in his eyes. Edgar could see how worried he was and he wished he could say something to make it better but there was nothing he could say at all.

'So how long you staying with us?' Edgar asked quickly, glad to have a friend around for company but also terrified by the fact that the truth was set to come out. Soon Alvin would know of Vicky's fate – but how would the story be covered up? Somehow Edgar couldn't imagine *"Vicky was burned alive by an angry mob,"* being the cause of death on her death certificate. Unless the Wright's were secretly travellers too?

No. It made no sense. None of it.

'I'm with you until they get back...so the next couple of weeks at least, maybe 'til the end of the holidays,' Alvin said, forcing an injection of excitement into his voice as he tried to cover his heartbreak.

'Does my mum know?'

'I've just been talking to her.'

'And what did she say?'

'She said it would be a pleasure for me to stay with you because you'd have someone to hang around with. Mum and dad had already arranged it with her.'

Edgar was confused. It was too much to think about and all of the things that could have been buzzed around inside his mind like angry flies trying to escape in the form of words. He didn't have the courage to tell Alvin anything yet.

There was a time he would have loved to have Alvin be around for so long but this was not one of those times. There was too much going on in his life. He had his adventures and a war to prepare for. He held a dark secret about Alvin's sister that he couldn't confess and the mere sight of him reminded Edgar of the guilt in his heart. It was his fault Vicky was dead. His fault.

He forced a smile and did what he had learned to do best; pretend everything was alright.

– CHAPTER TWENTY-TWO –
A GRAVE MISTAKE

Edgar woke up early the next day feeling like the entire weekend had been a dream.

He climbed out of bed, yawning and went down stairs. Alvin was already awake and watching TV. He sat there so innocently in his pyjamas, oblivious to everything his family were going through. Edgar hadn't been able to shift the thoughts all night; his conscience had been ripping him apart from inside and the pain was unbearable.

'Morning, Ed,' Alvin said cheerily.

'Morning Al. you're up early,' Edgar replied, feigning a cheery tone. Maybe now was the time to tell him.

'There was a load of banging at the back of the house and it woke me up,' Alvin said, stifling a yawn and stretching.

'The excavation!' Edgar exclaimed, remembering about the Damian and the archaeologists who had slipped his mind until Alvin had just reminded him. 'Look, Alvin. There's something I have to tell you,' Edgar said, looking at the floor guiltily.

'Yeah?' Alvin probed, eager to know more.

'It's about Vicky...'

The silence was palpable and Alvin raised an angry eyebrow.

'I know something...' Edgar stopped mid-sentence. There were footsteps on the stairs. Priscilla came around the corner.

'What do you know?' Alvin demanded in a quiet hiss.

'Shhh,' Edgar replied, looking scared and shot Alvin a wide-eyed look as if to tell him to be patient.

'Morning, how are you two today?' Priscilla asked kindly, completely unaware of the underlying tension.

'Fine,' Edgar and Alvin replied in happy unison, managing to sound convincing as they feigned their contentment.

Priscilla went past them, into the kitchen to make a coffee.

'Look. The thing about Vicky, I'll show you later. I'll introduce you to the people who were there with me. There was nothing we could do. I'm so sorry,' Edgar blabbed, struggling to keep the tears at bay. The secret was out and he felt such a strong mixture of both fear, relief and sadness.

'You're not making sense,' Alvin whispered, his expression twisting into a muddled glaze.

'I know it's hard. She's your sister... but you have to keep this quiet or we're both in trouble,' Edgar continued nervously, under his breath.

'I've got to go to work today and Ida's in so you two will have to stay here. I'm only doing dinner cover so I'll just be gone for a couple of hours,' Priscilla said morosely, her voice carrying in from the kitchen.

'Brilliant,' Edgar whispered to Alvin.

Priscilla came back in with her coffee and sat down, sipping at the warm drink., eyeing the boys over the rim of her mug with suspicion.

'Are you ok Alvin? You look a bit upset.,' she asked.

'Yeah, I'm fine, thanks, Mrs. Harold,' Alvin lied. He was growing increasingly worried about Vicky.

'Oh, I'll be having none of that Mrs. Harold stuff – you're a close friend – practically family and you're our guest so just call me Priscilla.'

'Ok, Priscilla...Yeah. I'm worried about Vicky... I can't stop thinking about how that woman looked at me. It was like she knew something was wrong,' Alvin said, shuddering as he remembered the event in the Madame Samara's tent. 'Vicky fell ill and my parents had to go and see her and it suddenly happened after that card reading. She hadn't been in touch with us for weeks,' Alvin explained his eyes wide in fear.

'Well, I told her not to do cards for kids anymore. I told her about you and she was really apologetic...if *"I'm sorry that fate hasn't been kind."* can count as an apology.' Priscilla said and her eyes caught the clock on the wall. 'Anyway, I've got to run, I'm meant to be at work in five; guess who's gonna be late. See you later. Bye boys,' she shouted over her shoulder as she ran to the door, dumping her half-empty, still steaming cup on the floor beside her chair.

'Bye,' Edgar said under his breath, not bothering to make himself heard because the door had already crashed shut with a tremendous slam and his mum was gone.

'Go on then. Tell me,' Alvin said anxiously as Priscilla exited.

'Just let me explain everything first before I show you,' Edgar said urgently. Alvin rolled his eyes. Edgar was stalling again and he wondered if there was anythg really going on at all.

Edgar told Alvin the whole story – from Betty's death, to his finding the travellers' token and he was about to explain about the adventures that followed but Alvin jumped up and stood defiantly with his hands on his hips. He didn't believe. This was ridiculous. He sighed and began pacing, ruffling his messy hair.

'Cut the crap, Edgar,' he snapped. Enough was enough.

'I can see I'm going to have to prove myself here. Follow me.'

Edgar dragged Alvin up to his room and sat him on the bed as he pulled his diary from a drawer in his desk. He sat down next to Alvin and flicked through the pages, showing him the long paragraphs of scruffy writing that he had scrawled to get his feelings off his chest.

'What's this got to do with anything?' Alvin sneered skeptically and Edgar glared at him. He pulled his travellers' token from his pocket and showed it to Alvin who just shrugged it off.

'What's that exactly?' Alvin asked, he looked a little closer lifted the diary, making the connection. 'That's the coin – the travellers' token thing you've written about in your story.'

'That's my diary. This is all true.'

'Edgar, you realise how insane you sound right now?'

'Keep reading, please. Keep going,' Edgar commanded and Alvin kept flicking through the pages until amid the messy words he spotted one that was legible; one word he had been searching for: *Vicky.*

Edgar noticed that Alvin had reached the passage about the Shrine of Saint Margarette and his heart skipped a beat and he turned away. He couldn't face Alvin.

Had he made the right decision? Was it sensible to share these secrets with him?

Edgar watched in silence as Alvin read. He kept peeking at the words to see how far he had gone and then it happened – the thing Edgar knew was coming, the thing he had been dreading but knew he had to share. Alvin came to the passage about Vicky. He read it out loud, his voice quiet and hoarse, the words trembling as he spoke them:

'It wasn't my fault. There was nothing I could do, it was like Charles said, I had to stay hidden or the same would happen to me. I didn't want to look as the executioner strung her up from the statue of Saint Margarette and left her dangling in the air like some kind of bizarre crucifixion. I didn't want to look but I couldn't help it. I wanted nothing more than to scream as he lowered the flaming torch to the bonfire beneath her but when I opened my mouth, no sound came. Vicky died because I did nothing. If I had done something, I would not be here writing these words. I can still hear her screaming, I can still see her writhing and smell the fire and smoke and burning flesh. I am racked with guilt. I sat there. I watched. I did nothing. *Nothing.* Now how can I ever look Alvin in the eye again, knowing what I know and having seen what I have seen? How can I face the family knowing that Vicky is gone because of me?'

Alvin looked at him as if he was crazy, his eyes swimming with tears. He swore and flung the diary at Edgar.

It hit Edgar square in the face but he didn't feel it. He was too numb.

'I'm sorry you had to find out this way,' Edgar whispered, taking Alvin's hand in his – it was a pathetic attempt to comfort him.

'It's not true,' Alvin stated, sounding like he believed it.

'I'm sorry,' Edgar replied, his eyes also brimming with tears. 'Hold on to my arm.'

Alvin looked nervously at Edgar, unsure what to do.

'Why do I have to grab on to your arm?'

There was an anxious look in Alvin's eye – something that told Edgar he was sceptical but somehow, he maybe believed. Edgar didn't answer. He just remained silent and austere and, Alvin, sensing the severity of the situation, did as he was told.

Edgar jammed the coin into the groove in the bottom of his boots and set it for Grindlotha, just like Betty had told him. The metal pins like spider legs clicked into place and held the token in place. A warm tingling spread from Edgar's toes, up through his body and into his fingertips. The token glowed like hot metal.

WHOOSH

A strong gust of wind blew pieces of loose paper around his room as the draught blasted through the house just like when the mysterious monk had stolen Teddy twelve years ago.

Edgar's bedroom rapidly dissolved away into white fog and Edgar was aware that Alvin's grip had loosened on his arm so Edgar clung more tightly to him.

Suddenly they were falling through thick, white clouds and swirling mist. Wind whipped them as they descended faster and faster, blown all around by the strong air current. Edgar's hair whipped into his face – he could hardly see but in his stomach he felt that sensation of falling and falling. Alvin's eyes had rolled back on themselves and turned white. He was unconscious.

Is this what had happened to Edgar the first few times he had travelled?

Edgar held to his friend for dear life, scared of what would happen if he let go as they travelled through the place between worlds...then out of the mist a landscape appeared; a vast expanse of fields and forests. There was a stunning lake surrounded by trees with a massive waterfall crashing down and a crooked ruin stood atop a cliff overlooking it. A village in the distance – a short row of stony cottages and a statue of the Shrine of Saint Margarette watched over it like a silent sentinel.

Edgar was taken aback by the spectacular view. Grindlotha was such a natural world and it was beautiful. It was peaceful without the roar of engines and the buzz of technology; the air was fresh, untainted by pollution. Edgar's heard thumped faster as they approached the canopy of trees at breakneck speed but they passed through them like ghosts.

THUD!

They both landed flat in thick mud in the middle of a forest clearing. There was nothing around them apart from tall, twisted, trees with thick bare branches that had become deformed with age and the chirping birdsong among them was peaceful. Alvin sprawled across the ground, his tongue lolling out of his open mouth. His eyes were slightly open but only the whites were visible. He showed no signs of coming around soon so Edgar remained by his friend's side, still hanging onto him

The horrible thought crossed his mind that the last time he had trekked through the forest with Charles they had come across a pyramid...who knew if one was nearby right now? As lush and calm as the forest was, it was ancient and dangerous and Edgar wasn't confident that they were entirely safe. He unhooked took the token from his boot and placed it in his pocket for safe keeping.

He glanced back to his Alvin who had turned a pale grey hue and sweat rolled down his face in a steady stream. His eyes were shut but suddenly, as if struck by electricity, he bolted upright and retched and groaned in his semiconscious state.

Had Edgar looked that bad the first time he'd dimension travelled?

Alvin's pallid, clammy flesh was mottled and grotesque; he looked like he was dying but Edgar tried not to panic, remembering the first time he had travelled with the token. He had been violently sick over the streets of Deuathac. Alvin retched again and made another subconscious effort to vomit. This time, he succeeded.

Edgar turned away, fearing that he, too, may throw up if he saw the pile of smelly, steaming chunks that Alvin had just chucked up and they both groaned queasily in unison.

'Edgar,' Alvin whispered groggily, lifting his head out of the pile of sick that he'd just thrown up. Bile still dribbled down his chin as he looked up and strained to get up of the floor but wasn't very effective in his efforts and fell back down.

'What's up?' Edgar replied sympathetically, helping Alvin sit up.

'Are we dead?' Alvin asked collapsing onto his back and stared up at the sky through the branches of the trees. 'What the hell did you do?'

'We've travelled into a different dimension, that's all,' Edgar explained to an amazed Alvin. His eyes opened wide.

'Edgar? I feel...' he threw up again; splattering the chunky remainders of his last meal all over the grass.

'Sick...and you have *really* bad stomach ache and you feel like your head's going to explode,' Edgar interrupted, quickly reeling off the symptoms of dimension travel to prove to Alvin that it was normal.

'How do you know that?' Alvin asked amazed, struggling into a sitting position where he sat swaying, but kept upright as his condition improved.

'Well, I've been through it before haven't I?' Edgar replied as if it were daily routine. 'I've been through all of this. It'll wear off eventually. I promise.'

'Where are we?'

Edgar didn't answer but his expression spoke a million words. His eyes suddenly widened, his jaw hung open ever so slightly and his complexion flushed of all colour. He didn't know.

'Edgar, tell me where we are.'

'Grindlotha.'

'Where?'

'Like I said, another world. We need to get moving – can't stay here forever,' Edgar commanded confidently.

He set off at a steady pace, wandering into the trees as Alvin forced himself to his feet and staggered weakly after. Edgar hated the feeling of not knowing where he was and he didn't like this forest. It was gorgeous to look at but it was not a nice place to be.

The mud was thick and bogged him down; he worried that maybe the mud would break his boots and snap the metal pins that held his token in place when he used it. It also didn't help that he had to hold up Alvin who was still dizzy and every time his foot sank into the mud and he tried to pull it out, he wobbled drunkenly.

The forest reminded him of his harrowing journey with Charles where they had witnessed Vicky's demise. As they stumbled further along a muddy track, the surrounding trees changed and became bigger with twisted branches with ancient trunks and loud, unusual sounds filled the air coming from among the bare branches.

The woodland sounds of wildlife mingled with the smell of fallen autumnal leaves made the atmosphere feel rather spooky and as they passed a giant, black pyramid, Edgar didn't mention anything about what the structure was. He didn't want to scare Alvin who would be put off dimension travel forever if he knew about the monsters as well as the sickness. Edgar and Alvin kept walking and neither of them talked much, apart from checking if each other were alright or asking which direction they thought they should go in next.

They trekked along blindly until they noticed the trees thinning out and a familiar tune wafted through the air, it was a jolly tune played on a violin and voices could be heard laughing and chatting. Edgar knew exactly where he was as he rushed out of the trees, feeling elated as the panic evaporated out of him. He was so relieved that he had found the way back to the travellers' camp.

'BETTY!' Edgar shouted as he rushed out of the trees to safety.

Alvin staggered behind, his face still gaunt and his eyes rolling slightly. He looked seriously ill but it was partly fear, partly intrigue and partly a burning desire to know more about what happened to his sister that spurred him onwards.

Edgar led them towards the campers who sat around the same fire, although some of the company were absent this time. Kerridwen played the violin while Mary Dandy danced with Saldi and Ansé. Marianne and Fergus snuggled together as cute as any couple could be and Norma sat alone, staring intensely into the flames and there was someone with their back to them.

'BETTY?' Edgar shouted again.

'Betty isn't here right now,' said a gruff voice. The man facing away turned around and Edgar saw it was the chunky, bearded man who had looked down his nose at him the last time he had been there – Bardolph. 'Oh, it's you.'

'Yeah. It's me.'

Everyone else waved and seemed excited to see him but Bardolph grimaced.

'Like I'd ever forget. You're all Betty ever talks about,' Bardolph sneered irritably. His beady eyes fell upon Alvin and widened in anger. His nostrils flared and his cheeks turned red. 'Who is this and how did he get here?'

'This is Alvin. I brought him to see Betty,' Edgar explained. He could feel himself shrink under Bardolph's vicious glare. 'He needs to-'

'He shouldn't be here. You risk exposing us – our secrets!' Bardolph bellowed with a furious rage, which made Edgar and Alvin back away to avoid the spit flying from his mouth.

'He's my best friend, he's cool!' Edgar replied shortly. He struggled against the urge to lash out at Bardolph but he managed to bite his tongue and clench his fist. 'His sister-'

'Bardolph, he's our warrior, we can trust him,' Ansé said, flashing Edgar a cheeky wink. He nodded in appreciation and Bardolph just glowered.

'ADOLPHUS!' He shouted over his shoulder into the direction of the tents. Edgar knew what was coming and he swore silently to himself.

'What's wrong?' Adolphus replied running over the grassy camp to side by his furious, red-faced brother.

'This fool has dragged an outsider along with him but before we know it his *friend* will be telling everyone in Erathas about us,' snarled Bardolph. He looked Alvin up and down as if he were a piece of filth and turned to his brother. 'He's supposed to be our warrior and he's endangering us more than helping. Betty was wrong about him.'

'That's not fair!' Mary Dandy chirped up coyly and Edgar felt thankful that she had stuck up for him.

'He's going to ruin everything!' Bardolph grumbled. 'You know what happens when there's a disturbance – when they smell new blood.'

Everyone fell silent. The glanced among themselves, exchanging tense glances. Edgar could feel the physical change in the air.

Would they all turn on him this easily? How could he lead them if they didn't even trust him?

'He's going to bring nothing but trouble and you all know it,' Adolphus agreed, taking his brother's side of the argument. There was a tone of urgency in his voice. 'They'll be coming already. He has to go. He's going to be the death of us all.'

Everyone looked concerned and nobody spoke.

'No. I promise I won't. I'm just trying to find out about my sister!' Alvin blurted, his voice weak. He had been so quiet since he had travelled that it was good to hear him speak again. He was recovering.

'Your sister?' Bardolph sneered. 'Who's that?'

'Vicky,' Alvin replied, strength returning to his voice. 'Victoria Wright. Edgar says she died here. He was with Charles when he saw it happen.'

'Is that so?' Bardolph grimaced. His tone was light but dangerous and there was a nasty gleam in his eye. 'So Edgar brought your sister here before you and she got killed?'

'That's not what-'

'Ladies and gentlemen. This is your true warrior. Your hero. The one they think was prophecised to save us all. He's already got innocent blood on his hands. Betty is wrong.'

Bardolph's words seemed to have an effect. Everyone seemed to look at Edgar and Alvin with more uncertainty and distrust than ever before.

'He's wrong. Don't listen to him. Vicky was already here when I saw her. She was killed at the Shrine of Saint Margarette. If only I could just speak to Charles. He could prove it.'

Edgar was desperate. His voice broke as he appealed to the camp but it was no use. Their silence spoke more than their words ever could and he knew, he just knew, that they were no longer on his side.

'Norma?' Edgar begged, trying to get her attention. 'Is Charles around? We just need to speak to him and then we can leave. I'll never bring him back, it's fine. I'm sorry I caused such a problem.'

'He's gone with Betty,' Norma said timidly and Edgar felt a wave of frustration.

'Shit.'

Edgar could hardly contain himself. He kicked the long log that lay on the ground beside the fire to serve as a bench. His whole body burned with fury, the hairs on the back of his neck stood on end, every sense was heightened and his heart beat faster. It was a mixture of anger and frustration – *why could nothing ever go right?*

AROOOOOO.

Things just got worse.

'They're here for you,' Bardolph barked. He didn't know if it was the howl or Bardolph's words that hit him harder in the gut but he felt as though he might be sick.

He remembered his last encounter with them and how he had almost been killed – how he would have been torn apart had Betty not appeared to save him...now she was nowhere around and he had Alvin to protect too.

AROOOOO!

'RUN!' shouted Adolphus, his face contorted with fear as he took off at top speed and hid in the tent that he had come out of before.

'Protect your friend, warrior,' snarled Bardolph and Edgar was certain that he'd seen a flicker of an unnerving smile cross Bardolph's mouth. 'Call this a test. You pass, you live. You fail...well...we'll know you're not our warrior.'

'Please...' Edgar whispered but Bardolph simply hurried away, chuckling sadistically to himself. 'PLEASE! HELP!'

AROOOOOO!

The howl was closer now and bushes rustled nearby as the Hound moved through the undergrowth at the edge of the nearby forest.

'Someone! Please!' Edgar pleaded. 'Ansé? Mary?' Edgar grabbed desperately at the arms of the fleeing travellers' but they pulled away and continued in their hurry.

'We have no weapons at hand! Just take cover!' Ansé hissed as he broke free of Edgar's grasp.

The world whizzed around him in a blur of madness. Alvin stood rooted to the spot in fear, he still appeared weak and sickly but Edgar grabbed him by the hand and began to sprint for cover – they couldn't travel again with him still in such a vulnerable state. Alvin could hardly keep up and stumbled over his own feet.

Edgar was terrified – he knew what the Hounds were capable of, especially if there were more than one but this time it was about more than just him. It was about Alvin. He had to keep him safe; he had already lost Vicky. He would not lose Alvin too. It had been a foolish idea to bring him along. It was his fault the Hounds were coming now – by bringing Alvin with him, it had attracted them even faster.

Alvin stumbled and fell onto the ground. Edgar stopped and helped drag him back to his feet.

'The Hounds are coming, we have to hide,' Edgar said. He grabbed Alvin by the shoulders and looked deep into his eyes, deadly serious.

'What are the Hounds?' Alvin asked, his voice wavering in fear.

'We have to run,' Edgar commanded. His head spun dizzily and his heart pounded in his ears so that he could hear it pulsing.

Alvin did as he was told and ran as fast as he could in his current state. Edgar was already ahead but he could hear the *pitter patter* of the Hounds' paws coming closer and spotted a shadow dart past behind a nearby tent. They were close, stalking them and playing with their prey. Edgar stopped in his tracks and Alvin did the same. His eyes scanned the environment for a hiding place -

'Under there!' Edgar hissed, pointing at Betty's caravan. Alvin dropped to his knees and quickly crawled underneath the caravan to hide. Edgar followed him. The campsite was silent now; not a soul remained in sight. They had all escaped and found their own hiding places.

Edgar lay next to Alvin and held his breath, unlike his friend who trembled and began to breathe heavily. A sharp chunk of wood hung down from the bottom of the caravan, nearly scraping Edgar's back. He couldn't move without it digging in uncomfortably. It was sunset now and the setting sun cast a golden glow over the trees in the forest and the tents appeared to shimmer in the last of the day's light.

'You never told me it was this dangerous!' Alvin said out loud. Edgar glared at him.

'Shush. I've been through worse,' Edgar whispered, trying his best to remain calm.

AROOOOOOO!

At that moment a towering Hound stalked into the campsite. It walked to the middle of the camp and stood by the fire sniffing the air like a giant, standing on its hind legs. Alvin gasped at the werewolf-like monster and was just about to scream when Edgar clapped his hand over Alvin's mouth before he could before he could make a noise. His shrieks of horror were absorbed by the palm of Edgar's hand.

'That's a Hound?' Alvin said in complete shock, his voice muffled by Edgar's hand. His eyes rolled into the back of his head and for a moment Edgar thought he had fainted.

'Shush!' Edgar commanded seriously. He was scared but he had learned how to compose himself. Fear was the only thing to fear here and it was fear that could get them both killed. He closed his eyes, took a deep breath and kept calm. 'They're attracted by the smell of fear and movement. Stay calm and very still.'

The Hound continued to sniff around. It looked across at the caravan and lumbered over slowly. Alvin gasped. It was coming to get them. The Hound stalked over and sniffed. Its bald, leathery legs close enough to touch from where Edgar and Alvin hid.

AROOOOO!

The Hound howled and dropped down onto all fours. Edgar lay perfectly still, his breath held, his eyes tight shut. Beside him, Alvin squirmed.

'It's found us!' Alvin muttered, scrunching his face up in fear. 'We can't stay here!'

'Don't,' Edgar mouthed silently but it was too late.

Alvin rolled out from underneath the caravan and made a run for it. He had no idea where he would go – just that he had to get anywhere away from here.

The Hound turned quickly, its milky white eyes fixed on its target. It howled once more and took flight after Alvin. It all happened so fast that Edgar didn't have time to react. He knew he had to save Alvin – it was all he could do. He would not let this become another situation like Vicky. The Wright's would never lose their son as well as their daughter as a consequence of Edgar's inaction.

Alvin had only managed a few steps when the Hound pounced and landed right on top of him. He fell to the ground with a sickening thud and the Hound's claws slashed down and cut him across the shoulder, chest and stomach. He let out a terrific scream of agony that split the air and echoed in Edgar's mind.

Was it too late? Was he already dead?

AROOOOOO!

Its claws dripped with blood and it lowered its leathery muzzle to Alvin's torso and began to lap up the blood. From where he lay, frozen in shock, Edgar could see Alvin's blank eyes staring at him. His body twitched and he hyperventilated, unable to do anything else in shocked anguish as blood seeped from his body and his life ebbed away, pooling around him in a crimson puddle.

'H-h-help...p—please....Edgar....'

Alvin lay almost lifeless on the ground, groaning in agony as the Hound nibbled at his flesh and lapped up the blood. Edgar's heart pounded, near to bursting. The momentary shock had passed and Edgar found himself ready to burst into action – he had to do something but as he tried to shuffle out from under the caravan, the sharp spike of wood dug into his back...of course! Edgar rolled over onto his back and with all his strength, pulled at the loose wood.

Alvin had managed to curl into a ball, hiding his head in his arms, still squealed in pain as the Hound sniffed over his body, playing with him like a cat toying with a dying mouse and he whimpered pathetic pleas for mercy to the merciless Hound.

Alvin gasped and convulsed on the floor - another fit of shock that would kill him if Edgar didn't act fast. He kept pulling at the wood, straining to yank it off; the thought of his friend dying, the prospect of two people from the same family dying because of him and the worry of how he would have to explain Alvin's demise flooded his mind.

The wood wouldn't come off. He was desperate. His heart full of fear and anger and guilt. His mind buzzing with shock and with all this emotion held strong, Edgar pulled again; he tugged at it harder with the sudden strength that he summoned from his fears but still it wouldn't move. He yanked once more with all his might, screwing his red face up as he pulled with all his strength and finally the wooden plank came off with a loud *crack*.

Edgar rolled over so it wouldn't hit him straight in the face as it came down. He rolled over again and came out from under the caravan. The Hound sensed new prey and roared, baring its crooked, rotten teeth and sprayed flecks of saliva all over as it turned its attention to Edgar, glaring at him with its milky white eyes. It swung its long, yellow and bloodstained claws down at Edgar. He dodged but wasn't quick enough and the Hound slashed his arm.

Edgar screamed in sharp, searing pain and he felt as if his arm had almost been severed. He mustered all the strength he had with his good arm and lifted the wood, trying to ignore the stinging throb and blood pouring from the deep gash in his other arm. The pain was too much and he let the wood fall to the floor. He dropped to his knees, muttering insults at the Hound that stood over him, contorting its face into what looked like an intimidating smile at the wounded prey. *What had he done? Why did he have to play the hero again?*

This was it. The Hound had won...if this was the strength of one Hound then it was true. Edgar was not the warrior Betty had been looking for. He was just a weak and naive little boy who had been desperate to be something more. He really thought he might be something special, but who was he kidding? At least he had tried.

The Hound rounded on Edgar again. It crouched down so that its snout was inches from his face. He could feel its hot, rotten breath on his face. It sniffed him and then stood back up on its hind legs and howled to the heavens, as if to celebrate its latest victim. It was like it knew who Edgar was – that he was supposed to be the warrior, like it was gloating that it would be the one to kill him and spare the Hounds and their Nazakan masters a bloody and brutal war.

Edgar glanced down at Alvin who lay on the floor, shivering; his body involuntarily siezing as more blood pooled around him, staining the grass red. More death. *Why did death have to follow him everywhere?*

"Not this time," said a small voice in the back of Edgar's mind. *'No more.'*

Just like before, when all had seemed lost, Edgar found a strength inside that he never knew he had. He lifted the wooden plank, pulled it back over his shoulder and swung it swiftly, putting as much force behind it as he could. It connected with a solid *whack*.

There was a sickening crunch as the wood hit the Hound's legs and they snapped. The bones shattered to the side as it fell to the floor, looking confused and disorientated. It tried to get back onto its feet but the bone spliced through its thick, leathery skin with a squelch. Blood spurted out of the wound and Edgar cringed as a splatter of the gloppy substance hit his face.

They were face to face now. The Hound growled and flailed its arms, just missing Edgar. Its jaw snapped dangerously as it yelped and howled in agony but Edgar stared it right in the eye and drew the plank back over his shoulder. He put all his strength behind another swing. He aimed the blow at its head. There was a deep indentation in the Hound's skull which now spewed blood in a steady stream and the creature rubbed it vigorously, as if that would make the pain go. The blood clotted and matted its thick tufts of fur. It swung its arm again and tried to slice Edgar with its razor-sharp claws but missed as it swayed dizzily.

Edgar pulled the plank back again and aimed at the Hound's neck. He swung it with all his might. There was a horrific crunch as the Hound's neck dislocated, its eyes rolled back into its head and its lifeless body slumped to the floor, dead - nothing more than an oozing pulp of meat.

Edgar cringed at the sight of the bloody body on the floor in front of him. He stepped over it and staggered to Alvin.

'Alvin! Can you hear me?' Edgar pleaded. He clutched his wounded arm, which stung and burned as the blood kept oozing and he tried to wipe the residue of the Hound's hot blood off his face, only to smear it more thickly. Alvin had stopped shaking and whimpering; his pallid complexion and cold, lifeless eyes scared Edgar. There was nothing he could do. Alvin was as good as dead and there was no one around to help him. 'Alvin! Come on!'

Alvin didn't answer.

Edgar's worst nightmare had been realised; first Vicky and now Alvin. Both had died because of him and both deaths could have been prevented had he not been so stupid. He didn't know how to feel other than numb. The world seemed to have stopped turning, clocks must have stopped ticking. Everything stood still in a moment that lasted a torturous eternity. There was nothing to feel but cold, pressing horror.

'Alvin!' Edgar pleaded. 'ALVIN,SPEAK TO ME!' he screamed hoarsely, choking on his tears that welled up in his eyes.

There was no reply. He was too late.

– CHAPTER TWENTY-THREE –
THE WITCH'S CONNECTION

It felt like forever that Edgar stared into Alvin's dead eyes before he thought about checking for a pulse. He grabbed Alvin's wrist and felt carefully. There was a pulse still there. Very faint. He was still alive – but only just.

'Ed,' Alvin gasped in a hushed tone. His voice was frail. 'It hurts...' and that was when Edgar's eyes were drawn to the wound.

He had known the wound was there – the blood was hard to ignore – but he had not dared examine it closely. He didn't want to see. In a way, it was his responsibility. He took a deep breath and looked. The Hound's claws had ripped deep into Alvin's flesh and fresh blood squirted rhythmically with each weak heartbeat. Thankfully his innards were not exposed, but it was very close and Edgar could see bits of shredded flesh and sliced muscle hanging off his torso in bloody strips.

Edgar gasped, turning away from Alvin so he wouldn't get upset by his reaction and lose hope. He felt sick by the sight that met his eyes. He had known it was going to be bad... but not as bad as this; he had just expected a scratch – not a trauma case. Alvin needed a hospital and in one desperate instant Edgar remembered the times he had travelled and the journey had miraculously healed him. His hand reached for his shoulder where he still had the scar from the bullet wound when he had narrowly escaped Mr. Griffith's museum and the cut on his wrist from Merimalima.

Could the same theory work for Alvin? Could Edgar save him or did it only work for him? Would it work on someone who simply hitched a ride? Did it have a limit to how many times he could use that power?

No. This was too serious and there were too many potential outcomes and questions. Edgar still had no idea how the healing worked and to risk trying it on Alvin was something he would only dare to attempt as a last resort. All he knew for certain was that he had to cover the wound up to stop the bleeding and prevent infection.

He told Alvin that he would be alright and left him while he ran desperately around the campsite looking around anxiously to find something to wrap around Alvin's wound. There was a spare cotton groundsheet lying beside one of the tents. It looked clean enough and that would have to do. He ripped a long piece off and took it back to Alvin. Edgar glanced all over, hoping there were no more Hounds on their way. It seemed quiet and safe. He spotted a bottle sat beside the log circle, left when the others had run. He grabbed it and sniffed. Wine. He took a swig to calm his nerves and stared at it. Alcohol! Of course!

He ran back to Alvin, poured the wine over the wound, not particularly caring whether or not the science behind his actions was correct or would even help. This was an emergency; he needed to do all he could and wine was alcohol. Alcohol helped to disinfect wounds. As the blood red liquid splashed on the area of the wound Alvin screamed and thrashed violently.

'I'm sorry, I'm sorry,' Edgar whispered calmly, trying to hold him still with his other hand. Once the wine was all gone, he took the long piece of material, half-lifted Alvin who was much heavier than he looked, and wrapped it tightly around Alvin's waist to conceal the grotesque injury and stem the blood flow.

'Ed. Am I going to die… like Vicky?' Alvin asked bluntly, looking at Edgar, with his scrunched tight, his voice nothing more than a deadly whisper.

'No. You certainly are not,' Edgar said sternly to Alvin even though he didn't quite believe himself.

'Was it true?' Alvin asked weakly, moving slightly but wincing as he did so and deciding to remain still instead. 'What you wrote about her in your diary?'

Edgar could feel the tears burning his eyes but he tried to hold them back. He didn't want the current circumstances to be worsened by his blubbering but it hurt him so much. He was the cause of so much death and destruction and the guilt just made him want to cry the pain away.

'Yes,' Edgar confessed. 'I tried to tell you…'

Alvin's eyes watered and his lip trembled. He screwed his eyes tight shut and sighed. Edgar wondered if maybe he was forgiven, but he was wrong.

'She died because of you! You could have saved her!' Alvin grumbled. 'It's all your fault…now look at me. I'm in the same position as she was…because of you!'

Alvin turned to Edgar, his face unexpectedly full of fury. His cold, clammy skin drenched in sweat and blood – he was too weak to move, too stunned by the pain to even try but he sobbed. Tears streamed down his face and Edgar knew that if Alvin somehow managed to recover, their friendship would not likely survive this time.

'You're a selfish bastard! I'm dying. Vicky's dead!' Alvin raged, 'It should be you! It's your fault! It should be you!'

Alvin's words didn't help. Edgar had been trying to keep it together, but his friend lost control and sobbed harder. Alvin was right to be upset - the truth was out and Edgar knew he deserved everything Alvin through at him. He could understand his friend's anguish.

'Vicky was innocent, she never did anything wrong. *I* never did anything wrong!' Alvin wailed, grief-stricken. His wound seared with a white, hot pain, yet when he looked at Edgar, it filled him with so much anger he felt as though he could physically get up and beat him within an inch of his life.

'You don't mean that!' Edgar shouted, cracking under the pressure of Alvin's verbal attack. He knew he shouldn't have lost it because Alvin was his best friend and was wounded so badly that he might die, but he wasn't going to accept that. He was determined that things would work out differently than it had with Vicky – no matter what it took, he would make sure of that. 'You're going to make it,'

'You're going to let me bleed to death. This cloth isn't good enough,' Alvin spat back spitefully but Edgar couldn't look.

If he saw the blood seeping through the thin, flimsy material it would make him feel worse. It would remind them that he was responsible. He had brought Alvin along here and he had not bothered to explain about the Hounds; they had even passed a pyramid which would have provided the perfect excuse to start up a conversation about the dangers of creatures that come through them.

Once again, it was his fault. It was Edgar's immature fear of stating dangers because he thought it would scare Alvin that had nearly killed him. It was his own denial that his friend was now paying the price for.

'HELP!' Edgar bellowed, his voice echoing around the empty campsite. 'HELP!'

There was no reply and the only sound was that of Alvin's rapid, breathing and the gentle breeze through the nearby trees.

'HELLO?' Edgar bellowed. 'IT'S GONE. I KILLED IT, BUT I NEED HELP.'

A figure emerged from a tent. It was Bardolph. He stalked closer, his eyes on Edgar and Alvin and the dead Hound sprawled on the ground.

'Killed another innocent have you?' he snarled viciously.

'Please, Bardolph. I need help. He's going to die.'

'You dug the grave and now you can lay in it.'

Bardolph turned his back and walked off in the opposite direction.

'Stop! Come back!' Edgar cried. 'Please. Bardolph!'

The man ignored him and then he was gone.

There was a commotion and Edgar heard more people slip from their tents. They gathered around, staring in horror and pointing.

'You killed it,' Ansé said, nodding his head as if he were impressed with Edgar's skill.

'It's dead but Alvin will be soon if I don't get some help.'

'Let's have a look.'

Ansé rushed forward and dropped down by Edgar's side.

'Nice bandage work,' he said to Edgar who beamed, feeling proud of himself. Ansé sniffed. 'Is that wine?'

'Poured it on the wound. Alcohol. Dunno if it'll work.'

'Better than nothing. Good thinking, Edgar.'

Again, a wave of pride washed over him. He had done alright in the middle of this crisis.

Edgar was unaware of the others crowding round now. They muttered among themselves, whispering and staring. Their eyes all over Edgar and Alvin – but even more so all over the dead Hound that lay on the grass, beaten and broken. Ansé flicked his fringe out of his eyes, lifted the bandage and peeked underneath.

His eyes opened wide and he shook his head.

'Nothing I can do with this,' he said solemnly 'but there is someone who can. For now, we need to get you both somewhere safe and out of the way.'

'Is it that bad?' Edgar asked quietly and Ansé didn't reply but the anxious look in his steely eyes said all that Edgar needed to know.

'Mary, go fetch Devi,' Ansé commanded and in that moment Edgar could see the strong leader of the Knights Templar that Ansé had once been. 'Fergus, Marianne, give me a hand lifting Alvin. We'll get him inside Betty's.'

They hoisted him to his feet and lifted him, supporting all his weight between them. Alvin screamed in agony so they quickened the pace. It was a quick journey and it was no time at all until they climbed the steps and entered the caravan. Alvin whimpered in pain as they lay him down on the bed in the corner and made sure he was confortable.

'Do you want us to stick around?' Ansé asked and Edgar shook his head. 'You sure?'

Edgar nodded.

'Devi will be here shortly. She'll know exactly what to do.'

'Thanks.'

Ansé, Marianne and Fergus left and closed the door behind them. Silence. It was unbearable. Alvin lay on the bed, half-conscious, groaning in pain.

'Are you alright?' Edgar asked, already knowing the answer.

'What do you think?' Alvin spat venomously. 'I should have never listened to you – I should have never come here.'

'You wanted proof about Vicky's death!'

'You could have warned me about the monsters!'

'You should have listened to me and stayed hidden!'

Edgar clenched his fist as he raged at Alvin. This was all his fault! Yes, he had brought him along and yes he had neglected to mention the Hounds and the dangers but when it had mattered Edgar had tried his hardest to keep Alvin safe and it was Alvin who had brought this all on himself – he had tried to run when Edgar warned him against it. He had made that decision, nobody else. He had no sympathy...

That was cold. Even for Edgar whose humanity seemed to have faded over the course of recent events. Survival relied on detaching himself from situations and people – on seeing from a different perspective. Not everything was his fault and now he realised that. He could not have helped Vicky – he had always known that but never been able to accept it but now it made sense. All saving her would have achieved would have been more death; she would have died and then so would he, and most likely, Charles too.

'I'm sorry. I can understand why you ran,' Edgar mumbled, hoping his quietly uttered apology would be enough.

'You're not sorry at all,' Alvin wheezed, he lay on the bed, his expression even more sallow and deathly than before.

He could hardly keep his eyes open and the wrapping around his torso was stained with blood.

Edgar couldn't look at him. The blood seeped through and stained the bed beneath him. He needed help quickly.

'Hello?' shouted a voice from outside. Edgar could see a figure wearing a white cloak stood upon the porch.

Edgar ran over to the door, opened it to let the woman in.

She instantly saw the look of distress on Edgar's gaunt face and sprinted over, pushing Edgar out of the way as she crossed the threshold.

'I'm Devi,' she said, kindly as she strode over to Alvin, ignoring Edgar completely. 'I got your message from Mary Dandy.'

She was a tall, beautiful, young woman with long, black hair that hung over her shoulders in tight curls. Her bright emerald eyes sparkled and her complexion was so pale and flawless that her skin looked like snow.

'Devi?' Edgar repeated. He had heard the name before.

The woman ignored Edgar.

'Oh, dear God!' she whispered as she examined Alvin.

'Can you help him?' Edgar asked urgently.

'Count yourselves lucky that I'm the camp's healer,' Devi said, unwrapping the cloth that had covered Alvin's wound. Her jaw dropped and she shivered uncomfortably.

'Is it bad?' Alvin murmured, as if he were only just clinging to his life by a thread.

'Nothing I can't fix,' Devi beamed as she began rummaging through a little bag slung over her shoulder.

'You know, those Hounds are particularly dangerous to those who don't belong here, so let that be a lesson to both of you.'

'I didn't mean for this to happen,' Edgar snapped defensively and Devi shot him a dark stare. 'He just wanted to see Charles – to find out the truth about what happened to his sister.'

Devi nodded somberly as she knelt down next to Alvin pulled out some bright green leaves and a mortar and pestle from the bag. She put the leaves inside and combined them with some oils. She squished it all together and ground it about, while chanting strange sounding words. Eventually the ingredients had turned to a thick, sloppy substance like a grey, mud which Devi then applied over Alvin's wound.

'You should have known better, Edgar Harold,' Devi said disappointedly. 'You're supposed to be our warrior but at this rate, you're causing more harm than good.'

'How do you know who I am?' Edgar asked anxiously. It always unnerved him when strangers knew who he was.

'I've waited a very long time to finally meet you, Edgar,' Devi said with a bright smile. 'It was I who sent Charles to collect you.'

And then Edgar remembered where he had heard the name before. Devi had told Charles where to find him when he had been lost in the ice caves. She had received a vision of his location...she was a witch!

'You're a witch!' Edgar replied, the words sounding a little more hostile than he had hoped.

'A witch?' Alvin gasped.

'Yes, and if it weren't for my intuition, Edgar would have been slaughtered a long time ago. Be thankful for my gift. Not all witches want to harm you,' Devi snapped furiously and there was something there in her eyes, a flash of malice and ancient power that told Edgar to back down.

'I'm sorry,' Edgar replied, choking on his words. 'But how did you know-?'

He never even got to finish the sentence before Devi butted in.

'As a witch, my power connects me to the world and my power tunes into the raw energy of the worlds and those who shape them. That is how we are connected. That is how I know where you are. I was already on my way when Mary ran into me.'

'Alvin,' Edgar said, glancing at him. He lay on the bed, calmer than before. It was as if the magic mixture had soothed him.

'The Nazakan and Hounds are sensitive to dimensional disbalance,' Devi said sternly. 'As soon as they sense something wrong they will swarm to the area to eliminate the threat. In this case, Alvin.'

'If that's true, then why did only one come here?' Edgar asked. It was a logical question.

'Who knows? Perhaps the others sensed that the Warrior of Legends protected their victim and thought better than to attack?' Devi guessed, shrugging non-chalantly.

Edgar gulped. *The Warrior of Legends.* Was that the title they had come up with for him?

It sounded better than *The Chosen One* but it still felt wrong that any kind of heroic title could be associated with Edgar at all; considering all the death and destruction that followed him like a shadow, he was anything but a hero.

'Do you want me to have a look at your arm too?' Devi asked, turning to Edgar, her eyes lingering on the slash across his shoulder and arm.

Amid the drama and the chaos, Edgar had forgotten all about his injury. Alvin had taken priority and the adrenaline had taken the pain away, more effectively than any painkiller. Suddenly, his attention was drawn back to it and he saw the river of dried blood oozing down his sleeve and he didn't realize how much it hurt until he had been reminded. The throbbing, burning sensation came back with vengeance. He nodded silently, wincing in pain.

Devi turned to Edgar and smothered some of the remaining medicine over the cut. It was cold and refreshing – he could almost feel it working instantly like magic. Devi rubbed the sloppy mush into the wound, her fingers pressing hard against Edgar's flesh. She muttered quietly in her strange tongue once more as she worked the mush into the wound.

'Are you feeling ok?' Devi asked Alvin, turning her attention back to him.

'The pain's gone a bit,' Alvin blurted gratefully in amazement.

'Just as I expected. You'll be fine in no time.'

'Edgar? How's that feel?'

'Fine.'

Devi nodded and caught Edgar's eye. Their gaze connected and for a split second Edgar felt as if she could see inside him and read his mind. He tried to turn away but she held him transfixed.

'I'll always watch out for you, Edgar,' said Devi's voice in his head. He wasn't sure if he had imagined it or if she really was telepathic. His eyes opened wide in surprise and Devi grinned knowingly in return.

'You think you're not the warrior we need,' Devi's unspoken words whispered in Edgar's ear. *'Our connection proves that you are and I will do all I can to help you prevail.'*

'Thank you,' Edgar thought to himself and Devi smiled at him.

'I have seen into your future, Edgar Harold, and you have a purpose beyond this war.'

'What do you mean?' Edgar thought anxiously. There was something about Devi's words that felt almost like a warning. She had implied he would survive the coming war – but how could she know?

'Time will tell, Edgar,' her eerie words rang in Edgar's head. *'Time will tell.'*

She turned away from him and the connection was gone. Edgar shivered as he almost physically felt Devi remove herself from his head. It was a horrible feeling – almost like coming up for breath after being under water for too long. It was refreshing and a relief that his thoughts were once again just his own.

'I think we need to go home,' Alvin said, suddenly reminding Edgar that he was there too. He had almost forgotten.

'But you still haven't seen Charles!' Edgar replied and Alvin shook his head solemnly.

'It won't bring her back, will it?' Alvin sighed. 'You've told me enough about what happened. I should have trusted you.'

'I'm so sorry, Alvin. I'm sorry I brought you here. I'm sorry this happened to you,' Edgar whispered, his voice struggling to work. He blinked back the tears in his eyes. This was his fault and this time he could not deny that fact.

'Guess what?' Alvin said plainly and Edgar raised a curious eyebrow.

'What?'

'You're right. It was my fault.'

Edgar tried not to laugh. Alvin had finally admitted he was in the wrong but it wasn't enough – it didn't really fix anything. He was still injured, he had still learned the secret of dimension travel. Edgar had burdened him with a terrible truth, something he could never take back.

'So what happens next?' Edgar asked, there was a sobering edge to his tone as if he realised the full severity of all the potential outcomes. 'Are we friends still?'

'Forgiven...but not forgotten,' Alvin said seriously. 'I would have never believed you about Vicky. You had no choice but to bring me here.'

'I know,' Edgar replied. 'but I need you to promise me that you will never tell a soul about this.'

Devi watched them through narrowed, suspicious eyes.

'It was foolish of you to bring an outsider with you, Edgar. You risked the exposure of our lives, of our home.'

Devi was furious. The low, quiet words sounded almost like a threatening hiss.

'I promise, I didn't intend to-'

'That's why nobody helped you, you know. They wanted him to die.'

The words hit Edgar forcefully and he felt himself dazed by their weight.

'They...they wanted me...dead?' Alvin said, horrified. He suddenly looked paler than before.

Whether Devi was telling the truth or playing a trick, Edgar didn't know. He knew the travellers' of Grindlotha's camp and he didn't believe they were capable of being so cold except, of course, Bardolph.

'But I'm sure they didn't mean-'

'A stranger came here. A stranger who has no business in our world, who drew the Hounds to their camp and who could go home and tell people about our home. Easier to leave him to die than deal with the fallout of him spouting his revelations back home.'

'If that's what they think...I never meant-'

'Whether you intended to or not, it happened, but no fear, I can put it right.'

Devi raised her hands and walked, arms outstretched, towards Alvin. Her fingers wiggled rhythmically and she whispered more words of ancient magic. Alvin tried to cower from her but his movement was still restricted and he whimpered in fear.

'What are you doing?'

'Wiping his memory,' Devi said telepathically and Edgar shrieked, not expecting to hear her speak in his head again.

'No! No, Devi. Don't!' Edgar pleaded. *'He won't tell. I promise.'*

'Are you sure?' she hissed in his ear.

'Yes! Please...'

'Very well.'

Devi stopped in her tracks. She beamed at Alvin and chuckled innocently as if she had been joking all along.

'What's going on?' Alvin asked, looking as though he may pass out at any second.

'It's fine, she's just joking,' Edgar laughed, trying to play along with Devi, pretending it was all a joke.

'Can he be trusted?' Devi's words floated into Edgar's mind effortlessly. It seemed that now she had strengthened the connection between them, she could speak to him freely without even having to make eye contact.

'Yes,' Edgar thought in return.

'If you're wrong, I'm afraid there will be consequences.'

'You can trust him. I promise.'

Edgar didn't want to know what the consequences would be – he had an awful feeling he could guess.

'He speaks out, he dies,' Devi's words came cold and chilling, confirming what Edgar had feared. They sent a shiver down his back and he tried not to react. He merely smiled at Alvin blankly.

'We have to protect ourselves.'

'Understood.'

'We'll be off then,' Edgar said, finally finding the words and forcing them out loud. It felt strange alternating between telepathy and real speech. His hands dug in his pocket, feeling for the cold metal token. His fingers brushed against it and he pulled it out and rolled it between his fingers.

'Thanks again,' Edgar said gratefully and Devi simply pouted and raised her eyebrows in a kurt acknowledgement.

'Are you okay to get up, Alvin?'

Alvin nodded uncertainly and sat up. Edgar sat next to him took his hand and put his arm around his shoulder which suddenly felt no pain.

'It's healed!' Edgar gasped and it was true – Devi's magic had healed the cut and the only sign of Edgar having being injured was the tear in his t-shirt and the mixture of blood and muddy goo that stained his skin and the cotton.

'Mine too!' Alvin shrieked as he looked down and saw that the flesh had knitted itself back together over his wound as if he had never been injured in the first place – again, the only tell-tale signs of anything untoward was the blood and herbal mush smeared over his abdomen.

'That stuff's amazing, Devi.'

She smirked silently and Edgar wasted no more time in lifting his right foot up onto his knee and setting his token for Erathas.

'Thank you,' he said.

'Thank you,' Alvin repeated. 'I owe you one.'

Devi didn't reply but she merely grinned widely and waved daintily.

'One day, the debt will be paid.'

A warm tingle began in Edgar's toes and spread through his body. He didn't know if the tingle was from travelling or from Devi's sinister words.

A thin mist seeped in under the door and poured through the corners of the window. In an instant it grew thicker and darker until the whole caravan was just a haze of fog. Alvin's eyes had already rolled back and Edgar clung to him tightly, knowing what came next.

WHOOSH.

The heavy blast of wind, the sudden, solid pull as if he were lifted into the air by some unseen force – a sensation that mimicked the feeling of a sudden drop, but instead of going down, he was flying upwards. He soared into the mist, unable to see anything; the air-currents tossed them around like ragdolls and Edgar tried to picture home.

He imagined his room with the posters on his wall staring at him with their blank, papery eyes. He imagined the cosy, red living room and his new garden with the trenches dug by the archaeologists. He pictured his mother – her round, friendly face and her icy eyes framed by her rectangular spectacles that made her look so austere. He thought about his grandparents, Scarlet and Robert. He imagined Scarlet's Sunday roasts and her delicious homemade Yorkshire puddings that she always served on their own as a traditional Yorkshire starter.

Betty had told him that dimension travel worked better when you could picture where you wanted to go and right now, Edgar pictured all of these things so vividly. He could even taste Scarlet's mouth-watering meal. His senses were enveloped in the imagery of home; of the happiness and simplicity of his life before the revelation of his true identity had been revealed. He felt a surge of joy in his heart as he glanced at Alvin and slung tightly to him as they blasted through the barriers between worlds.

Despite everything, they had survived and Alvin had forgiven him – that was all that mattered. The meaning of home was safety and security; family and friends and Edgar knew that even though his life from now on was going to be dangerous and deadly he still had home – the once place he was safe. It was his sanctuary where he was free from the worries his new life threw at him.

They reached the apex of their flight and the clouds cleared and they began their descent. Far below was the headland of Scarborough castle, surrounded on one side by sea and then the town on the other with the vast, rolling fields and forests and hills beyond the urban areas. He thought of all the people down there, scurrying like ants, and then, in the inevitable fear of the fall towards the Earth, one person crossed his mind:

Damian.

Edgar was uncertain why Damian had surfaced, but he thought that he knew deep down the answer was because he was strong and fit, he was experienced in war and Edgar was none of those things. The more he thought about Damian, the more jealous he felt himself become.

Why couldn't he be just like him?

The reason he couldn't stop thinking about his new friend was because Edgar knew he was inadequate and that Damian would have been a much better candidate to be the Warrior of Legends.

– CHAPTER TWENTY-FOUR –

THE CAVE

THUD

They landed in a crumpled heap with a heavy crash. Alvin groaned in pain and Edgar scrambled to his feet, untangling himself from his friend. They had landed in Edgar's room and it was all too quiet.

Alvin was conscious. He was groggy but he was awake.

'Are you alright?' he asked urgently and Alvin rubbed his head.

'I'll be fine,' Alvin said, his voice quiet and uncertain. 'Now can we talk about what just happened?'

Right on cue, a loud scream came from the garden behind Edgar's house. What was going on? Was someone hurt?

'We'd better go and investigate. Somebody's probably fallen in a trench and broken their neck,' Edgar chuckled jokingly as he headed for the door.

Alvin and Edgar raced down the stairs in a dramatic hurry to find out what the commotion in the garden was about.

'Wait....' Edgar said, stopping suddenly behind the front door. 'We can't go out like this. We're still covered in blood!'

'But I haven't got anything to change into,' Alvin said, suddenly realising that he had nothing.

'You can borrow one of my t-shirts,' Edgar said and they trudged back upstairs.

They changed quickly, hiding their tattered clothes underneath Edgar's bed and quickly washed off the blood in the bathroom before they raced off again.

They reached to the gate, skidded around the corner, up the steps, going so fast they were almost ran on all fours and along the path to the dig site. Lara was there, along with a group of chattering archaeologists and Damian who stood next to the man with the horse-like jaw whom Damian had been talking to before Edgar had left for Conisborough. Lara stood beside the trench, staring down at the place where the big, black rock had finally been moved.

'Can you believe it?' she squealed with excitement, bouncing on the balls of her feet, upon spotting Edgar's approach. She waved him and Alvin over quickly and pointed to the area where the rock had once been.

'Hey, Lara! What's happened?' Edgar asked excitedly.

Underneath where the rock once lay, was a large square of wood with a rusted, circular handle. It was a trapdoor.

'What the hell?' Edgar gasped in shock.

'I know!' Damian said, flashing Edgar a kindly smile. There was something in his tone that made Edgar feel as if Damian saw him as a total stranger and not someone he had called a brother only days ago.

'Who's this?' Edgar asked, looking at the horrible man beside Damian. He simply stood, staring into space, pouting and looking miserable. He swept his fringe out of his eyes, pushed his thick rimmed glasses up his nose and looked Edgar up and down with disgust.

'This is Markus,' Damian said but the awful man didn't react. Edgar held his hand out politely but Markus just looked down at it and turned his nose up with a quiet sigh.

Edgar knew he didn't like him from the moment he had set eyes on him before. His attitude stank and Edgar had to bite his tongue so that he would not flip and say something he might regret.

'Come on, Markus,' Damian said hotly, shooting him a scathing glare but Markus didn't even react. 'Be polite. Shake his hand, man.'

'So this is the little kid you won't stop talking about?' Markus sneered. 'You know it's not appropriate to be friends with children.'

'I'm *not* a child,' Edgar said under his breath and Markus begrudgingly took his hand shook it.

'That's more like it,' Damian said, clapping his hands together happily. 'We're all friends here.'

'And who is this?' Damian asked, noticing Alvin who stood with Lara chatting animatedly and laughing nearby.

'Alvin. He's a friend. He's staying with us for a while,' Edgar explained, omitting the complicated reasoning behind it all. 'So has anyone told mum yet?'

Edgar's eyes were drawn back to the trapdoor that had been buried under the solid, mysterious rock in the deep trench. He glanced around – everyone was excited and eager to take a closer look.

'Not yet. Do you want to do the honours?' Damian said and Edgar nodded with great enthusiasm.

He called Priscilla and she answered the phone in a hushed whisper.

'What do you want? You're not meant to call me when I'm at work! If Patrick sees me using me phone-'

'Mum, listen, they've moved the rock in the garden and there's a trapdoor underneath it,' Edgar interrupted urgently.

Priscilla shouted a swear word which echoed around the enormous museum.

'Priscilla!' Edgar heard Patrick exclaim in the background and suddenly there was silence. Priscilla had hung up.

'I think she's excited,' Edgar laughed. 'Can we go down and see what's in there?' Edgar asked eagerly. He desperately needed to know what was underneath the trapdoor.

'Not yet. We need to check that it's all safe first,' Damian replied. 'We couldn't let you go down first if there was a chance that you could get seriously hurt or something,'

'What's going on?' a young man with a dark fringe asked, coming towards them. Edgar recognised him and waved. It was James.

'There's a trapdoor!' Lara exclaimed, grabbing James in a tight embrace. They kissed each others cheeks and Edgar noticed

James catch Damian's eye. Markus glared at him viciously and put his arm around Damian's waist and pulled him close.

'You okay?' James asked politely, looking right at Damian. His voice trembled like his lip as he forced the tears to stay down.

Damian opened his mouth to reply but Markus beat him to it.

'Never better,' his gloating tone wound Edgar up in a way he didn't understand. He found himself imagining how good it would feel to physically attack him – to smack him in the jaw...and that was not like Edgar. From the way James glowered, his lip curling in a sneer and his brow frowning, Edgar guessed he felt the very same way. There was a very tense hostility that hung in the air, crushing them all in its awkward silence.

'What's with your attitude, Markus?' James snapped after a moment of trying to play it cool. 'You know, you make me sick. Damian literally *just* dumped me and you wormed your way in straight away.'

'He never loved you,' Markus snarled and he pulled a face that looked as if there was an unpleasant smell under his nose. 'Don't bother fooling yourself that your relationship ever meant anything.'

SMACK

Markus' hand shot up to his face and he stared at James in shock.

'Rebound. That's all you are,' James hissed.

SMACK

James recoiled from the returned blow and retaliated with another. The fight was violent and brutal; the force behind each punch and kick connected with sickening thumps and cracks. Alvin's jaw dropped and Edgar felt himself almost inclined to dive in and break up the fight but something held him back. James had a right to be angry at Markus. He wanted to see the horrible man suffer – he deserved everything James flung at him. Had this been a school fight, Edgar would be chanting for James to win.

The group of huddled archaeologists stared in surprise, unable to understand what had just quietly kicked off in their midst without them even realising. The whole thing had started from nowhere.

'Stop it! Please!' Damian yelled. He jumped in and put himself between the two of them, feeling the full force of their blows as they struggled to get past him to beat one another but he didn't even flinch.

'Piss off!' James snarled and he flung a punch at Damian instead but he caught James' fist, bent his wrist back on itself and twisted his arm until James fell to his knees, pleading for him to stop.

The archaeologists covered their mouths and watched silently. Edgar was horrified by what he saw – the glazed look on Damian's face, the strength with which he twisted James' arm and the expression of pure agony scrunched across James' face made him feel uncomfortable.

'I don't want to fight you,' Damian said calmly. 'But I do want this to stop, right now.'

'I'm sorry,' James moaned and Damian let him go.

'James, go home and calm down. I'll see you later,' Lara barked, pulling herself together.

'But I just got here.'

'I don't care. Go. Home!'

James sighed, shook his head in frustration and stormed off down the path. His anger apparent as he flounced away. Then, with her eyes bulging and jaw clenched tightly in fury, Lara turned to Damian.

'If your relationships are going to cause problems, there will be consequences,' she said authoritatively. Damian stared, open-mouthed. *Why was he being punished for James' actions?*

'I'm glad that's over,' Alvin whispered to Edgar who nodded absent-mindedly. He stared at Damian who had turned his attention to Markus and nursed his blood-splattered face. It appeared that James had broken that skinny, hooked nose and Edgar was glad. He deserved it.

'You need to go to the hospital,' Damian muttered to him but just loud enough for everyone to hear. It was purposeful. Nobody reacted.

'Amelia, go with him to the hospital,' Lara commanded and a pretty, young girl with bright, red hair nodded enthusiastically. She rushed over to Markus, put a comforting arm around him and started to lead him away. Damian followed closely but Lara held her hand out and pushed Damian back. 'Beckett will look after him.'

'But-'

'No.'

There was a malicious flash in Lara's usually kind eyes that told Damian he should not push her any further. He sighed and took a step back. He looked to Edgar as if hoping he would defend him but Edgar simply looked unimpressed and Damian eventually slumped off to stand in the corner. Everyone moved away, muttering among themselves. Right now, he was the least popular person in existence and it was clear why.

'Markus has been a bad influence on him,' Lara whispered and Edgar found himself nodding in agreement. 'Rebound is never a good idea. It just means everyone gets hurt.'

Edgar nodded solemnly. Was that all Markus was – rebound? Just someone to fill the void after he dumped James? All of this relationship talk was new to Edgar. Is that what people did?

'Damian was lovely the other day. Today he's a different man,' Edgar said sadly as he wondered if he had ever even known Damian. The man he had met the other day and offered his advice to had been obviously damaged but friendly. He had been pleasant and kind; but this man had been angry and twisted.

He was just a shell of the other person and Edgar had never felt so confused or conflicted.

'War does bad things to people,' she said quietly, her eyes still lingering on Damian. 'I don't know what Patrick was thinking, getting him involved here. It's still so raw for him.'

Edgar remained silent. He couldn't imagine what Damian had been through or what he had seen in Iraq. It had been all over the news – bombs, shooting, killing – just all out chaos and Damian had been caught up in the middle of that.

Had he killed too?

That was a new question in Edgar's mind but he already knew the answer. *Yes.*

'Are you alright?' Lara asked softly, her hand touched Edgar's shoulder comfortingly.

'Fine,' he lied, unable to shake the confusion over his feelings for Damian. He truly thought he had made a kind new friend who genuinely cared for him and then he was suddenly gone and this new man was in his place – this dangerous shadow of what he had been just days ago.

'So, what do we think is down there?' he asked, changing the subject. He pointed to the trapdoor and Lara shrugged.

'Could be some kind of tomb. We're near the churchyard so that's quite possible,' Lara said, pointing along the vast expanse of weeds and soil that ran behind the other houses to a high, crumbling brick wall that separated the allotment from the back of the churchyard. The steeple of the church could be seen over the top and the bells chimed the hour.

'This would explain why there are rats behind the kitchen wall,' Edgar thought out loud.

'How long 'til we can have a look?' Alvin asked. He walked over to the trench and looked longingly at the trapdoor.

'It'll take as long as it takes to get the professionals here to have a look,' Lara said.

'Ugh,' Edgar groaned in frustration. 'But there are loads of archaeologists here. Why can't any of them go down?'

'Health and Safety,' Lara said miserably but then that adventurous gleam came over her eyes and she beamed. 'Bugger it, I'm going in.'

'Alone?' Edgar gasped. 'You can't!'

The thought of exploring a secret tomb alone sent a shiver down Edgar's back – he wouldn't like to do it.

'Damian!' Lara exclaimed and he looked over. 'We're going in!'

The chatter among the archaeologists ceased and a deadly quiet gripped the congregation as Lara took a series of deep breaths, pulled herself together and became suddenly solemn. Edgar and Alvin stopped instantaneously and watched as Lara crossed the garden and jumped into the trench with Damian. He reached down to the rusty handle of the old trapdoor and pulled it up. The crowd gathered close by the edge of the trench and stared down in awe. The inside of the hole was completely dark. Lara pulled out a torch from her pocket and looked up at the crowd.

'Damian. Grab the radios.'

He nodded, climbed out of the trench and grabbed a couple of walkie-talkies that had been left on the roof before climbing back down. Lara quickly showed Edgar how to use the radio to speak to them and he had a quick practice to show he could do it.

'Wait here. I'll get you if I find anything exciting,' she beamed and slid into the hole, followed silently by Damian. 'We'll stay in contact by the radio.'

As they descended into the darkness Edgar could see the light from her torch getting dimmer as she went further into the unknown. Within moments there was no light at all as Lara and Damian disappeared further in the abyss and there was pitch black once more.

Even though Edgar only waited beside the trapdoor in the daylight, his body rushed with adrenaline. His insides were tangled and knotted, butterflies fluttered in his stomach; he felt slightly sick with the apprehension and his head was elated, buzzing with amazement and wonder.

Edgar pressed the button on the radio and it crackled.

'Anything exciting?' he said. 'Over.'

'Just one long tunnel, so far,' Lara replied. 'Over.'

'Let us know if you find anything. Over.'

There was no reply.

Footsteps approached fast and Edgar looked up.

'What's going on?' Priscilla asked, gasping for breath as she staggered up the path, after just running half way across town from the museum. The crowd parted to let her through.

'Lara's just gone down for a look,' Edgar told her, pointing to the open trapdoor.

'Oh my God. First that weird artifact and now this. I'm beginning to suspect something funny is going on!' she exclaimed.

'I hope they're ok down there,' Alvin said.

Edgar reached for the radio.

'Anything new? Over.'

Silence.

'Lara? Damian? Anything down there? Over.'

Edgar was apprehensive. Why was there no reply?

Nobody spoke – the whole group just stood silent, their eyes fixed upon the hole, awaiting Lara and Damian's return with baited breath. Suddenly, from the darkness below, there was a scream. It wasn't just a frightened scream, it was a sickening, blood curdling scream that made them all jump.

'LARA!' Edgar shouted into the blackness of the hole.

There was no answer.

'Are you okay down there? Over.'

Still, there was no reply.

Everyone looked around anxiously, their eyes connecting widely and fearfully. Had one of them had an accident?

'LARA!' Priscilla screamed.

They waited for a tense moment and when there was no reply, Edgar dropped into the trench, crouched down beside the trapdoor and looked into the darkness.

'Right, I'm going in,' he said bravely. 'Wish me luck.'

He sat on the edge and slid off, dropping several feet onto a rocky ledge. Suddenly, a light shone in the darkness .

'Is that you, Lara?' Edgar asked cautiously as if he expected somebody else to be coming towards him. Slowly, the light came closer, getting brighter and brighter.

'Damian?' Edgar asked again, a shudder of panic tinged his voice. 'Answer me.'

A grubby hand reached up to grab the rock that Edgar stood upon but grabbed his foot instead.

He screamed and stumbled back, leaning against the solid wall of rock.

Lara pulled herself up onto the platform, a sparkle of glee in her eye.

'Got you,' she laughed hysterically.

'You absolute cow. I hate you!' Edgar whispered – his voice unable to reach anything louder in his sheer horror.

Lara looked up into the blinding sunlight of the outside world. She could make out Alvin and Priscilla stood eagerly by the edge of the trench.

'I think you ought to come and have a look,' she said, suddenly serious. A grim expression was etched on her face and Edgar wondered what could possibly be down there.

Alvin and Priscilla climbed in carefully too. They landed on a small ledge that was made of the same rare rock that had covered the trap door and when the light of the torch hit it the walls shone brightly and sparkled as if by magic. From the first ledge there was a drop between the next one, which was slightly lower down. The ledges continued going down like this in a zigzag. It was clear that it had once been a path but chunks had broken away over the years, leaving treacherous crevices.

'Where's Damian?' Edgar asked curiously.

'He's still in there,' Lara replied. 'You'll see why.'

Being careful not to fall down the crevices between the platforms all four of them climbed down the path and jumped across the ledges until they reached the bottom. It was as dark as night until Lara shone her torch around the black walls, illuminating a little tunnel that sloped downward, descending deeper into the Earth.

The walls were close together and the low ceiling consisted of jagged brown rocks and soil fell down from above in occasional trickles. Priscilla grabbed Edgar's hand and squeezed tightly. She hated small spaces. They had to walk in single file and duck down slightly as they crept down the steep tunnel with Lara leading the way, her torch lighting the black path ahead.

As the tunnel went on the ceiling began to rise higher and the walls began to spread steadily outwards, until it came to an end and opened into a vast subterranean cavern. Damian waited at the end of the tunnel and ushered them out into the cave, his face like nothing Edgar had ever seen before – a mixed expression of awe, terror and surprise. He didn't even speak. He just pointed and shone his light.

Massive black, stone pillars held the high, vaulted ceiling in place. The cavern spread out wide, easily behind every house on Edgar's street and could have easily gone as back as far as the cliffs behind the house. It was impossible to tell in the pitch black. It was like standing on the edge of infinity, the dark stretching forever in every direction, like it was just them and the darkness. In what appeared to be the centre of the cavernous tomb, spread a vast, dirty lake with a rickety old bridge that reached out across it to an island. Some of the planks on the walkway had been broken or were missing and the wooden rail was splintered and smashed. The lake looked deep but Edgar didn't want to know what was lurking in the murky, stagnant water - probably rats he thought to himself, shuddering.

'How the hell was all of this here without us knowing about it?' Priscilla gasped, awestruck; her eyes gleaming with amazement at the discovery that had been made and the impressive chamber astounded her, the torchlight glinting off the shiny, black pillars.

'I don't know but I don't like the look of that,' Edgar said as his eyes came to rest on the island in the middle of the lake. Something stood there – a tall, pointed structure fashioned from the same black stone as the tomb and the rock that had sealed it shut. Its sides were steeply sloped and reached to a high point. It was a pyramid.

Edgar's heart sank. That was why the trapdoor had been sealed shut and buried. How could this be a coincidence? He had grown up in that house with this right behind him, buried under the ground. Fifteen years he had grown up in such close proximity and had never known about it. Now he had learned he was a warrior who was meant to lead a war against the creatures who had taken over these pyramids.

'Wow. Look at that! It's beautiful!' Priscilla squeaked excitedly. She took a moment of silence to admire the grand sight and ran over to the rickety old bridge to get to it for a closer look.

'I don't think you ought to do that, mum. The bridge doesn't look too safe,' Edgar commanded.

'It's fine,' she muttered, waving off Edgar's concern.

'I don't think it's safe down here at all,' Edgar whispered and his voice echoed around the cavern. 'We should leave.'

'Leave? But it's incredible!' Alvin exclaimed as he wandered around, examining the beauty of the secret cave.

'I didn't expect a find this huge,' Damian said and Edgar jumped. He hadn't heard him creep up behind him.

'Neither did I.'

Damian put his hand on Edgar's shoulder and squeezed tightly. It made Edgar jump but there was something comforting in the way he gripped him so tightly. Edgar turned to him. Damian smiled, a true, wide grin and Edgar could see he was happy now.

'Markus won't believe this,' he said.

'Markus isn't very nice,' Edgar said bluntly. He hadn't meant to blurt the words out but they came so easily. He couldn't stop himself.

'He might not be the greatest person, but you might understand one day when you're older,' Damian said, patting Edgar on the back. There was a dreamy tone to his voice and Edgar felt the hair stand up on his arms. Hearing Damian talk about Markus like that made his whole body tense. It was frustrating that everyone could see Markus for what he really was – a horrible, slimy creep and still Damian liked him.

'I'm wise for my age, remember,' Edgar retorted. 'I know a creep when I see one.'

Damian didn't reply. Instead he skulked off to join Lara and Alvin who were admiring the pillars.

Edgar glanced around. It was quiet and calm – too much so for his liking. He wondered if the pyramid worked – if it was possible that Hounds and Nazakan had been using it all the years he had lived in the house and been so close, yet he had never known. He wondered if they might be in there now, lurking in the darkness, just beyond sight. The thought made him shiver and as he looked over to the pyramid his heart dropped into his stomach.

'MUM! NO! COME BACK!'

Priscilla was already half way across the bridge. The wooden boards creaked and groaned under the weight of her feet. She ignored Edgar's pleas and reached the island. She stood there before the gigantic stone structure and reached her hand out to touch it. 'MUM

NO!' Edgar bellowed again as he rushed over to the bridge and stopped, not daring to set foot on it.

'I'm only having a look,' she said, perplexed and put her hand on the pyramid, stroking it to feel the impossibly smooth surface of the stone. 'It's amazing - just like a bigger version of the artifact I found,' Priscilla continued quietly, staring up towards the pinnacle of the stony structure. 'Perhaps they're linked.'

'We have to go. I don't feel safe,' Edgar said quickly. He took a deep breath and cautiously crossed the bridge to reach Priscilla.

Each footstep groaned and creaked. The wood was rotten and the half-broken handrail was covered in soggy, green moss. He finally reached the island, thankful he had made it.

'Mum, please.'

'It's fine, we've got Lara and Damian with us,' Priscilla said dismissively but Edgar looked annoyed and grabbed her hand.

'Mum! I don't like it,' he begged as he pulled on her arm until she agreed to retreat to the allotment again.

'Alright then,' she said, defeated and they crossed the rickety bridge one at a time, hoping that it wouldn't break. Back on the main land, they gathered up the others and left abruptly. Together, they trekked back up the steep tunnel with the earthy soil beneath their feet and climbed up the steep stones. The distant sunlight was blinding and a blessing. They were finally out of the dark.

'Wow, I can't believe all that was hidden behind us for all those years,' Priscilla said admirably as the crowd of archaeologists cheered upon their return.

'Mmm,' Edgar replied somberly, pretending to agree even though he could not muster the enthusiasm because he knew what the pyramid meant. Maybe if he hadn't known the truth he might have been a bit more excited about it.

'What's wrong with you?' Priscilla said and she frowned suspiciously at him. 'This is life-changing, Edgar. We could be famous. A find like that is one in a million.'

Edgar knew that if only she knew what was really happening and what the pyramid actually was and what could come out of it she wouldn't be so joyful. She would want to move away as far as possible from the wretched thing.

It was dangerous...and then the thought hit him. He had to tell Betty. She had to see it. She had to know what was going on. Edgar, Priscilla and now Alvin were in danger in that house and they needed professional advice. Betty was the person to ask...

But how could he bring her back without Priscilla asking questions?

She would have to find out. It was the only way, Edgar concluded. He could pretend he had to go out, then go to Grindlotha, bring back Betty then either explain the whole story. This discovery changed everything, with the weight of this danger hanging above him, ready to drop at any moment like the sword of Damocles. It was time.

'Mum, I have to go into town for a bit.... I erm, I need to get... a present for Ophelia's birthday,' Edgar lied, winking at Alvin to show that he was making a story up. Alvin understood immediately and nodded to clarify that he knew Edgar was up to something.

'Oh, I'll go too… and keep him company,' Alvin interjected quickly, grinning as if he were trying to hide being up to something. 'besides, I need to buy some clothes for my stay here and stuff.'

'Okay, love. Just be careful,' Priscilla said. There was something in the way she looked at Edgar that told him she knew he was up to something. It wasn't quite her signature glare that chilled him to the core, it was something a bit more subtle – as if she were trying to read his mind like Devi.

Edgar and Alvin said their goodbyes to the group and made their quick escape. They ran down to the street and sprinted along, past Edgar's house and up the little hill and flight of steps to the churchyard where they ducked under the drooping, vine-like branches of the old willow tree. Hidden behind the green leaves of the dangling branches Edgar knew they would not be seen by anyone passing by.

'Harold! Was that you?' shouted a loud voice in the distance. Edgar could barely see through the long, spindly branches but he knew who it was. 'How about you stop hiding and face me like a man?'

'Who's that?' Alvin hissed quietly as Edgar dug his hand in his pocket to feel for his traveller's token.

Edgar didn't reply but the fact his face had drained of all colour and the way he fumbled in panic told Alvin that this was not a good sign.

'Harold. We're waiting for you,' the voice said again.

Alvin peeked between the branches and spotted a group of tracksuit-clad youths sat on the bench beside the front door of the church.

Chunks of litter were strewn across the grass before them, mostly ephemeral remains of plastic bottles, takeaway cartons and carrier bags filled with cardboard boxes and empty beer cans.

'Don't make me come over there,' said the boy who appeared to be in charge. He wore a grey tracksuit with a burberry cap. Even from a distance Alvin could see that he looked thuggish – his build, slight but athletic and his facial features were pointed and ratty.

Edgar pulled the token from his pocket.

'Go on Spencer. Kick his head in!' laughed another boy.

'Bring him here for me then, Julian,' Spencer snarled, pointing to the tree as Alvin peeked through.

'I'm not your slave though am I?' Julian retorted and Spencer rounded on him. He said something that neither Edgar nor Alvin could hear from a distance and Julian got up abruptly.

The others in the group laughed and jeered and threw empty cans at him as Julian reluctantly swaggered towards the willow tree. A couple of girls in scruffy tracksuits, with greasy hair pulled back into tight ponytails cackled like witches. They both wore the same tacky chain with a chunky golden clown encrusted with fake jewels around their necks. They chanted *"Churchyard Crew, coming through. Churchyard Crew, coming through"* as Julian approached, stomping with intent, cracking his knuckles, ready for a fight.

Alvin ducked back, hoping he couldn't see him.

'He's coming, Ed,' Alvin whispered and Edgar slammed the token into the bottom of his boot. He grabbed hold of Alvin and the mist rolled in from nowhere, coming closer and closer, just like Julian.

He was close now.

He approached the tree tentatively.

Edgar could see his vague shape on the other side, the fog swirled around him and Alvin and as Julian reached out to pull the branches back -

WHOOSH

The blast of wind almost knocked Julian off his feet.

Edgar and Alvin were falling. The wind whipped their hair around and blasted them all over the place; backwards and forwards, side to side and spinning in circles as they fell. Alvin's eyes rolled back into his head. He passed out again. Eventually it stopped feeling like falling and began to feel like flying and all Edgar could think of was Betty. He pictured her friendly face, the warm campfire and the gentle violin music. It was so clear in his mind but as the fog cleared and a landscape formed beneath him, he could see that while the land stretched out underneath them in rolling, green hills and rocky mountains in the distance, he couldn't be sure where he was.

It looked like Grindlotha – there was a vast expanse of forest, stretching for miles and there was a lake directly below him. He recognised it slightly from before but couldn't get his bearings. He clung to Alvin as they fell faster towards the lake, a giant black ruin stood on the precipice overlooking a treacherous waterfall.

They fell faster and faster and there was nothing Edgar could do to change the course of his journey. He clung to Alvin, terrified of losing him and as they came closer to the unfamiliar landscape. He realised that in his haste, he had not checked that he had set the token correctly. They could be anywhere for all he knew. Maybe he didn't recognise the ruins on the cliff at all...it was so close now and Edgar closed his eyes, hating the moment when he expected a heavier impact.

'Oh sh-'

SPLASH.

– CHAPTER TWENTY-FIVE –
THE HAUNTINGS OF FATE

The water was freezing cold and the flow of the river dragged them fast towards the edge of the cliff - towards the waterfall.

Edgar kept hold of Alvin and struggled against the current. He pulled his friend, keeping his head above the churning water and swam over to the side. It was hard work but he was determined and the shock of the cold kept him going. At least it wasn't as cold as the water in the ice caves where he had nearly frozen to death.

Alvin gasped as he came around. The tumultuous roar of the waterfall made it difficult to hear his screams. As Edgar half-dragged him to the edge, he glanced around. The rocky river-side was jagged and would give them enough footing to climb to the path beside the fast-flowing river.

Towering above them, the giant ruins of an ancient monastery sent a shiver down Edgar's back. It appeared to be fashioned out of a shining black rock – something similar to the stone that had covered the trapdoor in the allotment behind his house. It glimmered and glistened as if it were made out of the darkness of space itself and sprinkled with purple and white stars. It was beautiful. A single, tall tower rose from the back end of the building and the arched windows that looked out over the landscape.

When Edgar finally got Alvin to the side of the river and they clambered up the rocks to the overgrown path, they took a moment to catch their breath and Edgar couldn't take his eyes off the ruin.

'Where are we?' Alvin gasped, coughing up water. 'What's the matter?'

'I...I just...' Edgar couldn't find the words. He felt like he had been here before but he knew that he hadn't. Despite that, it looked all too familiar.

'Is this the right place?' Alvin said. 'Is this where we'll find Betty?'

'I'm not sure,' Edgar muttered, more to himself. 'It went wrong. I just wanted to get away from the Churchyard Crew.'

'Churchyard Crew?' Alvin asked, frowning.

'The bullies from school. It's what they call their gang,' Edgar explained, his voice low, as if he could hardly bring himself to say their name.

'Right,' Alvin laughed. 'Very original for a gang of chavs that hang out in a churchyard.'

'They're no joke. If Julian had caught us or if Spencer had come over with him-'

Edgar trailed off. He spoke of them as if they were horrendous monsters to be feared – the stuff of nightmares, even. And they were. The Churchyard Crew were responsible for every single moment of torment that he had suffered at school, and it was their leader, Spencer, who had locked him in the locker on the last day of school and left him for dead.

Even after everything he had been through on his adventure, Edgar was still scared of them and that proved a point. He could handle Unsterbliche and Nazakan and Houds. He could survive deadly situations with fearsome monsters that could physically harm him with relative ease but when it came to facing other vicious, unpredictable teenagers, he stood no chance.

They had made up rumours about him summoning the Devil, they had turned the entire school against him save for his handful of true friends. The Churchyard Crew were even responsible for beating him up for money. People paid them to kick the hell of out of Edgar so that they could watch and it was classed as entertainment – the perfect way to spend a breaktime. It was no different to throwing gladiators into the colusseum, except it was, quite thankfully, never a fight to the death although with the frequency of the attacks on the rise, Edgar often wished that perhaps it could have been. At least then it would be over.

The worst thing about the Churchyard Crew was that no matter how many teachers he spoke to, no matter how many times he complained or spoke out, the teachers did nothing. The Churchyard Crew had a certain influence, not just in the school, but in the town. Their families were well known and were mostly the unsavory types – known for being in and out of prison for committing crimes ranging from arson, to serious assaults with deadly weapons, to murder. It was safe to say they had people wrapped around their fingers out of fear. They could pull strings and things could happen –

bad things. This was why every time Edgar spoke out, he was the one persecuted and sent out of class. He was the one told to stop making things up. He was the one told he was lying and imagining things even though the cuts and bruises and black-eyes said otherwise. They were worse than the monsters he had fought simply because they were human and there was a monstrous darkness in their souls that allowed them to behave so despicably and they were allowed to get away with it.

'We're lucky we escaped,' Edgar said, managing to calm himself down at last.

'He's just a bully. You shouldn't-'

'He shoved me in a locker and I was nearly stuck in there all summer. I could have died if Mr. Wise hadn't found me.' Edgar snapped and Alvin looked at him, eyes wide in disbelief.

'You never told me that part.'

'Yeah. I don't like talking about it.'

Edgar sighed and contemplated just using the token again – to correct his mistake and leave straight away. Just as he was about to, he turned to Alvin and told him to grab his arm but as Alvin did as he was ordered, Edgar saw something unusual out of the corner of his eye. Further along the path, beside the doorway to the ruin stood a tall, flickering figure.

'No,' Edgar groaned to himself. 'It can't be. Not again.'

Alvin looked confused but Edgar didn't notice. He set off at a run, dripping a trail of water as he rushed over to the ghost. He was sure it was Brother Bradley – the height was a dead giveaway but the monk simply beckoned Edgar, turned, walked through the heavy, wooden door and vanished.

Edgar reached the door and tried to force it open. It towered over him and there was nothing he could do. It was too heavy and simply would not budge.

'Edgar! What are you doing?'

'It's Brother Bradley. He's here.'

'Brother Bradley? I didn't see him?'

'Just get over here and help me.'

Alvin raced to his side and they pushed together, straining hard and pushing with all the strength they could muster to no avail.

'It's no use, Edgar. Why don't we just give up and go find Betty?' Alvin said dismissively.

'No,' Edgar insisted, throwing himself at the door again. 'This is important.'

He shoulder-barged the hard, rough wood, throwing all his strength against it but the door refused to even shudder.

CLICK.

There was a sound from the other side, like a click of a latch and the door swung open to admit himself and Alvin inside. Alvin stumbled back and tripped over a rock, but Edgar managed to grab him before he could fall and seriously injure himself.

'The door...' he whispered hoarsely, pointing a trembling finger.

'All the more reason to go inside,' Edgar said, pushing the heavy door open further so that they could squeeze inside.

The long corridor was dark, lit only by the dim sunlight that shone through the open door and through the large, round window above the door; a circle with intricate intertwining lines. Its shadow crossed the black, marble floor. It was cold and the whole monastery glittered and gleamed. Brother Bradley stood at the end of the corridor, watching as if making his presence obvious so that Edgar would follow and that was exactly what he intended to do.

Edgar and Alvin crept along, even their softest footsteps echoed as loudly as claps of thunder and as they came closer to him, the ghost walked away into the next room.

'Come on,' Edgar said, pulling Alvin along impatiently.

They rushed along and followed the ghost through the door into the next room.

'Hello?' Edgar said apprehensively.

Brother Bradley stood in the centre of the cavernous room. Hefty, wooden bookcases filled with ancient tomes lined the walls and long tables stretched across the centre of the room with equally long benches next to them. Twisted candleholders sat upon the tables, dripping with wax that had accumulated over the years, hiding what once had been the holder underneath the many layers of wax.

At the far end of the room, four arched windows looked out over the cliff to the lake below and the almost deafening crashing waterfall echoed through the room. He had been here before. He knew it. He remembered it – like a deja-vu. He could feel it, this moment, him standing in the middle of this exact same room had happened before...but it couldn't have. He had never travelled in his life until that first journey a matter of days ago.

Despite all the wonderous sights of the all-too familiar library, the thing that made Edgar's jaw drop – the thing that almost made him scream was that Brother Bradley was not alone. Scattered across the library, going about their business, were several other monks. All as ghostly as Brother Bradley, flickering and distorting as they moved, barely paying attention to Edgar and Alvin who were insignificant to them.

'You...' Edgar spluttered, unable to believe his eyes.

Brother Bradley turned to Edgar and he entered but Alvin hesitated by the doorway.

'Who are you talking to? I can't see anyone,' Alvin asked, peering over Edgar's shoulder, trying to catch a glimpse of the invisible person.

'Brother Bradley obviously,' Edgar snapped. He turned to face his friend and held a hand up to signal for him to shut up.

'Well I can't see him!'

'Can't you see any of them?' Edgar snapped irritably.

'There's more than one?'

Alvin glanced around, a curious brow raised as he looked around the empty library and then eyed Edgar worriedly.

'Yes,' Edgar said, his eyes darting around, trying to take in all the figures.

Alvin remained quiet and stared at the floor, shuffling his feet.

'What are you doing here?' Edgar asked, directing his words at Brother Bradley, softly, hoping for a decent explanation as he turned back to face him.

'Oh, come on! If there was a ghost, I'd be able to see it,' Alvin insisted pompously but Edgar ignored him and shuffled closer to Brother Bradley.

'He calls us ghosts but ghosts we are not,' Brother Bradley said, his tone deadpan and Edgar found his attention drawn to the others who had finally stopped in their tracks and turned to face him. 'We are neither living, nor dead. Those of our Order were granted the gift of an eternal half-life for our sacrifice.'

'What sacrifice?'

'The great sacrifice of Krinka,' Brother Bradley replied solemnly. His voice crackled and hissed like static and Edgar's jaw dropped. He distorted, stretching and shrinking frantically.

'Krinka? But that was just a story…'

Alvin watched Edgar with disbelief as he spoke to the invisible person. He could not see or hear a thing – only the empty room where the wind whistled through the open arches and the waterfall crashed outside.

'Krinka is much more than a story, Edgar, and our sacrifice made us worthy of a prolonged life on Earth. We are the guardians.'

'Guardians of what?'

'Edgar...I'm worried about you,' Alvin mumbled but Edgar just turned and *shushed* him again.

'Guardians of peace and balance,' Brother Bradley said as he inched towards Edgar who wanted to retreat but stood his ground. 'It was our sacrifice that created the barriers that hold the Nazakan at bay.'

Edgar's eyes widened. Suddenly it made sense.

'But it was all for nothing. They created the Hounds to cross the barriers.'

The other monks around the room, who up until now had been going about their business peacefully, turned their attention to Edgar and glared at him.

'How dare you?' Brother Bradley snapped. He flickered dangerously and there was a look on his face that terrified Edgar. 'We sacrificed ourselves selflessly!'

The other ghosts muttered among themselves, glaring darkly at Edgar. He shivered, feeling their scathing gaze cut right through him. He had offended them without truly meaning to and now they were angry.

'Who are the others?' Edgar asked, as he glanced around the vast, black marble library. He hoped that changing the subject might make things right.

'Brother François,' said a tall man with a heavy French accent. Under his white robes he appeared to be quite bulky but not fat – it was all muscle. His face was young, handsome and he had dark, sparkling eyes and a thick, black beard.

'Brother Benedict,' said another young man – this one was much smaller than François in both height and build. He was much thinner, his face drawn and sharp.

'Brother Jacunda,' said an older man with a long, grey beard and a gruff voice. He looked wise and his dark eyes glistened as if he were still angry about what Edgar had said before about the sacrifice.

'Brother Sergio,' said a handsome young man with a Spanish accent. His face was fresh with a neatly trimmed beard and a heavy brow over his dark eyes.

'Brother Alexander,' said a middle-aged man and he gestured towards another man who looked strangely alike. 'And this is my real brother, Brother Anthony.'

Edgar waved and smiled coyly.

'Nice to meet you all...' he said, his voice catching as he tried to speak.

'You truly believe he's the one, Brother Bradley?' asked Brother François, eyeing Edgar suspiciously.

'The prophecy tells us that it is so,' said another monk who stepped forward from behind a bookcase. He lowered his hood and Edgar could see that he was only young. His hair short and red, his eyes bright and blue – there was something strangely familiar about him. 'Hello, Edgar Harold,' he added kindly, nodding curtly at Edgar.

'Hi,' Edgar whispered hoarsely. 'You know me already then?'

The monks' chuckled among themselves and Alvin looked at Edgar with his brow furrowed and nose wrinkled in confusion.

'Brother Dominic,' the ghost said gliding over towards Edgar.

His jaw dropped.

It was him!

'*The* Brother Dominic?' Edgar gasped, staring at Brother Dominic gormlessly. 'From Krinka?'

'*The* Brother Dominic from the City of Krinka,' he confirmed.

Edgar turned to Alvin but he paid no attention – his focus still upon the books that were stacked on the high, black shelves around the library.

'How come only I can see you? I don't understand…' Edgar asked. 'Why can't he?'

'You became susceptible at a young age, to the presence of all who learned the secret of dimension travel,' Brother Bradley explained but Edgar still had no clue what was going on.

'But why can-'

Brother Bradley shot Edgar a cold stare, as if to shut him up so he could continue.

'When you were young you wanted a friend, therefore I showed myself to you and taught you how to read. Your open mind and links to our kind allowed me to appear to you.'

'I still don't understand.'

'It was known that you were to become one of us – that you were to discover the secret of dimension travel that we worked tirelessly to keep undercover. The hauntings you experienced as a child were the beginning of the journey leading you to become the man you are today. Those hauntings of fate bound you to us.'

'Hauntings of fate? You make it sound like my life is a story that's already written,' Edgar sighed anxiously – it was true.

Prophecies, fate, destiny, legends. These words had been thrown around an awful lot since he had begun his journey.

'Your fate is sealed, Edgar Harold. It is known how this ends,' Brother Dominic said, his tone sombre.

He could barely keep eye contact with Edgar, as if there were something he didn't want to reveal – some terrible, dark secret. Edgar knew the reaction well. It was how he had felt around Alvin after seeing Vicky die.

'Then tell me,' Edgar demanded angrily.

Brother Bradley and these monks knew too much. Perhaps they would be able to soothe Edgar's mind, to put his fears at rest...or perhaps they knew something terrible. Edgar noticed his even though his ghostly form flickered and distorted, like Brother Dominic, he couldn't quite keep eye contact and his lip quivered as he was caught unaware by what Edgar asked of him.

'You truly are the Warrior of Legends, Edgar,' Brother Bradley said and the other monks gathered nodded solemnly like a jury in court condemning an innocent man.

Edgar gulped hard. His stomach flipped and he felt sick. All the colour drained from his face and he almost fell to the ground, unable to support his own weight.

'But will I survive?' Edgar asked, forcing the words out past the lump in his throat. 'I have a right to know that much.'

The monks remained silent.

They glanced at one another awkwardly, as if waiting for someone else to say the words that none of them wanted to say.

'It will end in tragedy,' Brother Dominic said finally and Edgar glowered.

'Will I survive?' Edgar demanded and Dominic gulped. He looked to the others for support but received none.

'Your path leads you to the plains of Hell where you will face your final battle.'

The words hit him forcefully – so hard they nearly knocked him over. He couldn't breathe. His brain couldn't process the information. His world was spiralling into a freefall and soon he would crash and burn. This was it – hard confirmation that he would die.

He refused to believe it. Whatever prophecy this came from was wrong – whoever wrote those ancient words that condemned him before he was even born would be proven incorrect. He would fight. He would win. He would survive. An expression of grim determination crossed his face and instantly, with the defiant thoughts, he felt stronger.

'This prophecy, I've heard a lot about it but I've never actually heard it,' Edgar said.

It suddenly hit him that though he had been told about it and he had been convinced by all the stories, that he truly was the Warrior of Legends, he had not once heard the prophecy that supposedly put him in this position.

'That may be for the best,' Brother Bradley said, his form trembling and shifting even more dangerously than before. Edgar wondered if perhaps it were to do with his anxiety. He could tell the ghost was scared – but why?

Because he knew it was finally time to give answers?

'If I'm your warrior I need to know everything,' Edgar said sternly and Alvin turned to him and rolled his eyes.

'Can't you just stop it? You're scaring me now,' Alvin said as he crossed to the window and looked out over the stunning view of the lake and the forests, far off into the golden horizon. He turned back to Edgar, unable to see anyone besides the two of them.

'You still can't see them?'

'No,' Alvin said. 'But if you're going to hang around being weird, I'm gonna go explore.'

Alvin stalked past Edgar and out of the library into the long corridor they had entered through.

'Sorry about him...' Edgar said. 'Now it's just us, if you don't want me to keep running from my responsibility, you can't run from yours. If you're my guardians you *have* to tell me.'

Brother Bradley sighed and Edgar caught a glimpse of his sad expression. His eyes glistened and his mouth twitched into a feigned smile. The other monks expressions weren't much more optimistic – all of them grim and solemn.

'If you're sure,' Brother Dominic said.

Edgar nodded. He mouthed *'I am,'* the words sticking in his throat as he wondered what truth could be so bad that the monks wanted to hide it from him. Brother Dominic took a breath.

'No, I'll tell him,' Brother Bradley said. 'It's only right.'

'But it's because of-'

'Dominic. Please. Let me.'

Brother Dominic nodded and Brother Bradley sighed. He took a deep breath and made the sign of a cross over his chest, muttering to himself. He smiled weakly at Edgar and began:

'The child born of a wandering traveller to a woman as pretty as a flower upon the foundations of a sanctuary by the sea will be protected by the White Brothers and raised in the way of the warrior until he is fifteen years old. So begins the first trial – a test of intellect and worthiness. The boy will pass, so begins the second trial – a journey of courage and bravery in the face of adversity and death, but this he will overcome. Thus, this lover of man, learns the truth and begins to prepare. The end begins in a far off land; and under the blazing sun by the shores of a foreign sea, the Warrior will face his final trial. In the Tomb of the Iconic Templar, should he finally pass, he will be delivered by angels to the truth he sought his entire life. He will lead the battle upon the burning plains of Oona Rab – the deserts of Hell itself. Here, the warrior with hair of flame and eyes of ice will be powerless as those closest to him are thrust into the arms of death. He survives to defeat the Nazakan and their Hounds…all but one; and he will give chase and hunt it down but even he, this Warrior of Legends, cannot escape the clutches of that treacherous place for when the battle's over and the last beast lays slain, he will be drawn back to those deserts of damnation where he will be lost forevermore.' Brother Bradley fell silent and Edgar stared grimly.

The words rang deafeningly in his ears and he just gazed, his eyes glazed and catatonic. Brother Bradley appeared to be speaking but Edgar had no idea what was being said. The words were distant and incoherent. His world closed in around him; his heart filled with a dark, crushing blackness that threatened to pump around his entire body, tainting him. He wanted to curl up – to hide, to give in.

The prophecy could easily have been interpreted as him – hair of flame and eyes of ice. Born to a wandering traveller and a woman as pretty as a flower, his dad had been a traveller before him and his mother's middle name was Hebe, a type of flower. He had been born on the foundations of an ancient sanctuary; the Cistercian monastery that had once stood where his house had been built and the White Brothers, the Cistercians, like Brother Bradley, had watched over him. He had been raised in the way of the warrior with the re-enactments he had attended.

The prophecy was accurate enough for it to be a genuine worry. The loose strands of questions and mysteries that had followed him for his entire life suddenly tied together and they tied him to his fate. He knew now how it would all end:

In Hell.

'Well, shit,' Edgar whispered to himself as he came out of his daze. His voice was hoarse.

'I'm sorry, Edgar,' Brother Bradley replied downheartedly.

There was silence as Edgar tried to wrap his head around it all.

'So Hell's a real place?' Edgar muttered to himself. The hairs on his arm stood on end as he thought about all the paths before him leading to the place of eternal damnation.

'Not quite the way you understand it. Its existence and truth has been somewhat lost in translation through the years, but yes, Hell is real,' Brother Dominic explained, interjecting before Brother Bradley could say anything.

'And if I'm the Warrior of Legends, if I win this war, I can't escape from there?'

'If you *are* the Warrior of Legends and if the prophecy *is* true.' Dominic replied.

'Seems like a lot of if's,' Edgar said – at least that was a consolation. These were all *if's*. It was not like anything were set in stone. He might be fine – it could all be wrong. He could survive after all. This was denial, and he knew it.

'I'm afraid it *is* your fate,' Brother Bradley butted in before Brother Dominic could speak.

'And just what makes you so sure?'

'Every second has a meaning...' Brother Bradley began solemnly, as if reciting a prayer.

'Oh,' Edgar sighed. The realisation physically hurt. All hope was snatched from him, his heart was torn from his chest and his breath caught again. 'The poem. My name. It's all connected, isn't it?'

'More so than those poor souls we previously thought to be the Warrior. I'm afraid all the lines converge on you. It is you who stand at the crossroads of fate. It is you who must carry this burden,' Brother Dominic said. His tone was indifferent, cold even and Brother Bradley glanced at him, his eyes shining with ghostly tears. His shape flickered more violently than ever before, he was clearly distressed.

'And I'll do it. I just need time,' Edgar said, giving them what they wanted to hear. His whole body, mind and soul were numb. He felt nothing and even though Alvin wandered back in and went almost unnoticed, Edgar was so alone and scared.

'What about the pyramid behind my house?' Edgar said. 'Is that part of this too? Was that what your last warning was about?'

Brother Bradley nodded soberly and Edgar's heart sank even further. He was about to speak out again but the door creaked open and Alvin re-appeared.

'There's not much out there. It's just a ruin. Beautiful though,' Alvin said as he crossed back over to Edgar.

'Yeah. Gorgeous.' Edgar replied absent-midedly.

'Are you still talking to yourself and pretending it's a ghost.'

Edgar didn't reply.

Alvin patted him on the back as he walked past and stood right beside the ghost but he really didn't see him.

'He's right beside you!' Edgar said, the words feeling robotic. He could hardly process the information and emotion that coursed through his body.

'There's nothing there.'

'There is!'

'Not!'

'Is!'

'You're just like your father. I wouldn't have liked to have been on his wrong side either,' Brother Bradley said and Edgar's jaw dropped. Suddenly the prophecy didn't matter anymore.

'You knew him? What happened to him?' Edgar asked anxiously, taking a step forward. For his whole life he had grown up with no knowledge about the man, but now he knew that he followed in his footsteps as a traveller, wearing his old boots, he wanted to know more.

'They thought he might have been the Warrior of Legends, once upon a time,' Brother Bradley said and Edgar's eyes opened wide. His father had been considered to lead the war he had now been appointed leader of –

But what did that mean for him? Had his father's disappearance to search for his brother been a simple cover up? Had he really gone off to lead a war and perished in the process?

'But now they think I am. Did he fail?' Edgar asked, not sure he wanted to know the answer.

'He was not the one.'

The ghost grew anxious and his flickering intensified again. Edgar's questions had hit a nerve.

'I guessed, but did he survive?'

'The last time I saw him, he asked me to watch over you. He demanded I saw you came to no harm and to protect you. I swore an oath and kept my promise.'

'But that doesn't answer my question,' Edgar said, growing more and more agitated. 'As for protecting me, you did a great job! You abandoned me!'

'You let Priscilla convince you I was an imaginary friend,' Brother Bradley continued, ignoring Edgar's probing questions. 'I was there all along, right by your side!'

The other ghosts had wandered away again to carry on with their business around the library but Brother Dominic remained by Brother Bradley's side like an intimidating shadow.

'Is my dad sill alive?' Edgar tried again urgently.

'Why did you stop believing in me?'

'You answer first.' Edgar insisted. He had come this far and was not going to play games. He wanted answers and he wanted them now.

'It's been a long time, but I believe he is still alive,' Brother Bradley said coldly. 'Your turn.'

'When Teddy was taken, I was terrified. I had never been scared by you – even though that wasn't you, was it?' Edgar admitted. 'It wasn't fun anymore. I wanted it to stop – for the hauntings to just go away. I started to believe my mum when she told me I had been imagining it all... even when part of me wanted to see you again, the stronger, more logical part of my brain told me you were just made up.'

'And you need to *want* to see us,' Brother Bradley said quietly. 'Like I said, I never left your side, waiting patiently for the day to come, when we could meet again.'

It was all too much.

All those years that Edgar had never even heard or seen a sign of Brother Bradley and it had been because he let his mother convince him he had been an imaginary friend. All those years he had lost out on – the years of answers that he could have had. He might have been a totally different person had Brother Bradley been around to help him, to shape him into the Warrior they needed.

Instead he was the quiet, nerdy goth who was bullied and weak – he should be strong but he wasn't.

'Edgar, why are you crying?' Alvin asked as Edgar wiped a tear from his eye. He couldn't tell if he was crying because he was happy or sad or overwhelmed or all of them together.

'I just want to know where he is,' Edgar said, stifling more tears.

'Edgar, please...' Alvin snapped. 'Don't make me smack you again.'

'Alvin, do you really want to see Brother Bradley?' Edgar asked him.

'*Who*?' Alvin asked, puzzled, looking at Edgar. His eyes scanned the room for any signs of another person again but there were still none.

'Brother Bradley! He's right here with the others You just need to *want* to see them before they can show themselves to you. When I was young I *wanted* a friend, hence Brother Bradley – Biggy and then he vanished for years because I convinced myself he was imaginary,' Edgar explained as if it were as simple while Alvin just stood staring blankly at Edgar, looking as thick as a plank of wood.

'Then he kept coming back recently when I was confused, scared and wanting answers.'

'Ok, I want to see these ghosts so it proves that you're telling the truth.'

Alvin rolled his eyes.

'Do you *really* believe it? Do you *want* to see him, or are you just saying you do?'

'Yeah, whatever,' he sighed.

'Seriously?'

'*Fine!* I want to see them!'

Slowly, he began to believe that he did. He looked around, straining to see the secret monks and he let out a discreet squeal as Brother Bradley slowly came into focus out of thin air in front of his eyes and the others faded into view from their places around the room.

'OH MY GOD!' screamed Alvin, covering his mouth and nearly fainting in astonishment.

'That is blasphemy. Now would you please mind your language and refrain from using the Lord's name in vain?' Brother Dominic said sternly, his bright eyes flashing in anger.

Alvin's mouth flapped open and closed. He couldn't speak in shock.

'Ghosts!' he gasped, pointing rudely.

'Not ghosts. Echoes,' Brother Dominic corrected him.

'Now you know the truth, Alvin,' Edgar said. 'I told you so.'

'But...they're...'

'Not ghosts, yeah.'

'And we...'

'Need to go. We need to find Betty. I've got enough answers for now. We've got more important things to worry about.'

Edgar turned to Brother Bradley who looked confused.

'The cave behind our house. The pyramid in there. You know what that means.'

Brother Bradley looked solemn and didn't utter a word in reply. Brother Dominic and the others turned and watched him darkly as if they knew more than they let on as usual.

'Maybe we don't need Betty,' Alvin said, grabbing hold of Edgar's arm as the idea struck him. 'We could avoid having to take her back. We don't need to rock the boat with Priscilla.'

'Sadly there is nothing we can do,' Brother Dominic replied. 'We cannot interfere.'

'Then we need to go.'

Edgar stormed towards the door but he stopped dead in his tracks. In the distance, heavy footsteps clumped along the corridor.

'Someone's coming,' he whispered and Alvin looked around at him in horror.

The ghosts muttered among themselves and began to fade away. Edgar waved frantically, hoping to stop them but it was futile. They were gone and Edgar was alone with Alvin with the footsteps only thundering closer.

'What do we do?' Alvin whispered, hoping he wouldn't be heard.

'Who's there?' shouted a voice from outside. 'I know you're here. I can hear you!'

Edgar sat on the long bench beside the table and slotted the token into place, making sure that it was definitely set for Grindlotha. It was. He grabbed Alvin's arm and the warm tingle spread from his toes, through his body but the fog didn't come. Edgar's heart sank.

'Come on!' he squeaked, praying that the token would work.

'Who's there?' came the voice again. Edgar's eyes were fixed on the door – a long shadow swept over the wall in the corridor and a figure appeared. Edgar could barely make out who they were – in the encroaching darkness it was impossible to make out any physical features but he wasn't particularly tall and had short hair. That was all that was certain.

'Why isn't it working?' Edgar whispered to Alvin, his eyes wide in fear. He stamped his foot hard on the ground again. 'For f-'

Edgar's words were cut short by a blast of wind but this time there was no mist, there was no falling or flying. Instead there was a heavy force from behind that grabbed him and pushed him forward at a million miles an hour. It was like the first few seconds of a rollercoaster ride or that moment when the aeroplane boosts its speed on the runway.

Edgar screamed and held Alvin's arm tightly but felt himself almost pulled out of his grasp. Alvin trailed behind, unconscious, his arm almost pulling out of its socket and keeping hold of him was all that mattered. Edgar didn't catch the man's face as they hurtled past him. He didn't recognise the pale, bearded face and watery eyes.

Before he really understood what was happening, they were flying through the front door of the monastery and through the blurred forests but the more he tried to feel it, the more he couldn't tell if he was moving or if his surroundings were moving and he stood still. It was such a surreal experience that Edgar reeled in confusion but despite that, all he could think of was Betty and the travellers' camp.

They hurtled through the forests, passing through the trees like ghosts, past the Shrine of Saint Margarette and over fields and meadows until the speeding journey slowed down. Everything was still and he fell flat onto the grass with Alvin.

'What the hell was that?' Alvin groaned as he slowly sat up, rubbing his shoulder.

'I guess we were in Grindlotha all along,' Edgar replied, thinking of the only logical reason that he could.

Edgar clambered to his feet and offered his hand to Alvin and helped him up. It was dark and the tents stood in long lines like a ghost town.

'Come on, we need to find Betty's caravan,' Edgar said, walking off ahead and leaving Alvin behind.

'We can't. What would your mum say? Betty's supposed to be dead,' Alvin reminded Edgar, beginning an awkward silence in which Edgar wrestled with his morals.

He remembered back to the memorial - to the day Priscilla had told him about Betty's death. She had really believed it and was so taken in by the unequivocal illusion of Betty's death but now things were too important to ignore. They needed Betty and it was a simple fact that Priscilla would have to face the shock of Betty's revival. She had kept enough secrets from Edgar – Betty being his real grandmother, just one of them. She had a lot of questions to face from Edgar. It was time for revelations on both sides – time to clear the air and put everything out in the open.

'That pyramid behind my house is dangerous and Betty's the only one who can do a thing about it,' Edgar decided. 'It's time to tell mum everything.'

He walked away, heading off to Betty's caravan among the various tents and caravans that filled the campsite.

He found it quickly as it was the biggest and the most decorative and sat by the ring of logs where the travellers gathered by the campfire. He walked up the wooden steps, knocked on a glass panel on the front door and hoped beyond hope that Betty would be home this time. Nobody else was around.

There was a shuffling sound on the other side. Clumpy footsteps moved over the wood and he saw a shadow on the other side of the frosted glass. The door creaked open.

'Oh, Edgar,' Betty smiled kindly, her green eyes twinkling.

'We need your help. It's something that we can't say here. Can we explain inside?' Edgar blurted out at once; he had to tell her everything.

'Yes, come on in.'

Betty stood aside and welcomed them in. The inside of the caravan was dark; she lit a candle and placed it on the table. It cast sinister, flickering shadows over the walls. Betty sat down at her table and Alvin perched on the bottom bunk, where he had laid when the Hound wounded him. Edgar remained standing. He was too anxious to sit down; his feet shifted around underneath him and he fidgeted uncontrollably, pacing back and forth across the caravan.

'We found something behind our house. It was an artifact. A black pyramid with this symbol scraped into the bottom of it,' he showed Betty the token with the same insignia engraved on it. 'The museum bought it for the collection.'

He told Betty about the excavation and how they discovered the trapdoor. She listened rapturously.

'And then we went through and there was a tunnel. It led into a massive cave and there was a *pyramid* in there,' Edgar finished, his voice wavering with terror - every word feeling harder to spit out. He knew that Betty would be powerless to do anything, but there was the possibility that she knew something that they could do.

The face that Betty pulled at the sound of Edgar's shocking news only confirmed just how serious things were and that action should be taken immediately.

'Please. Tell me you can help.'

Betty looked serious. The wrinkle lines on her forehead were deep and her eyes had lost their sparkle.

'God help us. It seems that fate is at work once again,' Betty murmured, every word coming out fast and hoarse.

Alvin remained quiet and Edgar sank onto a chair, looking at Betty in concern.

'Betty, can you come back with us? We need you,' Edgar looked desperately at Betty and clasped his hands together as if in prayer. He could tell she was seriously thinking about the request.

'This is important, I'm sure I can make up an excuse to tell your mum, or I could tell her the truth. What would you rather I do?' Betty asked Edgar, solemnity etched into every wrinkle on her face.

'It's time to be brave,' Edgar said honestly, staring down at his clasped hands, then up into Betty's gleaming eyes. 'I've got to tell her the truth.'

A chilling silence filled the caravan and Betty simply beamed at Edgar. She took his hands in hers and gripped them tightly, looking him right in the eye.

'I'm so proud of you.'

'She's going to find out sooner or later.'

Betty nodded solemnly.

'I don't think it'll be as hard as you think. She knows more than you'd expect.'

Edgar smiled weakly. Knowing that he was about to tell his mother the truth about his adventure and his fate to become the Warrior of Legends made him feel anxious. He didn't want to do it – he just had to. By speaking about it, that made it real.

Too real.

How would she take it? Would she understand? Would she still love him?

His stomach gurgled and tightened as he thought about the million ways the conversation should go – a million possibilities all playing in his head at the same time. It hurt. It was dizzying. As soon as he confessed, everything would change and his life would never be the same again. He had come to accept it himself, on a personal level, but telling other people still felt like an enormous step.

'Come on, there's no time to waste.'

Betty fitted her travellers' token into her slipper. She fiddled with it as Edgar grabbed Alvin's arm and she grabbed hold of

Edgar's and Alvin's hands. Together, holding on to each other in a circle, through the thick, swirling mist they fell upwards, as if being forced up by a sharp force and Alvin screamed at his side.

'I'm doing it properly. I haven't passed out!' he yelled excitedly. 'WOOOOHOOOOOOO!' he yelled as they fell and Alvin experienced the fullness of dimension travel for the first time.

Betty gave him a friendly smile as the wind rushed past them, blowing them around in its wild currents, their hair getting caught in their faces as it blew all over.

The air cleared and they fell. The familiar view of Scarborough headland hurtled closer and Alvin screamed louder and harder than ever before.

'We're going to die!' he shrieked, his voice high-pitched. Edgar could have sworn he was even crying, tears streamed his face but they may have just been watering from the wind.   Relentlessly, the ground rushed nearer.

There was no stopping it and suddenly they landed with a heavy *THUD*!

They had landed on the allotment behind Edgar's house, right in the middle of the dig site. Luckily, it was evening now and the archaeologists had gone home as the setting sun cast its last glow of golden light over the rooftops of the town.

Edgar and Alvin got to their feet, dizzily and helped Betty before walking casually down to Edgar's house.

Edgar knocked on the door. A rush of footsteps could be heard from inside and Edgar's heart pounded in his chest as he braced himself for Priscilla's reaction to Betty's resurrection.

The door opened slowly. Priscilla poked her head around the corner. Her eyes fell on Betty who beamed and waved coyly. Priscilla screamed loudly her voice echoing down the street. Her wide eyes seemed to pop out from her head and her mouth opened and closed wordlessly. For a moment Edgar thought she might faint.

'BETTY!' she flung her arms around Betty and smothered her in a choking hug that nearly crushed her. 'You're not dead!' she whispered as a solitary tear streamed down her cheek.

'You thought I was? After everything?' Betty said, a trace of hurt in her voice.

'They found your coat!' Priscilla exclaimed, as if that were a good enough reason to believe in her death.

'I found my token!'

Priscilla gawped with an expression somewhere between extreme happiness and shock.

'Oh, Betty! Why didn't you just tell me?'

'Wait...you knew about this?' Edgar gasped, All that worry had been for nothing. 'About her looking for her travellers' token?'

'Of course I did! So I assume you know now...' Priscilla said seriously. 'About...things?'

'Alvin knows too, Priscilla...about travelling. It's okay.' Betty said, just to confirm.

'Yeah. we've been travelling...' Edgar said.

And it was out.

The truth was in the open and it felt like a huge weight off Edgar's shoulders. If anything, he couldn't believe that Priscilla had already known and she had been keeping it all secret from him for his whole life. Since learning the truth about Betty, he had suspected but had kept quiet to protect her.

Still, it was a relief.

'By the way Alvin someone's coming to see you. I expect they'll be arriving soon,' Priscilla said ecstatically with a smile on her face as she ushered them all into the house.

'Who?' Alvin asked, perplexed. His brow wrinkled as he looked to Edgar and Betty wondrously.

'I can't say but it'll be a nice surprise for you,' Priscilla replied as she strolled into the kitchen to get the kettle on.

A sudden scratching, scraping sound came from behind the wall at the back of the kitchen again and she sighed.

'Bloody rats. At least we know where they're coming from now, what with that great big cave back there and everything,' she said as she put the kettle on and stood there, listening to the sound which only reminded Edgar of the secrets hidden behind the wall and made his stomach tie in knots.

Brother Bradley's words suddenly came back to Edgar's mind:

"This house is not as safe as it once was. Its defences are weakening so who knows what might break through in the dark. I shall keep watching you, Edgar Harold but I cannot assure your safety." And as the words replayed in his mind, out of the corner of his eye, near the back of the kitchen, right beside the wall, he saw the flickering figure of the man who had given him that same warning.

He watched Edgar gravely and Edgar smiled weakly at him. Nobody else could see him but Edgar – Brother Bradley was invisible to all those ignorant to his presence but it chilled Edgar to the bone that he had appeared right then out of all the times he could have shown up.

Was this an omen of impending danger?

Edgar didn't know and he didn't particularly want to find out but he knew, that as Brother Bradley kept telling him, only time would tell.

– CHAPTER TWENTY-SIX –

A KISS GOODBYE

They waited in Edgar's living room, apprehensively, wondering who it could possibly be that was coming to visit Alvin. They sat in silence, fidgeting on the edge of their seats and twiddled their thumbs impatiently. Brother Bradley had vanished again. It happened when Edgar took his eyes off him for a second and then looked back and there was nothing there – just an empty space where the ghostly figure had stood only seconds before.

The front door opened and the wind chimes that dangled above it jingled to announce the arrival of guests. Alvin jumped up excitedly, hoping it was his mysterious visitor but Damian shuffled in from the hallway and looked sheepish.

'Are you alright?' he said coyly. Alvin and Edgar stared at him – was this going to be a petty attempt at an apology for his behaviour earlier?

'Hello,' Betty said, beaming at him. 'I don't believe we've met.'

'No, we haven't. I'm Damian,' he said politely as he extended his hand for her to shake. She took his hand gently and shook it.

'Betty,' she replied and Damian forced a kindly smile. Edgar could see that behind his deep, dark eyes something more was troubling him. He opened his mouth to speak but couldn't find the words and stopped.

'Erm, well, I guess I've just sort of come to...' Damian began eventually. He gulped. There was something on his mind – a heavy burden that he struggled to say 'to kind of...say goodbye, I suppose.'

'What do you mean?' Edgar blurted out loudly – perhaps a little louder than he had meant to. His booming words startled Star who had been sleeping on the pile of cushions on the floor by the window. She woke from her slumber, looked dazed and then fell asleep once more.

'Higher powers have decided that Markus and I should move to another site,' Damian explained. There was a regretful tone to his voice. 'It was lovely meeting you all. Thanks for all the sandwiches, Priscilla. And Edgar, thank you for the advice.'

'No! You can't go!' Edgar exclaimed, shaking his head furiously. 'Absolutely not.'

It was unfair. Damian couldn't leave now! He had only just arrived.

'I'm sorry, guys,' Damian said. He fell silent, completely lost for words. Edgar could see in his eyes and from the way the corners of his mouth turned down so sadly that he was genuinely upset about the decision. 'We can still visit though. It's only Whitby.'

'But it's miles away!'

'It's twenty miles, an hour on the bus. Half an hour by car. We'll still see each other, Edgar,' Damian said defensively. 'It's not the end of the world, I promise.'

'I know but...'

Edgar couldn't complete the sentence.

"I Need you," didn't sound right. He didn't *need* Damian but he would have very much liked him to have stayed around. He needed all the friends and allies that he could get. He needed someone who could help him get stronger – to fight and get fit for the coming war. He needed someone he could talk to and there was something about Damian that made Edgar feel so comfortable – or at least there had been when they first met. There was also something dark in him too; something that had scared Edgar when he saw him snap before and hurt James but but the way he was now was equally as charming as when they met and if this was the true Damian, then yes, Edgar did need him.

'But what?'

Priscilla eyed Edgar with a raised brow but while he didn't notice, Damian did. Her phone bleeped loudly and she jumped to her feet without saying a word and dashed outside.

'My room,' Edgar said, leading the way upstairs. He grabbed Damian's arm and pulled him after him. Together they climbed the stairs two at a time. Once they reached Edgar's room, Edgar pulled him inside, slammed the door and pressed himself against it.

'You can't leave,' Edgar insisted.

He squared up to Damian but the man before him simply shook his head.

'You can't. I need you.'

'I've got to. It's that or get sent home to London.'

'But I need you,' Edgar snapped exasperatedly. 'You're my brother, right?'

'I am,' Damian replied, grimacing and it seemed like he was trying to hold back some tears. 'I always will be.'

'Then tell them to get stuffed!' Edgar said stroppily.

He sat down on the edge of his bed, arms folded.

'Tell them to send James away instead! He started it! Make him move!'

'It's not that easy, I'm afraid.'

'It is! Just do it!'

Damian turned aside and laughed. He tried to hold it in but it was no use.

'It's not funny, Damian!' Edgar grumbled. 'You can't go!'

Damian wrapped his bulky arms around Edgar tightly and he squeezed firmly. Edgar felt his whole body tremble slightly as Damian squashed him in his tight embrace. He returned the crushing hug with all his strength but felt like his strength didn't even half Damian's. Edgar closed his eyes to try to stop the tears that welled in his eyes – tears that he couldn't explain or even begin to guess where they had come from. They just had.

Damian felt the splash of Edgar's tears on his bare shoulder, gently pushed Edgar away and looked into his eyes. He smiled sweetly and wiped the tears away.

'Seriously, don't cry. You'll only set me off,' Damian said, stifling his own tears. Edgar made a funny sniffling sound as he tried to stop himself but they kept coming. 'What's the matter?'

Edgar brushed Damian's hands from his shoulders and sat down on the bed.

'I got you into this. I told you to dump James-' He gestured for Damian to sit next to him but instead he pulled out the rickety wooden chair from under the desk and sat facing Edgar.

'You didn't cause this. James started that fight. I ended it.'

'So why are you being punished?' Edgar spat irritably. It was not fair at all that Damian was in trouble for something he didn't even start.

'To be honest, it's Markus,' Damian said quietly and Edgar felt his stomach twist in disgust and a fire raged in his heart, burning him from the inside out. The mere mention of the name was enough to make the hairs on the back of his neck stand on end. *Was this what hatred felt like? Is this how he made Spencer and his Churchyard Crew feel?*

'Oh,' Edgar said, unable to say any more.

'He wants me away from James. Says he's a psycho...but we have a real chance to make this work, Edgar,' Damian said, his eyes lighting up. He grinned dreamily and sighed a little dazed sigh. It was pathetic.

'Make it work with Markus, you mean?'

'Yes.'

'Oh.'

Edgar felt like he had been hit by a speeding train.

The feelings hit him so hard and fast that he didn't even know they had struck him and he was left with a numbness that just lingered over him. It was an empty feeling, like his world and his life was devoid of light, of meaning, of feeling but in that moment it was just him and Damian – he could see the man before him, that vision of sheer physical perfection that he could only ever wish to attain – the man who against all odds had labelled him a friend, a brother.

'He's not right for you,' Edgar whispered, his hoarse voice catching in his throat. 'You haven't been you when you're around him.'

Damian didn't know what to say. He stared at Edgar, a dark gleam in his eye, as if he were furious Edgar would dare to dictate to him.

'And what makes you think you know me?' Damian snarled – and there it was again. That darkness sparked within him. The vicious curl of his lip, the malicious flash in his eye. 'You met me once and you know all about me? You know nothing, Edgar!'

'I'm not a child!'

'You're fifteen. Of course you are.'

'You said I was-'

'Wise. Yeah, but physically and from the way you're acting now, I'd say mentally, you're still a child.'

The way he looked at Edgar was uncomfortable. There was a cold gleam in his eyes and Edgar couldn't understand the feeling deep inside that it triggered. His heart sank into the black-hole that was his stomach and it physically hurt.

'I'm still wise. I just wish you'd listen,' Edgar said, forcing the words and holding back the emotion that caused a turmoil inside his head. 'What's so great about *him*?'

'He understands me,' Damian replied shortly. His face flushed a little red and the muscles in his neck seemed to spasm. 'He's not as bad as you all think.'

'He's a massive cu-'

'Right. I get it. You don't like him but I do, Edgar. *I* like Markus and he's *my* boyfriend so thanks for your concern but I don't need it right now.'

Damian had snapped, his voice raised and Edgar felt a little nervous as he towered over him, looking down at him on the bed. His handsome face was redder now and it was clear that he was trying to hold his frustrations back. He sighed, sat down again next to Edgar and took his hand in his own. Their fingers locked together and then Damian covered their joined hands with his other and gripped them tight as if forcing them together.

'I'm sorry,' Damian whispered softly. 'I didn't mean to snap.'

A tingling jolt of something Edgar had never felt before shot through his body. Damian's warm hand gripped Edgar's tightly, crushing his fingers and from that small connection Edgar almost felt as if they were one – two souls combined as one, like two parts of a jigsaw that were designed to fit together.

His heart beat a little faster as he looked at Damian beside him and his eyes scanned every inch of solid muscle. Damian's strong jaw and sharp cheeks looked much more defined close up – the neat flecks of short, dark stubble only enhanced their shape. His deep, brown eyes sparkled as they bore into Edgar's crystal blue and Edgar felt himself tremble. The connection was strong, so much so that Edgar felt himself drawn closer.

Edgar was terrified. It was a feeling he had become accustomed to lately but this time he wasn't scared for his life. He couldn't quite pinpoint what it was that made him so anxious. It was like the world turned to slow motion and he saw all of the beautiful details of Damian at once.

No.

Edgar pulled his hand away from Damian's as it were a burning flame.

'What's wrong?' Damian asked quietly, eyeing Edgar suspiciously.

'Nothing,' Edgar whispered hoarsely. 'If you've got to go - just go.'

'Edgar I-'

'Just go!'

Damian huffed and got to his feet silently. He turned back to Edgar and pointed at the tattoo on his shoulder.

'This represents-'

'Eternal life and constant rebirth, I know,' Edgar replied. He didn't know why he remembered such an odd fact but it had stuck in his memory and he hadn't been able to shift it.

'Exactly. Life chucks crap at us but we have to let it help us to grow. We all change and evolve every day,' Damian said, flashing Edgar a cheeky wink. 'I'll see you soon.'

'Yeah,' was the only reply Edgar could muster as Damian leaned over, kissed him on the cheek before turning away. He opened the door and slid out without saying another word.

Edgar watched him leave and his heart sank. He could still see him stood there, so vivid and bright like a shining ghost. His cheek burned. He could still feel Damian's soft lips upon him. He didn't want him to go but as the moment passed, and he heard Damian saying goodbye to Betty and Alvin downstairs, Edgar's perfect vision faded.

The windchimes above the door tinkled to signal Damian's exit and he heard him say goodbye to Priscilla outside, his voice through the crack in the bedroom window sounded so clear. Edgar pulled the net curtains aside and peeked out onto the street. Damian didn't look back and Edgar stared after him, watching him walk away. After a moment that felt like both an eternity and a split-second, Damian was gone.

Edgar closed his eyes, sighed and flung himself face first onto the bed, burying his face in his pillow and thrashed around, beating the duvet and mattress with his fists. The feelings that surged through him were more intense than anything he had ever felt before – anger that Damian could just leave him like that, frustration that he couldn't explain the feelings that spun dizzyingly in his head, jealousy of Markus who would now get Damian all to himself...

And that was it. That was Edgar's answer. All these feelings, the hero-worship, the security, the comfort, the desire to be close to Damian – it all made sense. Damian wasn't just a friend, a brother. He was closer than that – or at least that was what Edgar wanted more than anything. What if his doomed relationship with his friend Ophelia, the one where he couldn't even bring himself to hold her hands, had never been to do with him being awkward or shy or prude or any of the other names that the kids at school called him? What if it just meant that he was different?

Edgar's heart sank.

Different was such a kind euphemism.

He considered it for a moment and he couldn't breathe.

His hand reached up to his cheek – to the place where Damian's lips had connected.

Could he be really *different?*

Could he be...gay?

What if he were gay? What would that mean?

Edgar knew nothing about being gay – it was something that was covered up at school and he knew why:

Bullies.

If Spencer and his Churchyard Crew ever found out Edgar had felt these feelings even just this once, he would be as good as dead. Even if this was a curious phase – a complicated mix of teenage hormones combined with the sheer awkwardness and confusion of relationships and trying to figure out how he felt about them. It might be nothing. There was no need to worry – he could keep it to himself. He could ignore it. It didn't mean a thing.

While he respected Damian for being so open about who he was, Edgar didn't want that to be him. Being gay meant living in a different world. It meant alienation. It meant living as a second class citizen – he would never be able to fall in love and get married (he had heard on the news that Civil Partnerships for gay couples would soon be available, but it wasn't the same as marriage.) He would have to keep his relationships quiet – pretend to just be friends. He would have to worry about HIV and AIDs – both things he didn't really understand but knew that people could die from the latter.

He had seen a couple of people come out at school and how it ruined them. Scott Livingston had been one of the most popular people in the school; every boy wanted to be him and every girl wanted to be with him. He was handsome, athletic and clever. He had it all and had been a perfect student – more so a perfect specimen of humanity. It all changed over one night when he came out. He was shunned by his friends, mocked by the boys who had idolised him and degraded by the girls' who would jealously never get to be romantically involved with him.

Yes. In one night, Scott Livingston's world was torn apart. He lost everything and over the following days, Edgar, along with the whole school saw him quite publicly fall from grace and the straight-A student barely made it through his exams.

Bullied. Beaten. There were even rumours of him having started self-harming and attempting suicide. It had hurt Edgar knowing that the poor young man had faced such trouble over something that, to him, was no real problem. It was dreadful.

No. That wasn't Edgar's fate. He had enough to worry about.

Denial.

He sighed and swore to himself under his breath.

'Edgar!' Alvin shouted from downstairs. 'Are you coming down?'

Edgar took a moment to pull himself together but the panic of what had just happened gnawed at his innards like there were live rats trying to nibble through his guts from the inside out. He couldn't shake the thought of Damian and his bulging muscles and that striking tattoo. His hand still tingled from where Damian had held it – he could still feel his touch, like a static electricity stored in his skin. His cheek burned as if Damian's lips had been made of flame. Edgar was helpless and that kiss had branded him forever.

'Yeah. Fine,' Edgar replied, swallowing his pain. He took a deep breath and headed back downstairs.

'Everything alright?' Betty asked as Edgar came around the corner of the stairs into the living room.

Edgar took a deep breath and rubbed his red eyes to hide the tears.

He didn't reply.

The windchimes above the door tinkled as Priscilla stepped back in.

'What's going on? Who's coming?' Edgar asked curiously. 'Can't you just tell us who the mystery guest is?'

Priscilla shook her head and beamed.

'It's my parents isn't it? They're coming up to tell me about Vicky,' Alvin guessed. He hung his head sadly and stared at the floor. Edgar was overcome with a surge of guilt. 'They're taking me to her funeral aren't they?'

Alvin's voice broke as he spoke and his lip trembled as he fought back the tears.

Priscilla looked perplexed and put her arm around him in a kind embrace.

'What? Alvin you shouldn't think like that. Your sister's not well but it doesn't mean she's dying. But yes, your parents are coming,' Priscilla sighed bluntly, though very confused.

She mumbled to herself, clearly annoyed that she'd given away the secret, oblivious to all the secrets that had happened behind her back. Edgar's heart felt like a lead weight and it sank deeper as the guilt rose up inside him.

How had he been stupid enough to keep it all secret from his mum – the one person he had promised he would talk to about absolutely anything. He had betrayed her and now she was telling Alvin his sister was alive when he knew that she wasn't made him feel even worse than he had done before.

'Get off me!' Alvin exclaimed snappily. Priscilla let go of him as if he had sent an electrical surge through her, while Betty looked on in shock at Alvin's reaction to being comforted. Betty opened her mouth to say something but outside there was the roaring sound of an engine and a toot of a horn.

Priscilla leapt out of her chair and rushed over to the door. She pulled it open enthusiastically and Betty mumbled to herself.

'Come on you two,' Priscilla said, waving them over to the door as she pulled it open and exited onto the street. Edgar and Alvin followed.

A car was parked just outside and there were three people inside. A tall, stern looking man with short graying hair and bright green eyes was sat in the driver seat and beside him in the passenger seat was a plump, round faced woman wearing a gigantic grin. Her plaited grey hair was tied up so tightly that it only made her face appear even more round and friendly. Edgar recognized them instantly as Mr. and Mrs. Wright – they were unmistakable.

But the third person in the vehicle made Edgar's stomach flip. It was someone who Edgar never thought he would see again in his life. The images of her death flashed through his mind when their eyes met - her smile seemed to be an illusion and the wave of her hand was a mirage... after all it was nearly dark now. Perhaps his imagination was playing tricks on him. Edgar clutched his chest; his heart was beating so fast he couldn't believe it and he began to hyperventilate.

He didn't know whether he should laugh or cry. He could only just try to keep himself together. *Was she alive or just a figment of his imagination? Was she a ghost, filling in the empty void to complete the happy family gathering that could never be possible after the terrible experience that Edgar had suffered when he saw her die?* Victoria Wright sat in the back of the car looking pale and groggy but alive, all the same.

– CHAPTER TWENTY-SEVEN –
REVELATIONS AND REVIVAL

'What's up Ed? You look like you've seen a ghost,' Vicky said through the rolled up window, but Edgar could still hear her.

'Oh. You've no idea,' Edgar laughed hysterically, a tear of joy rolled down his cheek and his heart felt lighter - he felt it flutter and inflate for the first time in days. His mind buzzed with confusion, relief and excitement. He moved closer to the car, leaned close to the window stared at her.

It was really her.

She was alive!

Alive!

Alvin glared at Edgar with deep disgust. A wave of hatred surged through him.

He wanted to punch him again. He wanted to make him suffer as much pain as he had caused him with his lies. After everything, this had crossed the line. He had nearly died because of Edgar's lies.

Edgar caught a glimpse of this dark glare and knew he was in trouble but he was as confused as Alvin.

Alvin's head spun in circles. He couldn't make sense of it all. Tearfully, he stared at his sister, unable to speak.

Why had Edgar told such a sick joke?

Why had he said that Vicky was dead?

Alvin was angry with him and wouldn't have cared if the Earth had swallowed Edgar up there and then but Vicky was alive and that was all that counted to him. He waved at her with tears streaming down his face. Vicky waved back and grinned, she was happy to see her brother.

'How come you're back then? I thought you were on your mission still,'

Edgar asked excitedly, covering up all that he had seen at the Shrine of Saint Margarette.

'I got some nasty bites off some mosquitoes. They became infected and I got sent home early,' Vicky explained, showing Edgar several inflamed scarlet pimples on her neck, arms and face, which were seeping clear liquid. They looked quite disgusting and painful.

'Do you want to come in for a cuppa?' Priscilla asked politely but Mr. Wright shook his head.

'No time, I'm afraid. Just a quick visit to drop off Alvin's stuff. He's gonna need some changes of clothes if he's staying.'

'Staying?' Alvin hissed. He glared again at Edgar and it was clear he wanted to be gone – he didn't want anything to do with Edgar anymore since the lies.

'No choice, I'm afraid. The doctors said Vicky needs time to heal for a few weeks. She's in and out of hospital so we'll have to leave you up here for the summer and into your first term of college. We can't take you away from your education so-'

'But-'

'It's all sorted. We should be okay to visit at Christmas. Priscilla's already had a word with the college and sorted it all out,' Mrs. Wright said sadly as she smiled weakly at Alvin who didn't seem too thrilled by the news.

'But that's like five months?'

'I thought you'd be happy! You get to stay with Edgar!' Mrs. Wright exclaimed.

She had no idea. There was a time when Alvin would have been thrilled about having to stay with Edgar but she didn't know about his betrayal. He had lied about Vicky – he said she had died, yet here she was as alive as could be. Alvin wondered if he were dreaming, if this was all just a trick of his imagination but he knew he was awake and this was real. He grimaced to himself and there was an awkward silence. Alvin didn't know what to say. Priscilla practically bounced around in excitement, oblivious to the tension between Edgar and Alvin and the bitter, hateful glances they exchanged in silence. Mr. and Mrs. Wright seemed downhearted to leave him there but glad he would be with friends.

'I hope you get well soon,' Alvin beamed, reaching out to touch Vicky's hand through the glass of the window. 'I wish I could come home now. I miss you all so much.'

'Me too, little brother,' Vicky said. 'That mission has really opened my eyes to the world. It made me realise just how lucky our family is to have each other.'

'Where's Charity? Why isn't she staying here with us?' Alvin asked.

The talk of family hit him hard and he wondered why his little sister hadn't been evacuated to stay with them too.

'Oh, mum said she's too young to stay too far from home but she's fine - living with Aunty Julie until I'm better,' Vicky explained, pushing her glasses up her nose.

'She's far too young to be so far away.'

'Can't I come back to stay with Aunty Julie?'

'She hasn't the room.'

They chatted for a while longer, sharing small talk until Mrs. Wright climbed out of the car and pulled out several black bin bags full of Alvin's clothes and personal belongings that he might need over the duration of his stay with Edgar. She grabbed Alvin and squeezed him tightly and whispered words of love into his ear and kissed him on the cheek.

Her usually bright, rosy cheeks were dulled; she looked pale and sad as she forced a handful of notes into his hand. They argued about how much she had given him – she insisted but Alvin refused and so it went round and round in circles. Eventually Mrs. Wright turned to Edgar, grabbed him and pulled him in for a tight cuddle too.

'Look after him,' she whispered in his ear and Edgar felt a cold shudder shoot through his body.

He had already put Alvin in danger and shared adventures with him that he shouldn't have. He had exposed Alvin to a dangerous world which he ought not to be a part of but he looked Mrs. Wright right in the eye, crossed his fingers behind his back and nodded.

'I will,' he lied, knowing that it was impossible. He could not keep Alvin safe. That was a promise he could not truly hold – he could try but trying meant nothing. Anything could happen out there.

He felt a pang of guilt somewhere deep inside. It wasn't the betrayal itself that bothered him, it was the fact that he had changed so much as a person through the recent events that he had become a different person to anything he ever recognised as himself. He had become a cold-hearted, lying, murderous monster and that made him stop and think.

'Thank you,' Mrs. Wright whispered, a tear in her eye. 'God bless you, my love. God bless you.'

Edgar smiled weakly as Mrs. Wright turned to Priscilla and began to thank her too. He hated it when people said *"God bless,"* as a non-believer it felt patronising. He didn't need blessing by a man on a cloud who didn't exist. It was the same way he felt about people who prayed for others in tragedies. Why pray? Praying did nothing. Helping, donating, physical actions – they helped. Not praying.

The family shared a brief moment of sorrow as the reunion reached an end. Alvin and Priscilla waved them on as the engine began to rumble. Alvin put his hand on the glass of the window and Vicky put her hand on the other side right where Alvin's was. For a brief moment, they smiled at each other and Edgar watched, feeling guilty. Vicky was alive and for a brief moment they shared a moment of happiness together.

Edgar's heart leapt as the vehicle moved slowly away. He bit his lip to hold back the squeak of excitement that wanted to escape from him. He felt inflated like a balloon – Vicky was alive. The guilt washed away and he smirked to himself. The car sped up and Vicky was whisked away down the street, Priscilla, Betty walked back into the house ahead of Edgar and Alvin who remained on the street, watching the car as it turned the corner onto the hill.

'You owe me an explanation,' Alvin hissed as soon as the car was out of sight. 'You lied to me.'

'I'm sorry...I had no idea...I saw Vicky die. I swear it. I don't know how...' Edgar gasped the words breathlessly. The question of how Vicky had survived swirled dizzyingly around his head.

'You told me that my sister was dead!'

'I saw her die!'

'Then how was she here?'

'I don't know...'

Priscilla peeked out onto the street to see the boys stood together, looking tense.

'Everything alright?' she asked.

'Fine,' Edgar said, walking away from Alvin. He headed back in and Alvin took a moment to collect himself and follow.

'Right. Before we get this business done, we all need to talk,' Betty began solemnly as she sank into the squashy red sofa and Edgar remained standing. He couldn't sit down now – not at a time like this.

He was too tense.

His whole body was itching, his muscles were tight and he had to keep moving.

'It's a long story,' Edgar laughed sheepishly.

'When did you get your token?' Priscilla asked and Edgar cringed. It felt so strange to hear his mother asking questions about his travelling life as if it were nothing. It was wrong. This was his secret.

'The museum. I found it on the day of the flood,' Edgar explained and Priscilla's eyes opened wide. She smiled and nodded, suddenly it all made so much sense.

'And then what happened?' she asked.

Edgar took a deep breath, unsure whether he should tell her. He knew it would upset her but he knew she would also be proud of all he had survived so he told her.

It was uncomfortable to watch her reaction. She cringed in all the right places, she covered her mouth in horror at his story of the Unsterbliche, she shed a tear over the story of Mr. Griffith's sudden death and her face turned a shade of grey when he showed her the scar from the bullet wound on his shoulder. She stood up and grabbed him tightly when he told her about Merimalima and the trials he faced there with the thief and the bounty hunters. Her eyes filled with tears and she couldn't stop herself from sobbing.

'I'm so sorry, Edgar,' she cried as she lifted her glasses and wiped her tears away with the back of her hand. 'This is all my fault. I was scared to tell you-'

'It's done now.'

'You reminded me so much of your dad, I couldn't bear to think of losing you too,' Priscilla wailed, pulling Edgar into a tight embrace. 'I tried to protect you.'

'We can't run forever and there are some secrets that catch up to us sooner or later,' Betty said, shooting Priscilla a scathing look, similar to her own that struck fear into Edgar's heart.

'I know, but...'

'I'm not done yet,' Edgar said, his tone flat and tired. He knew the worst was to come.

He continued his story about the ice caves and the Nazakan frozen in the ice – about how they had awoken in his presence and then how he had been saved by Charles, seen Vicky burned at the Shrine of Saint Margarette and met the Hounds in the Grindlotha campsite. He winced as he explained how he crossed paths with Betty again and he told Priscilla how he had learned about his fate as the Chosen One – *the Warrior of Legends*.

Priscilla couldn't take much more. She broke down and sank back into her chair, crying hysterically into her hands. Her whole body heaved as she sobbed and Edgar put his arm around her. He had never seen her like this before.

'It's fine, mum,' Edgar said. He had accepted it now. 'It's my fate. I can't change it. You can't change it.'

Priscilla couldn't reply and Edgar caught Alvin roll his eyes.

'The prophecy is unclear. Edgar might not even be our warrior,' Betty said, hoping to comfort her but Edgar shook his head. He had dealt with enough lies, enough euphemisms and they only caused more hurt. From now on, he would deal in cold, hard facts.

'No.' Edgar said coldly. 'All the evidence points to it being me. I *am* the Warrior of Legends and I *have* to lead the war against the Nazakan.'

'You're fifteen, Edgar!' Priscilla shrieked. 'You can't lead a war. You can't...you're just a little boy. You're *my* little boy.'

'I've changed, mum,' Edgar replied. He could feel tears filling up in his eyes but he refused to cry. He had to be strong; not just for himself but for them too. He had to prove he wasn't weak. He had accepted his fate.

It was like a peace washed over him – gentle and calm. Yes, there was still fear – that much was natural, but it was nowhere near what it had been.

'You're still my little boy,' Priscilla sobbed. 'You're still him.'

'I've had to fight to survive and that did something to me. I'm not the weak, innocent kid I was before. I've killed and I have to kill again.'

His words were shallow – heartless.

'You don't have to. You could walk away from this and protect yourself.'

'I can't,' Edgar laughed, wishing he could. He was too far in now, he had learned the truth and his fate was written, set in stone. He could not abandon that. 'In fact, if I want to protect myself, protect you and Alvin and the rest of the world, I have to fight.'

Priscilla wiped more tears from her eyes and Edgar sank down on the sofa next to Betty.

She took his hand in hers and held it tightly for moral support. It felt comforting.

'Edgar is right. The reason he brought me back was so that I could have a look at this pyramid in the cave. If it is in use, you are all in danger.'

Betty's words cast a spell of silence over the room. She glanced around her audience, all deadly solemn as if they were at a funeral.

'If we're in danger, we'll just leave. We can go and live with Robert and Scarlet.'

'That is the worst thing you could do. If the pyramid is active, it must be kept in check.' Betty hissed. She scowled at Priscilla for being so irresponsible.

'And if something happened? If someone died?' Priscilla retorted. 'You think I'll risk losing my son like you lost yours?'

Betty glowered and gritted her teeth. She trembled slightly as if she were going to speak but she held back.

'It's all Cad's fault. If he hadn't been so reckless, if he hadn't been such a bad influence on Aidan-'

'How dare-' Betty hissed, her face contorting in a mix of rage and agonising sadness. Her eyes filled with tears.

'I loved Aidan. You know I did and when he went off to search for Cad, I always thought he might come back but he never did.' Priscilla's voice wavered, a dangerous trace of anger. 'I waited, perhaps more anxiously than you. I mourned, I grieved but there was never any closure. Nothing. Yet you carried on as if nothing had happened, like you knew more than you would ever let on.'

Betty clenched her jaw tight shut, her eyes burning into Priscilla's.

It killed Edgar to see them both so upset – to see them both arguing like this. He opened his mouth to speak-

'Aidan is still alive,' Betty spat venomously and the silence that fell across the room was so solid it was almost tangible. 'He's still out there.'

Silence. Priscilla's jaw hung open, her tears began to flow once more and Edgar was glad Betty had beaten her to saying the words out loud. What had he been thinking?

'He's-'

'Alive. Out there. Somewhere.'

'And you never thought to tell me?' Priscilla bellowed, jumping up from her seat. She began to pace, her head in her hands.

'I'm not even sure where he is myself. It has been too long since I last saw him.'

'How long?'

'A few years. Before I lost my token.'

'But he...he...was...alive?'

'I think I know my own son when I see him. Yes, he was alive.'

'And why did he never come back?'' Priscilla gasped, on the verge of hyperventilating. 'Did he find Cad?'

'He did.'

'And?'

'I'm afraid it was bad news,' Betty muttered quietly, barely able to bring herself to speak about her lost son. 'He couldn't come back. Not after everything. He was too hurt.'

The revelation hit both Edgar and Priscilla hard. Edgar knew his father was still out there somewhere, thanks to Brother Bradley but the truth of his absence knocked him sick. It felt like his whole life had been a lie – like everything he ever knew had been a sanctuary to keep him safe and protected but it had been built from flimsy excuses and dangerous lies but now the truth was out it began to crumble and fall down around him and he was left in the ruins, trying to deal with all that was left: destruction and pain.

'No more lies,' Betty said, wiping a tear from her eye. 'Look at the harm it's caused. I'm so sorry.'

'We're all guilty of hiding secrets, I suppose,' Priscilla said and she smiled weakly. She looked at Betty and nodded. 'I forgive you.'

'I forgive you too. We're family after all and we need to stick together,' Betty said. They wiped their tears and shared a group hug, a sign of their re-forged friendship and forgiveness and suddenly everything was fine once more.

As fine as it could be, at least.

It was as if nothing had happened but beneath the surface, Edgar knew that nothing would ever be the same. The consequences of this moment had caused ripples on the surface of a still lake, ripples that would grow into tidal waves. There was no turning back from this, there was only forwards and under the circumstances it felt like he was being forced into a corner, hands tied, blindfolded and with a gun to his head. He could not escape and all he could do was ride the wave and hope to survive.

'So,' he began. 'Back to business. The pyramid.'

*

They all traipsed up to the garden, following Edgar's lead.

There was an unusual fog in the air and it clung around them as if to smother them in its icy grip. Edgar led the way over to the trench where the trapdoor was hidden under the great bulky piece of rock. They jumped carefully down into the trench and came together to help each other to lift the bulky, shimmering slab.

Betty screwed up her face as she helped to lift up the heavy rock and drop it to the side. Edgar took a torch off the grass at the side of the trench and led the way into the dark hole once the trapdoor was open.

They descended deeper, stepping carefully as they climbed down the narrow ledges and jumped over the crevices. When they reached the bottom, they walked, stooped over, along the tunnel which grew higher and wider as it continued to descend steeper and steeper into the deep cavern.

Betty gasped in wonder and shock at the colossal, black marble vaulted ceilings that towered above her, held up by massive marble pillars that ran along the edges of the cave. She wandered over to the wooden bridge that jutted out across the dirty underground lake to the small island where the pyramid stood. Edgar followed her across.

'This is definitely one of them, all right,' Betty said strongly, her quiet voice echoed off the walls and reverberated in Edgar's ears. 'There's absolutely no doubt.'

'One of the ancient ones?' Edgar asked, trying to hold back his unease. 'Used by the Nazakan?'

'See the little mark at the top, the two crossed swords and the glowing light, all inside a pentangle star,' Betty said looking at Edgar with a raised brow.

'The symbol off the travellers' token!' Edgar exclaimed.

'Right you are, right you are,' Betty said absentmindedly as she fiddled with a brick on the side of the pyramid now. 'That symbol is all the proof we need.'

'But why is it buried under here?'

'I have no idea but it must have been here for years – hundreds of years,' Betty said thoughtfully as she examined the pyramid.

'Exactly...strange isn't it?'

'Everything happens for a reason, Edgar – fate, you know, but why has this been uncovered now? It could have been discovered long ago but it is only now that we find it.'

'Like you said, it's just fate isn't it?' Edgar whispered intently as he looked up at the imposing structure. 'My fate.'

Edgar turned to go back. He wanted to talk to Alvin - to apologize about the mix up about Vicky and to say he was sorry for upsetting him when he needn't have done but half way across the splintery, rickety old bridge, something distracted Edgar.

A fuzzy, flickering shape had just appeared on the land at the other end of the bridge. It was one of the monks. He was taller than anyone Edgar had ever met and wore a long white habit with the hood up over his head so his stern features were hidden in shadow –

there was no mistaking that it was Brother Bradley and he pointed straight at Edgar. He screwed up his face in confusion, trying to work out what the monk wanted.

'GET OUT!' he bellowed and Edgar realised he was pointing over his shoulder. 'LEAVE! NOW!'

Brother Bradley faded away, his voice still echoing eerily around the cave. Nobody else reacted – they couldn't see him.

Edgar glanced back over his shoulder. The hairs on the back of his neck stood on end and his eyes widened in horror. The pyramid started to resonate a strange, pale green light. The shimmering glow reflected off the shiny, black pillars where gaping cracks showed up in the growing light. The floor rumbled, throwing them off balance and small fragments of rock crumbled away from the walls and ceiling.

Betty froze in terror, staring up at the glowing pyramid before her. Alvin and Priscilla stood behind Edgar, on the other side of the bridge staring at the scene in front of them completely immobilized by their fear and Edgar was caught in the middle, trying to keep his balance on the rickety bridge, not knowing whether to run or grab Betty. Various ideas of actions he could take buzzed through his mind but he couldn't think straight.

It was on the spur of the moment and he needed to act now.

There was no time to think.

'RUN!' Edgar screamed at the top of his lungs, thinking of the only possible thing that could be done.

His heart was in his throat and pounded so fast that he felt dizzy. Adrenaline kicked in as Edgar began to sprint towards the pyramid. He reached the other side of the bridge Betty stood as still as a statue before the towering, stony structure - as if she had been entranced by it, looking up at its peak.

Edgar ran towards her as the pyramid's ethereal glowing light reached an unbelievable shade of bright, emerald green that was almost blinding. He couldn't leave her behind.

There was an earth-shaking rumble that threw Edgar off balance followed by a smash and an earsplitting roar. He stumbled, fell hard onto the jagged stone.

'BETTY! RUN!' Edgar repeated, screaming so loudly that his throat felt sore, like his tonsils had just been ruthlessly ripped out. He scrambled back to his feet and brushed the dust from his clothes.

His heart beat faster and faster still - a dozen beats a second, making him feel dizzy and disorientated in his panic and shock. He stared around in wide-eyed fear as he examined the scene that was laid out before him hoping to spot an escape by some sort of miracle.

Several bangs echoed from inside the pyramid itself. There was a CRASH as the heavy wooden door flew off its hinges and through the cloud of dust he could see the hulking shape of a Nazakan, illuminated by the slowly dimming glow.

He screamed again and tried to run but he was frozen to the spot. He bellowed Betty's name one last time before he was powerless to do any more.

– Chapter Twenty-Eight –
The Creature in the Cave

Edgar was frozen with fear. His heart pounded faster and faster, sinking to his twisting, churning stomach at the same time. Betty stood in front of the pyramid, staring up in horror as it resonated with its unreal glow that slowly faded away and the shadow of the Nazakan blended into the darkness. Betty choked on the cloud of dust that consumed her and as Edgar stared ahead, he could see only her silhouette illuminated by the dull, green glow of the pyramid.

'BETTY! GET OUT!' Edgar yelled, struggling to find her amid the debris and he swallowed a mouthful of dust and dirt that made him cough violently. 'BETTY!'

His throat was hoarse with shouting.

'Edgar... what's going on?' screamed Priscilla from the other side of the bridge, hardly even able to make her voice heard over the tumultuous racket that filled the rocky chamber. The pyramid rumbled, making the ground beneath their feet quake uncontrollably – it was hard to keep balance.

The black pillars crumbled and enormous cracks opened up like gaping mouths about to devour them; heavy, sharp rocks of all sizes showered down onto Edgar and everyone in the cavern below. They hit the lake and made ripples, creating the illusion that there was frenzied life down beneath the surface trying to escape from its watery confinements.

They all shielded their faces with their arms as the rocks fell like killer raindrops upon them but still Betty stood in front of the pyramid, completely transfixed to it as the Nazakan growled somewhere nearby. Its shape could no longer be seen but the sound of its hungry growls echoed all around.

'BETTY! COME ON!' Edgar shouted again, pleading with the old lady. She ignored Edgar's desperate pleas. Her face was solemn and it seemed that the reality of the situation was finally sinking in but fear rooted her to the spot.

'Betty! What are you playing at?' Edgar begged, his voice strained with emotion. 'We need to get out of here!'

The dust still swirled around the island, slowly settling and Edgar had no choice other than to grab Betty and pull her away. He stumbled through the thick cloud, barely able to see her ahead of him. Edgar coughed and gasped for breath as he fought his way forwards to find her among the choking dust. Somewhere in the near distance he heard shuffling footsteps and stopped dead as a shadow loomed out of the darkness, lumbering towards him.

'Edgar. We need to leave,' Betty gasped, coughing as she ran past him, pulling her blouse up to cover her mouth and nose.

It was Edgar's turn to freeze now. Betty had finally responded to him and he glanced back to see her cross the bridge towards Priscilla and Alvin who watched in open-mouthed, wide-eyed fear. He saw Priscilla take Betty in her arms and check she was alright.

'EDGAR! WE NEED TO GO!' Betty shouted, her voice was hoarse from the dust.

Priscilla shone her torch over the murky lake and over at the island, casting a faint light over Edgar and the pyramid.

'COME ON! BETTY'S RIGHT!' she screamed but Edgar couldn't move.

Edgar was terrified but he had to fight the creature. He had to stop it from escaping but he had no weapon nor any plan. His mind whizzed in dizzying circles as he pondered what to do. If he didn't kill the creature now, who knew what it would do if it managed to break out into the world.

As it came into the light, the shadowy figure's flesh turned ghostly white with an ugly, green-grey tinge. It stood still for a second; then as the last few particles of dust and debris settled it came closer.

Edgar stumbled back a few steps, his eyes fixed upon the monster. It growled and looked directly at Edgar with its piercing lilac eyes. As it shuffled towards him it seemed to slope to the right – its weaker side with the limping leg. The bone below the knee stuck out at a sickening angle as if it had been broken and never healed properly.

Its face was actually quite normal with no mutations or deformities like the other Nazakan in the ice tomb and that scared Edgar most. It made the creature appear too human and though he knew it was a violent monster that would murder him without hesitation, he could sense some kind of humanity inside it.

Despite having no deformities, its skin was pale and wrinkled, smothered with black bruises. A chunk of flesh missing from its forehead revealed a fragment of its skull beneath and a hole in its cheek showed right through into its mouth through which Edgar glimpsed its broken and rotten teeth that leaked a stench like death, so horrendous that Edgar retched. It had long, straggled black hair that hung in clumps. Some of it had turned white and there were areas of baldness where it had ripped its own hair out, standing as a mark of its tortured insanity.

It was horrible.

Edgar looked the Nazakan up and down, taking in every minute detail of its appearance. It was such a sad and lonely thing that for a moment, despite the shocking appearance, Edgar felt as though he wanted to help the pitiful monster.

It was only when the creature raised its arm and hit Edgar hard across the face that he crashed back to reality – it was going to kill him and everyone else. He recoiled, his hand shooting to his face. There was no blood. They had to get out before any was spilled.

'EDGAR!' Priscilla screamed, her eyes wide with horror upon seeing her son attacked.

Edgar began to back away from the Nazakan, retreating across the rickety bridge. It roared and loose rocks fell from the ceiling again as the sound echoed around them deafeningly.

'GET OUT!' Edgar shouted at Priscilla and Alvin who stood with Betty beside the lake, watching in silence.

'Edgar!' Priscilla gasped. She looked at her son and she didn't recognise him anymore. Her innocent, little boy was gone.

Instead there was a man, strong and brave. His face set and his deep, blue eyes piercing, much like her own. He gave her the look that she often gave him and for the first time, she saw he meant it. This was serious.

How much had his adventures changed him? How had he coped with so much going on behind her back without telling her?

'GET OUT! I'LL FOLLOW YOU!' Edgar yelled. His voice ripped his throat apart again but he ignored the pain.

'Go, Priscilla. Take Alvin. I'll get Edgar out,' Betty commanded and finally, after many serious warnings Priscilla and Alvin rushed back up the tunnel into darkness to climb up to the garden. They didn't look back – they couldn't.

'Edgar, you can't fight it. You have to leave,' Betty said calmly, over the din that resonated around the cavern.

'No. You go. *I have to fight it,*' Edgar said, grinding his teeth, determinedly. This monster had been living behind his house - it was a dangerous creature. As far as he was concerned it needed killing and he was the one to do it if the prophecy was true.

He stood on edge of the wooden bridge, his eyes fixed on the monster that slowly approached and Betty loitered near the entrance to the tunnel.

Why wasn't she leaving?

'Just leave me!' Edgar demanded. She shook her head and remained still.

Edgar bent down and ripped a piece of splintery wood off the walkway beneath his feet. He held it in his hand like a baseball bat and watched as the creature lumbered nearer.

Edgar raised the piece of wood in defence.

The creature held its arm out, waving it around as if trying to swot a fly as it stumbled forwards clumsily.

Edgar whacked the wood at its outstretched arm and cringed at the crunch as the creature's forearm splintered into a right angle. The elbow pivoted backwards, splattering blood everywhere as the bone broke into a compound fracture and shot through its thick, leathery skin.

It howled in pain, piercing the air with a bloodcurdling, almost human scream. It bared its black teeth at Edgar who waved the wood before him, warningly as he took a few steps back. He wanted to scream but couldn't. His voice had lost all use in his fear.

'Edgar, just run!' Betty exclaimed. 'You can't do this! Not now!'

Her cry took him by surprise and as he turned to face her, the creature slashed him across the shoulder with its snapped and bleeding fingernails. Edgar backed away, still clutching the blood-splattered wood. The Nazakan shuffled after Edgar and tripped over the gap in the walkway where Edgar had removed the wood to use as a weapon.

It grabbed Edgar's foot as it fell down flat on its face with a loud CRASH. Edgar stumbled backwards, not feeling its long fingers wrapped around his ankle and he stumbled, just managing to keep his balance. He swayed on the spot for a second, trying to keep upright and shook his foot to try and loosen the monster's grip but he, too, lost his balance and fell down.

He landed with his face only centimetres from the monster's – it's lilac eyes bore into his own and Edgar couldn't move.

'*Ekkdar...*' it hissed, '*Ekkdar Harrok.*'

It felt like forever that Edgar looked into the monster's sparkling eyes. He felt like they told the story of his life, silently - as though his body had been battered and broken but all of his life was preserved in his eyes, like a prison of his soul. They were eyes that were full of fear, fury, joy and hurt all at once. It was the scariest thing Edgar had ever seen – even worse than the Unsterbliche.

"*If the eyes really are the window to the soul then this creature isn't actually that bad,*" thought Edgar before realising his situation and he stumbled back to his feet.

Edgar looked down at it, and was tempted to bring the wood down on its head with a quick crack and have it all over with – but after seeing the eyes he couldn't do it. Edgar had learned enough from just looking into them – those haunting eyes that had shown him the thing's soul.

It was still his enemy and he had a prophecy to fulfil. If he truly was the Warrior of Legends, he told himself he had to kill it. He could put it out of its misery so he raised the splintery wood high above his head and the monster looked up at it. It growled and whimpered.

'I'm sorry...but it's better this way,' Edgar whispered quietly, squinting – all he had to do was smash its brain in. He could do it. He could end its pain.

The monster looked at him, eyes wide and desperate. Their eyes connected again. The creature was scared to die. It had been through so much – had been tortured and mutilated but he was still scared to die. A pang of remorse split through Edgar as he towered above the monster that was finally getting to its feet. He had the power to kill it but he wouldn't use it. He would just walk away and let the creature go back to its pyramid and go away.

He took one last sad glance at the monster.

'Go! Leave us!' Edgar commanded strongly but the creature growled treacherously. Edgar held the plank defensively, ready to swing. 'Go back to your pyramid and leave us alone!'

'*Ekkdar. Pezillar. Makkar,*' it groaned, shuffling closer to Edgar with its arms outstretched.

'Leave now and I won't hurt you.'

'*Nazakan...kill...*'

The monster roared. It writhed on the spot, its arms clutching at its own body, as if wrestling with itself. It screamed and stopped. Its head lifted slowly and it looked at Edgar. It froze...and then it ran.

Edgar turned and sprinted as fast as he could towards the tunnel leading to the exit. He didn't dare look back at the monster – he had given it a chance. He knew he should kill it but it didn't feel right. Edgar finally caught a glimpse of Betty just up ahead, beginning to climb up the ledges towards the trapdoor. The sunlight streamed in from above and the natural light made Edgar's eyes burn.

'Go Betty!' he shouted.

'Edgar...did you-?'

'Quick. Keep moving!'

Betty began to scramble up the ledges as the creature let out a bloodcurdling roar and Edgar could hear the patter patter of hurried footsteps hurtling up the tunnel behind him. He screamed. Betty struggled to climb up the ledge to the path so Edgar gave her a boost and just as she pulled herself up, there was another roar. Edgar turned back to see the monster rushing towards him.

Its horrible face was contorted with rage and malice – it wasn't itself now. It was like it was possessed and something else had taken control. Edgar scrambled up onto the ledge but the monster leapt at him. It narrowly missed Edgar's dangling feet by millimetres. He pulled himself up fast and glanced at the monster below while Betty rushed up the path and jumped over a crevice.

The creature's skeletal fingers grabbed hold of the ledge that Edgar stood on. He stamped on it and it squealed in a high-pitched tone and dropped back down.

In its anger it jumped again and grabbed hold of the ledge. Edgar ignored it and ran up the sloping path. The Nazakan pulled itself up and Edgar looked back to see it follow him. He turned his attention forward again and almost fell down a crevice in the path. His heart leapt into his throat but his legs moved on their own accord and jumped across the gap. The creature limped quickly in pursuit and launched itself over the deep crack at Edgar. He dodged but the monster landed right next to him. It grabbed him and they began to wrestle violently.

They battled on, locked together in furious combat, the sour stench of rotting flesh filled Edgar's nose and he retched again. The horrid stench made him lose all concentration and strength that he had - the creature was winning. It bent Edgar's arm behind his back. There was a sharp crack and Edgar screamed in pain while the monster just snarled, baring its sharp, black teeth and made a sound like choking, which Edgar guessed was a laugh.

It stared into his blue eyes with its own piercing lilac ones and as Edgar struggled to get free. The monster tightened its grip but Edgar kicked his foot backwards and sliced the serrated metal on the back of his boots sole down the monsters leg, leaving a deep cut that oozed thick, black blood. The creature howled in pain and let Edgar go. It wobbled weakly near the edge of the ledge. Edgar pushed it hard and it fell down, screeching in terror and pain. He had managed to buy some time.

Edgar ran. He sprinted fast up the path, jumped up the sloping rock and hopped across the final crevice to the last section of the path. From this final slope he could climb up into the garden. He was so close now he could see the square of light spill through the open trapdoor – he was almost free.

He paused for a second and looked over the side of the path to depths below. The creature was down there - it had started to climb the sheer wall in an attempt to catch up quickly. Edgar ran faster towards the top of the slope, his legs burning from running so much. He reached the top and jumped up to reach the ground above. His fingers clamped onto the soft earth and he pulled himself up in to the garden with assistance from Alvin whose face was still gaunt and petrified. There was a roar from below. The creature bounded up to the top the slope and stared up in to the air. The late evening sky was golden and the moon had just started to show through the blanket of quickening darkness.

It looked up innocently, a gleam of unsettling madness in its lilac eyes. It took a deep breath and closed them as if it enjoyed the fresh air that drifted into the cave through the open trapdoor.

Edgar felt pity for it again, imagining how it must feel being locked up in that cave with nowhere to go and then it occurred to him...It was never the rats scratching behind the kitchen wall. It was that vicious monster trying to get out, scratching and scraping with every spare moment - trying to escape into the world even if it could only go so far and still be trapped within the confines of its magical barrier. It would still be able to see daylight and moonlight, feel the red hot sun and the refreshing cool of rain. He would be able to hear the thunder and see the lightning. Even though he would be trapped, he would still be free.

Why did it have to care so much about this dimension though?

It could go to another place and be free...why was it so obsessed about being behind Edgar's house?

This must have been what Brother Bradley had warned him about when he said the house's defences were weakening and it was no longer safe. He must have meant that the Nazakan was trying to get out of the cave and was coming closer to its goal with every scratch.

As Edgar thought this over in his mind he didn't notice that Priscilla and Alvin stood at the other side of the gate, gripping it to keep their balance, still shaking with shock and fear and he didn't notice Betty beside him, stood staring down through the trapdoor at the snarling monster with a tear in her eye.

It reached up and tried to climb out of the hole, its dirty hands clawing at the soil with long, broken nails.

Edgar looked to the others for assistance and his eyes fell upon a shovel leaning against the fence. It had been left by the archaeologists.

'Pass the shovel,' Edgar commanded. Alvin grabbed it and rushed over.

'Give it to me,' Betty said sternly and Alvin handed the shovel to Betty who in turn swung it at the Nazakan that backed away so that Betty narrowly missed it. 'Damn you!'

There was a harshness to her voice and her expression was solemn and cold.

'Go away,' she said weakly as its haunting lilac eyes looked up at her, almost human and full of sorrow. It reached its hand up and there was a look of desperation in its gleaming, tearful eyes.

'It's like it wants us to help it,' Edgar whispered quietly.

Betty heard and looked up at him with a dark, warning look in her shining eyes. She shook her head and swung the shovel at the monster.

'Be gone, I said!' Her voice strained but the Nazakan merely cowered from her, whimpering softly.

'*Makkar,*' it whispered, daring to reach its hand out for Betty again.

She stood her ground and raised the shovel as if she were going to swing it again. There was fury etched in every wrinkle of her face.

'Get back to where you came from. You have no business here, beast!' she bellowed as she forced the shovel into the hole and prodded the Nazakan with it viciously.

'Gnar, ach lab foo,' the creature shrieked. It spent a moment staring up into the sky, admiring the golden glow. It frowned balefully and shrank into the shadow.

'Be gone,' Betty whispered hoarsely again.

The Nazakan remained silent. It took once last glance up, right into Edgar's eyes and it was as if it begged him to help. He shook his head gravely and the monster turned to Betty instead.

'Ach lab foo,' it repeated but Betty simply closed her eyes, passed the shovel to Edgar and turned away.

'Close the trapdoor,' she commanded.

'Gnar Makkar!' the monster shrieked.

Its deep, rattling voice broke and Edgar thought he caught a glimpse of a sparkling tear trickle from its eye.

'I showed you mercy, now go before I have to kill you,' Edgar said to the Nazakan. It looked right at him again, as if his voice had interrupted its thoughts.

'Ekkdar...' the Nazakan hissed, 'Ekkdar Harrok.'

The words hit Edgar hard. The unintelligible growls and snarls that had come from the creature's lips until this point had no meaning but this...this was something else. It made Edgar freeze, his blood turned cold and he stared at the creature as it repeated itself, a hint of urgency in its wavering tones, tears welling in its bright eyes and Edgar knew it was no threat. It was angry, confused and scared but this creature surely couldn't be violent, could it? After all...

'It's trying to say my name,' Edgar thought aloud, turning to Betty. She held the shovel defensively in her trembling hands, ready to fight in case it attacked.

Betty listened but remained silent, caught up in her own thoughts. She stared down at the ground, her face solemn and stern. There was an icy quality to the glare she bestowed upon the monster – something like the one Priscilla gave him all the time. The creature lurked in the shadow and stepped forward slowly, raising its hands. Suddenly, Betty turned and screamed.

'BE GONE, BEAST! I SHALL TELL YOU NO MORE!'

The creature remained silent. It looked up dolefully, then hung its head and turned around and vanished quickly into the darkness of the chamber below.

'How did you do that Betty?' Edgar asked quietly,

'It's difficult to say. I can't explain,' she said sternly, biting her lip as she slammed the wooden trapdoor shut.

'I think it knew my name,' Edgar said to Betty.

'Impossible.' Betty replied indignantly.

'It did!'

'The Nazakan speak in grunts and gurgles. They have no words – I doubt it would know your name,' she said quickly as if she wanted to avoid the topic.

'It called me Ekkdar Harrok and if that's not an attempt at Edgar Harold, I don't know what is.'

'Help me move this rock back,' Betty said, changing the subject quickly as she strode over to the heavy black marble rock that lay in the trench beside the trapdoor.

'You can't go lifting that, Betty, it'll break your back,' Priscilla said. She patted Alvin on the back and he followed her. They tried to lift the rock but even their combined strength was nowhere near enough.

'Edgar, can you help too?' Alvin asked, straining to carry the weight of the rock. His face scrunched up and turned red. Edgar didn''t hear. He stared at the trapdoor, his head reeling and his emotions all over. He knew the Nazakan has said his name – fair enough, the rest of its words had been garbled and incoherent but *Ekkdar Harrok* was clearly *Edgar Harold* and there it was again – another link, his name and his fate, entwined.

'Edgar! We need your help!' Alvin groaned, struggling to help the others move the rock.

'Yeah, sure,' Edgar muttered, coming back to his senses.

'It's just up here,' said a voice in the distance and she appeared within second. It was Lara and she was escorting a couple of geologists who had come to identify the rare rock that they were trying to move.

'Ah, so you're putting it back then? What's going on down there?' Lara asked looking slightly curious.

'It's a...'

'It's nothing. It's just...' Alvin continued.

'A gas leak - just a gas leak,' Priscilla covered as Edgar and everyone else breathed a sigh of relief. 'We could smell gas.'

'Oh, good idea. Best to stop the gas getting out and causing a problem. 'til someone can get here, eh?' said Lara smiling and Edgar couldn't tell if she was being sarcastic or not.

'We'll phone the gas man in the morning and get him to come and have a look at it,' Priscilla said sheepishly, hoping not to give her quick thinking lie away.

'Would you mind helping us put it back before you examine it, I mean, the gas could leak through the cracks around the edge of the trapdoor,' said Betty, raising an eyebrow at Edgar who took the hint and nodded in agreement. Everybody followed suit, knowing that it would be disastrous if the Nazakan burst out while they were examining the rock.

Together, they moved the rock back to its original place on top of the trapdoor. As they heaved it back into place, Edgar couldn't stop thinking about how he felt sorry for the creature but at the same time there was the constant nagging fear; the fact that it was behind his house and that it was constantly scratching, trying to get out.

One day it could escape and that day would be soon – Brother Bradley had already warned him about it…but maybe he was wrong. The creature seemed friendly and may have only attacked because it was confused, frightened even. He knew that was wrong. It was a pathetic thing to pretend – it was a Nazakan, sworn to destroy the traveller community and Edgar was the Warrior of Legends. Whether he liked it or not, it was time to face up to that fact.

The house was no longer safe. The place that had provided comfort and shelter and hope for so many years was compromised.

They had nowhere else to go. Scarlet and Robert would ask questions if they asked about moving in with them and they were two people Edgar knew he could never tell about his secrets. As lovely as they were, his grandparents were very old fashioned and would never believe a word. Instead they'd just have him locked up. There was no alternative. They'd have to stay but remain on constant red alert.

Edgar didn't take part in the excitement and relief as the geologists studied the rock in search of an answer to its origins and could only come to the conclusion that it was an unclassified type of rock – somewhere in the middle of metamorphic and igneous with no explanation as to where it came from. The geologists and Lara waved their friendly goodbyes and went off to report their findings at the offices before Edgar noticed what they had concluded.

Priscilla had been chatting with Betty while Edgar was wrapped up in his thoughts and decided that she could stay with them for a night until she plucked up the courage to visit Doreen the next day and explain her reasons for faking her own death.

Betty was so overcome with gratitude that she offered to take them to York - a nearby city which was reached by an hour long train journey as a little getaway and some time to de-stress. Edgar had been there plenty of times since he was young and it felt completely familiar to him by now. He loved the place and enjoyed strolling around the ancient streets within the old wall that surrounded the outer edge of the city, all overseen by the gigantic cathedral in the centre.

When they went back to Edgar's house to make their last hot chocolates before bed Edgar felt alienated in his kitchen – like he should have known that the scratching was something different all along. There it was again.

Scratch, scratch, scrape, scratch.

It sent a shudder down his spine just to think about it. He tried to force himself to believe that he was only imagining it but it was no use. He knew the truth now and there was no ignoring that. When Alvin came in he banged his fist loudly on the wall and shouted:

'Hasn't Edgar taught you anything?'

Behind the wall, the Nazakan let out a low and only just audible hiss of hatred at Alvin who punched the wall in anger again. Edgar drank his chocolate in silence, repeatedly standing up out of his seat and pacing back to the kitchen to check that the wall hadn't burst open. The anxiety was too much – it could happen any moment.

'What if it's friendly? It didn't seem to want to hurt us,' Edgar said, wishing that he wasn't hoping for too much. 'It kept struggling with itself.'

'No. The Nazakan are never friendly. They are cunning and devious. Whatever happens, never trust them.' Betty hissed, rolling her eyes. 'We've been through this before, Edgar. They want us dead and as for you, it's up to you to fight them – to put an end to this for good.'

'But what if I'm not? What if I'm just a victim of circumstance and this is all a massive coincidence? What chance do I stand?' Edgar replied defensively; he slammed his mug down on the table and stared at Betty defiantly.

You keep saying that but you know that it isn't. You know this is very real and you are a key player in what is yet to come. Have your ghosts taught you nothing?' Betty replied sternly and Edgar hung his head, unable to argue.

He nodded silently in agreement as his mum put her arm over his shoulder and pulled him in close.

He had accepted his fate. He couldn't live in denial – not anymore. Not after all he'd learned, after all the signs pointed to him.

'You're right...but what can I do? I'm not even half prepared to fight the Nazakan. I'm useless.'

Edgar's heart leapt to his throat and stuck there, he felt scared. There was no way out of this. Everyone seemed adamant that he was some great hero but he was only fifteen. He was a kid – he hadn't even lived yet. Things like this only happened in books and films, not real life.

A young boy, fresh out of childhood and only just beginning his journey on the road to adulthood, yet there he was forced to deal with everything; with life, with growing up and with this...with this responsibility that had been shown to him by ghosts since he was just a toddler. His fate had been laid out before him and there was no way to escape that. The clues that he was destined for something massive were there since the beginning of his life and yet he had dismissed them, he had shunned them aside and not bothered to look deeper into it, to prepare for the future.

Edgar jumped to his feet, unable to sit down any longer – sitting down was resting and resting was wasting time. If he was going to survive, he would have to prepare. All eyes were on him as he jumped up and began pacing.

'Put it this way, if it does break through we'll have a free extension on to the house and we can clean that lake out and use it as a swimming pool,' Priscilla joked and Edgar froze, he turned and shot her the same icy cold glance that she would shoot him – a look so piercing and cold that it shut her up instantly. Edgar had finally mastered her talent.

'It's not a laughing matter, mother. We are not safe anymore and all you can do is joke about it,' snarled Edgar angrily and stormed off to bed.

He lay there unable to even close his eyes with the vision of his kitchen wall breaking through in the middle of the night and the creature murdering him, his mum, Alvin and Betty in their sleep.

'No. That would be impossible,' he told himself. 'We'd hear it break through.'

Even if the creature broke through the wall and they heard it Edgar still wouldn't know what to do. He wasn't strong enough to fight. He'd always said that he'd rather die in his sleep and not know about it rather than spend his last moments in fear of what would happen to him to make him depart from this world. He would hate to stare death in the face with brave determination and fail. The idea of having his life swept away in one swift stroke after the torture of wondering, of thinking of every possibility out of the situation – of the enemy winning.

He imagined his last memories being those of the creature murdering him and in some cases, torturing him, before killing him in many horrific ways and each time he was helpless against its power. He thought about how it would feel to be won over by the enemy - an enemy that could threaten and terrorise the world – even if it was just a small portion of it. If it could bring Hounds through, what might happen then? There was no limit to the danger.

Edgar tried to fall asleep but his mind was in alert mode.

There was no sleep planned for him. He would stay awake in case the creature broke through.

When all of the other lucky people staying with him had managed to fall asleep he sneaked downstairs, grabbed his new sword as he passed the fireplace and sat facing the kitchen wall, guarding it in darkness. The frantic scratching began again.

His heart began to pound faster. Each second brought the creature closer to breaking through the wall and into his house. His heart was soon pounding as frantically as the scratching.

Scratch.

Scratch.

Scratch.

They both sounded at the same time, in tune and perfectly timed as if they were one and the same. Still, Edgar sat, cross-legged, his sword laid casually across his lap as he stared at the wall with determination. He refused to move.

If it happened tonight or tomorrow - if it happened in a week or a month he was going to fight. He would be ready. He would be prepared. He would not be the victim. He would be victorious.

Printed in Poland
by Amazon Fulfillment
Poland Sp. z o.o., Wrocław